FIGHTING WORDS

Davey's voice wasn't trembling any longer. Now he sounded mad. "I'm thinkin' you're a low down cheater, jus' like Zeke said you was."

The smile left the gambler's face in a big hurry. He tilted his hat back a bit to get a better look at Davey. "My, my," he said mockingly. "If you ain't all dressed up as a shootist!"

"Davey," I said louder, moving toward him, "for god's sake shut the—"

"Hold it there, hero," the gambler said. "You ain't gonna jam yourself between me and this little turd. You stand right where you are."

"He's just a kid," I said.

"Right. A kid with a Colt on his leg and a bloodlust that makes him want to show that he's faster than I am, better than I am. Thing is, that isn't going to happen. If I stand up from this bench again, it means one of us is going down dead." He struck a match and put it to his cigar.

I started toward Davey again.

"You stop right there, hero. You heard what I said before and I meant it."

Davey's eyes were hot, dark embers that blazed against the paleness of his face. His Adam's apple bobbed a couple of times, but that was his only outward show of fear. His right hand—hovering near his Colt, fingers curved slightly inward—was steady.

The gambler drew on his cigar and blew another smoke ring. "Lookit, kid," his voice now sounding aggravated. "If you're going to do something, you go ahead and do it..

Other *Leisure* books by Paul Bagdon:

BRONC MAN
DESERTER
PARTNERS

OUTLAWS

Paul Bagdon

LEISURE BOOKS

NEW YORK CITY

This one is for our Wednesday Group: Ms. Bonnie, Joe, Art, John, Peter, Blanca, Louise, Kevin, Emily, Willow, and all those who've been in and out of our jolly crew. I love them all, even though each of them finds great joy in poking and prodding hell outta me.

A LEISURE BOOK®

December 2008

Published by

Dorchester Publishing Co., Inc.
200 Madison Avenue
New York, NY 10016

ISBN 10: 0-8439-6073-6
ISBN 13: 978-0-8439-6073-0

Printed in the United States of America.

10 9 8 7 6 5 4 3 2 1

OUTLAWS

Chapter One

"Hotter'n Satan's ass in here," Davey whispered.

I'd learned quite a bit about my cellmate, Davey, when I was waiting in jail to be hanged and Davey was awaiting a trial on a statutory rape charge. He wasn't quite sure how old he was, but he'd been too young to fight in the War of Northern Aggression, and that had ended a half-dozen years ago, so I figured he was seventeen, perhaps eighteen, now. He tended to run his mouth maybe a bit more than he needed to, but waiting to be strung up is a difficult way to pass time, and listening to Davey helped there.

"Hush," I told him. "I'm not exactly sitting on an ice block either."

The two of us were in a space that seemed to be about the right size for a chicken, a little cave in the center of a full freighter load of baled hay.

We heard some riders—we couldn't tell how many—come up close to us. "Where you boys headed?" one of the riders asked. Zeke answered. He was the father of my partner, Zeb, who was killed in the pissant little town of Paris, Texas, as we robbed the bank.

"We're headin' home with a load of hay for the winter, Sheriff. Our pasture doesn't grow nothin' but rocks and scorpions."

"That bottle you just shoved under your seat for the winter too?"

Even though there were layers of hay above and around us, we could hear the voices quite well.

"Seems to me a man can take a sip of whiskey every so often should he care to, without bein' harassed by a buncha lawmen," Zeke said.

"Ahhh, shit," we heard the sheriff say. He was quiet for a moment, and then went on, "Lookit here, you ol' geezer, I don't care nothin' about your liquor. We're lookin' for a pair of men—one maybe thirty or so, the other a kid. Sonsabitches locked me in a cell an' hauled ass. You seen anything of either one of them?"

A moment passed before Zeke spoke again. "No, we ain't seen nobody. Ask my boys here—Howard an' Randall—but they'll tell you the same thing."

"What about it?" the lawman said, obviously addressing himself to Zeke's sons.

"I seen one hell of a rattlesnake," a voice said. "Sumbitch was every bit of seven feet long with a head on him big as a melon. We don't carry no guns, so I couldn't do him in."

Another voice said, "I seen the snake, but Howard, he tends to build things up bigger'n they are. The rattler was a five footer, but no more than that. Why, hell, once I was up near Laredo and I saw this—"

"I ain't interested in no snakes," the lawman interrupted. "You seen anything of the men I'm after?" His voice had gone from normal to that of a mean dog about to bite.

"Nossir," the two voices answered together.

"You boys keep a sharp eye out for those fellas," the sheriff said. "There's paper out on the older one—he's worth a thousand dollars dead or alive."

That thought made me swallow hard.

"What about the kid?" Zeke asked. I could tell it was his voice; it was whiskey-scarred and tobacco-smoke gravelly, and his sons hadn't lived enough years to sound that way.

"He was in for messin' with a underage gal," the sheriff said. "No paper on the little bastard, but I figure the two of them will stick together, for a while, at least."

That was the end of the conversation. Davey and I heard the riders swing out past Zeke's freighter and ride on. When the hoofbeats could no longer be heard, Davey said, "A thousand bucks is a insult, Pound. Hell—you're worth five times that."

I sighed. "Having a price—any price—on a man's head is no honor, Davey. All it means is that the fellow is a killer or thief or both, and the law will pay to have his ticket punched. It's not a badge—it's a disgrace."

"Well, still," he said, "it's a good disgrace, ain't it? If a fella does the best he can at somethin', be it killin' an' stealin' or whatever, he deserves to be recognized for it. Wouldn't it make you feel right good an' proud to walk down a street an' hear someone say, 'There goes Pound Taylor—he's worth ten thousand dollars'? I know if it was me, I'd sure—"

"Davey," I said, "shut the hell up. And I've told you a hundred times, my name isn't Pound."

There was a bit of warning in my voice. Davey shut up.

The Pound name will stick with me, I guess, whether I like it or not, and there's nothing much I can do about it. It'd started when I was teaching school in Burnt Rock and signed for some items at the mercantile with my legal signature—L. B. Taylor. The mindless dolt of a clerk thought that the L.B. was an abbreviation for pound. I told him I was given the name Lawrence Basil by my parents, but it was too late. A few cowhands hanging around the store picked up on it, and I've been Pound ever since.

All that aside, Davey had been quite correct in his assessment of the heat in our minute cave: It was, indeed, hotter than Satan's ass. It was mid-August in West Texas, and the sun pounded down like a sledgehammer on everything and everyone. Farmers had their crops in the ground, but needed to get water to the plants if they were to survive and grow to fruition. Good friends came to blows, or worse yet faced one another with pistols about the diversion of the selfish streams that became yet stingier with their water during the hot spells. Rain was as rare as teats on a fence post, and when it did come, it came hard, driving down, strangling plants and washing away good soil.

Cowhands didn't have much to do at this time of year except get liquored up, play poker, and shoot one another. Until the trail drives were put together in the early fall, a 'hand was a liability to a cattleman, and he'd cut loose all but the most essential workers with their final pay in their pockets. Then, the boozing, poker playing, and gunfights would begin.

The fact that Davey and I hadn't bathed in a couple

of months didn't make our confinement any more pleasant. The freighter creaked and jolted along endlessly, and the boy and I were as drenched in sweat as we'd be if some Jesus-shouter had just baptized us by immersion in a river.

Davey was dozing and I was in a stultifying state of semihypnosis, not quite asleep, but not fully awake, either. When the wagon stopped both of us came to full consciousness. It took several minutes for Zeke, Howard, and Randall to free us. The taste and feel of fresh air was almost orgasmic. Davey pushed himself out first and I followed right behind him. We stood on wobbly legs, soaked with sweat, and got our first good look at the sons of Zeke Stone. We'd seen Zeke when he brought the gun concealed in a Bible, but had scrambled into our hutch too fast to pay any attention to his boys.

"I'm Howard," one of them said, extending his right hand. Howard was tall, as lean as a rifle barrel, with long blond hair that ended below his shoulders. He had the sort of piercing blue eyes that looked like they could see through a person's skull, right into his mind. His features were even, and much like those of my deceased partner: high cheekbones, straight nose, and a mouth that liked to smile. I shook his hand and he turned to Davey and repeated, "I'm Howard." He and Davey shook hands.

Randall wasn't quite as tall as Howard, who probably topped six feet, but he was broader, wider, more powerful appearing. He was dressed like his brother and his father, in beat-up denim pants, work shirt with the sleeves rolled up, and boots with high riding heels. "I'm Randall," he said to me, and we shook hands. He repeated the phrase to Davey and again offered his hand.

"Water," Davey croaked.

Zeke, who'd been hitting his bottle pretty hard, pointed vaguely in the direction of his house and the well in front of it. "Plenty there—all you want," he said.

We didn't need a further invitation. I knew my voice was completely gone—I couldn't have gotten a single word out. My mouth and throat were far beyond being dry—it was as if I'd eaten a bale of straw and washed it down with a glass of sand.

Davey grabbed the crank and hauled up the bucket, the metal gears grinding from lack of lubrication. There were a pair of good-sized ladles hanging from the pump apparatus by strips of latigo, and Davey and I put them to work. The Stone well yielded sweet water, cold enough to make my teeth hurt. That didn't stop me from drinking it. We emptied the first bucket in a hurry and Davey dropped it in and brought it up full a second time.

When we were both sated, Davey looked at me and grinned. "Damn," he said, "I never tasted anything as—"

"Now, see," Zeke said. I was too busy sucking water to see him behind us. "The ol' lady, she's a bit churchy, an' she don't hold with no cussin'. Other'n that, she ain't half bad as a wife. She purely cooks the ass offa anything she has around or me or the boys bring in." Zeke handed over his bottle to me. I accepted it and took a good slug, expecting the throat and gut fire that always accompany the raw coyote piss that passes for liquor in West Texas. I was very pleasantly surprised. That whiskey was as smooth as a baby's ass, with none of the foul, metallic taste or smell that comes from pushing the process of fermenting too fast—like some of the Mexicans do, tossing a hog's head or some dead prairie dogs or a sack full of rattlers into the vat to get things churning.

"Where'd you get this?" I asked.

Zeke's eyes weren't focusing too well and he seemed a mite unsteady on his feet.

"Some of the customers I sell to drop off a bottle now an' again," he said.

I looked around the ranch. The barn and house were respectable enough, but the fences were sagging in some places and on the ground in others. There were a few scrawny head of beef wandering about, looking for grazing, but it was immediately evident that the cattle were range-bred, ribby, and had some bison back in their bloodlines somewhere. I saw no evidence of crops in the ground and the place certainly wasn't a cattle operation.

Davey had been looking around, just as I was. "Jesus," he said, "lookit them cattle. There ain't enough meat on them to roast on a stick. And I don't see no . . ."

All of a sudden, Zeke had Davey shoved against the short stone wall around the well, both hands on the boy's neck, but standing close enough to him so that even if Davey could swing at him, he couldn't do any damage. I was real surprised that Zeke could move as fast as he did. Davey was a hell of a horseman, or so he said, and if a man attempts to break mustangs he either has to know what's coming or he's going to eat dirt. Now, all he was doing was making choking noises, squirming a bit, and banging his fists on Zeke's back, doing no harm whatsoever.

I liked Davey a lot and I wasn't about to see him choked to death by some wild-ass dirt farmer. I picked up the empty bucket and whacked Zeke a good one on the back of his head.

Zeke released Davey, took a step and a half backward and hit the dirt ass first, where he sat, dazed.

I crouched down next to him. "What the hell was that all about? The boy didn't do anything wrong. Why'd you . . ."

Some life was returning to Zeke's eyes, chasing the dullness. "He up an' used the Lord's name in vain," he said. "I don't care what else a man might say, but I can't abide with that sort of cussin'. It just ain't right an' I won't have it."

"So you need to strangle the kid? Look: Davey was just commenting on your cows—he didn't mean any harm. If you'd explained to him about your objection, that would have been the end of it."

"I'll admit the cows are a sorry lot," Zeke said. Howard and Randall helped their father to his feet.

"We're not talking about cattle here," I said, keeping my voice as level as I could. "I agreed to ride with you boys, and I'll do it. But if you have any more idiosyncrasies, you damned well better tell me about them right now."

"What's a erdosinker?" Zeke asked.

"It's a habit kind of thing," I said. "Something a person does different than others would, just like you jumping on Davey for no reason."

"The reason . . ." Zeke began.

I held up my hands to silence him. I was standing maybe a foot away from him, eye to eye. "I know what you think the reason was. Fact is, Davey don't care about your Lord any more than I do, which is none at all. If you'd have said something, none of this would have happened."

Randall became a peacemaker. "Pa doesn't have no other bad habits 'cept wantin' folks not sayin' Jesus," he said.

"That's true," Howard said. "How's about we all forget about this little do-si-do an' go on to the house and chow down?"

"I'll say this first," Davey said, glaring at Zeke. He hadn't spoken since the attack, but that could have been because he was gasping to suck in breath. "You don't get but one free ride. Next time, we'll finish whatever gets started."

"The boy's feisty," Zeke observed. "Got some grit to him."

For a long moment the five of us stood there by the well, like a bunch of those store manikins mercantiles use to show dresses and suits and so forth. Then Davey broke the silence and the tension. "That grub Howard jus' mentioned sounded real good to me. I say we get to it."

"My ma," Randall said proudly, "can take a ol' boot and a cow flop an' make the finest damn meal you ever ate. You see if that ain't true."

We started to the house, Zeke weaving a bit, Davey walking between Howard and Randall, and me kind of following along behind them. Randall laughed at something Davey said, and so did Howard and Zeke. That felt good to hear. I had a stack of doubts about the outlaw thing working, but having any acrimony between the others would make it completely impossible.

The Stones weren't exaggerating even a tiny bit about their mother's cooking. She'd prepared a venison roast and mountains of mashed potatoes that were as creamy and white as an angel's underdrawers, and some candied carrots, fresh-baked bread, and an apple pie for dessert. It wouldn't take much to do a lot better than the jail food Davey and I had been sustaining life with, but that slop wasn't fit for a rabid hog. What Mrs. Stone prepared was purely a delight.

Mrs. Stone introduced herself as Agnes. She looked a good deal like Zeke—not tall, sort of rounded with no sharp edges, and those striking blue eyes that must have run in her blood.

There are some folks who are just naturally happy, and by being so, they spread their happiness around them. Agnes Stone was one such person. Any residuals from the Jesus confrontation were long gone, and it was much like Davey and I were brothers in the Stone family.

After we'd eaten we went out back to see the sunset. Zeke and I smoked cigars. Randall rolled a pair of cigarettes and offered one to Davey. He said he didn't care for it, but thanked Randall anyway. When I caught a whiff of the brother's smoking mixture, I knew Davey had made a wise choice. The smoke smelled a bit like camphor and fuel oil, is about as close I can come to describing it. Zeke kept a bottle in the bushes at the base of the house, and he fetched it and pulled the cork. Zeke didn't offer whiskey to Davey, Howard, or Randall, which, it being his home and all, was up to him.

After a bit the conversation dwindled, but the silences weren't uncomfortable. We watched the lightning bugs flit about, making little rails behind them in the darkness. I glugged the bottle once more and then asked a question that had been in the back of my mind since Davey and I crawled out of the hay.

"Just what is it you boys do here, Zeke?" I asked. "You sure couldn't make a living from the beef we saw, your fences are piss-poor, and I didn't see any indication of corn or wheat or anything else around here."

Zeke reached out for the bottle and I handed it over. "Well," he said, "since we're pardners now, I'll tell you. What we do is grow a kind of hemp, is all, and there ain't much hard work to it."

"Hemp? You mean like for rope?"

"Not exactly, but it's pretty much the same plant. The kind we grow, though, we dry out and clean the stems an' seeds out an' sell what's left to the Mexicans. They've really took to smokin' that stuff."

I thought he was pulling my leg. "C'mon, Zeke," I said. "I'm serious."

Zeke chuckled. "So am I. Me an' the boys got not quite half a acre of hemp an' we draw enough money from it so we don't lack a thing, an' we can even buy the occasional frippery for Agnes and somethin' for ourselves."

"Is that hemp that you boys are smoking?" I asked the brothers.

Howard answered dreamily, "Oh, yessir," stretching the S-sound out until it was a yard long. "It sure is."

"Damn," I marveled. "Smokin' hemp. A fellow sure can learn something new every day."

The conversation pretty much died down after that. It was a nice night—but any night where a man could see the sky and the stars after being in prison is a nice night. I stood to go into the barn and the cot the Stones had prepared from me, a few feet from where they'd set up for Davey. "We don't have much of nothin'," Davey said, through a yawn. "We need some clothes and horses and guns, 'fore we can do anything like robbin' a bank."

He had a good point. "I'll talk to Zeke in the morning. Maybe he'll front us the cash we need to get equipped." I thought for a moment. "You any good with a pistol, Davey?"

"Some. I never drawed against a man, though."

"Let's hope we can keep it that way," I said. "You'll do a fair amount of holding a pistol on folks to keep them still and not to raise a ruckus, but pulling iron against a man who wants to kill you is a different story."

"You done that, Pound?"

"Yes. I have."

"What did it feel—"

"Let's let it go for now, Davey. It isn't a topic I like to discuss."

It's a whole lot more pleasant to be awakened by a rooster than it is by a lawman banging keys against the bars of a man's cell. Davey and I were at the well, washing the sleep out of our eyes and cleaning up a bit, when Zeke came out, a mug of coffee in his hand. "Pot's on the stove, boys," he said. "Help yourselfs. Agnes, she's got some side meat cookin' and she'll do up some eggs too."

"Sounds real good," Davey said.

"It does," I agreed. I turned to Zeke. "As things stand now, Davey and I don't have horses or guns and our clothes are about to rot off of our bodies. I'm wondering if you'd care to advance us some money and lend us a couple of your horses and point us toward a town with a stable and a mercantile—and where they don't much care what happens over in Paris, where we were being held."

"Glad to, boys," Zeke said. "Sooner we get you some gear, the sooner we can ride on outta here an' make some money. Matter of fact, I already thought about it. There's a town called Dobbins not more'n thirty, maybe thirty-five miles dead east from here. They can fix you up with what you want. It ain't much of a town, but they got most everything a man needs: a livery owner who usually has some good stock for sale, a mercantile with clothes and a pretty full line of Colts and Smith & Wesson pistols. Got a couple of whores, too, at the saloon, but I'd sooner bed down with a damn boar hog." Zeke reached into his pocket and pulled out some folded bills. "Here ya go," he said. "That's a hundred and fifty. That should do you, right?"

"Sure," I said. "It'll be plenty. Thanks."

Zeke nodded and then stood back from us for a moment, scratching his head. "I'll say this," he said. "That mercantile has pants an' shirts an' hats an' you boys best pick some up. You look like a tall pair of piles of buzzard shit." He took another step back. "You might wanta try a bath at the barbershop too. Both of you smell real rank."

"You'd smell some too, you'd been in that jail as long as me an' Pound was," Davey said. "It ain't like we could stroll down the hall an' get a bath an' a shave. Jes—Goshdarn," he quickly amended, "the place was like a slop pit."

The breakfast was delightful. Agnes had flapjacks along with the side meat, and I swear those things were so light they'd have floated on out the window if we'd not held them down with molasses. I don't think it was the jailhouse swill I was accustomed to that made Agnes's food so good—it was simply that she was a wonder in the kitchen. When I complimented her on her skills she blushed a bit.

It was hard for me to figure out why Zeke would care to leave a woman like Agnes and go out on the outlaw trail and more than likely get his ass shot off or be publicly hanged. But—the man and his sons had saved my life and I owed a real big debt to them, and I wasn't about to back off from that.

Davey and I set out for Dobbins, me on Randall's quiet, easy to get along with, blood bay gelding named Boy. Davey rode Howard's horse, a tall, lanky paint named Paint. Zeke's horse, a tall black named Ranger, watched the saddling of the other horses with the bemused look on his face that almost always appears when other horses are being put to work. When we were about a mile out from Zeke's home and couldn't be seen from there, Davey let Paint out and then spurred him a tad. There was no doubt that the horse could cover ground; he had that smooth gallop in which it didn't look like his legs were moving awfully fast, but they reached out far in front of him and pulled yards of earth under him, much as a mountain lion runs. Davey reined Paint in about a mile away from me and began walking him in a big circle to cool him out. I put Boy into a jog to catch up.

Davey's grin was as wide as the horizon. "This boy won't lose many races," he said. "Sumbitch flies."

I'd been a bit concerned about prairie dog holes during Davey's ride; if the horse had stepped into one of them he'd tear up a leg bad enough to earn him a bullet, but Davey was so excited about the animal's speed that I didn't bring it up just then.

We'd left early for Dobbins, hoping to make a good part of the trip before the heat got too bad. Even so, within ten minutes or so of the sun being up, both of us were wet and sticky with sweat. When we hit a small water hole we were glad to see it. We refilled our canteens and let the horses drink. We had to drag them back from the water with reins and curses, but letting them fill up when they're hot could have a real bad effect on them.

In spite of the heat—and that sun hung in the sky a few feet over our heads and burned with a white fire that could melt the nails out of a horseshoe—we made decent time and rode into Dobbins about mid-afternoon.

There's a dreary sameness to West Texas towns. The wooden sign stating DOBBINS, TEXAS was barely legible because of the number of bullet holes in it. It appeared that someone with a buffalo rifle had been sighting in on the sign; some of the holes were the size of a big man's fist. The street was rutted and potholed, and there was little pedestrian traffic. The livery and stable was at one end of the street and a church at the other. There were a pair of saloons, one on each side of the street. Dobbins Trust Company, the local bank, was in a small two-story building about midblock. The mercantile was good-sized, with a large sheet of glass that allowed passersby to look in at the goods displayed.

Even the semiferal dogs that skulked around in the alleys seemed interchangeable between towns: they were ribby, dirty, and moved about with their tails between their legs, as if expecting a kick.

We tied up in front of the stable and walked over to the corral where the sale stock was held. There were a dozen or so horses there, standing in the sun half asleep, their tails swishing desultorily at flies. Davey climbed over the fence and walked among the horses, feeling a foreleg here and there, opening a couple of mouths to check ages, and generally poking around. I stayed outside, leaning on the fence, rolling a cigarette.

Davey had talked quite a bit about horses while we were in the lockup. He seemed to know them, but talking about a horse and selecting, riding and using one are two different things. The way the boy threaded through the herd with such unconscious confidence made me pretty certain he knew what he'd been talking about all those days and nights in jail.

There was a coil of rope slung over the fence. Davey took it, shook out a loop, and tossed it over a roan gelding's head. The horse shied and backed but Davey went down the rope to him and calmed him, gently rubbing the roan's muzzle and kind of humming to him. I'd seen that done before, mostly by Indians. It wasn't singing, but it wasn't exactly humming, either. Whatever it was, it had a calming effect on horses.

A portly fellow with a long, droopy moustache stepped out of the barn and into the corral, watching

Davey. He reminded me of the few buffalo hunters I'd met in my day: big but not fat, with biceps the size of hams, and a way of moving that looked slower than the way most fellows moved, but actually wasn't. It was the smoothness of motion that gave the impression of being slow. I'd never seen a buffalo hunter waste a single motion in any situation, and I doubted that I'd ever see this stableman waste one, either. His voice had years of booze and cigarettes behind it. "That roan ain't a bad horse," he said to Davey, ignoring me.

Davey looked over at the man and then bent and lifted the roan's right rear hoof. "Maybe not," he said. "But his pasterns don't have no slope to them—he'd give a rough ride."

"Well, shit," the stableman said with a grin. "Your grandmother gonna ride him, maybe get her ass banged up a bit?"

Davey returned the grin. "I'm just saying, is all."

The stableman strode over to Davey and extended his right hand. "Lucas," he said.

"Davey." He paused for a moment, looking around. "You got some decent stock here, Lucas," he said.

"Damn right I do. I can fetch a saddle and bridle—would you care to try out a couple?"

"I don't need no saddle, but if you got a bridle with a low port bit to it, that'd be good."

Lucas liked that answer—his grin turned into a full smile. "I got one of them copper port jobs. Gimme a minute." He headed back to the door to the barn.

"Looks like you made a friend," I called over to Davey.

"Maybe so—but there won't be no friendship when the dealin' starts, Pound." He pointed at a buckskin near the fence. "What'd you think of him?"

"He looks good, but I can't ride good looks."

"I'll give him a try after I ride this here red roan," he said.

As it turned out, nothing Davey had said in jail about his skill with horses was untrue. He rode bareback with the easy grace of an Indian—never off balance, even when the horses did a couple of sunfish leaps at the sky—and never hauling on the horse's mouth. Lucas let him out of the corral and Davey turned the roan in a few big circles, ran some figure eights on him, and then galloped him for a short stretch. He rode back to where Lucas and I stood. "Ain't too bad of a horse," he said. He put the roan back into the corral, bitted the buckskin, and went through the same riding routine on him. When he came back to us, he said, "This boy might could take a man down the road."

As he was sliding down he asked Lucas, "What'll you take for the pair of them—the roan an' this one?"

"I gotta get ninety dollars for those two. They're the best I got here."

Davey handed the reins to Lucas. "Good meeting you, Lucas," he said. "C'mon, Pound. I got a throat that's fulla dust an' needs a beer."

"Now hold on, Davey," Lucas said. "You know those horses are worth every penny of ninety dollars. An' I'll tell you what: you don't buy 'em today, they'll be gone by tomorrow—lotsa boys been lookin' at them."

"That's good," Davey said. "It'll save you from

feedin' them, what with the price of decent hay these days. C'mon, Pound," he repeated.

We got maybe a dozen steps toward the nearest saloon. "Ain't you gonna make a offer?" Lucas asked.

Davey stopped and turned back to face Lucas. "I'll go maybe sixty-five dollars for the two if you toss in a pair of saddles an' bridles."

"Yer plumb crazy, son. Sixty-five for them horses is crazy, an' the saddles an' bridles, even if they're Mex made, are worth another twenty-five dollars."

Davey thought that over for a long moment. Finally, he said, "Are you a man who would maybe drink a beer with me an' my pardner?"

"I might do that, boy—but my prices ain't goin' any lower."

"Fair 'nuff," Davey said.

As we walked up to the batwings, Lucas pointed to a pair of horses tied to the hitching rail. "You might find crowbait like them two for your sixty-five dollars, but you ain't about to buy a horse worth havin' for it."

Lucas drank seven schooners of beer, I had three, and Davey had one that he sipped at and pushed around on the table; when we left, the schooner was still almost half-full.

Davey and I walked out of the saloon owning the buckskin, the roan, two Mexican-made saddles, a pair of raggedy saddle blankets, and two bridles with bits, for which we paid $83.50. Lucas went back to the stable to write up the bills of sale and Davey and I went into the mercantile.

The scent of a mercantile is one of the most pleasant on earth, in my mind. Maybe it's the mix of the odor of leather and wood and steel and penny candy and cloth and such, but whatever its source, it's delightful.

We looked at pistols first. We decided on Colt .45s with six-inch barrels—a dependable weapon and one with enough punch to get the job done. We bought gunbelts and holsters that seemed as stiff as they would had they been made from oak, but we know some oil rubbed into the leather would fix that. We bought two hundred rounds of ammunition, denim pants, a work shirt each, and hats that weren't Stetsons, but looked to be well made.

We each had a bath at the barbershop, and the wrinkle of the barber's face as he first approached us indicated how foul we'd become. I got a shave too, but Davey didn't need one. We walked out of the shop talcum-powdered and bay-rummed in our new clothes and figured we'd had a real good day. We took a meal at a boardinghouse down the street that cost us each fifteen cents, and we both packed away more food than most men would eat in a week.

Neither of us cared to spend the night in Dobbins so we collected our new horses, tied a couple of lead lines onto Howard's and Randall's horses, and set off for the Stone ranch—or farm, or whatever the hell it was. The new horses were tractable enough and we left enough room between them and the two we were leading to avoid friction and ass-biting.

We rode on through the day's heat and continued after the sun set. We hit that water hole and let the horses drink and we filled our canteens. We thought a bit about making a camp right there and finishing the trip in the morning, but we had no food or coffee, so we decided to keep going. There was plenty of moon but we didn't dare go faster than a brisk walk. The moonlight made the shadows sharp and angular, so that the shadow of a rock formation or a seguro was clearer and more defined than the object itself.

There's something mesmerizing about a trek like that. We were cool enough, our horses were behaving, we still had our guts full of boardinghouse food, and even the creaks and groans of our saddles seemed pleasant. After a while, I asked Davey where he'd learned so much about horses.

"My pa was a trader," he said. "He sold lots of remounts to the army and supplied cowpokes with ridin' stock too."

"And he taught you the business?"

Davey's voice changed suddenly, became lower and his words came out faster. "He didn't teach me a goddamn thing. I learned what I learned from watchin', not bein' taught nothing."

"Sounds like there was some bad blood between you and your pa."

"He hit my ma every time he got drunk. Hit me, too, but I could take it. It was Ma I was worried about. That's why I did . . . what I did."

"And what was that?"

"I gunned the ol' bastard with his own twelve-gauge. He came home from sellin' off a bunch of stock an' started right in on Ma. The shotgun was standin' right there next to the door in the kitchen. I picked it up an' gave him both barrels. I didn't shoot him in the back, though. I called out, 'You touch her again ever an' you're a dead man.' He shoved Ma and turned to me an' I fired." I could see Davey shake his head slowly from side to side, like he was having trouble believing his old story. "Sure did take him apart, those two loads of single-ought shot—painted the kitchen wall with him."

We rode on in silence for what seemed like a long time. "My ma," he finally said, "never shed a tear over him an' I sure as hell didn't either. He'd turned a good dollar on the sale and had better'n four hundred dollars in his pocket. I gave Ma the money, picked out a good horse from what stock was left, and rode west."

"Headed where?"

"Hell, Pound, I dunno. I picked up some ranch work an' some bronc work here an' there an' I didn't have much money, but I didn't need much, neither. I ended up in Paris and was already in jail by the time you an' Zeb tried to rob the bank. I can say this for true: I ain't ever again gonna statuate no daughter of a blacksmith. He near 'bout killed me—had fists on him bigger'n a hog's head."

I began to explain for perhaps the fiftieth time that statutory rape had nothing to do with statues—and that there was no such word as statuate—but then gave up. It hadn't sunk in any of the previous times, and there was no reason it would now.

"You done some killin' too, right?" Davey said.

"When I had to. I never dropped a relative of mine, though."

"That make a difference, Pound?"

I thought that over. "Not that I can see, Davey. A dead man's a dead man regardless of who his kin are."

We rode on in silence for quite a while, watching the vague orange hue at the horizon become more and more vivid, until the sun swept it away with the day's first burst of light.

"What say we let the horses breathe and put some rounds through these new Colts—see if can they shoot straight?"

I nodded. "It'll be good to see how the new horses react to gunfire. If they get crazy, we need to bring them down, because it's a good bet that they'll hear people shooting at us and us shooting back."

Davey smiled at me. "I shoot better'n any fat-assed lawman, Pound. I ain't scared."

That remark irritated me. Here this silly seventeen- or eighteen-year-old kid was yapping about taking on all the law in Texas, and there were some very hard men who carried a badge in Texas.

"Lookit, Davey," I began.

"Whoa," he said. "Hold on. Me tellin' you I can handle iron don't prove nothin', right?"

"I'm certain you can shoot rocks and cacti and so forth, but they're not shooting back at you. That's the difference, Davey."

Davey tugged his Colt out of his stiff new holster and turned it about in his hand, enjoying looking at it. "Pull yours, Pound," he said.

I did. There's something about a newly oiled handgun that makes a man sure he's invincible. Of course he isn't, but the pistol comes close to convincing him otherwise. I eased the cylinder open and filled it with six rounds. The metal-to-metal mating always sounded good to me, and today it sounded even better. I spun the loaded cylinder and it made a sweet, perfectly lubricated *whir.* It seemed to be a quality weapon, but I hadn't yet fired it. The hard rubber grips didn't feel right at all—I'd used bone grips just like my previous pardner.

I spun the cylinder again, and the tick and lubricated sweetness of the quality of the weapon promised that it'd always be there for me. Maybe that's idiocy, but I'd traded lives a few years before, and rode with Zeb Stone. He made me real sure that a good weapon could—and would—save my life.

Another thing: there's most definitely something about the smell of gun oil. It was Hoppe's that the storekeep took care of his guns with. Guns are machines, and the best tuned and lubricated machines are the ones that do what they're supposed to do.

Anyway, as Davey said, we'd best see if our guns fired at all straight and true.

"I can't draw worth a goddamn outta this holster," Davey said. "What I'll do is shoot at somethin', Pound—somethin' you name."

I looked around us. "See that segura—the stunted one that looks like its head is a whole lot bigger'n its body?"

"Wahl shit, Pound," Davey said, "That cactus is fifty, maybe sixty feet off from us. Plus, I'm shootin' a pistol I ain't shot before. I'll give her a rip, though."

Before I could speak, Davey stepped forward, and stood there, left foot maybe a foot behind his right, slightly crouched. I'd seen that same position before, once in Yuma and once in Dodge. In both cases the gunman who employed it killed his opponent.

Davey extended his right arm to aim his Colt and fired, punching a good-sized chunk of pulp out of the cactus. "Not bad," he murmured. The next five rounds he fired fast, with the pistol about level with his waist. He pulled the trigger so rapidly that the shots sounded like a single explosion. Shards and bits of cactus seemed to fly out of the plant, several arcing perhaps ten feet in the air.

Davey held the barrel to the side of his face and smiled. "Ain't even hot—this here's a good pistol. I'll get bone grips put on her and I'll have one hell of a weapon. Go on, Pound—try yours out."

"You didn't leave me much cactus," I said. "I'm not a shootist or a gunman. I'm fairly handy with a pistol and I can usually hit what I aim at, but in a draw down I'd be lying in the dirt before I could clear leather."

The Colt felt right in my hand—cool, my index finger sliding naturally onto the trigger. I didn't have the skill to hit anything firing from the waist. Instead I held the Colt out in front of me at shoulder's height. My first shot dug a furrow in front of the remains of the cactus. My next one socked home, tearing off a good ball of pulp. I fired slowly, aiming each shot, easing the trigger back instead of jerking on it. My final four slugs beat to hell the cactus nicely.

"Like you said, Davey—these Colts are good pistols. Not much recoil, either. It's easy enough to keep the gun on aim."

The two new horses did some dancing and fidgeting when we began firing, but they calmed down after a few minutes. "Those boys been around shootin' before," Davey observed.

We each fired maybe fifty rounds at various targets. I watched Davey from a bit behind him and slightly off to the side. That Colt .45 became a part of his hand, doing whatever it was he wanted it to do. He never wasted a motion and didn't seem to be firing fast, but he was, putting six slugs into whatever he was aiming at faster than it took to think about it.

We pulled our cinches and mounted, ears ringing and buzzing from the racket, and set out again to the Stone place.

"Now all we gotta do is rob us a bank," Davey said.

Chapter Two

When we rode in with the new horses the Stone family, including Agnes, gathered around us like kids around a birthday cake. "Looks like a fine pair," Zeke pointed out. "I reckon they can run some?"

"They've got good wind," Davey said, "but we haven't been able to run them yet, haulin' you boys' horses along after us like we was."

"I'd sure like to see which one is the quickest," Howard said.

"Me too," Randall said.

"There's nothing wrong with a little horse race," Agnes said, "as long as there's no wagerin' going on. Wagerin's a sin."

Davey and I looked at one another. Our new horses had come from Dobbins pretty much nonstop, but stout young animals like ours, there ought to be lots of grit left in them.

"Fine with me," Davey said. "Only let's keep it fairly short."

Agnes patted my buckskin on the neck. "He's a pretty boy," she said. "What's his name?"

Neither Davey nor I had given much thought to naming our horses. There's little sense to it—it's much like naming a chicken or a fence post. The names are fun for the owners; the horses recognize the sound of grain in a feed pan, but wouldn't know their own names if a flaming chariot came outta the sky and an angel called out to them.

"Buck," I said.

"And yours?" she said to Davey.

"Uhmmm . . . Red. Yeah, his name is Red."

Zeke had stepped off to the side a bit and was shielding his eyes from the sun with his hand. "See where that busted-down cart is out there? Kinda next to the desert pine tree?"

Davey and I nodded.

"Suppose," Zeke said, "you start from here, circle the wagon, and come on back—first horse 'cross the line wins."

"Ain't no prairie dog holes or nothin'," Randall said. "That little path is where we go out to tend our hemp."

Randall and Howard stood by, holding the reins of their horses, the men's eyes full of the glitter of anticipation.

"You go on three, OK? One," he began the count without waiting for an answer from us.

Davey and I eased our horses a few feet apart and held them on tight rein. The excitement got to both animals—I was real sure they'd been raced before. I reached ahead a bit to pat my horse's neck. He was so tense that it was like stroking a warm length of steel.

"Two . . ." Zeke waited an inordinate amount of time before shouting, "Three!"

Both horses hurled themselves ahead like juggernauts, shod hooves flinging clods of dirt behind them, stretching their bodies into an immediate gallop, reaching far ahead of themselves in a sweet rhythm, hooves thudding hollowly with each impact with the earth.

I'd planned to hold my mount in slightly as we raced to the wrecked wagon, in order to have plenty of fire left for the dash home. I might just as well have attempted to hold back a speeding locomotive—Buck had the bit in his teeth and nothing but a bullet or a broken leg would slow him down. Davey was leaning far forward in his saddle and I used the same tactic.

I'd raced a few times before, a couple times because my partner and I were being pursued by the law, and once and again in a flat race for a beer or a couple of dollars. It's strange how in a race the riders hear nothing but the beating of hooves; all other sounds are swept away by the power and speed of the animals.

Davey and I were neck and neck as the broken-axled wagon seemed to rush toward us. The turn would be crucial; taking too wide of a turn would give the other horse an advantage, but cutting it too tightly would cause the horse to scramble and could drain off some speed and momentum. I decided to do it conservatively and swing a tad wide. Davey was obviously of a different opinion—he looked like he was attempting to crash Red into the wagon. As it turned out, he made the right choice. He gained about a horse length in the turn, and that's all he needed. The gallop back to the street was intoxicating, exhilarating: the rushing air tasted sweet and the heady odor of the sweat of a healthy horse was as pleasant as any scent I'd ever known.

We finished with Davey the horse length he'd picked up at the turn ahead of me. We reined in and walked the horses, listening to them suck air after the burst of exertion.

"You got an eye for horses, Davey," I said.

"I'm not certain 'bout that," he said, "but I sure as hell picked a fine pair this time."

Davey and I spent most of the remainder of the day on our cots, dozing off the sleepless night before. After that, I walked around some, not headed anywhere, thinking. The Stones were brand-new to bank robbery, and although Davey was handy enough with a pistol, he'd never stolen anything other than a few licorice straps at a mercantile. Zeke, Howard, and Randall were all for robbing the bank in Paris where my partner—and their son and brother—met his end. I felt no compunction about robbing the bank; my concern was that my life could well depend on four fellows who'd never been involved in such a thing. I had the veto power, I suppose, because without me the Stones would probably be tripping over or shooting each other in that bank. I had a bit more trust in Davey, but not a ton.

I came across Zeke on the front porch sucking on a jug, and I pulled a rocker next to him. He offered the whiskey and I took a glug. It looked like he'd been out there for a while. His eyes were somewhat glassy and he slurred the occasional word. I suspected that intoxication was a standard aspect of Zeke Stone, but, like most men who drink heavily daily, he seemed to handle it fairly well. Still, asking for a drunk's split-second decision was like asking a rattlesnake to play a violin.

"I ain't bein' pushy or nothin'," Zeke said, "but when do you plan for us to ride out? The boys are pantin' hard to knock over that Paris bank."

"We'll have to discuss that a little later," I said. "What about equipment? All three of you have guns an' bedrolls?"

"Damn!" Zeke snorted and slapped his knee, laughing. "Maybe it's a good thing we got you with us, Pound. I purely never thought of that shit. I got me an ol' Army Colt but it don't work very well. Howard, he's got a .22 squirrel rifle. Randall might have a gun—I ain't sure."

I sighed. "Look—you need to send your boys into Dobbins to buy what the three of you need at the mercantile. Also, I want one of you to check out that little bank, make a drawing showing what's where—where the safe is, like that."

"I'll do her," Zeke said. "Hittin' that little tin-can bank in Dobbins is a good idea. If we don't take enough in Paris, we jus' ride on over to Dobbins."

I let that go, thinking we could discuss the whole operation at supper time.

By the time Agnes began whacking the iron triangle hanging outside the kitchen Davey was up and around, running a brush over his roan.

When we were all seated at the table, Zeke at one end and me at the other, we ate and talked at the same time. Zeke paid good attention and his eyes were no longer fogged. That was good; I wanted him to remember everything that was said.

I explained to Randall and Howard that they were to take a trip to Dobbins for supplies. "What kinda pistols should we buy, Pound?" Randall asked.

"Colt .45s. They're a good gun. Get belts and holsters too, and ammunition. Pick up a sack of Arbuckle's coffee and a blanket each for a bedroll."

Howard looked puzzled. "What?" I asked.

"Thing is, I already got me a good blanket."

"Howard," I said, "use any blanket you care to, OK? Just make sure you have one."

I put a large scoop of creamy mashed potatoes on my plate and passed the bowl to Randall. He loaded his plate similarly and passed the bowl on to Davey. We'd all taken hefty helpings but the bowl was still damned near full. Seems like Agnes felt she was feeding an army. The potatoes ended up in front of Zeke.

"Now," I said, "I know you boys are thinking on robbing the Paris bank. We can't do that." The Stones' eyes—even Agnes's—swung to me as if I'd just suggested that we run a spit through one of the new horses and slow-roast it over a firepit.

"That was the agreement," Agnes said, "because of Zeb an' all."

"There may have been an agreement amongst you people, but there never was one with me. We need to start out small, get our moves down, get rid of some of the jitters, and make sure each of us can do what we need to do once we're in a bank."

Randall's sarcasm fell flat. "Well, if that ain't jus' dandy. We gonna rob us a Sunday School picnic."

"Pound's right," Davey said. "An' if Pound don't go to Paris, neither do I."

Strangely, Zeke had nothing to say. He listened quietly, nodding slightly every so often.

When the boys' grumbling wound down, I said, "Think about it. You ever heard the saying, 'Practice makes perfect'?"

"No," Howard said. Randall shook his head. Zeke stared straight ahead. "Well, it's true," I said. "It's like—I dunno, maybe riding a horse. The first time you mount up you'll probably end up on your ass on the ground. But each time you give it a try you'll learn something, and in a time, you'll be riding as good as Davey, here."

"That may be true," Howard said. "But we all know how to ride good. Why do we got to—"

"Ah, Jesus," I said disgustedly.

I was fortunate Zeke hadn't heard my slip. His face had fallen forward into the bowl of mashed potatoes deep enough to cover his ears.

Randall smiled. "Ain't no problem, Pound. We'll jus' tell Pa tomorra that he agreed to everything you said."

"Pa, he takes a drink now an' again. Doesn't cause no problems, though. This ain't nothin'."

Agnes's eyes flashed her anger. Her chubby face flushed crimson. "Ain't nothin?" she bellowed, with about the same tone and volume I once heard from a bull moose during rutting season. "I wash them dadburned spuds an' peel 'em an' smash 'em all up for supper, an' now we're goin' to have strands of hair in our leftovers!"

Randal grabbed the hair at the back of Zeke's head and pulled his face out of the potatoes. "Lookit there, Ma," he said. "There ain't but a few bits left behind."

Davey and my eyes met across the table. Neither of us had ever heard a conversation even remotely resembling this one. "OK," I said, pushing my chair back from the table. I noticed that Zeke was snoring and was blowing tiny bubbles of mashed potatoes from between his lips. I looked away quickly. "It's settled then: You two boys will head to town tomorrow an' the first bank we'll take will be the little one in Dobbins."

I stood up from the table and headed out the kitchen door. I'd known some families are somewhat strange, but the Stones went way the hell beyond strange. Davey followed me and we ended up leaning on the corral fence, watching our horses eat hay.

"I dunno, Pound," Davey said after a long silence during which the only sound was the snuffling and grunting of the horses as they ate. "I'm real thankful to Zeke and the boys for bustin' us outta jail. But I sure wonder how they'll act when we're in a bank."

"I do too, Davey. But look: if you're too worried, why not mount up and head out and all of us will part as friends. All the Stones did was get you out of a statutory rape charge, but they saved me from dangling at the end of a rope. I owe them a hell of a lot more than you do."

"I thought a bit 'bout that," Davey answered. "But then I figured that you an' me, we'd kinda become pardners, ya know? We stick together."

"Davey . . ."

"No—hold on, Pound. All I'm sayin' is that we jailed together an' got busted out together an' we're gonna rob banks together, an' if that don't make us pardners, well, Jesus, I don't know what does."

Both Davey and I quickly looked over our shoulders, half expecting Zeke's wrath to come down on Davey again, even though the man was passed-out drunk in the house. We both laughed, a little self-consciously.

"What we need to do," I said, "is to rehearse the

Dobbins robbery just like it was a play on a stage: who'll hold the horses, who'll go in the bank first, who'll gather the tellers' money, and who'll get the bank president to open the safe. If we practice it enough, the whole thing might just work. They'll bring back a sketch of the bank tomorrow, and we can set up in the barn and run through the whole thing a few times until Zeke and the boys have it down solid."

"S'pose Zeke is drunk when we hit Dobbins?"

"Then we'll tie him up and leave him here."

"He ain't gonna like that."

"I don't suppose he will, but that's not our concern. I'll talk with him, though, tell him he's gotta stay sober for the robbery."

Davey decided to swing a leg over his roan and take a little ride. I went to the porch and sat down in one of the rockers. Before long, Agnes came out and joined me, bringing each of us a mug of her coffee.

"I suppose," she said, "you boys are some worried about Zeke on the outlaw trail."

"The thought's crossed my mind more than once, Agnes," I said. "I'll admit that."

She rocked easily in her chair, sipping at her coffee. "Zeke drinks, there's no doubt 'bout that," she said. "But when somethin' needs to be done, why, he'll do it sober, or real close to sober. He gets the shakes a bit of a mornin', but a pull at his jug takes care of that."

The coffee was very strong and very hot and tasted wonderful. We rocked together for a few minutes, neither of us saying anything.

Agnes broke the silence. "Zeke's got a pair of brass balls the size of watermelons on him, Pound," she said. "He won't turn scared on you an' he won't run out on you. I can flat-out-damn-guarantee that."

"That's good to know," I said.

"You know," she said, "when you was outlawin' with our boy Zeb, you couldn't have found a more proud pa than Zeke Stone. See, Zeb was the first in the family to accomplish anythin' much. Howard and Randall are good boys, but they ain't brave or smart like Zeb was. In truth, they're kinda no-account."

I nodded as if I agreed with—or at least understood—what Agnes was saying, but in actuality, I didn't. I'd never heard a parent before who was proud of a bank-robber son or a pair of hemp-smoking miscreants.

"Now, Zeke," Agnes went on, "he's a bright man. He most always took care of us good. When he heard that Zeb was killed in the Paris robbery, he could hardly lift his jug, he was so sad. Then he came up with the plan to get you outta jail an' go outlawin' with you, an' he wanted to share that with his two remainin' sons, such as they was."

"It's awfully dangerous, Agnes. You must realize that."

"Well, sure it is. So is bustin' broncs or runnin' cattle or jus' 'bout anything else. An' Zeke said he wasn't never goin' to kill no one an' made the boys promise that too. So, if y'all get captured, Zeke and the boys will only do some time, is all."

And I'll be hanged, I thought.

"I was thinkin'," Agnes said, "how nice it'd be if Zeke, Howard, an' Randall all did their time in the same prison—keepin' a family together is always a good thing."

"You sound pretty sure we'll get captured," I said.

I tried to keep the venom out of my voice, but I'm not at all certain I did.

Agnes took no offense. In fact, she leaned over from her rocker and patted my shoulder lightly, the way a mother does to a little boy. "You hush now about that, Pound! I don't think you'll get captured. I was just sayin', is all."

Zeke, Howard, and Randall left before dawn the next morning on their run to Dobbins for supplies and to check out the bank. Agnes had a big breakfast ready for Davey and me when the scent of coffee pulled us into her kitchen. The sun had barely cleared the horizon, and it was uncomfortably hot already. That shouldn't surprise anyone who's lived in West Texas for a year or more, but still, the stultifying heat—the raw, sweaty intensity of it—was something no one could really become accustomed to. Natives assured one another, "This'll break soon," but no one actually believed it.

Davey and I saddled up to give our horses some exercise. We loped off to the hemp field, neither of us having seen one before. The plants were tall—many better than six feet—and skinny, articulated spires and branches that bore spikey, serrated leafs about five inches long for the top ones, then decreasingly shorter toward the base of the leaf.

Buck reached out his head to snag a mouthful of a plant but I hauled his head back and advised Davey, "Don't let Red get into this stuff. It can't be too good for a horse, seeing what it does to Randall and Howard."

I noticed that the plants were in nice, straight lines a foot or so apart from one another. The open spaces were pretty much weed-free.

"Looks like they put some time into their crop," Davey commented.

We rode on, leaving the small cultivated field behind us. There hadn't been rain in several weeks, and the soil was dust-dry. Even the undergrowth and scrub was suffering, turning a lifeless brown that crunched under our horses' hooves. I turned in my saddle and looked behind us. A line of dust and grit we'd raised when at the lope pointed to where we'd been like an arrow headed dead-on to its target. At the walk, as we were doing, we didn't raise a cloud.

We came upon an almost dry water hole with wagon wheel and boot tracks all around it. The water was sulfury and that thick, rotten egg stink was all around us. "I heard sulfur water is real good for crops," Davey said.

"I heard that too. That hemp field back there goes to prove it, I guess."

We swung back to the way we'd come, loped the horses again, and then slowed to a fast walk. "How do you think Zeke an' the boys will do in the robbery?" Davey asked.

"You worried about them?"

"Worried? Not exactly. I'm just wonderin' how they'll do when we get into the thick of it. Seems to me there ain't much room for screwups once we get in the bank."

"Yeah. That's why I wanted the sketch and why we'll set up a kind of stage in the barn to look as much like the bank as we can, using bales of hay and so forth. We can run the Stones through the whole thing—right down to holding the horses out front—until they've all got their jobs down tight."

"That should work," Davey said.

"Well, that's the thing. It *should* work. But if something strange happens to mess up the plans, there could be trouble."

"Like what?"

"It's impossible to say. Like once Zeb and I were taking down a bank in some little jerkwater town I can't even remember the name of. Everything was going just fine and then this coot hauls out a beat-up old cap-and-ball pistol and held it on Zeb, saying he'd shoot if we both didn't drop our guns and raise our hands."

"What happened?"

"My Colt was already in my hand and all I needed to do was swing it a few inches to shoot the ol' codger—which I did. But the gunshot drew the law and Zeb and I had to shoot our way out and we never did make a penny on that robbery."

"I see what you mean," Davey said. "Things can always get screwed up no matter how good the plans are."

"Sure. Robbing banks isn't easy. If it were, everybody would do it."

"What about the old man?"

"What about him?"

"Well . . . did he die?"

"I don't know. I never did find out. Zeb and I ran pretty hard from that bank."

Davey was quiet for a moment. Then, he said, "Jesus, Pound, I never figured you'd . . . I dunno." He swallowed hard. "Kill a old fella . . ." He let the sentence die away, but the thought in his mind certainly didn't. "Maybe you coulda . . . I dunno . . ."

"Davey," I said, choosing my words carefully.

"That's the business I was in. After a few days, it'll be the business you're in. If it bothers you, the best thing you can do is ride on. You've got a good horse and you'll find cattle work or whatever you want to do. I won't think the least bit less of you. Agnes would put up some trail grub for you and you could head out within a couple of hours."

For a long moment, I thought Davey would take my advice. Then, I knew he wouldn't. "I just felt a little sorry for the guy, is all," he said. "I ain't about to ride out, Pound. I'm in this all the way. If the Stone boys can't cut it, that's their problem. But either way you an' me is ridin' out together."

I didn't have an answer for that, so I just shut up and sat my horse and we got on back to the ranch. We washed the horses down a bit even though they weren't sweated or frothed. We didn't talk as Davey fetched buckets of water and seed sacks to rub the animals. It's that way with good friends; they don't need constant chatter in order to prove the friendship.

My Buck was truly a fine horse. Maybe I don't know stock as well as Davey did, but I was smart enough to see a horse that was better than most. I could check a mouth, and look for abuse, and gauge the slant of a fetlock, and all that because Zeb had taught me, but it takes a better, more experienced eye than mine to pick a superior horse out of a herd.

I found the porch to be an excellent place to sit in the shade and think, or maybe just sit and rock. Either worked extremely well.

Davey had scrounged up a piece of latigo in the tack room of the barn and sat on the rocker next to mine. He'd already worked teat balm into his gun holster, and its color was a few shades darker than it had been. He measured out a length of latigo and cut it away from the original piece and eased the end of it through the small hole he'd cut in the bottom of his holster. Then he tied the holster in place.

"That'll hold 'er down good," he said, "right tight to my leg." Davey let his right arm and hand hang naturally at his side, grumbled, "Shit," and let his gun belt out another notch. This time the grips of his Colt hit his hand maybe an inch down from his palm, just where his fingers began to curl inward toward his leg. "Good," he said, and sat back down.

"I filed the front sight down," he said. "It's as smooth as a virgin's tit. There's no way this pistol is goin' to hang up in my holster an' slow down my draw."

"Davey," I said, "you look and talk like a gunfighter." I didn't mean it anywhere near a compliment, and my voice must have conveyed that to the boy.

"That's what we are, no?" he said, sounding hurt, or at least confused.

"No, dammit, that isn't what we are. We're bank robbers. There's a big difference. We don't go out looking for people to kill—we steal money and do our best not to hurt anyone. The best robbery is the one we ride away from without a shot being fired."

Davey considered that for a long moment. "Yeah. I guess you're right. But look: someday someone in a bank is going to try to get the drop on us. If I can outgun that man, we're just fine. If I can't, some of us are gonna get dead."

I rocked some more without answering.

"Jus' stands to reason," Davey went on. "We're gonna be robbin' banks for a long time, an' it's—"

"Davey," I said, "I'll let you in on something. As soon as I have twenty-five thousand dollars or better in my poke, I'll be headed for Mexico, saying good-bye to the Stone family and to you."

"Ain't many banks in Mexico, Pound."

Davey can be very thickheaded at times. "I'm not going there to steal—I'm going there to live. I'll buy a little spread and maybe run a few head of cattle, and maybe find a nice Mex lady and settle in for the rest of my life, my stealing days long gone."

"What about me, then? I thought we was pardners, gettin' busted out of jail together an' now goin' out to rob banks an' all."

"I never referred to us as partners, Davey. Zeb Stone was my partner and now he's dead and I don't need or want another one. You go ahead and do what you want to do after I pull up stakes to go to Mexico, but don't be thinking that I'm going to be any part of your plans, because I'm not."

Davey stood and kept his back to me as he walked down the porch steps. He stopped for a moment, said, "Well, hell," and strode over to the barn.

Agnes made a fine stew for dinner, along with biscuits and candied carrots and buttermilk to drink. Davey was quiet through most of the meal, but he joined me out on the porch afterward. Neither of us spoke of our earlier conversation.

Zeke, Howard, and Randall pulled in late afternoon of the next day. All were dressed in brand-new work shirts and denim pants, and each wore a stiff gun belt with an even stiffer holster containing Colt .45s, the same pistols Davey and I had purchased. Zeke picked up a new scrub board for Agnes and she near swooned over how much better it was than her old one. The boys had coffee, canned peaches, hard candy, and loose .45 shells in their saddlebags. Zeke's saddlebags tinkled quietly as his horse walked, the bottles inside sounding almost musical.

The boys were all frothed up about showing Davey and me the drawing they'd made of the bank's layout. We sat at the kitchen table with mugs of coffee in front of us. Howard flattened the page of foolscap he'd drawn it on and pointed out the features on the diagram.

"Here's the door, see? There's no back door. The tellers are right over here behind a counter that has glass winders in front of them with little slots at the bottom to pass money through. There ain't but two tellers, although there are three teller stations. This right here is where the president sits at a big rolltop. He's as fat as a hog in August and won't give us no trouble. There's a couple other small desks here . . . an' here, each with a fella at it with ledgers open in front of them. They was wearin' those green eyeshade things. The safe's back over here behind the tellers an' it's a big sumbitch for such a small bank. The steel door was open a hair and the president, he waddled in and after a bit come out. We couldn't see inside the safe. There's a counter here away from the tellers for customers to use, I guess. Wasn't nobody much in there."

"Is there a guard?" I asked.

Howard laughed. "I guess you could call him that.

He was a good two hundred years old, and sits in a chair inside the door. He's got a holstered pistol. He was asleep while me an' Randall was there."

"How about a lawman?"

"The marshal's name is Thad McCrossen. He ain't a bad guy for a lawman. He locked Pa up for drunk an' distorted, an' didn't charge him nothin' when he let him go in the mornin'."

"Is he handy with a pistol or rifle?" Davey asked. I thought that was a pretty clever question for a beginner in the bank-robbing business.

"Nah," Zeke said. "On Independence Day two years ago there was shootin' contests an' McCrossen didn't hit nothin' at all."

I took the diagram from the table to study it more carefully. "What's this?" I asked, pointing to what appeared to be a bucket.

"There was a fella in there moppin' the floor. That there's his bucket."

"Where's the man? Where did he go to empty the water? Is there some sort of back room or anything like that?"

Randall answered. "The mopper, he'd went out an' was rollin' a smoke, standin' near the hitchin' rail. He's a old fella an' nothin' to worry about."

"OK," I said. "Good. Now, let's go out to the barn and set up our own little bank an' then you boys should get some sleep."

All along the rafters inside the barn, harvested hemp plants were hung, drying. The entire barn had a cedarlike scent to it. We started hefting bales of hay—which were old and moldy but probably good enough for the sorry beef the Stones owned—and placed them within an area about the size of the bank. I checked the diagram frequently, trying to create as accurately as possible a replica of the Dobbins bank.

"This'll be the front door," I said, "and this bale here is where the guard sits." I turned to Howard and Randall. "Are the distances about right? Like from the door to the tellers?"

"Looks fine," Howard said.

"I want you boys to just stand here and look at what we've done very closely—see if there's anything we've left out or misplaced."

After a long moment, Randall said, "The bucket ain't there."

My eyes and Davey's met. I'd say we were both thinking the same thing: *Can these morons pull off a bank robbery?*

Randall saw the expressions on our faces. "Well, hell, if it was there, one of us could trip over it," he said. "Or maybe step right into the sumbitch an' get a foot caught."

I let that settle for a few heartbeats and then said, "You boys get some sleep and we'll talk again at supper time."

The Stones trooped out and Davey and I stood looking over our bank. "Looks fairly straightforward, Pound," Davey said. "The guard's a fossil an' the lawman can't shoot, and I don't think we'll get no grief from the tellers."

"Don't forget where our information came from," I said. Davey nodded.

"Now," I said, "here's how I see it. We leave one man outside holdin' the horses. One man charges into the bank and scares hell outta whoever's there, shouting, 'Raise your hands! This is a stickup! Stay still and you won't get hurt.' That man also keeps his gun on the customers, watching them real close. At the same time the other three of us rush in. I go directly to the president"—I pointed to the hay bale representing the man's desk—"and the other two of us get to the tellers. Smash those windows with the butt of your gun—shoving money through those slots takes too long. Watch for a hideout gun on a teller—they sometimes carry them."

"What're you going to do with the president?"

"If the safe is open I'll take him to it, and if it isn't I'll have him open it."

"How long you figure this whole thing'll take?" Davey asked. He asked fine questions for an amateur.

"No more than three or four minutes—we're in, we grab the money, and we're out, mounted, and riding hard."

"What do we put the money in?"

"Grain sacks," I said. "We fold them up and tuck them inside our shirts."

"Then what, Pound?"

"We ride east to the foothills, make a camp, and decide whom we're going to visit next."

Davey grinned. "Whom?"

"Yes, dammit, *whom*. There's nothing wrong with good English."

"Try tellin' that to the rest of the gang. They make me sound like one'a them college professors."

Davey had a sound point.

Agnes had her usual wonderful spread out for supper: two-inch-thick buffalo steaks with those sweet, wavering stripes of fat that tell a man that the meat came from the hump or real close to it. She had big bowls of candied yams and a large bowl of mashed potatoes. I'm not generally at all picky, but I more or less drew the line at the potatoes, being much concerned about Zeke's goddamn hair. I noticed that Davey passed by the potatoes too.

Agnes fixed that all up for us. "Look," she said, "I ain't about to serve spuds he up an' buried his face in. These are new, fresh, and hairless, and if you're partial to them and don't take any, you're idjits."

Davey and I scooped grand mounds of mashed potatoes onto our plates.

When we were all as full as a stern-wheeler running cotton, Agnes brought out coffee.

There's a thing about coffee. I've known hard-core bar rags who had to have a cup before they took up the booze for the day. And one time, when Zeb and I were holed up in a cave with a posse after us, we didn't have coffee and we risked going to the nearest town—which wasn't near at all—to procure some. I don't think it's any more addictive than booze is, but how we miss it when we can't have it—the coffee, I mean.

Agnes made coffee strong enough to melt a horseshoe but it was never bitter or burned. If I ever find a woman, she needs to make coffee like that.

I told the Stones essentially what I'd told Davey: about the positioning of the men and the time involved and the responsibility of each of us, and then we went out to the porch and sat back and sipped coffee.

At first, none of the Stones had anything to say. Then, it seemed like the question hit them all at once.

"Who's gonna do what, Pound? 'Cause I'm tellin' you right now, I want to be in that goddamn bank," Randall said.

"I ain't holdin' no horses," Howard said.

"I'll be the first man in," Randall said.

I'd anticipated this sort of thing and had prepared a speech. "You boys have never robbed a bank," I said. "But I have—lots of them."

"Goddammit," Zeke broke in, "get to it."

"OK," I said. "For the first few times out, I want Zeke keeping the horses ready. It's an important piece of work, and Zeke's the only one who can do it right."

That, of course, was a crock of shit—both Stone boys were handier with horses.

Zeke's mouth dropped open and his complexion turned crimson.

"Look," I continued, "what we're going to do is shift men around the first few banks we hit—see who's good at what, who does the right thing."

Zeke's eyes were like embers to the side of a hot fire. "Hell no, Pound. I ain't holdin' no goddamn horses while we're robbin' a bank. What'll my ol' lady think, should the story make the newspaper? Pound an' Davey an' the two Stone boys robbed a bank an' left Zeke Stone to hold their goddamn horses? Shit." He spat at my feet.

I held his eyes for a bit of time and then carried on. "I'm thinking Howard in first, warning the people, then. . . ."

Howard grinned broadly. "Like you said earlier: 'Raise your hands—this here's a stickup! Move an' I'll kill you.' "

"Close enough," I said. "Zeke, like I said, we gotta switch men around the first couple of times. This time in Dobbins, Davey and I will follow Howard in, and then—"

"No. I ain't gonna do it an' my boys ain't gonna

do it. If stuff was different and you wasn't my dead son's pardner, I'd gun you right now."

"It'd be a whole lot better if you didn't talk like that, Zeke." I kept my voice placid. "Davey and I are real grateful for you men busting us outta jail. That was a good thing; it was a thing that brought your son Zeb back to you, at least in a sense, no? So I'll tell you this: you Stones have to follow my orders or the whole bunch of us will get our asses shot off."

I took a step back and got my balance and said, "Zeb Stone and I robbed banks. I didn't know a goddamn thing about all that when we met in Burnt Rock. Zeb carried me along, showed me how it was done. He was good."

"Dammit, Pound, seems like you want to give all the orders," Howard said.

"Yeah—that's pretty close."

I had to think a moment, and I did. I wanted to say something to the Stones that'd calm them down, but I wasn't about to lie to them. I swallowed a couple of times.

"Here's the way it can go or not go. Davey and I could knock any bank we cared to. Davey is new, but he'll do what I need him to do. You men figure bank robbing is easy. It isn't. It's dangerous too—some of them have guards who're good with their weapons, and some towns have lawmen who'd rather shoot down a robber than lock one up."

"We ain't scared," Zeke said. "An' I'm speakin' for Howard an' Randall too."

"Zeke," I said, "let's go for a little walk and leave the boys here so we can get a little privacy."

We followed the path to the hemp field for no particular reason, ambling rather than walking. "Please try to see this thing my way," I said. "For the first few jobs we need to try each man at a different position. Holding the horses is just as important as any other part of the robbery—maybe more so."

"How do you figure that?"

"Look: suppose the four inside men run out of the bank with bullets flying and haulin' sacks of money, and the horses either got free of the hitching rail or started a fight. Without the horses ready we wouldn't have a chance. See what I mean?"

Zeke thought for a few moments. "Yeah, I guess maybe you're right, Pound. But I ain't gonna do it permanent, I'll tell you that right now."

"Fine," I said, and held out my right hand. Zeke took it and we shook, formally, almost, as if we were sealing a big business deal.

On the way back I brought up another point that'd been circling about in my mind, ever since Davey and I got to the Stone ranch. "What about Agnes?" I asked. "It's not likely that we'll be back in this area for months—maybe a year or more. That's a long time for Agnes to live there alone, with no help."

Zeke grinned at me, looking proud. "We already thought of that. Agnes's brother Orville is comin' to stay here an' take care of the chores and the hemp. He's a no-account sumbitch who ain't bright enough to step in outta the rain, but he'll follow Agnes's orders."

"Good. That's real good. One other thing, if you don't mind, Zeke."

"Sure. What?"

"It seems to me that you and Agnes are church people, what with saying grace and not taking the

Lord's name in vain and so forth. How does that fit in with robbing banks?"

"We discussed it," Zeke said seriously. "You see, there ain't no sin so great that God, He won't forgive it. Also, our church says once we up an' give ourselves to God, we're saved. So, we ain't goin' to hell if we get killed, an' Agnes figures robbin' banks ain't such a big sin, anyhow—the sonsabitches got more money than they need. See?"

There was a certain imbecilic logic in what Zeke told me. In a sense, I kind of envied his belief. I have no idea at all what's at the end of the road, and I don't give it much thought. Still, believing as Zeke did would make a man more comfortable in his life, wouldn't it?

Chapter Three

The next day we practiced our routine, even though there wasn't much to it. Zeke held the saddled and ready horses, Howard went in first and made his announcement, then Davey and I and Randall barged in. I went right to the bank president's desk and made as if I was walking him over behind the tellers, where the safe was. Davey and Randall worked the teller. They both remembered to break the glass in the tellers' windows, just as I'd told them. We went out in the reverse order: Howard first because he was nearest the door, then Davey and Randall and then me.

We even tucked grain sacks inside our shirts and filled them with straw, to represent money. We ran through the entire scheme a half dozen times. I didn't see any flaws in the plan, and neither did any of the others.

We'd planned to set out that night, make a fireless camp, and head into Dobbins at opening time for the bank. We were ready, primed, practiced—and in a hell of a hurry to get the whole affair in motion.

Rain started about midday, heavy at first, driving down in sheets, pounding the parched earth and turning it into a soupy quagmire. When the initial storm was over, the rain turned into a steady, monotonous shower that came straight down—an indication that there was no wind behind the rain clouds, and that they had decided to settle in for a spell.

We sat at the dining table drinking cup after cup of coffee—except for Zeke, who was sucking at an unlabelled quart bottle that gave off the aroma of shellac. Conversation started abruptly and stopped just as quickly. The main topic focused on the condition of the street in Dobbins. It'd be damned near impassable, Zeke said, because the mud would be as thick as cow shit and would slow the horses by half. The rain tapped on the roof as if mocking us.

I made the mistake of asking if the Stones had a deck of cards so we could entertain ourselves with a few hands of poker. That set Agnes off.

"Playin' cards are one-way tickets to hell," she said. "I'd no sooner have them in my home than I'd tuck a scorpion into my bed. Even when they ain't played for money, they're pure evil—what with them Lucifer pictures on them an' numbers that mock the books of the Bible. Why, I had a uncle back home when I was a youngster who went to a friend's place to play with cards. On that very day he fell off his horse dead drunk an' busted his neck. I recall his head bein' all twisted around, ugly as a pig's ass. *That's* the sort of thing playin' cards bring with them."

"I guess that's it for poker, then," Davey said, and mumbled, "Shit," under his breath.

Agnes continued with her rant until she drove us all out to the barn. Our gear didn't need checking, but we checked it anyway. Nobody wanted to rehearse the robbery again, which was fine with me.

Too much practice dulls the senses and doesn't allow a man to make a good decision in a tough spot—he's too bound up with what he'd rehearsed that he can't think his way out of trouble.

Zeke was the only one of us who was at all relaxed. He sat on the bale that'd been the president's desk with his bottle, not saying much of anything, and when he did speak, he was generally talking to himself. Davey brushed out his horse, keeping pretty much to himself. The Stone boys became fractious, snarling at one another and arguing about nonsense. Finally, I told them to shut the hell up, and they did.

The rain stopped just before dark. The next day wouldn't work because of the residual mud and muck, and we had to wait that one out too—at least until late afternoon when we'd start toward our camp outside Dobbins.

Riding toward a bank to rob is, I guess, an experience not many men have had. In a sense, it may be like a soldier feels on the night before a battle. The difference is, the soldier has to be there, has to fight. In our case any one or all of us could have turned back or gone in any direction we cared to go, but we elected to do this robbery instead.

We found a decent place to put up just before dark. Since we weren't going to build a fire, we didn't have to gather up kindling or wood. We ate venison jerky, drank water—except for Zeke, who was tapping at his bottle—and sat around, not saying much. The horses grazed on some scrub grass that had almost miraculously turned from a desiccated, lifeless brown to a shade of green. I don't think any of us did much sleeping that night.

The following day promised to be a fine one. The

sun peeped over the horizon like a huge orangish-red ball, but there was a slight breeze moving, which would help further dry the mud. We ate jerky until we figured it was close to opening time for the bank and rode at a walk into the town, saving our horses for the rush after the business in the bank was finished.

There was a saddle horse and a surrey tied to the hitching rail in front of the bank. Down the street a couple of cow ponies stood listlessly at the rail in front of a saloon. A freighter with three teams of mules hauled a huge load of baled hay.

We pulled up in front of the bank and stepped down from our saddles, handing the reins to Zeke. Davey and Zeke looked calm enough, but Randall and Howard were both pasty-faced and I noticed the trembling of their hands as they handed over their reins. All their eyes swung to me.

"Let's rob a bank, boys," I said, my voice businesslike, just as I wanted it to be.

We formed a loose V, with Howard at the front. He drew his Colt and slammed through the doors, yelling, "Raise your sticks! This a hand up!" He hesitated for a heartbeat and shouted, "No—that ain't right, goddammit! Nobody kill or we'll move you!"

The four customers at the tellers' windows got the message and they raised their hands. The tellers did too.

Davey plucked the pistol from the holster of the old guard, who stood next to his chair, looking like he'd been stunned by a blow on the head. I headed to the president's desk. He was in the process of lighting a cigar and the match burned down to his fingers; he yelped and tossed it and the cigar to the floor. He was a corpulent fellow of about fifty, and his nose had the choleric red hue of a heavy drinker. "Look here . . ." he began. I whacked him lightly on his forehead with the barrel of my pistol, not hard enough to knock him out. "Get up," I said, "and go to the safe. I'll be a step behind you. Get cute and you die."

"The safe," he said. "The safe is open. You don't need me to . . ."

I jammed the muzzle of my Colt into his back. "Of course I need you, lardass—as a hostage if things get sticky." I heard the sound of glass shattering as Davey and Randall cleared out the tellers' drawers.

The safe was open a crack, just as it'd been when Howard had visited the place a couple of days ago. I pulled the heavy steel door open and goaded the banker inside. It was a room of about eight by eight, with steel walls and ceiling. It was a claustrophobic little cave and its only illumination was the light from the outside. There wasn't much of anything there. Most of the steel shells were empty, but there were a pair of canvas sacks sitting alone in a back corner. I grabbed them, keeping my gun on the banker, and was a tad disappointed at the lack of weight of the bags.

I shoved the banker out. Davey and Randall held their grain sacks in one hand and their pistols in the other, watching the customers and the guard.

"Listen up and listen close, everybody," I said. "We have nothing to lose by shooting you people—but I don't want to do that. My boys and I are leaving now. I want everybody to look at the clock over the tellers' cages. If anyone moves from this moment until five minutes have elapsed, I'll find out about it and your life won't be worth a plugged nickel. Everybody clear on that?"

Everyone nodded.

One old man spoke. "Mister," he said, "your boys grabbed my money right offa the shelf here, an' it wasn't the goddamn bank's money—it was mine." I thought for a second, held both the sack and my pistol in the same hand, and pulled out some bills. "This should be enough, old timer," I said. As I was turning away I saw that at least a couple of the bills I'd handed over to the old guy were fifty-dollar notes. That felt good.

We backed out of the bank pretty much the way we entered. Zeke was in his saddle, holding the reins of the others. While we'd been inside he'd knotted each pair of reins together with itself, so that if there was trouble we wouldn't be grabbing the wrong reins. I hadn't thought of that. It made good sense. We mounted up and rode hard to the east. When we reached the end of the street and hit open prairie, I turned in my saddle and looked back. The town was as somnolent as it had been when we rode in. The bank doors were still closed.

We rode until nightfall, alternating between a gallop, lope, and fast walk, with the gallop, of course, being the shortest run in the sequence. A good western horse can settle in at a lope and go damned near forever without wearing himself out. Still, we walked fairly often, wanting to make certain we had enough horse left, should we need the speed.

Just before nightfall we flushed a half dozen or so of prairie chickens. I shot two down and Davey accounted for one. The birds were big and summer fat, and they'd make one fine meal. The flavor isn't far from that of a farm hen—maybe a bit more stringy and gamey—but they made good eating. We gathered up our kills and then rode on until dusk.

We camped on the lee side of a small rise and picked up wood from a scraggly stand of desert pine. I wasn't worried about a fire giving us away; I doubted that anyone even bothered to follow us or put up a posse to do it. The truth is, most folks don't care much that a bank gets robbed. If someone's hurt or killed that's a different story, of course, but if it's just money that's taken, nobody works up a sweat over it.

We dumped our money into a pile away from the fire and counted it. We did better than I thought we would, given that Dobbins was a dusty little jerkwater town in the middle of West Texas: $4,700.00. We divided it up equally, each man receiving $940.00.

"Whoooooeee!" Howard exclaimed. "I like this here bank-robbin' business!"

Davey looked at the stack of bills in his hand as if he'd discovered the secret of life. "Jesus Christ," he said reverently, "I never held no more than a twenty . . ."

That's as far as he got before Zeke whacked him a good one on the back of his head with his whiskey bottle, knocking him silly.

"Dammit, Zeke!" I bellowed at him. "You got to cut that shit out. Suppose the bottle broke—you'd have cut hell outta the boy's head."

"I already warned him," Zeke said defensively, almost petulantly. "If it takes a little tap once an' again to put an end to Davey's mocking the Lord, well then, it's worth it."

"You're wrong there, Zeke. Davey's a good kid who does what he's told and has all he needs to rob banks. You slamming him on the head needs to stop. I don't give a flying goddamn what he says—you lay offa him or you and me are going to have big trouble."

Zeke stood and looked at me, his eyes boring into mine. "I ain't scared of you, Pound. Your kid partner has no goddamn respect, an' I can't abide by that."

I searched Zeke's stance and his eyes and the way his right hand hovered over his pistol. The Colt was much too high for him to get a rapid grip. "You don't want to do this," I said. "You really don't. Maybe it's the booze giving you courage or maybe you're plain mad at me, but Zeke—you don't want to challenge me."

The heat left Zeke's eyes slowly. "It just ain't right, Pound," he said.

Davey had pulled himself up to a sitting position with his legs out in front of him. He held the back of his head tightly with both hands, as if he could squeeze the pain away.

"What the hell?" he said. "What happened?"

"Just a misunderstanding, is all," I said. "It's not going to happen again." I glanced over at Zeke. "Right, Zeke?"

"Yeah, OK—it ain't." He walked over to where Davey was sitting, still holding his head, and hunkered down next to him. "It ain't that I don't like you, boy. I do. But when I hear them words, I kinda lose control."

"I gotta tell you this, Zeke," Davey said. "If it does happen again I'm going to draw on you. That's a promise. Hear?"

"I hear. Look: might be a little toot of red-eye help

out your head." He stood and fetched his bottle from where he'd left it. Davey looked at it rather dubiously and then upended it and took in a pair of glugs. After a few moments he sat up straighter and grinned. "Works right good," he said. He held out his hand to Zeke for the bottle. "'Nother little taste wouldn't hurt."

I needed to talk to Davey, but away from the Stones and when he didn't have a snootful of Zeke's whiskey.

We cleaned our prairie chickens. Instead of trying to pull feathers we ripped their skins pure off. We lost a bit of meat from each of them, but not enough to worry about. We spitted various pieces on sticks and held them over the fire. The fat dripping into the fire made it flare up high enough to not only cook but singe the meat. It was a fine meal.

I saw no reason to post a lookout that night, and we didn't put out our fire, either—we just let it burn down on its own. That might sound a little cocky on our part, but I'd been involved in a slew of small-town bank robberies and like I said earlier, unless someone is hurt or killed no one would be dogging us. The talk around the fire as we drank our coffee turned, naturally enough, to where we were going next. I didn't know the territory well at all, so I had to rely on Zeke and his boys.

"There's a town maybe two, two and a half days' ride from here," Zeke said. "It's called Injunhead, 'cause when the railroad was comin' through they'd stick an Injun's head on a post every so often to keep the hostiles in line. Some good-size cattle drives end up in Injunhead, so the bank's bound to be bigger'n the one in Dobbins."

"Any of you ever been there?" I asked.

Zeke shook his head. "No, but I know it's there 'cause my cousin, Lucas, worked at a mercantile for a bit 'til the owner caught him stealin'. I don't know nothin' about the law there, though."

"Could be worth a try," I said. "The cattle buyers stash their money in the banks where the drive ends, so the bank could be nice and fat. I say we go there. What about you boys?"

"Let's do 'er," Zeke said.

"Sounds good to me," Davey said.

Randall and Howard spoke together, mimicking their father's words. "Let's do 'er!"

We did pretty well on water the first couple of days of our ride to Injunhead. The rain had been a toadchoker, and even the unrelenting sun took some time to lap it up. The third day we didn't do as well.

By midday we'd emptied our canteens into our hats for our horses and a sip for ourselves. All five of our mounts were dragging their hooves as they walked, and my buckskin was beginning to weave a bit. Both those things are bad signs. We needed water and we needed it badly.

There was no sense in stopping to rest; there was no escape from the pounding of the sun, no shade of any kind. We didn't talk as we plodded along. For one thing, we had nothing to say, and for another our mouths felt as if they were stuffed with cotton. My lips had cracked earlier in the day and when I looked over at Davey I saw speckles of blood under his lower lip.

I'd heard men—mostly miners and buffalo hunters—talk about mirages. Miners and skin hunters tend to exaggerate a good deal, so I didn't pay much attention to their tales. One old gaffer told me he almost beat his mule to death trying to get the animal to run toward the big city the miner saw just ahead. Others had seen lakes and ponds that were always just a little farther away.

There's a difference between a real mirage and sheets of what looks like water rising from the prairie floor. Mirages are more real. I was dizzy in my saddle when I thought I saw a copse of desert pines way out ahead of us. I wasn't sweating any longer; my skin was dry and felt clammy. I shut my eyes for maybe a minute and hoped that the trees would be gone when I opened them. The trees were still there. It didn't seem like we were drawing any closer to them, but they were there. I reached over and poked Davey, who was riding next to me, on the shoulder and brought him out of his feverish half sleep. His eyes were red-rimmed and crusty. I pointed ahead. He squinted, shading his eyes with his hand. There was disbelief all over his face when he looked back at me and he shook his head slowly from side to side. He'd evidently heard the same mirage stories I had.

Then, of a sudden, his roan's head popped up from where his snout had almost been dragging in the sand. My horse did the same thing, alert now, ears ahead, drawing in huge drafts of the superheated air and testing it with his nostrils. Behind me I could hear the Stones scuffling with their mounts. Then, like a stampede all five of our horses began to run—and run hard, in spite of their condition. It probably wasn't the brightest thing in the world for us to do, but we gave them all the rein they wanted and launched a headlong charge at what *wasn't* a mirage.

It was perhaps a half acre in size and all but the

very center of the pond was thickly covered with green scum. The water was about ten inches deep at the shoreline, and it didn't get much deeper farther out into the pond. There was a pervasive, almost sickening stench of rot in the air, and we'd apparently irritated a bunch of bullfrogs whose croaking was almost loud enough to be deafening.

Neither us or the horses gave a damn about all that. We charged in, pushed off our saddles, cleared some scum from in front of us, and drank. The horses buried their snouts and sucked the tepid, metallic-tasting water, grunting like satisfied sows. We had to goad them out with curses and our heels banging on their sides to get them out of the pond, but letting them drink too much too fast could cause a ton of major problems, such as founder, which can cripple a horse.

We were so frantic for water that we'd ridden into the pond with our pistols in our holsters, which meant that we had some cleaning and oiling to do. The bunch of us stripped down to our skin when we let the horses have another drink and took the first bath any of us had for a good long time. Even with the water as foul as it was, it felt wonderful on our parched skin.

I looked around at the other fellows as they played about in the water, splashing one another, acting like a crew of grammar school kids skipping school for a dunk in the swimming pond.

There aren't many people who've seen a cowhand or a sodbuster naked: maybe their wives and perhaps a barber after the 'hand's paid twenty-five cents for a bath in a barbershop. Other than that, these men don't see bathing water for half a year or more.

Those who've viewed cowhands and farmers in the flesh hope that people they care about don't have to see the same thing.

A cowhand's or sodbuster's face and hands—or maybe part of their arms if they rolled their sleeves—are a dark, ineradicable, chestnut color. It isn't unpleasant to look upon. The rest of the man's body, though, is enough to make a maggot vomit. Their skin is a sickly, pallid, corpselike white. Even the black men who work cattle showed much the same thing. Dark flesh does indeed grow darker, and black flesh constantly clothed becomes a washed-out nutmeg sort of hue that doesn't look a bit healthy.

I suppose that the scum sticking to our hair didn't add much to our beauty—but what the hell. The midfloor of the pond was a slippery, silt-muddy mess. Close to the shore, though, the sand was gritty and firm and could readily be employed as soap. It was quite abrasive, but it for sure did the job of scraping off months of sweat and trail grit and so forth.

After we'd sanded ourselves off, we began discussing our next step. Of course, we were going to Injunhead. Here's the thing: having five men obviously together ride into a town when there's no cattle drive being completed, just doesn't look right.

"I'm gonna get me a steak as big as a saddle blanket," Randall said, "and there ain't goin' to be enough of it left to feed a goddamn flea."

"That steak sounds good," Davey said. "Maybe some mashed potatoes wouldn't hurt, neither."

"I'm going to have a meal an' then play me some poker," Zeke said. "I'm feeling lucky."

"You won't feel so lucky if Ma finds out," Randall laughed. "What about you, Pound?"

"Seems like I haven't had an egg in a 'coon's age. I'll have a cook scramble up a half dozen or so and cook up some bacon. Then I'll check out the bank, see what we might run into when we're ready to get to work. There's no hurry—we can all use a couple of days of not doing much of anything. One thing—check your horse's shoes, and make sure they're set right."

We decided to let our clothes dry in the sun and then ride into Injunhead. Randall, Davey, and Zeke would ride together, and Howard and I would pair up. We figured there had to be a couple of hotels in town and decided we'd split up in lodging, just as we did in entering town.

Injunhead was about twice the size of Dobbins. The buildings were nicely false-fronted and white-washed, and there were even wooden sidewalks in front of some of the stores. The mercantile was a large one, with a long plate glass window that must have cost a pretty dollar to ship and erect. There was a church at one end of the main street. The tinkling of piano music snuck into the street from three saloons. The bank was roughly midblock, and was a solid-looking structure. It was closed for the day, but I hadn't planned to go in and do any snooping until the following day, anyway.

Zeke's, Randall's, and Davey's horses were tied to the hitching rack in front of Joe's Restaurant. Howard and I rode past them and swung in at a hotel called Travelers Rest. We got a couple of rooms and gave the hotel restaurant a try. The food was good and there was plenty of it. Then we both lit cigars and walked the town. The walking made us thirsty so we pushed through the batwings of a saloon. The first words we heard were bellowed by Zeke Stone: "You're cheatin', you dirty sumbitch!"

Zeke had been playing poker with four men. Three of them had backed way the hell out of the line of fire. The table was upended and there were bills and coins soaking in spilled whiskey and beer. Zeke's face was scarlet, his eyes crazy-wild. The man Zeke had challenged stood easily, one foot a few inches behind the other. He had a long cheroot in this mouth. He was dressed like a banker in a nice suit and vest and a string tie, and the gold chain of a watch crossed his stomach.

"Shit," I said aloud.

It wasn't so much the man's stance or his clothing, or even the Colt .45 holstered low on his right side and secured to his leg with latigo that frightened me. It was the look in his eyes. They were flat, almost uninterested, like those of a fellow ready to doze off in church when a sermon got to be too long on a Sunday morning. His right hand hung casually at his side, fingers barely touching the bone grips on his pistol. His fingers were marble-still, with no tremble whatsoever. It was clear he'd done this before; he wouldn't be standing there if he'd lost.

In contrast, Zeke looked like a damned clown. His feet were a yard apart, his new holster was strapped way too high—up to his waist and a bit more—and the untreated leather of his holster made it stick out to the side like a cowlick on a boy's head.

The place had gone tomb-quiet. Even the piano player stopped in the middle of "Buffalo Gals." So, my exclamation of "Shit" was heard easily enough. The gambler's eyes flicked to me for a second and then returned to Zeke.

"Mister," I said, "my friend has had too much to drink. He's in no shape to go up against you or anyone else. I'll make up any losses from when he dumped the table and buy you a drink. Will that settle things?" Then, I added, "My friend doesn't mean any harm, mister. It's the booze that's talking for him."

The gambler had a rusty, tobacco-and-whiskey sort of voice. He didn't speak loud, but each word was clear. There was no anger, no emotion at all in his voice, but there didn't need to be. His words said all he needed to.

"This drunken fool called me a cheat a few minutes ago. I let that go. But nobody calls me a cheat the second time. There are men in pine boxes who tried it."

I pushed forward, wanting to get between Zeke and the gambler, which probably wasn't a terribly bright thing to do. Zeke made a clumsy grab at his pistol. I slammed my hand and forearm down, knocking the Colt from his drunken grip. He took a swing at me and I put everything I had into a roundhouse right that took him on the jaw. He went down like a tossed sack of grain. I turned back to the gambler. The muzzle was pointed at my chest.

"You looking to die?" the gambler asked in that same unexcited voice.

"No—no, I'm not," I said, keeping my hand a good distance from my pistol. "We have no argument with one another, and this chucklehead is down and out. How about that drink?"

It was an eternity before the gambler holstered his weapon and said, "Sure. Why not?"

I grabbed Howard by the arm. "Look," I said, none too gently, "you get this imbecile to his room.

Tie him up if you need to, but keep him there. Understand?"

Howard understood. He pulled Zeke up from the floor, slung the man over his shoulder, and wobbled his way to the street. The piano started up again and the conversations continued from where they'd broken off. The whole life-or-death matter was instantly forgotten.

The gambler and I walked to the bar. I asked the barkeep for the best he had and to leave the bottle. I filled a pair of shot glasses and we both drank.

"Your friend isn't going to last too long if he doesn't get his mouth and his booze under control," the gambler said. "He came within a frog's hair of catching a couple of slugs a few moments ago."

"Yeah. I know. I'll tell you something, though—that's the last time I step between him and a man who handles a gun the way you do."

The gambler nodded. "Good advice," he said. "You in Injunhead long?"

"No. A couple, three days. We have some business to take care of and then we're heading out."

"Business?"

"Land speculation—nothing very interesting."

The gambler poured us each another shot. "I thought the army owned all the land around here," he said.

The army? "We're looking into bits and pieces."

I steered the conversation away from business, but I couldn't help but wonder what need the army had for Injunhead. After a couple more drinks I paid for the bottle and handed it to the gambler. We didn't shake hands.

I figured Howard would take Zeke to the room in

the hotel where we were staying, and I was right. Zeke was passed out on the bed in Howard's room, hands and feet bound. "He give you any trouble?" I asked.

"Nah. He passed out soon's he hit the bed. I trussed him up a little just to be on the safe side."

"I don't have to tell you that your pa was in some deep trouble with that gambler," I said.

"Nossir, you surely don't."

"If he gets screwy in a bank he's liable to get himself and some of us killed."

Howard nodded but didn't meet my eyes.

I stretched and yawned. The whiskey and the big meal earlier had made me sleepy. "When Zeke wakes up tell him I'll be here early to talk with him about what went on tonight. You might let him know I'm damned angry about it and that I can't tolerate such horseshit."

"I'll do that, Pound," Howard said. "Maybe he'll listen to you. He ain't much good at listenin' to nobody else, 'cept maybe my ma."

"He'd better listen real well tomorrow, because I'm not going to ride with him if he's going to cause trouble. Robbing banks is more than risky enough without having to babysit a crazy man."

"Yessir," Howard said. "I'll tell him all that."

I decided to walk off some of my frustration and anger. I came across Davey and Randall sitting on rockers in front of the mercantile, which had been closed for several hours. They both smelled a bit boozy, but I wouldn't call either of them drunk. I told them what happened with the gambler. Davey shook his head. Randall stared down at the ground in front of him. "I'll be talking to Zeke early tomorrow," I said. "And either get things straight or break up this gang. There's nothing in between."

I sat in a rocker next to Davey and rolled a cigarette. The three of us were quiet for a bit. Then, Davey said, "We found out a little about the marshal. His name's Jack Corey. He gets lot of respect around here. He's said to be handy with both a pistol and a rifle."

"That doesn't sound real good," I said.

"No," Randall said, "but he's outta town for a few days deliverin' a prisoner. If we get the bank, say, tomorrow or the day after, we'll be long gone 'fore he comes back."

My cigarette tasted raw and dry. I flicked it out into the street and stood. "I'm going to get some sleep. You boys best do the same. We'll make more plans tomorrow."

I couldn't hear much street noise from my room. I stretched out on the bed and, although I was tired, I couldn't seem to capture sleep. For whatever reason, I kept turning over the fact the army owned much of the land in the area. I didn't see what difference that would make, but the thought bothered me like a mosquito buzzing around. I finally slept—but not for very long.

The sun was barely up when the trumpet jarred me awake. I pulled on my pants and a shirt and went downstairs to the restaurant. "What lunatic plays a goddamn trumpet at this hour of the morning?" I groused to the cook.

"Why, that's the wake-call from the camp," he told me.

"Camp? Where?"

"Not more'n a half mile that way," he said, pointing with his spatula.

"I didn't see any soldiers in town last night. Seems like the bar would be full of them."

"Well, they usually are. Thing is, Marshal Corey banned all of them for a week for racin' their horses in the streets an' fightin' drunk an' so forth. Hell, half my business comes from the camp."

"How large is it?"

"Maybe four or five hundred mounted men. They built it right after the end of the war."

"Jesus Christ," I muttered. "We might just as well try to rob Fort Knox."

"Sir? I didn't catch that."

"Never mind—just talking to myself. That coffee almost ready?"

I drank a couple of mugs of coffee and went up to the room where Howard was holding Zeke. The old man was untied, and he looked like hell. As soon as I walked in he started on me. "Dammit, Pound, I don't need you to fight my battles for me. That sumbitch was cheatin' sure as you were born. If you hadn't busted in I'd have—"

"You'd have caught a couple rounds in the chest and you'd be dead right now," I snarled back at him. "That fellow was a professional. He'd have no more trouble killing you than he would swatting a fly."

"Professional, my ass! A professional cheater is what he was."

I'm not generally a violent man, but sheer, raw, unreasoning stupidity riles me. I had a very strong desire to punch the old fool just as I had the night before.

"Pa," Howard said quietly. "Pound, he saved your life."

"I don't need nobody lookin' after me."

"You did last night, Pa."

"Horseshit." Zeke stood from the bed, tucked in his shirt, and pushed his way past me to the door.

"Where ya goin'?" Howard asked.

"I'm goin' to get me some grub an' a taste of eye-opener."

"You come back here drunk and the whole thing is over, Zeke. I mean it. I won't ride with you and I won't let Davey, either," I said. "This goddamn town you brought us to is about a half mile from four hundred mounted and armed soldiers. We wouldn't have a chance robbing the bank. And if your cousin Lucas had paid more attention when he was here than on how much money was in the boss's till, we wouldn't have had to ride through hell to find out there's an army camp right next door."

Zeke mumbled something as he went out the door. I doubt that it was a compliment to me. I sat on a rickety chair in the corner and said to Howard, "Get Davey and Randall and bring them on up here. We need to talk."

It didn't take Howard long to find the others. They, too, had been awakened by the trumpet and assembled at a restaurant for coffee and breakfast.

The room was small, and seemed much smaller with four men in it. I led things off. "Some of the things I'm going to say will probably upset you boys, maybe make you mad at me. If that's the case, so be it." I took a breath. "Zeke damn near got himself killed last night, and I had a good chance of dying because I mixed into it. Zeke had a snootful and accused a gambler of cheating. Then, after that godawful ride to get to Injunhead, we discover there's an army fort a stone's throw from here with a slew of mounted and armed men. We wouldn't have gotten a mile away. That'd mean jail for you boys and a rope for me."

A silence ensued before Randall said, "Pa don't mean nothin' by what he does."

"I realize that and it doesn't make a damned bit of difference. Fact of the matter is, he's going to get some of us or all of us dead."

"Are you sayin' you won't ride with us no more?" Randall asked.

"I don't see any way around it. Unless Zeke straightens out, I'm ridin' out of Injunhead alone—or with Davey. But I won't be riding with the Stones."

"Don't seem fair," Howard said. "Pa's a good man."

"Maybe so," I admitted. "But like I said a minute ago, unless he changes a whole lot, he's going to get some or all of us killed."

"We got you outta jail," Randall said. "You didn't complain about Pa then, now did you?"

"No, I didn't. But we're talking about two entirely different things. What—"

"Jesus!" Davey exclaimed. He had shifted to look out the window, which had a good view of the street. "Pound—look at this!"

We all hustled to the window. There, on a bench outside one of the saloons, the gambler was sitting, smoking a cigar, his hat tilted far forward to keep the sun out of his eyes. Zeke stood in the middle of the street with a bottle in one hand and his Colt in the other. "Come on an' get on your feet so's I can knock you down, you goddamn cheat."

The gambler blew a perfect smoke ring that hung in the air for quite awhile before it broke up.

Zeke fired somewhere in the gambler's direction, his bullet punching through one of the batwing doors.

"This is awful stupid, ol' man," the gambler said. "Fact is, it's deadly stupid."

I rushed to the door with the others on my heels. We got down the stairs and burst out of the hotel—and then stopped. The gambler was standing, his cigar set between his teeth. He'd pushed his coat back so that it wouldn't impose on his draw. Zeke was taking a long glug from his bottle. He wiped his mouth on his sleeve and raised his Colt.

"Don't do it, Zeke!" I yelled. "Don't—"

Zeke fired again and this time his slug dug a hole in the wood maybe a foot and a half away from the gambler's head. I was looking right at the gambler and I didn't see his pistol appear in his hand—he was that fast. He fired what sounded like a single shot but was actually two. We could tell that because two red spots about the size of a nickel appeared in Zeke Stone's chest. Zeke took half a step back and then went down suddenly and silently, as if there was nothing left in him to hold him up.

The gambler holstered his pistol, sat back down and took a pull on his cigar. He knew what he'd done was purely and simply self-defense, and everyone watching from behind windows would swear to that. He blew another smoke ring.

The Stones ran to their father and Randall cradled Zeke's head in his lap. Tears streamed down Howard's face. Davey stood a couple of feet away, his face white.

"You didn't have to kill the ol' guy," Davey said. His voice quivered with either anger or fear. I wasn't sure which.

The gambler laughed. "No, you're right. I should have let the old bar rag throw shots at me until he got real lucky and hit me with one."

"That ain't what I meant and you know it. You could have slugged him in the mouth or shot him in the foot or somethin'. He didn't do nothin' that called for killin'."

"Davey . . ." I began.

Davey's voice wasn't trembling any longer. Now he sounded mad. "I'm thinkin' you're a low-down cheatin' pile of shit, jus' like Zeke said you was."

The smile left the gambler's face in a big hurry. He tilted his hat back to get a better look at Davey. "My, my," he said mockingly. "If you ain't all dressed up as a shootist! Why, lookit that Colt tied down to your leg, and the easy, comfortable way that pistol sits in your holster like a baby in its mama's lap."

"Davey," I said louder, moving toward him, "for God's sake shut the—"

"Hold it there, hero," the gambler said. "You ain't gonna jam yourself between me and this little turd the way you did with the drunken fool last night. You stand right where you are."

"He's just a kid," I said.

"Right. A kid with a Colt on his leg and a bloodlust that makes him want to show he's faster than I am, better than I am. Thing is, that isn't going to happen. If I stand up from this bench again, it means one of us is going down dead." He struck a match and relit his cigar. "A man can't have a moment of peace of a morning, without some pup or drunk stirring things up." He sighed. "Gets right tedious."

I started toward Davey again.

"You stop right there, hero. You heard what I said before and I meant it."

Davey's eyes were hot, dark embers that blazed against the paleness of his face. His Adam's apple bobbed a couple of times, but that was his only outward show of fear. His right hand—hovering near his Colt, fingers curved slightly inward—was steady.

The gambler drew on his cigar and blew another smoke ring. "Lookit, kid," he said, now sounding aggravated. "If you're going to do something, you go ahead and do it. I don't care to sit here for the rest of the day waiting on you to get your courage up."

"You said you were going to stand," Davey said.

"Why, so I did, boy. And I'm always a man of my word." He drew on his cigar a final time and tossed the nub into the street.

From that moment forward, everything slowed down until it was barely moving. The gambler was on his feet, crouching slightly, the barrel of his pistol picking up the early sun and glinting. He moved to his side rather than standing straight up as he had when he shot Zeke, but to me it looked like he was moving underwater, his actions foolishly, ludicrously slow.

I watched Davey's draw. It was a single, slow, smooth motion. He held his pistol slightly above waist height and a pair of puffs of blue smoke rolled out of the muzzle. One took the gambler in the neck, the other in his chest.

Then things speeded up. Blood gushed from the

man's neck and he crashed to the ground next to the bench, where the thick stream of blood slowed and stopped. His pistol hadn't yet cleared leather.

"Dumb bastard," Davey said.

Chapter Four

I took a good look at Zeke. There was no way a doc or anyone else could do him any good. Randall and Howard were hunkered down by their father's body. Randall was slapping at Zeke's face lightly, as if to awaken him from a nap. Howard gaped at the body, mumbling.

"We've got to get the hell out of Injunhead," I said. "There are a crateful of gawkers at windows and they'll all say Davey goaded the gambler into a gunfight and then dropped him. It wasn't self-defense; Davey began his draw first. The law will see it as murder."

"I'll get the horses," Davey said, starting toward the stable and livery.

I crouched next to the boys. "As far as I can see, neither of you had anything at all to do with the gambler being gunned. If you want to stay here and see to a decent burial for your pa, that's fine. I don't suppose you want to ride with Davey and me and I can't blame you for that. But, Davey and I don't have any time to think things over."

Howard looked up at me, his eyes still tearing and his face a mask of anguish. "I'll ride with you,

Pound. I got nothin' else to do, an' Ma is well took care of."

"That's up to you, Howard," I said. "Randall?"

"Yeah. Me too. Pa ain't gonna be any more or less dead no matter what we do. I like outlawin'. I'm comin' with you boys."

Davey hauled his roan to a stop next to me and handed over my reins. "I saddled an' bridled Randall and Howard's horses but didn't want to lead them down here, not knowin' if they were comin' with us," he said.

The Stone brothers stood up from their father's body. Randall swung on my horse behind me just as Howard did with Davey. We collected the horses at the livery and lit out, riding in an east-northeast direction. There were railroad tracks that pointed that way and I figured there must be something down the line.

We left Zeke's horse and gear with the stable owner in payment for boarding and feeding our mounts.

We rode hard and long, using the walk-lope-gallop sequence to avoid burning out our horses. We cut water a couple of times and let the horses drink while we filled our canteens. Nobody said much of anything, particularly the Stone boys, who were as quiet as statues.

"Well, hell," Davey said once as we rested our horses, "looks like the man with the rope is looking for both of us now."

"Looks that way."

"I don't see that it makes no difference, Pound. Nobody ever said bank robbin' was easy. That gambler got what he had comin' to him, an' I don't give a goddamn what a jury says, 'cause I'll never stand in front of one. Thinkin' about being strung up scares the piss outta me. No matter what happens, I'm saving a bullet for myself. I'd rather check out that way than provide entertainment for a bunch of gawkers."

I couldn't think of a way to argue with Davey. Before we pulled our cinches and saddled up, I felt for the single .45 bullet I'd been carrying in my pants pocket ever since we bought supplies. It'd gotten to be a habit with me to feel for it every once and again. I wasn't going to swing either, regardless of what happened. Davey and I both had cartridges in the loops in our gunbelts and plenty more in our saddlebags, but it seemed like a good idea to have one set aside, kind of like insurance that I'd never see a damned rope with a noose at the end of it.

We kept the railroad tracks in sight until it became too dark to see them. We hauled in to camp under a couple of trees with some buffalo grass around them like a big apron to let the horses graze. We decided against a fire, but we all sure would have loved a cup of coffee.

We were quiet for a long time, gnawing on jerky and looking up at the stars. Howard spoke first. "This don't change nothin'," he said. "Pa is dead. I loved him, I guess, although it wasn't hard to see that he was gettin' more an' more loony as time went on."

"Seems like the whiskey rotted his brain," Randall said. "I loved him an' he was good to Ma most of the time, but—tell the truth—bustin' you boys outta jail didn't make no sense to my brother an' me. We done it 'cause it was what Pa wanted real bad."

"We could wire some money, and have your pa's body shipped back home," I said.

"What good would that do?" Randall asked. "He'd be pretty ripe by then and Ma would have to get a box and get a hole dug an' her brother might get around to that about Christmastime."

Howard nodded in agreement. "Injunhead has a Boot Hill and they'll plant Pa there. That'll do. We can write Ma a letter soon's we get some paper an' a pencil an' envelope."

"Ain't neither of us can write. We can do some sums good, though."

I nodded. "You tell me what you want and I'll write it down as pretty as can be for you. I was once a schoolteacher."

"How'd you ever swing to robbin' banks, Pound?" Randall asked.

"It's a long story. We'll get to it another time."

Davey grinned over at me. He knew the whole sordid story: how I got fired by the school for being a drunk, how I partnered up with Zeb Stone, and what went wrong in Paris, where Zeb was killed. That was a good thing about Davey; he didn't flap his gums unless he had something to say, and I was positive he'd die before he'd break a confidence.

After another silence, Randall spoke. "You an' Davey gonna take us with you, Pound? Robbin' banks an' all?"

"Is that what you want to do?" I asked. "I thought we already discussed that."

"Well, growin' hemp ain't real interestin' an' it don't pay all that much. Plus, Pa spent a good part of the money on pulque," Howard said.

"What's pulque?" Davey asked.

"Mex booze," Howard said, "made from cactus and other shit they throw in the pot. Tastes like a coyote pissed in it."

I gave the boys some thought. I rolled a smoke and said to Davey, "Let's take a little walk."

"Jus' you boys?" Randall asked.

"Yeah," I said. "We have things to discuss."

When we were far enough from the Stones not to be heard, I said to Davey, "What do you think?"

"I ain't one to leap at the first idea that comes along," Davey said. "How about this. We try another bank and see how Howard an' Randall do. If they screw up, we cut them loose, an' if they do their parts, we keep 'em." After another second, "Hell, Pound, we got their pa killed."

Sometimes Davey spoke and thought like a man; other times I was forced to remember how young he was. "That's pure bullshit," I said. "Sooner or later Zeke would have gotten juiced up and mouthed off to the wrong man and he'd be just as dead as he is now."

"Maybe so. But we owe them the chance. An' I got an idea too. If we follow these tracks we're bound to come to some sort of town or settlement. We haven't had much to eat an' my gut's talking to me. Even if the town don't have a bank, I say we take the mercantile—not only for the money but some canned meat an' such. The horses could use a good feed too—some crimped oats, maybe, with a touch of molasses to keep their fire up."

I smiled at Davey but I don't know if he could see it in the dark. "You know, boy," I said, "I always figured you for a smart fellow. I like your idea just fine.

There's bound to be a town up ahead and I'd wager we'll come to it tomorrow. Come to think of it, my boots are about shot to hell, and a box of cheroots—those long, black ones—would be right handy."

"I was kinda thinkin' of a new hat," Davey said. "A Stetson, if they got them. An' I've had a hankerin' for canned peaches for weeks an' every mercantile I ever been in has them. Canned ham don't make bad eatin', and it won't go bad on us too quick. Hell, we better make a shoppin' list for tomorra."

As it turned out, we didn't need the shopping list for almost three days.

It's hard for anyone who hasn't been to Texas to imagine the size of it. It goes on forever in all directions, and a man will wonder if it ever really ends. I had a gent tell me one time that Texas was like a good watch that was wound and cared for every day—it just kept on going beyond anywhere there was to go.

Water was getting more and more scarce. We came upon rank water with no animal tracks around it and we had to beat and spur our horses away from it. If the desert and prairie animals couldn't drink it and stay alive, neither could our horses—and neither could we for that matter.

For all three of those days we rode we never saw a train going in either direction. This was a double set, you see, and double sets usually indicated there was commercial hauling or goods or even passengers, although who'd want to take a goddamn train to hell?

We had nothing to bitch about but the heat and our thirst and that of the horses, so we turned our venom on the railroad.

"Sonsabitches in New York and Chicago run these tracks wherever they please, whether or not anybody ever uses them," Howard said.

"Should we come on a depot 'fore we make a town, no matter what size it is, I'm gonna kick that ticket clerk's ass up through the top of his head and take every penny in the till, and his own money too," Randall offered.

"Look," Davey said, "these tracks go somewhere. All we need do is keep us an' our horses alive an' we'll get there."

I had nothing to add to the conversation, but I admit I was thinking along the same lines as Howard.

We hit a spring about the size of a spittoon and let the horses have first crack at it. It wasn't more'n a couple feet deep, and the water was the temperature of fresh piss, but there were coyote and prairie tracks around it, so we figured it was fairly safe. The horses sucked it dry, shoving and biting one another, trying to get more. It took maybe an hour for the spring to recover and the four of us dropped to the dirt and stuck our faces in and drank crazy. When it next filled, we let the horses have another run at it. We must have spent two, three hours out there with the sun so blazing hot and near that a man with a short stepladder could touch it, emptying that muddy little hole and then letting it replenish itself.

Of course there was next to no grazing for the horses and we were down to our last shreds of jerky. We saw a couple hares, and Davey and I each took a shot, but we missed them because they were running right into the sun. "Prolly stringy sonsabitches anyway," Davey said.

Just before dark, when the temperature had dropped a couple of degrees, we saw a thin wisp of smoke rising to the sky a few miles on down the tracks. We would have whooped, but there wasn't enough saliva among us to give a flea a footbath. What we did was urge our horses into an unsteady lope. At first they resented that—they were as weary as we were—but as we drew closer to the smoke, they picked up the scents of man, which meant water and feed to them.

About a half mile out there was a shot to hell sign stating, TOWN OF DOREEN. We had to draw rein to keep the horses from going nuts, and we held them in tight check walking down the street of Doreen. The town was about Dobbins's size or a bit smaller. There were no sidewalks at all and the street was deeply rutted, with potholes big enough to swallow a Brahma bull. A church was the first thing we heard or saw at the very end of the street coming in. It was small, unpainted, and the entire structure seemed to lean quite a bit to the left. A sign stuck in the ground said, HOLEY TEMPLE OF JESUS. ALL WELLCOME." The misspellings or the building itself wasn't what caught our attention, though. From inside the church came the barking of dogs, mooing of cows, coyote yelps, and screams of "Jesus!"

The front doors were wide open and so were the windows. As thirsty as we were and as antsy as our mounts were, we simply had to take a little peek inside to see what all the racket was. Davey stepped down from his roan, took a good grip on the reins, and walked up to the door. "Holy shit!" he exclaimed, and waved us on. The rest of us dismounted and joined Davey.

Inside the church there were a dozen or more folks rolling about on the dirt floor, making the animal noises. A heavy fellow in a black robe with a Bible in his hand was bellowing something about ". . . taking up the vile serpents . . ." One man, tall, thin, stoop-shouldered, pushed past a mooing lady and went to the front of the church. There was a wooden crate there with a cross painted on its top. He opened it, reached in better than elbow deep, and withdrew a handful of six or eight writhing, twisting snakes and held them over his head, a look of pure ecstasy on his face. His mouth gaped wide open and the few teeth he had were yellowed and chipped or broken. I recognized a few of the reptiles he held: a couple of harmless bullsnakes, some common grass snakes—and at least two full-grown rattlers. Another fellow came up and reached into the box and then another.

"Goddamn," Randall said. "Is they all crazy?"

"Close enough to it to touch it," I said. "C'mon—let's get these horses to the livery." It wasn't but a short walk so we didn't mount up. There was a mercantile, a pair of saloons, a livery stable and blacksmith shop, an undertaker and furniture maker, and that was about it.

"Pound, what the hell was them folks doin'?" Howard asked.

"I saw it once before at a tent revival," I said. "They believe that the Bible will protect them from vipers or some such stupid thing. I got a chance to look into the snake box afterward and saw that none of the rattlers had fangs—they'd been yanked out."

"The ones we saw tonight had fangs," Davey said. "I seen 'em."

"Yeah. So did I."

"What's the snakes got to do with rollin' around in the dirt mooin' and barkin' an' such?" Randall wanted to know.

"Beats hell out of me," I said.

The blacksmith who ran the livery was built like an oak tree, and probably just as strong. He said he'd ration water to the horses and then, later on, grain them good and check the set of their shoes. He said he'd give them each a flake of good hay for overnight. That sounded real good to us.

"Where you boys from?" he asked. "You lookin' for cattle work?"

"We're originally from San Antone," I said. It was the first name that popped into my mind. "And yeah, we're looking to pick up a season of cattle work."

The blacksmith spat on the ground and shifted the wad of tobacco from one side of his mouth to the other. "Cattle work, my ass," he said. "Not one of you has a rope on your saddle an' none of you got the look of a cowhand to him. I'll tell you what: Doreen is a decent little town. You mind your business an' we'll mind ours, an' then you'll ride on out. That suit you?"

"Suits us fine. Just now, we're about dying of thirst and hunger too. We'll be back to even up with you tomorrow, OK?"

That was fine with the 'smith.

The first saloon we came to was a ramshackle affair, but they were cooking steaks outside on a barrel cut lengthwise to use as a grill. That's what put up the smoke we saw. The cooking meat smelled as sweet as honey. We sat at a table inside and drank several buckets of beer. I was surprised that the beer was cold, but the owner explained they cut and stored ice in the winter from a pond nearby. If I'd ever tasted anything finer than that beer, I'd be awful hard-pressed to say what it was.

Each of us had a steak that hung over all sides of a large plate, and the meat was tender and bloodred inside, which is the only way to eat beef.

After we'd finished up at the saloon I bought a cigar and we walked the length of both sides of the street. It was pretty dark by then so we couldn't see much in the mercantile, but I didn't have any doubt that they'd have everything we needed.

We met the sheriff, who seemed to be a decent enough fellow. He was young—not much older than Davey—and I noticed his badge was cleaned and nicely polished. We didn't get his name.

There wasn't a real hotel in Doreen. There was a small whorehouse, but that isn't a place where a man stays overnight. We found a little rooming house that served us just fine. For a quarter apiece we each got a bed and a breakfast in the morning.

Early the next morning after a fine breakfast of bacon and biscuits and fair to middlin' coffee—which was nowhere as good as Agnes's had been, but was still tasty—I gave the landlady three dollars. She acted like I'd given her a handful of diamonds.

"My boys and me appreciate a comfortable bed, good cooking, and good service, ma'am," I said, "and you provided us with all three. You have a nice day now, hear?"

Cooler air had moved in from somewhere overnight, and it was a pleasure to be walking down the main street of Doreen, in no hurry at all, enjoying the sweet freshness of the breeze. We sauntered into the sheriff's office and found him with a mug of coffee, looking over some papers.

"Mornin', gents," he said. "This coffee ain't half bad. Help yourself. I even got some fresh cream." The little stove he used was a few feet behind his desk, right near to the two cells he had.

"Be glad to," I said. I walked behind him, drew my Colt, and gave him a solid whack on the top of his head with it. He didn't bleed much, although head wounds do generally tend to bleed copiously. We gagged the sheriff, tied him up nice and snug, and dragged him into one of his cells. The keys were in his desk; we locked the cell door and tossed the keys into his trash basket. Then we left.

As we walked past the mercantile to the stable, the storekeep was just opening up for business. We "Howdy'd" him and he gave us a smile and a "Fine mornin', ain't it?"

The 'smith was bringing the fire in his forge to proper heat, pumping the bellows.

"Good stock you boys have," he said. "I reset a shoe on the black and another on the bay. They've been fed—both grain and hay—and they're ready to make tracks."

Davey picked up a heavy, broad-faced hammer from a workbench and slammed it down on the blacksmith's head. The sound was like that when a steer is slaughtered with a sledge. The 'smith dropped to the floor. We gagged and tied him and dragged him into an empty stall.

The mercantile was small but tidy and it smelled as good as all such stores do: of leather and wood and metal tools and gun oil and brand-new clothes. Randall closed the door after we entered and turned the sign that hung in it from OPEN to CLOSED.

The storekeep got a little feisty about that and after a bit we had to tie and gag him too. I don't doubt I could write a full page of what we took from the store, but I'll just list some of it: canned peaches, canned ham, three Stetson hats, several boxes of ammunition, a Case knife for each of us, several handfuls of beef jerky, six canteens, and a dozen or better licorice straps from the penny candy counter, a box of cheroots, and a coffeepot.

I fought and cursed my way into a pair of fine-looking boots with a sharp riding heel. I knew my feet would be sore for a few days, but after a bit the boots would fit perfectly. We each took a Winchester 30.06 lever-action rifle and ammunition.

Of course, the boys picked up knickknacks: harmonicas, bandanas, hard candy, and so forth. I took a creamy white envelope, a few sheets of good paper, a quill, and a bottle of ink.

"Come on, boys," I finally said. "We're going to need a couple pack mules if we take anything else out of here." We'd tied our horses out back and that's where we filled our saddlebags. It was Howard who remembered that we needed saddle scabbards for our new rifles and went back into the store to fetch them.

We rode out of Doreen happy as can be, me sucking on a cheroot.

We'd gone maybe a couple of miles—I know that because my cheroot was down to a nub—when Randall pulled his horse up to the right side of mine. I looked over at him enquiringly. "What's up, Randall?"

"I jus' been thinkin', is all. It ain't criticism, mind you—jus' thinking."

"About what?"

"Well, see, we coulda paid for the things we took outta that mercantile without makin' a dent in our money from the bank job. 'Stead, we stole the stuff. I can't figure that out, Pound. I've chewed it over an' twisted it around in my head and it still don't make no sense."

I paused a bit, wanting to form just the right words. I noticed Howard and Davey had come up closer to us. "You need to understand," I said, "that you're completely different men than you were a couple of days ago. Except for me and Davey, you fellows had no squall with the law. Now you have. We robbed a bank and one of our people was killed and Davey gunned down a man. Like I said, everything's different. Every lawman in Texas will be watching out for us." I lit another cheroot.

"We stole from the mercantile because that's what we do, gentlemen. We don't buy—we take, we steal. We don't spend the money we've robbed until we're ready to, and we weren't ready back there in Doreen. Keep this one thought in your mind: we're different men now. Our whole lives are changed."

Nobody spoke for a few moments. "But, Pound," Howard eventually said, "you and Davey already had your asses in a crack, right?"

"And so have you since we robbed the Dobbins bank—and even before that when you broke us out of jail."

"Yeah, but we ain't killed nobody, right?"

I reined in and the others stopped around me. I was getting a little sick of Howard and Randall and their worries. "Look," I said, "there are a whole bunch of directions you boys can ride off in. If you're scared, or if you don't care to stick with me and Davey, just point your horse in one of those directions and light out."

"No need to get all prickly," Howard mumbled.

"How about this," Davey said. "There's no need for you boys to hang on with us 'less that's what you want to do. We can part friends if you ride off. Hell, you ain't done but one pissant bank an' a little mercantile. Let your beards grow in and nobody will recognize you. Fair 'nuff?"

"Who gets Pa's share?" Howard asked,

"Your ma," I said. "That's why I took the paper and envelope at the store—to write her Zeke's deed and send his share to her."

"Me an' Randall, we got to talk for a minute. You boys stay here, OK?"

"Fine with me," I said. Davey nodded.

When the Stones had ridden a hundred yards or so they dismounted and faced one another, talking.

"Truth is," Davey said, "I ain't real sure I want those two with us, Pound. Them an' their pa have gave us nothing but trouble. 'Raise your sticks—this is a hand-up.' Jesus."

"I can't disagree with you, Davey. But, I owe their pa and I owe them. If they hadn't come along, I'd have stretched a rope. No doubt about that. So, I can't just shag them off like a pair of pesky dogs."

The Stones had remounted and were riding toward us. "Looka like they ain't cut an' run, anyway," Davey said.

Randall pulled in next me; Howard hung back a

bit. "We wasn't meanin' to rile you, Pound. 'Course we got some questions—this robbin' is a new perfession for us. But we like it an' we like you boys an' we'll learn the business as we go along." He waited for a moment, his face slightly flushed. "Can we all shake on that?"

Howard moved his horse a few steps ahead and we each shook hands with one another. Then Randall turned in his saddle and pulled out a bottle of whiskey. "This kinda fell into my saddlebag back at the mercantile," he said, grinning. "I don't see no sense in wastin' it." He pulled the cork with his teeth and handed the bottle to me. I took in a pair of healthy glugs and handed the booze to Davey. Davey had a slug and passed the bottle to Randall, who hit it pretty hard before he handed it off to Howard. There were only a few inches left when we finished up.

We rode through most of the day, stopping only once to loosen our cinches to give the horses a break. The day had stayed the way it started—a far cry from being cool, but even farther from the heat that'd melt the nails right out of a horseshoe and send Beelzebub back to hell, where it was more comfortable.

We came upon a few desert pines and a little water hole about dusk and decided it was a good place to make camp. "You think anybody's after us?" Davey asked.

"Hell, no," I said. "Who'd ride a slew of miles over some stuff from a mercantile and a blacksmith with a knob on his head?"

"We locked the sheriff in his cell," Davey reminded me. "I don't suppose he liked that much."

"He's a kid, Davey. In his mind we were like the James brothers and the Cole brothers combined. The farther we are away from him, the happier he'll be."

We gathered up some kindling and some dead branches and dug a little pit and got a real nice fire going, all of us hungry and all of us hankering to try out the new coffeepot. That canned ham was singing to us, and the canned peaches sang yet louder than the ham.

We tried the coffeepot first. It made a hell of a cup of coffee. We added the remainder of our whiskey to our second cups, and then we opened up the ham, cut it into thick slices, skewered them on sticks, and roasted them over the fire.

Folks in the West eat a great deal of beef, which is natural enough because the West is where most cattle are raised. Ham, on the other hand, is hard to come by at times, and when we do get it, it's a real treat. Between the four of us we finished that entire three-pound canned ham, plus a can of peaches for each of us. We grunted like sows as we laid back on our blankets and watched the shifting of the stars and the sparkling tails of the shooting stars.

Randall grunted himself to his feet and said he was headin' for the privy. Of course there probably wasn't a privy within fifty miles of where we were, but we all knew what he meant. "Stay downwind," Davey suggested.

Randall hadn't been gone for more than five minutes when our coffeepot exploded, flipped a good ten feet in the air, and thunked down to the ground. The boom that followed the explosion of the pot was an authoritative one. I'd heard Sharps .54-40s fired before and there's no weapon less than a cannon that makes such a thunderous, deafening roar.

"Anybody reaches for a gun dies right now," a deep, raspy voice told us as the blacksmith from Doreen stepped into the scant light of our dying campfire. He'd set the single-shot Sharps aside and was holding a pair of Colt .45s on us. "Take them pistols outta your holsters one at a time, using only your thumb and your first finger and toss them over here by me. You first," he said, indicating me with the muzzle of his pistol. I did exactly as he said. He pointed to Davey next and then to Howard.

"Where's your other litter-mate?" he asked. "I been following the tracks of four horses."

"He's long gone," I said. "He never had the balls of a field mouse and he lit out on his own."

"On foot? Bullshit."

"Nossir, he bought a horse off a cowhand. These four are mine an' my horses don't go to cowards."

"Cowards?" the 'smith spat. "It ain't cowardly to knock a man on the head an' tie him up?"

"You were the only man in that goddamn town we had any worries about. The sheriff is a kid still in diapers. Sodbusters and ribbon clerks are as useless as a one-legged stool. We had to knock you out to get done what we needed to get done."

"What I'm goin' to do here," the blacksmith said, "is shoot each of you in a knee. I'm goin' to take your horses an' your gear—an' your water an' whatever else you got in your saddlebags. If one of you should happen to crawl back to Doreen or up ahead to Broken Rock, that's fine with me. I ain't a killer, but I'll punish a man who wrongs me—an' you men wronged me real, real bad."

None of us said anything for a long moment.

The 'smith said, "I don't doubt you're contemplatin' on if the three of you rushed me, you might could take me down, grab up a pistol an' blow my brains out. I s'pose it's worth a try, anyway. Way I see it, it'd be better'n crawling long like a goddamn snake. 'Course, that's up to you."

I swallowed hard a couple of times so that my voice would sound as natural as possible. "Seems to me like a coward's way to settle things," I said. "Shootin' three men in the knee, knowing they're not going to get anywhere before they die. How about this: I holster a Colt and you do the same and we have a go at one another—a fair contest."

The big man laughed. "I'm a blacksmith an' you sonsabitches are shootists. Who do you think would win? Don't take me for a idjit just 'cause I'm big, outlaw."

He took a step closer to me. "You get to make your choice—right or left knee. It makes me no never mind. Either one will likely hurt like you never hurt before." Even in the darkness I could see his teeth as he smiled. "C'mon," he said. "I ain't got all night to screw about with you—I got other knees to shoot."

Randall must have slipped a boot on a rock. It didn't make much of a sound—but it did make a sound. The blacksmith spun toward it, his Colt raised. It seemed passing strange to see the 'smith's hat fly off, at least until we saw that the top third or so of his head went with it. He stood there for what seemed like a long time. Randall pumped five more rounds into him before he fell.

"I'll be goddamned," Davey said. "You done real good, Randall—real good."

"Shore did," Howard said.

"You did just fine, boy," I said. "You did what needed to be done."

Randall stood there with his Colt hanging limply in his hand at his side. "What I was plannin' was to stick my gun in his back and tell him to drop his pistol. Then we coulda tied—"

"It wouldn't work that way, Randall," I said. "As soon as he felt your muzzle on his back he'd have started firing, knowing he was gonna be dead either way. You saved your brother and Davey and me."

"I didn't set out to kill him, though."

"Doesn't matter," I assured him. "It was him or us."

Randall sighed. "Well, damn," he said.

"Least we know where the next town is," Davey said. "That Busted Rock isn't a long way down the line, I guess."

"Broken Rock—but yeah, it can't be too far. Let's drag this knee-shootin' sumbitch off a ways and then get some sleep. And Randall—don't you spend any time worrying about the 'smith. Like I said, it was him or us. Better him, right?"

"Yessir, Pound. But I didn't mean to . . . ahhh, the hell with it. The guy was going to kill us with as much pain as possible. All I done is punched his ticket with my first shot."

"Good point, Howard," I said.

"I wonder where his horse is," Davey said. "If he hobbled him the poor critter is going to die of thirst—if he doesn't first kill himself wrestling with the hobbles. We'll need to find him in the morning, untack him, and set him free."

"And then head for Broken Rock to see if we can

maybe make us some money," I said. "For now, let's get some shut-eye."

It was barely light when the cackling, screeching, and flapping of wings of the vultures got started. At first they circled over the blacksmith's body, but they became more courageous and landed near and on the corpse, tearing away strips of flesh and chunks of meat.

I think it's fair to say that buzzards are the most disgusting creatures on earth. They live on carrion—apparently the riper the better, although they'll tear apart fresh kills with equal hunger and enthusiasm. I shot one once and walked over to it. The stench from that bird was so putrid, so vile, I had to back away quickly before I vomited.

Davey sat on his blanket feeding rounds in his new Winchester. Howard and Randall followed suit, and so did I.

There were at least a couple dozen vultures circling and dropping in for a bit of breakfast. The four of us walked closer so we'd have a good line of fire. I sat, while the others prepared to fire from a standing position. There was a bird quite industriously attempting to get the 'smith's eye out of the bone around it. We heard the cheekbone snap—it sounded like a dry stick being broken. Davey fired and at first we thought he missed. Then, the vulture attempted flight, fell on its side, and was still. Two or three of its peers were immediately on it, feathers flying. I took out one of them and Randall another.

Howard wasn't doing real well. He was shooting but not hitting anything. Davey took Howard's rifle, used his pocket knife to make a minor adjust to the front sight, and pumped two shots into a buzzard.

"There ya go," he grinned, and handed the rifle back to Howard.

We put lots of rounds through our Winchesters, and there was quite a scattering of dead and dying vultures on the ground. Above, more of them circled. It's funny; I'd never shoot an animal for sport, although I've killed deer for food. But it's as if vultures are meant to be foul and repulsive targets that a man could kill all day without a second of remorse. Come to think of it, rattlers and cottonmouths fall pretty much into the same category. Still, if I saw a rattler a distance away from me, minding his own business, sliding along, I wouldn't shoot him. It'd be different, of course, if the snake was close to me or my horse, or on my blanket.

We decided to break up so that all of us wouldn't ride into Broken Rock together. Davey and Randall would track down the 'smith's horse, take anything worth having from his saddlebags, untack him, and set him free. There were enough herds of wild mustangs around for him to find somewhere to fit in. Howard and I would ride on to Broken Rock and look things over, get a room, and so forth.

Howard didn't have much to say as we rode. It was yet another decent day—not quite hot enough to melt us and our horses as if we were made of candle wax. About midday, Howard took out the harmonica he'd taken from the mercantile and began blowing into it, bringing forth screeches, honks, blats, and almost any other sound in the world but music. I listened for as long as I could stand it.

"Howard," I said, "put that thing away. It's driving me pure crazy."

"Takes a bit of time to learn, is all. Hell, Pound,

I'm catching on right quick. Listen up: Here's 'Camptown Races.' "

"I don't want to hear 'Camptown Races,' Howard. Put the damned thing up before I take it away from you and shoot it."

"You think you could do that, Pound?" There was the tiniest taint of challenge—or at least menace—in his voice.

"I know I can, boy. And I wouldn't suggest you trying me."

Howard put his harmonica back into his saddlebag and we rode on for another hour or more before he said, "We still got some peaches an' we could make some coffee, in the cans, and give the horses a rest." That's exactly what we did.

As we waited for the scorched cans to cool enough to pick up, Howard said, "I didn't mean anything back there, Pound. 'Bout my music, I mean."

I had to grin at Howard's use of the word "music." "Let's just forget it," I said. "Eventually, you or Randall or even Davey are going to try me. That's just the way things are when a few men ride together. Hell, most of the busted noses and missing teeth cowhands ride in with at the end of a long cattle drive didn't come from cattle—they came from each other's fists and boots."

The first thing we saw of Broken Rock was the spire of the church. The building sat up on a rise, I guess, so that it could look down on the town for any sin that might be going on. What it'd do about the sin I couldn't say.

Broken Rock was a midsized town, substantially larger than Dobbins or Doreen. At the railroad depot there was stout fencing in good repair—enough of it to hold maybe eight hundred or a thousand head of cattle at once. The street obviously had been dragged every so often because its surface wasn't rutted too bad. There were stores on both sides of the street—a mercantile, a feed and grain store, a barbershop, a doctor's office, a lumber company, and even a ladies' clothing shop. There were three saloons, two on one side and one on the other. There were horses tied at the hitching rails of each, desultorily swishing flies with their tails. There was a good bit of pedestrian traffic—mothers with young ones in tow, folks coming in and out of stores, a few old gaffers sitting in front of the mercantile, whittling and arguing politics, cowhands going from one saloon to another, laughing and horsing around as they did so. The sheriff's office was midtown and the door was open. The Broken Rock Trust Company was directly across the street from the lawman's office.

Both of us had a strong thirst going and I figured I could use one of the tables in a saloon to get the letter to Agnes Stone written up. It'd been in the back of my mind and I was pretty sure about what I was going to write to her.

I got my paper, ink, envelope, and quill from my saddlebags and we went into The Inn, the first saloon we came to. There were a couple of poker games going on and a half dozen cowhands stood at the bar, drinking beer. I told Howard to sit at a table and I walked to the bar. I ordered a bucket of beer. There was a stack of newspapers on the bar and I spent a nickel on one of them. I carried the beer, two schooners, and the paper on a tray the bartender handed over.

The headline on the front page of the *Clarion*

caught my eye. Howard poured beer as I read the article:

> Vicious Desperados Critically Injure
> Sheriff, Blacksmith, in Doreen—Loot
> Town Mercantile!
>
> Four heavily armed and murderous thugs rendered the sheriff unconscious in an attack in which the lawman was vastly outnumbered. The lawman staged a valiant battle but was overcome and locked into one of his cells at the jail. Also attacked was the town blacksmith who was struck with a hammer, tied, and gagged. The owner of the mercantile says the value of the goods and cash taken amounted to more than six thousand dollars. Firearms and jewelry were also purloined, and . . .

Later in the article we were referred to as ". . . a band of six vicious miscreants led by murderer Lawrence Basil Taylor, who had been awaiting a date with the hangman's rope . . ."

I laughed out loud and Howard looked at me quizzically. "Somethin' funny?" he asked.

"Yeah," I laughed. "There sure is. I'll tell you all about it when we get together—all six of us."

"Six? There ain't but four of us, Pound."

"I'll tell you about this later, OK?"

The task of writing to Agnes Stone was a grim one. It was the sort of thing that's almost harder to think about than it is to do. It took considerable lying to make Zeke's death sound like anything but a drunk being shot down for running his mouth, but I did my best. I told Agnes he had put down the bottle for good when he'd gone on the outlaw trail, in respect for her and for Zeb. I wrote that he died bravely, in an attempt to save the life of his sons in the course of a dastardly ambush by unscrupulous lawmen. I signed off, tucked Zeke's share of the money in the envelope with the letter, addressed it, and walked it over to the barbershop—which was also the post office.

I felt good to have done it—as if a heavy weight had been taken off my shoulders. When I got back to the saloon, Howard had refilled our bucket of beer. After we drank that down, we decided to stroll over to the mercantile to pick up a new coffeepot. We walked the aisles of the store, checking out various goods. Howard spent several minutes looking over a stock saddle that was about the prettiest thing we'd ever seen. It was full double rigged and the leather was so perfectly tanned that there wasn't a flaw or discoloration anywhere. A little sign told us the tree was solid ash. I moved a stirrup far forward and heard not a sound. Most new leather will squeak or complain a bit until it has been oiled and broken in. The price on the saddle was an astronomical $95.00.

"Damn," Howard said, "I'm gonna have a saddle like this one day—see if I don't."

"You have the money, Howard," I pointed out. "Why not buy it right now? It's a fine saddle—the best I've seen."

"I . . . I can't, Pound. Not right now, anyway. I . . . jus' can't."

"Why?"

"Well, 'cause the saddle I ride now is a good one an' there's no sense in wastin' that kinda money on another."

"Bullshit, Howard. If you want the saddle, buy it."

"Oh, I want it, OK. Thing is . . . there's this gal I was courtin' back home and I kinda promised her I'd save up the money I robbed an' we'd buy ourselves a spread somewhere an' have a family an' all that." After a moment, he said, "You won't tell my brother or Davey, will you? It's kinda a secret engagement."

"I won't tell anyone, Howard. You have my word on it. Now look, let's pick up a coffeepot and get together with the other boys."

A couple of hours later the four of us sat around a table in The Inn. I'd looked at the bank; cashed a twenty for fives, and saw that it was logically set up. The guard looked straight enough until I concentrated on his hands. Either he had a terrible case of palsy, or he needed a drink. His weapon was covered by a leather army-type flap. It looked to me like a .38. A .38 isn't a toy, but it sure doesn't have the stopping power of a .45. I liked the flap; if he tried to draw on one of us he'd be dead before he got his pistol free.

"Should we get rooms?" Randall asked.

"Why screw around with—" Davey began.

I held up my hand to stop him. "I know what Davey is going to say and I agree with him. We've got fresh horses, the bank guard is either a drunk or sick, and it's a slow business day throughout the town. My thought is, boys: let's finish our beers, walk on out of here, go to the Broken Rock Trust, and rob."

Davey looked at me and nodded. Howard and Randall were incredulous. "We ain't made no plans or nothin'," Randal protested. "We ain't thought it out."

Davey laughed. "Randall, once when you decide

where to dig a fence-post hole or where to set some hemp plants, there's not much plannin', is there? Robbin' a bank ain't like makin' a watch, for Chrissake. We go in, rob it, and haul ass."

The brothers looked at one another for a moment and then Howard, said, "Let's do her."

Chapter Five

Sometimes a bank robbery ticks along as nice and smooth as one of those expensive Regulator clocks. There's a nice till, none of the customers or employees decide to play hero, not a shot is fired, and the escape is like a Sunday ride to visit a friend.

That's the way the Broken Rock Trust Company worked out. I went in first, waving my pistol. Right behind me was Howard, who said "This is a stick-up. Don't move and you won't get hurt."

Davey and Randall cleaned out the tellers' drawers and I escorted the bank president to the safe. He opened it without trying to argue with me. In fact, he said, "Damn, Mr. Outlaw—insurance is a wonderful thing, isn't it?"

The safe was good-sized—maybe five feet by eight feet with a seven-foot ceiling. There were six Wells Fargo metal cases in the corner of the safe; I tried to lift one and it was either filled with rocks or gold, and I doubted that Wells Fargo much cared to haul rocks around to banks. There were shelves on both sides of the safe, holding coins and bills of various denominations. I filled my grain sack with twenties and fifties; hundreds and larger bills draw a lot of attention to a man. I looked longingly at the gold for a few moments, but then marched the president back out of the safe. I gave them my "Anybody who comes out of this bank before five minutes have elapsed, I'll track down and kill," spiel, and they all seemed to accept that.

Howard was holding the horses and we all mounted up and rode down the street as if we were headed to a Sons of the Confederacy meeting. Where the hell the lawman was, I have no idea. Howard said the lawman spent a good deal of time with a whore named Suzanne, but I don't know anything about that. All I cared about was that he wasn't throwing lead at us.

When we rode out of Broken Rock we made some time, asking quite a bit from our horses. The ground was dry and we put a long, brown finger of dirt and grit in the air that pointed at us, but as far as we could see, nobody was following us.

When Howard was outside holding our horses he gave a kid some money to run to a saloon and buy a quart of whiskey. Howard gave the kid a five-dollar bill and the booze only cost two dollars, and Howard said that kid was the happiest youngster he'd seen when he told him to keep the change. The bottle came out of Howard's saddlebags, and we all had a couple of glugs.

"This bank robbin' ain't half bad," Randall said. "A man could get to like it a lot."

"I thought I'd end up following a mule's ass with a plow or ridin' trail drives. Neither of them appealed to me. I thought I might take a crack at breakin' broncs for ranchers, but that never paid much. I like bein' a outlaw just fine, and that's God's own truth," Davey said.

We made a camp with a fire that night. We drank the booze but didn't have a ton of stuff to eat. Davey went out about dusk to see if he could bring us a prairie chicken, but the only thing he saw was prairie dogs and a rattlesnake so big, his warning rattle was like shaking pebbles in an empty tin can. Davey said this boy was a full ten feet long. That's possible, I suppose.

I've eaten snake and I'd have eaten the one Davey saw, if he'd brought it in. Howard said he'd just as soon eat a bowl of buffalo turd, and Randall agreed—and so did Davey.

The next town was Hopewell. It didn't have a bank, and didn't have anything much else, either: a saloon/restaurant, a small mercantile, a church, and a livery. Seemed like the predominant source of employment in Hopewell was drinking and whittling.

We picked up some good stuff at the store: several sacks of Bull Durham with rolling papers, three canned hams, a half dozen quart containers of canned peaches, several different types of penny candy, both .45 and 30.06 ammunition, a couple of bottles of whiskey, and so forth.

Davey was fascinated by the patent medicine case. "Look here," he called to the rest of this. "If this ain't somethin'! There's a medicine here guaranteed to work for every disease I ever heard of." He pointed at a bottle in the case labeled DR. P. S. DELONG MALE RESTORER. "That's for a fella who can't get it up real good," the clerk told us.

"Here's another one's guaranteed to cure drunks. It says right here that the potion will 'remove the desire for alcohol and subsequent intoxication . . .'"

I'd had some experience with that sort of snake oil. Of course the goddamn stuff would remove the desire—it's so loaded with morphine that a couple of tablespoons will damn near paralyze a man.

I found a nice coffeepot and got it and a large sack of Arbuckle's dark roast.

Strangely enough, we paid for everything that left the store with us. The storekeep with the big, flashy window could afford to take a hit—this fellow couldn't.

"Funny," Randall said as we rode out of Hopewell, "we paid here but we didn't at the last place."

"Look," I said. "This is simply a matter of business ethnics. Suppose you had a powerful need for milk and had two choices—a big dairy farm or a broken-down shack with sick kids and a ma who had a peg foot and an almost dried up milk cow. Which are you going to pay for the milk you need?"

"Don't seem like the lady with the twisted-up foot would have much milk to sell," Howard observed.

"Jesus Christ," I mumbled.

Good luck is much like a tornado: it can sweep homes and barns away so fast you can hardly see it done. And yet if you're lucky your own home is as it was—how you built it and improved it, and ran fences, and got a solid barn.

It's a hard thing when a man loses his place.

Luck isn't—and can't ever be—something that lasts forever in a person's life. Some folks get more good fortune than others, and some take a solid screwing lifelong, but no matter how long a string of luck holds out, there's an end to it.

The end to our string came in Sweetwater, Texas, in a scruffy little bank that we hit about noon on a pleasant, sunny day. Davey was emptying a teller's drawer—a sweet-looking old lady who looked like she could bake a cherry or an apple pie worth dying for. After Davey cleaned out her drawer, he said, "Thanks, ma'am."

"I like a boy with manners," the ol' gal said. "Doncha want it all?"

Davey was a bit confused. He looked into the cash drawer and said, "But, ma'am, I believe I got it all. Look for your ownself—the drawer is empty, ain't it?"

"Don't say, 'ain't,' boy, it's crude and shows no breeding." She snapped at him as if he were a schoolboy who hadn't done his lessons, rather than a bank robber.

That sweet lady laughed a bit and said, "No, silly goose, I mean this." She pointed to a small drawer under her cash drawer that was inset a few inches so's it'd be hard to see. "Here's where we keep anything over a twenty, you see, when the cattle drivers come to town."

Davey tugged open the small drawer and found a thick bundle of fifties and another smaller bundle of hundreds.

"Damn, ma'am, I sure do thank you," Davey said.

The ol' gal's face got tight and serious. "I've already corrected you once on your mouth. You don't need to thank me for the money—it certainly isn't mine—but you'd best watch your mouth when there's ladies around. I know it's a man's world, but that doesn't mean a lady has to listen to profanity."

"I'm right sorry," Davey apologized again. "An' I'll watch the cussin' round ladies from this day forward." He raised his right hand—with which he still clutched his .45—in a pledgelike motion as he made the promise. Her smile could have lighted a deep coal mine at midnight.

Davey told us later that of course he went down the line of the three tellers and cleaned out their small drawers too. It was simply a matter of good luck that the lady took a liking to Davey.

Anyway, back to luck: Good luck, in my mind, is like that Russian Roulette game where you put a single cartridge in a wheel gun, spin the cylinder, point the gun to your head, and pull the trigger. You either die or you don't. I saw a couple of chowderheads in a whorehouse in Yuma playing the game. After each spin, if the man lived, he had to add a twenty-dollar gold piece to the kitty. Then, the other fellow would spin and pull the trigger.

The click of a hammer on an empty cylinder has a distinctive and unique sound: it should be a sharp, clean, oiled *snap*! If it isn't the pistol probably isn't worth a damn.

In this crazy-assed game the pile of gold coins in the middle of the table grew and the sound of the hammer punching any empty cylinder was loud enough in that totally silent saloon to be heard in Galveston. Eventually, one of the boys ran his string of luck to the end and he put a .45 slug right through his stupid head.

That's the way I see runs of good luck: they're bound to run out sooner or later. There's no way around that; it's going to run out, no question and no doubt.

We'd hit five banks in about a month and each robbery went fine. The newspapers said there were prices on our heads: $5000 apiece on Davey and me and $1000 apiece on the Stone brothers.

But when we left that bank in Sweetwater with our usual warning and were on our horses within a couple of seconds, at that moment the town sounded like the battle of Gettysburg in Pennsylvania. Men were firing from all over the place: rooftops, windows, behind water troughs. We returned fire but we had no real targets. Men would shoot at us and then duck back under cover.

The way Sweetwater was built was that there were two sides of the main street with stores, but one of those lines was intersected like a T—a space maybe twenty yards wide for freighters to rest horses and so forth. Getting out of Sweetwater via that alley was our only chance. Even though the men shooting at us were piss-poor shots, they'd have to get at least a couple of us eventually.

We asked our horses for all the speed they had, making tracks to the alley. The opening was to our left side and we were going to have to take the turn at a full gallop. Davey was first, a horse length ahead of me, and Howard and Randall were neck and neck a few feet behind us. The horses ran like they knew this was real bad trouble and they had to get away from it.

Davey and I took the turn, our horses' hooves scattering dirt and grit behind us. We were leaned forward in our saddles, pistols holstered, running like hell.

That's when the wheels came off the whole goddamn affair. Maybe ten feet ahead of us a heavy Indian lady, holding the hand of an Indian kid of maybe three or four years old, stepped into our path. There was absolutely nothing Davey and I could do: stopping a galloping horse, or even swerving him hard in a matter of eight or ten feet is damned near impossible.

Davey's roan hit the woman front-on, and he hit her hard. Like I said, she was stout, but that made no difference; Davey plowed into her like a locomotive. I got the child. The sound of the two impacts are things I'll never forget. The woman had started a scream, but it got cut short when Davey hit her. The little kid had huge brown eyes that peer at me in nightmares to this very day.

It's unlikely that either of them could have survived after we hit them, but Howard and Randall galloped over the bleeding forms too.

I looked back over my shoulder. The woman was splayed on her back, arms outstretched, motionless. I thought at first, for the tiniest part of a second, that I was seeing her underclothing, white, shiny, with red striations. Then I realized it was her intestines I was seeing. The bile rose in my gut so fast I vomited onto my saddle horn and my horse's neck.

The child—a little boy—was a couple feet beyond his mother. A human head, I guess, isn't built to support the weight of a 1200-pound horse's steel-shod hoof. The boy's face was caved in. His eyes were no longer big and brown. In fact, they weren't there at all. The hoof must have struck him a bit beneath his nose, and squashed his head like a goddamned rotten melon.

I knew absolutely that there'd be a posse after us—and they'd ride through hell if they had to in order to catch us. A kid is a kid, and a woman is a woman, Indian or not.

If we were captured, of course, we'd never see a jail cell. They'd either put enough slugs into us so that our bodies would fall apart, or string us up—slowly—raising us from the ground with a rope over a branch and then watch us do a macabre, spastic dance of death as we dangled there.

Davey had looked back too. He was dazed, pasty-faced, and he'd let his reins fall slack. His horse was slowing and shaking his head, not knowing what was going on with no direction from his rider.

I slowed and shouted at Davey, "Ride, Davey—ride like hell!"

By then his roan had slowed to a clumsy lope. "Did you see the kid?" he asked in a flat voice.

"I saw them both. We don't have time for this. Take up your reins and ride, dammit!"

The Stone brothers had swung about to ride next to us. "What do we do, Pound? Them people—the Injun woman an' the kid are sure 'nuff dead," Howard said.

Randall started, "The lady's guts, they were hangin' right outta her like—"

"Shut up!" I snarled. "Just haul ass. That's all we can do."

I slapped Davey hard across the face. His lower lip began bleeding almost immediately. He put his fingertips to the wound and tasted the blood. "Pound . . ." He said. "The kid . . ."

"Yeah, I know," I answered. "We need to get moving now, pard."

I heeled my horse into a gallop and Davey stayed alongside me. Randall goosed his mount up next to me on my right. "Wasn't but Injuns," he shouted over the drumming of hooves.

I couldn't quite reach him without falling off my horse, so instead I hollered, "Ride, *pendajo*, and keep your goddamn mouth shut."

Randall eased back to ride beside his brother.

I contemplated a bit that I may have just bought myself a slug in the back of my head. I didn't much care, though. All four of us were dead already. There's a kind of a code in the West: You can do pretty much anything to a man but shoot his dog or his horse, or kill his wife and his kid. When those contingencies come into play, law and order is all finished—even for most lawmen.

We pushed our horses as hard as we dared, using the walk-lope-gallop routine. There was little or no conversation; none of us had much to say.

About dusk I held up my arm in a "stop" command and then pointed to the sky to the northeast. "That's about the best thing that could happen for us," I told the others. "From the size of the clouds we're going to have one hell of a storm with a pounding-down rain—and rain washes away tracks."

We sat there and gawked at the sky for a couple of minutes. I hadn't been exaggerating at all about the coming storm: the front was not only gray—it was black. And the clouds themselves rolled on and over one another, tearing loose tendrils that quickly closed on other clouds. The motion was hypnotic. It was a bit frightening too.

We were in the foothills of a stand of small semi-mountains. "There must be caves over there," I said, "and we're going to have some shelter between us and our horses and the storm."

"That ain't no real storm," Randall disagreed. "She's all jus' dark clouds, no?"

The timing was perfect: the sky lit up with sinuous, twisting streams and random broken fingers and forks, and as we sat in our saddles trying to control our horses, a ragged ball of pure, sharp, sizzling white traveled along the prairie floor maybe a couple of hundred yards ahead of us, looking for a home. It found one: a tall segura cactus exploded, bits of burning pulp creating a searing white fountain high into the air. That lightning ball apparently used itself up on the cactus, but there was another one zigzagging across the prairie floor, its hissing, crackling sound louder than anything around us—the wind, the booming, still far-off thunder, the neighing of our on-the-edge-of-panic horses.

"We gotta find a goddamn cave," Randall shouted.

I looked around us. "We need to split up. There's no sense in all of us riding to the same places." I pointed to the south and said, "Randall, east, Howard, west, Davey and I'll take north. When you find a cave fire your pistols three times, wait a bit, and then fire it three times again. Keep on doing that until we're all together again."

It was Howard who came across the cave we needed. It wasn't huge but it was adequate, and the river that'd carved it was now a lame little stream. The mouth of the cave was about a yard higher than the stream. We got ourselves and our mounts into the cave. I lit a match and the flame and smoke were immediately sucked upward. "Good," I said. "There's a natural flue. At least we won't have to smell each other while we're here."

It's always amazed me how Texas weather can suddenly turn a decent day into a hard time. The temperature dropped like an anvil down a well just moments before the rain came. It seemed like the rain was coming from different directions—*all* directions—and the drops were sharp and hard because of the power behind them. The horses backed as far into the cave as they could, and so did we.

It was impossible to see outside the cave. The rain, in sheets now, was a constant, screaming force. The flue I'd mentioned earlier became a waterfall, splashing from the cave ceiling and puddling on the floor. That puddle began to spread, to broaden, to encompass more and more of the cave floor. We'd all had wet feet before, so that was no big deal. It wasn't what you'd call comfortable, however. More important than the water from the flue was the rate at which that stream I mentioned earlier was growing. It had a sound of its own, separate and distinct from the rain and the thunder—a sort of scraping, whistling, hissing sound.

About ten minutes later, the water was lapping at the edge of the cave floor—the picayune little streamlet had turned into a roaring river. Randall, who was standing closest to the mouth of the cave, said, "Holy shit—look at this!" A cow was entangled in scrub and brush and was being hustled along by the power of the current. Her head must have hit a rock; a good part of it was gone. Her left front leg was twisted and broken in at least a couple of places.

A storm with the sort of furious velocity this one had generally can't last too long.

Within ten minutes everything slowed down. It was still raining hard, and the stream was still rushing, but the drainage from the flue had settled from a gusher to a small, steady stream—like that from a good pump in a kitchen.

The four of us stood together, our horses behind us.

"We need to figure out what we're gonna do now," Randall said.

"Yeah," his brother answered. "Things is different now. We gotta—"

"Things are different, OK," I interrupted. "But some things haven't changed at all. We're outlaws and now we're killers too. I already had a noose around my neck, but all you boys would have done was to draw some jail time. Now, all of us are killers—killers of a woman and a kid."

"Well, hell, Pound, our army sure killed off a whole lot of Injuns and that didn't bother nobody," Howard said.

"For the most part, those were hostiles—and they were killed out in the prairie somewhere, where nobody but Indians and the army knew what went on. We were in a town, and that lady and her kid sure weren't hostiles. Could be she's one of the wives of some Indian who carries some weight—has white friends, maybe, or is a respected warrior."

"I ain't scared of no Injun," Howard said. "Warrior or not. Plus, that woman's man is probably a drunk hangin' around beggin' for nickels for a beer."

"We don't know that," Davey said. "But I think we'd best find out—we need to know who might be doggin' us." He looked to me.

"Yeah. But all of us were seen in the bank, so there'll be no slipping back into town to hear what they're saying in the saloons."

"What, then?" Randall asked.

"After this storm is over we keep riding. Eventually we'll come to a town and almost every town has a weekly newspaper. Maybe we can talk up somebody in a saloon. I don't know. The thing is, we gotta keep moving, putting as many miles between us and that woman and kid as we can."

What'd been a voracious flood an hour ago was once again a tiny stream, the type of which poets write—except for the dead cow, which had snagged on a jagged outcropping of rocks.

"Been a while since I had a nice, big steak," Davey said.

The other three of us looked at one another, smiling. After all, the beef was already dead. All we had to do was hack steaks out of it, and we could wash them right there in the stream.

Finding anything to burn was problematic. Howard, though, was the sort of fellow who could start a good fire by rubbing two handfuls of water together. The beef was a bit tough, but that didn't slow us down. We tore into that meat as if we hadn't eaten in a month. Then we kicked the remains of the fire into the stream, so there'd be no sign we'd stopped.

There was a bright three-quarter moon, so we decided to keep on moving and lay up somewhere the next day. It's strange how moonlight softens some things and sharpens others. For instance, a segura startled me and I drew on it before I recognized what it was. But, some outgrowths of rock that were sharp-edged and angled appeared as soft as a goose-down mattress.

Any conversation dwindled out pretty rapidly and we rode alone with our thoughts. I knew there was no way I could have swerved to avoid hitting the woman but that didn't make it any easier to live with. I glanced over at Davey and it was clear that his thoughts were following the same paths mine were.

We rode through the night and into the midday heat and when we crossed a little copse of scraggly desert pines with a bit of buffalo grass around them and a small water hole, we decided to put up there and head out again at dark.

We ate some jerky, refilled our canteens, and rode on at dusk. It was another bright, clear night. A couple hours later I noticed wagon ruts and pointed them out to the others. The ruts were soon joined by more ruts as well as shod hoofprints. "All these folks are going somewhere," I said. "And there's been traffic since the storm. We'd best pull off a good bit. If the news has gotten around, four men traveling together will be awfully suspicious."

We rode a half mile or so away and dismounted, letting our horses breathe a bit. "I might be the best one to go in alone," I said. "I'm older than you boys and I don't look much like a bank robber or a killer."

"What's one look like?" Howard asked.

"Usually bigger than me—and, well, there's a look to a hired gun. Hard to describe, but it's there." I unstrapped my gun belt and untied my holster from my leg and handed them and my pistol to Davey.

"Goin' in unarmed?" Davey asked.

"Yep. No reason for an out of work book salesman

to carry a sidearm," I said. Funny how naked I felt without that .45 at my side. I removed the rifle scabbard from my saddle and gave that to Davey too. "How about you boys set up a camp a bit farther out? If Howard plays a couple of notes on his harmonica, I'll find you easy enough."

"Can we have a fire?"

I thought that over for a bit before I spoke. "Make a fire. If anybody comes on you, you're lookin' to pick up work with a herd somewhere around here. If anyone asks, tell them you worked for the Goodnight organization, but got fired for drinking on the job. Stick with that story and you'll be fine. Don't do a thing but answer questions—don't add any information about anything. If anybody asks if you've been to Sweetwater, you tell them you never even heard of Sweetwater. Another thing: put your gun belts in your saddlebags."

"Shit, Pound—" Randall protested.

"Look," I said. "I want you boys to look as much as down on your luck drifters and crazies from the war as possible. There aren't but maybe half a million defeated Rebs riding around the South and West. You boys'll simply be three more of them. Do as I say."

There was no further argument, although I knew damned well that Davey would never be more than a short reach from his .45. I figured the Stones would get liquored up and go to sleep and it'd be Davey honking on the harmonica every so often, beginning in a few hours.

I read once that boozing is a disease and it can be passed down from father to son. Well, hell. As far as I know, there are no whiskey salesmen around tying down folks and pouring booze down their gullets.

I went on back to the rutted road and rode at a fast walk. Sure enough, before I saw the town sign, I heard the discordant rattle of a saloon piano. When I did come to the sign it was shot to shit: it looked like everything but a cannon had been used on it. It read, CHAMBERRY.

I'll admit I felt a tad of trepidation riding into Chamberry. No one paid the least bit of attention to me, but I felt like I had the sights of a marksman on my back. I pulled in at the first gin mill I came to and tied my horse. Saloons in the West are interchangeable, except that some have whorehouses and others don't. The place was lighted pretty well with coal oil lanterns, especially back near the tables where the poker games were going on. This one had a darkie playing the piano. There were a dozen or more men bellied up to the bar, all with schooners in front of them, and maybe two-thirds with shot glasses. These men weren't desperados or gunfighters, that was easy enough to see. About a third of them carried sidearms—mostly those big, awkward army Colts—and they were dressed like farmers or ranchers, which I suppose they were. They were a jovial bunch, mostly drunk, having a fine ol' time.

I squeezed in at the end of the bar and bought myself a schooner and a shot. The whiskey tasted like goat piss, but the beer wasn't bad. There was a small stack of a newssheet with the title, *The Chamberry Intelligencer*. I picked one off the top of the stack, slid a nickel across the bar, and began to look the rag over.

The front page was the usual bullshit—mindless stories about residents of the town who'd given parties, been injured, been locked up overnight for public intoxication, and a list of birthdays of readers coming up. I breathed a deep sigh of relief and ordered another beer and shot.

Then I looked into the second page with the story headlined, TWISTED FOOT LOSES WOMAN, CHILD TO DEPERADOS.

"Ain't that a bitch?" the fellow next to me said. "Them desperados might just as well dig holes for theirselves and lay down in 'em, 'cause they ain't going to be living long."

I swallowed the whiskey in a single gulp and shoved the glass out in front of me. "What do you mean?"

"I'll tell you: Twisted Foot is every bit as mean as Blue Duck ever was. He won't take lightly to some bank robbers smashin' down his woman an' kid. Why, I could tell you stories about Twisted Foot that'd curl your hair, was you to put a beer an' shot in front of me."

I waved the 'tender over and put some money on the bar. "Give my friend here what he wants, and keep it coming," I said.

"This hunk of horseshit'll drink his way through your money," the bartender said.

"You heard me," I said.

I took a close look at the fellow next to me. He was scruffy and had a good deal of beard. He wore a Reb jacket with the sleeves hacked off and a pair of Union parade pants. His boots were sorry things, but I noticed right off that a couple of inches of the heft of a Bowie knife protruded from his right. He had a long scar that ran across his forehead and down the right side of his face. I guess it hadn't healed well; the pinkish-gray flesh was raised its full length and looked like some sort of disgusting worm. He dumped down his whiskey and immediately held his shot glass up to the 'tender.

His right hand was clutching his right ear as he talked, as if, if he let go of it, he wouldn't be able to speak any longer.

"See, here's the thing," he said. "Twisted Foot, he was born of Lakota and a white man. When he came outta his ma, his left foot was twisted way the hell in, kinda pointing at his right foot." He sucked down half a schooner, belched loudly, and continued. "Some of them Lakota Sioux, they think a baby messed up in one way or another at birth might have strong medicine. Some of the tribes, they woulda killed the baby an' tossed it to the dogs. Anyway, Twisted Foot was allowed to live."

He waved the bartender over. When his glasses had been filled, he said, "Twisted Foot didn't much give a damn 'bout his foot. He rode a pony better'n the other Injun kids, and he could purely run like a son of a bitch. I seen him when he was maybe twelve or so in a big race with a slew of other young braves, trying to show how strong an' fast they was. Ol' Twisted Foot, he dusted the whole goddamn bunch." He shook his head, grinning. "That there was a sight to see."

"An Indian with a lot of grit," I said.

"Sure enough he had grit up his ass, my friend. He killed his first Injun at thirteen—damn near cut the man in half. It was a grisly sight, I don't mind tellin' you."

"Why did he fight the Indian?"

"It wasn't a fight. The Injun had laid his eyes on the squaw Twisted Foot was livin' with, an' Twisted Foot went after him. Scalped him after he killed him too—an' he still carries that scalp on his belt."

"He ever kill a white man?"

The drunk laughed. "Jesus Howard Christ, boy, he's killed more goddamn white men than you can count—with a rifle, a pistol, a knife, or his hands. I heard tell he took him one soldier an' tied the poor sumbitch over a branch and made up a small fire and sat there with his woman, watchin' the poor kid get his brains baked 'til his head come right apart."

I thought a moment. "Why didn't the army set off after Twisted Foot? Seems like you could send out four or five good men and they'd bring back Twisted Foot's balls as a necklace."

"Yeah. Well," the drunk said. "The army done just that. What they got back was a string of five scalped heads wrapped around a Lakota pony's neck like a garland for a parade or something."

"An' the army put up with that?"

"Didn't have much choice. See, by then, Twisted Foot was some kinda hero to the Lakota, an' if the army or anyone else, dropped him, there'd be a ton of trouble. See, there's a whole slew of hostile Lakotas out there—a whole hell of a lot more than most folks know. And here's the truth, much as I hate to admit it: them goddamn redskins are better fighters than our army boys."

"Is Twisted Foot still around?" I asked.

"Oh, yeah, he's around. Not more'n a few days ago some men rode down an' killed his kid and' his woman. Wouldna been so bad if the kid was a girl, but it wasn't. It was a boy. An' I'll say this: Twisted Foot won't stop searchin' 'til he finds them men an' kills them. Like there was the freighter Twisted Foot raided and then tied the drover and his wife to the floor of the rig, cut the horses free, and burned the freighter. I heard tell Twisted Foot ate some of the less scorched parts of them two people, but I can't promise that's true 'cause I wasn't there.

"Twisted Foot," he slurred on, "don't have too much truck with a pistol or a rifle. He carries a bow and a quiver of arrows and I've heard he can trim a hair off a flea's nuts at a hundred yards. Sumbitch milks rattlesnakes to dip his arrowheads in. Then, there was the time—"

"OK, OK," I said. "I've heard enough. I was just wondering, is all." I motioned the bartender over. I didn't much want another drink, but I *needed* one. I slugged down the whiskey, drained the schooner, and left a quarter for the drunk an' another for the bartender.

I rode back the way I came, not asking my horse for anything beyond staying on the road, as I thought things over. I wasn't responsible for just myself any longer. There was Davey and Randall and Howard who depended on me—on my decisions—to keep us alive and to make sure we stole enough money so I could go to Mexico and the others could go wherever they cared to go.

There was a little breeze and it smelled like rain.

The images of the woman and the child stayed in my mind, and it wasn't only because I was afraid of Twisted Foot. I never planned to live forever anyway, and if it was Twisted Foot who took me down, well, there you go. Like I said, I hadn't planned on living forever. I guess it was the fact that this mother and kid were doing absolutely nothing wrong and ended up dead for simply walking across an alley.

I reined in, rolled a smoke and lit it. The smoke was harsh and abrasive as I sucked it down, but in a sense it felt good. There were a pair of riders coming toward me, going to Chamberry. They nodded and so did I, but no words were exchanged.

I had a thought that made me feel dirty. It just kind of popped into my mind from nowhere, and I had no control over it. I thought about hauling my horse off the road to a different direction and keep riding until I found something or some place that made me feel good inside, not like a killer or a bank robber. I certainly had enough money in my saddlebags to carry me through whatever I decided to do. I felt small having that thought, and yet I entertained it, twisted it over and over in my mind, trying to see all the parts of it.

I couldn't do it.

Davey depended on me and so did the Stone boys. How the hell I came to be the leader of an outlaw gang is beyond me, but I was, and I was responsible for those three young fellows who trusted me. I rode on, finished my smoke, and flicked the nub off to the side.

It wasn't too long when I heard a discordant honk that sounded like someone was twisting a goose's head off. I swung over that way and found the camp.

They'd built a small fire and were all drunk. I guess there wasn't much else to do, and they had the bottle in Randall's saddlebag, so what the hell. I dismounted, unsaddled and hobbled my horse where there was a bit of grazing, and held out my hand to Davey for the bottle. He passed it to me with a lopsided grin that told me he was going to be hurting in the morning. There were only a couple inches of booze left in the bottle so I finished it off and hurled it out into the darkness.

Davey asked, "You find anything out, Pound?"

"Yes," I said, "a great whole lot, none of which you clowns would remember in the morning if I told you about it now."

"Prolly not," Davey agreed. "We had us a little drink."

"I noticed. Now how about we bed down for the night and we'll figure out what we'll do in the morning."

Randall had already passed out. Howard was about to blow his harmonica but I took it away from him before he could make a sound with it. "I'll give the goddamn thing back in the morning," I said. "But I'm not about to listen to it all night."

There was little sense in telling the others about Twisted Foot and the reputation the Indian had for cruelty and revenge. All I knew for sure was that we'd bought ourselves a passel of trouble, and we'd have to be on the lookout at all times—a man posted all night, never having our weapons more than a few inches from our hands, and so forth.

I didn't get much sleep that night.

Chapter Six

As it turned out, our biggest worry just then wasn't Twisted Foot.

At the end of the war a whole lot of men with scrambled minds rode away from Appomattox. It wasn't just the Confederates who left their minds on battlefields either; there were bands and gangs of flat-eyed Union men who couldn't rid themselves of the thrill of the kill—if that's what it was—and rode in groups both small and large, going nowhere in particular, killing, burning, looting, attacking any groups of settlers they came across. It wasn't so much money they were after—it was blood.

It was providential that I didn't get much sleep that night. I drifted in and out of semiconsciousness, but never really fell into a deep sleep. So when our horses began to shift and nicker a bit, become restless, huffing every so often, I was certain that something was going on that I needed to know about. I crawled out of my blanket with my rifle and my Colt in my hand and moved toward where we'd hobbled the horses, crawling along on my belly as silently as possible. It could have been a coyote coming too close, or a couple of mounts were having a disagreement and stirring up the other two, but I couldn't afford to take any chances.

There were maybe a dozen men spread out in a line moving toward our camp. Maybe half sat horses. They stepped quietly and moved slowly. Every so often the moonlight would glint off a badge or button of one of the men. *Military?* Nah—it couldn't be. If it was the army after us they'd charge, shooting at anything that moved. *Indians? Twisted Foot?* No—it couldn't be. Most Indians won't attack at night, and if it was Twisted Foot, the whole bunch of us probably would have been trussed up, awaiting whatever torture he had in mind for us.

I held my position where I was. The very dying embers of our fire still glowed a faint orange, but that apparently gave one of the raiders enough light to shoot. He raised his rifle to his shoulder, grunted quietly as he worked the lever action—and then appeared to have been knocked off his feet, his rifle flipping in the air. The echo of a pistol shot rang out a second later. *Good ol' Davey,* I thought.

Then, the whole goddamned night was lit up like the Fourth of July. It seemed like there was fire coming in from all sides—and there might have been if they'd circled us. We wouldn't know about that since we were either drunk or sleeping.

I had to assume my boys were either behind cover or looking for it, because their return of fire was good and steady. Sure, Howard and Randall are chuckleheads, but any man who's dragged out of a drunken sleep and can defend himself and the men with him is just fine with me.

It's amazing to me how much light a muzzle flash puts out at night. In a daylight gunfight it's possible, at times, to see a foot long or so flash from a .45, but that's not the standard thing. One of the raiders was firing a .54-50 rifle, though—probably a Sharps—that put out a blast of flame that was six feet long, an orangish-yellow color. That's a hell of a weapon. One of those thumb-sized slugs could hit a man almost anywhere and kill him.

My boys were doing well. A staccato burst of pistol and long-gun fire had begun a few seconds after we were attacked, and raiders were going down—at least according to their screams.

I needed to get the buffalo gun out of play. I listened over the rattle of gunfire for the thunderous, percussive voice and flash of the .54-40. I loaded my rifle and my Colt and spread some ammunition out in front of me. I was in the sitting shooting position, which generally works well for me, allowing my knee to serve as a muzzle rest. Of course, that didn't mean a damned thing in a pistol fight. But as soon as I heard that huge boom and saw the tongue of light, I opened up with all I had. My face was peppered with the stinging blowback of my 30.06. One of my rounds got lucky. There was a harsh, gurgling scream, an explosion of light like that a photographer makes when he sets off his magnesium—and that was it for that raider.

My boys were giving a whole lot more than they were receiving. They'd spread apart not in a line at all but with each man positioned alone, throwing lead at a prodigious rate.

We didn't have a lot of visibility, but neither did the raiders. And the waning moon was behind them, giving us the advantage.

I hadn't realized how many rounds I'd run through

my rifle, but when my hand touched the barrel it burnt like a sumbitch, and raised a fat blister almost instantaneously. I set the .06 aside and picked up my Colt—but there didn't seem to be anything left to shoot.

That dead, eerie silence that follows a military engagement set in: there were no birds, no crickets, nothing.

One of my boys loaded the fire and it blazed up nicely. Then, we went out among the raiders, pistols and rifles at the ready. There wasn't much to see: one bullet-riddled corpse looks pretty much like another.

Davey led an emaciated Appaloosa in close to the fire. There was a bearded man in a Reb outfit hanging from one stirrup, his boot turned almost completely around. He was moaning and crying out for help. I took a closer look in the flickering light of the fire. The raider had taken a slug in the shoulder and another in his right leg.

"He doesn't look too bad," I said.

"Look here, Pound," Davey said, leading the horse closer to the fire. There were spur marks on the sides of the Appaloosa that looked like they'd been cut into the poor animal with a dull knife. Davey stood at the horse's head, stroking his muzzle.

"Looks like this one is the only one alive," I said. The raider was still hanging from his stirrup. "Ma," he called out, "help me. Jesus—please help me."

"Kill the sumbitch," Davey said.

"Let's just free him up from his stirrup, send his horse on its way, and let him get his ticket punched when the coyotes and buzzards come around. We can't kill an injured, unarmed man."

"Sure we can," Davey said. He drew and put a .45 slug directly between the raider's eyes. And then he spit on the corpse.

We went through the raiders' belongings the next morning, much of which consisted of ammunition and whiskey.

What bothered me the most was that when I picked off the man with the buffalo gun, my slug must have hit his loaded chamber, exploding the round in there, spattering the raider and, more importantly, parts of the rifle all over the prairie. I'd wanted that .54-50.

There were a couple of decent rifles and a twelve-gauge double-barrel that looked pretty good. Their tack was Mexican junk held together with goose shit and baling twine. None of them had more than a few dollars in cash in their pockets. They may have stashed their funds in their boots, but none of us needed the dollars bad enough to drag off their boots. They were more than a little rank with sweat stink, the metallic odor of blood, and the full loads in their denim pants from when they died and their guts released.

We took what was worthwhile—which wasn't much of anything—unsaddled the horses and sent them off with a slap on the rump. We left the raiders right where they fell. The buzzards were already circling and some of the braver ones were landing a dozen yards or so from the corpses.

We rode for about a half hour with no conversation. In my case, at least, my thoughts weren't about the dead raiders. The thing was, I didn't know where the hell we should go next.

It must have been obvious to the law that we were following the railroad tracks—they'd have to be morons not to see that. So, it was a question of when and where a passel of Pinkertons, Texas Rangers, and bounty hunters would be waiting for us. The next town? The one after that?

I motioned Davey up next to me. "We can't do this anymore," I said. "We need a new direction, somewhere we won't be expected."

"I been thinkin' on the same thing, Pound. We keep ridin' the way we are, we're goin' to end up with our asses shot off in some Podunk town. So look: the Big Bend area is over that way"—he pointed vaguely west—"and once we're near there, I'll be OK. I been there before. I was just a kid, maybe eight, ten years old, but old 'nuff to remember. What's important is that eventually we'd strike El Paso, which is a big city with at least a couple of banks—maybe more. Also, it ain't too far from places in New Mexico like Deming and Las Cruces, which was small ten years ago but mighta built up by then. Mexico ain't real far from El Paso, so if we cross the Rio Grande, all we'll have to worry 'bout is bounty hunters."

"We have guns and ammunition," I said, liking the plan more and more, "and there's game all through there, right?"

"Right. We ain't gonna starve."

"Another thing," I said, "is that the time we're travelin', folks are getting the opportunity to kinda forget about us—maybe think we broke up or something."

"Except for . . ." Davey began.

"Yeah. Except for Twisted Foot and his band. They're not going to forget and they're not going to quit doggin' us until there's a showdown."

"I guess it'll come to that eventually," Davey said. "From what we heard, there ain't no way around it." He turned in his saddle and waved Howard and Randall up to us.

"There's a new plan," I said. "We're fixing to go to El Paso and take off a big bank and maybe after that head into Mexico."

Randall looked disappointed. "We don't get to rob no banks 'til we get to El Paso? I was gettin' to like it a lot. Plus, El Paso is a hell of a long haul, ain't it?"

"It's a good distance," I agreed. "But while we're covering it the news about our banks and about killing the woman and kid will die down quite a bit. We'll be just like any other drifters and saddle bums in the West."

"We ain't got provisions for goin' that far," Howard said. "Tell you the truth, I ain't real sure me an' Randall are in with you on that, Pound. I don't like that goddamned Injun trackin' us down, an' if we split up, there's less chance he'll catch us."

"Me an' Howard can rob a bank good as any man," Randall said. "I'm thinkin' we jus' might go on about our ways."

"Up to you," I said. I looked over at Davey. He nodded slightly at me. "OK," I said. "We're going on from here. The money is split, your ma has been written to, so I guess everything is taken care of." I paused a moment. "Good luck to you boys," I said.

It was as simple as that. Davey and I climbed down from our horses to let them blow a bit and Howard and Randall rode off in the direction we'd been heading.

"Them two are going to end up dead if they try a

bank by themselves," Davey said. "They ain't got the common sense of a peanut between them."

"Isn't our problem any longer," I said. "I figured I owed Zeke and his boys a real big debt. Now, it seems like I've pretty much paid it off. Maybe they'll go back to their hemp farm, or do something else. Whatever it is, it's not my business."

"Still, it'll seem strange travelin' without them two. It's not that we've been together all that long, but I spent time talkin' to both of them, gettin' to know them."

"You spent more time talkin' with them than I did, Davey. But I'll tell you this: I'm not about to spend any time grieving."

Just before nightfall I shot a nice, fat rabbit. A few minutes later, Davey picked off a prairie hen, so we ate real well that night.

We were in the saddle at first light the days following. The heat during the day sapped the energy—the life—out of our horses and us, as well. Water wasn't too much of a problem, and there were stands of desert pines that kept the sun off us midday. On good nights, when the moon was near full, we rode right on through. We weren't in a big hurry, but we were both aching to get to El Paso. Why? Beats me. Maybe because the kind of traveling we'd been doing just naturally makes a man want to see that there really are other people in the world, and buildings, and good feed for horses, and meals man didn't have to shoot for himself.

It was three days later at dawn that we saw the dust trail far behind us.

"Could be almost anyone," I said.

"Could be Twisted Foot too," Davey said.

"Yeah. A blind man could have tracked us from our hoofprints and our trails, and the rooster tails we put up behind didn't help much either. What we need is a place to fight from. It's not likely we'll surprise whoever that is, but we need to have cover between ourselves and them. If it turns out to be a traveling preacher or a snake-oil salesman we haven't lost anything. If it's Twisted Foot and we're fighting from a decent position, maybe we can drop him."

We came to nothing for the balance of the day but scrub and dirt and heat. The trail didn't seem to be gaining on us, but it was still there, hanging in the sky like an elongated brown cloud. I got a crick in my neck from turning to look back at it. We rode through the night.

The next day we got lucky. There was a bunch of desert pines and a boulder setup that looked like a miniature variation of the Little Round Top at Gettysburg. It wasn't settled any higher than the ground around it, but it was the best cover we'd seen in a good long time. We got the horses settled—hobbled them instead of ground-tying them, because there could be a lot of noise, even for those boys, who were used to gunfire.

We had jerky and water and some cover, so all in all, we weren't in bad shape. Davey was situated twenty feet ahead of me, with a boulder on either side of him. He had his rifle and Colt, and he had the shotgun we'd taken from the raiders. I was off to Davey's left, without quite as much cover, but with the ability to see a bit better what was going on. Each of us had our ammunition spread in front of us. Depending on how many followers Twisted Foot had, I thought we might have a chance at coming out of this mess alive. The problem is, a man like Twisted Foot—with the reputation he had—would make things awful hot before he went down.

Neither Davey nor I are real fond of waiting, but there was nothing else we could do. Maybe an hour after we got settled in, Davey said, "This ain't right, Pound. That trail in the sky ain't bein' put up by a bunch of riders—maybe two or three at the most."

I took a close look and saw that Davey was right. "A messenger?" I asked.

"I can't see Twisted Foot sending no messenger."

"I can't see a white flag or anything like that," I said.

As the rider drew closer we could see that his face was painted red, and so were his arms and hands and feet. His horse was weaving, frothed with sweat, mouth gaping to drag in as much air as possible. There was nothing we could do but wait and wonder what the hell was going on.

After a bit, Davey said, "Jesus Christ," and it sounded like a fervent prayer.

"What?" I asked. "My eyes aren't as good as yours."

He was quiet for a bit before he spoke. "That ain't warpaint on that fella's face," Davey said. "It's blood. He's been scalped, Pound, but they were careful not to kill him." We watched as the exhausted horse came closer. "They cut off his fingers," Davey said, "left him his thumbs to get a grip on his reins. He's naked."

The rider was now close enough for me to make out details. "They cut off his toes too," I said.

We gaped at the figure as he rode up to our cover. "It's Randall," I said.

Davey moved to help him down from his horse, but all the blood must have made Randall's body slippery and he fell to one side, landing on his back. It was very clear that Twisted Foot hadn't cut off only scalp, fingers, and toes—Randal's manhood was missing. Davey turned away and vomited.

I crouched down next to Randall. "Kill me," he said in a coarse whisper. "Please kill me." I hated to ask him questions but I had no choice. "How many Indians, Randall?"

It took him awhile to form the word. "Six," he said. Then, he added, "Please kill me, Pound."

"Do they have Howard?"

"They . . . they made him watch. They put my scalp on a string around his neck. They . . . made him watch."

There was no doubt that Randall would bleed out soon, but until he did he'd be in unbearable agony. I whispered, "You're going to be OK, Randall." I turned away from him for a second and when I turned back I fired my pistol between his eyes.

"Well," Davey said, wiping his mouth on his sleeve. "Well."

"I don't suppose Howard's going to get any better than Randall did, Davey. You must know that Howard's dead. And, if we fall into Twisted Foot's hands, we'll fare yet worse. You understand that, right?"

Davey vomited again, less copiously this time, mostly bile. He went to our saddles and pulled out a quart of whiskey we'd taken from the raiders. He pulled the cork with his teeth and drank as a man would drink water after a day in the desert, booze running down his chin and onto his hands. "No man deserves to die like that."

"No," I agreed.

"So, we've got to take this animal out, Pound. We've got to kill him and kill him and kill him again." His voice was low, barely above a whisper, but there was steel in it, steel and fire.

I held out my hand for the bottle and hit it hard.

"That's not going to happen," I said. "At least the way you're seeing it. It'll come down to a fight, you can bet on that. We can kill Twisted Foot, but not by attacking him or dogging him, but by keeping on going ahead with what we planned—do our robbing and go to Mexico. He'll follow us there and that's where the whole thing will end."

"Maybe," Davey said.

"What's your suggestion, then, Davey? Sneak into his camp and cut his throat? That's about as likely to happen as Randall here coming back to life."

He stood there and looked at me, and for the first time in awhile I realized how young he was. He hadn't been in the war, hadn't see that butchery.

"It's getting dark, Davey. You get some shut-eye. I'll take first watch. It's going to be a long time before both of us can sleep at once without fear of being hacked to pieces. I'll take Randall out a bit and get some rocks and dirt over him—keep the coyotes away for a time, anyway."

The whiskey hit Davey fast. He stumbled his way back to his watch point, put his head down, and within moments was snoring sibilantly, moaning every so often. I watched him for a few minutes.

I dragged Randall with my hands under his

armpits. I found a little spot just outside the pines and dug a hole with my knife. There were rocks and roots and it was like digging through cement, but I managed to get a shallow pit dug. I put Randall in it and covered him with rocks. It was the best I could do without a shovel.

I took the entire night watch, because Davey wasn't really used to booze and he'd hit that bottle hard on an empty gut—after all, he'd puked his guts out when he got a good look at the torture Randall had suffered—so, anyway, I let him sleep.

I really wasn't expecting a night attack. That isn't the Indian way. Nevertheless, I'm sure Twisted Foot was as unpredictable as whether or not it'd rain two weeks from Wednesday, so I sat there, rifle across my lap, rolling and smoking cigarettes. Of course, the red nub would show to anyone who was watching, but I simply didn't give a damn.

As I think about it now, what had been done to poor Randall needed to be revenged. It wasn't as though the man was my brother or partner, but he was with us—with me—and he wasn't a bad sort at all. I wanted a whole lot to drop Twisted Foot for what he'd done to my friends, but I wasn't about to attempt to track him and hunt him down to do it. I guess that's the way lots of Indians are different from whites: they'll dog a man until they finally catch him, no matter how long that takes, and then kill him. There's some sort of honor in that, I suppose.

Davey and I struck the outskirts of El Paso early on our fourth day of riding. That damned trail in the sky from Twisted Foot and his men was a constant; I never looked back at it any longer, knowing it would be there. I also knew that any lawman—and almost every other man—would shoot Twisted Foot on sight, so I didn't think he'd come into the city after us. We hadn't seen the paper that was out on us, so we weren't sure whether or not we were shown with scruffy beards or clean shaved, or whatever. I thought our best bet was for one of us to ride on in and get a room and then see if posters or newspapers could be found.

"What I'll do," I told Davey, "is that I'll get a room for us at the hotel closest to the barbershop. I'll look around for posters or news sheets and whatever they show, I'll do the opposite. If they show us bearded, I'll get shaved as smooth as an infant's ass, and if they showed us clean-faced, I'd just keep my beard and get a bath. We've got more money than we need and we can rest up real good until we decide which bank we'd visit."

"Well, hell," Davey said. "That leaves me out here with them Injuns, Pound."

"Not if you hang close outside town, Davey—even Twisted Foot wouldn't dare to ride into El Paso with the reputation he carries."

"Yeah, I guess that's right. But look: there're bound to be a few hotels an' barbershops in a place as big as El Paso. Suppose there's more'n one next door to another?"

"Just say you're looking for a fellow named Coleridge—Sam Coleridge. If I haven't been there they won't know the name."

"Good," Davey said. "Let's do her."

El Paso was bigger than I'd imagined. There were side streets running off the main street, and those streets had houses already on them, and more going up. The main street had sidewalks on both sides, the length of the whole street, and had gaslights too. There were stores where a fellow could buy most anything. Beyond the mercantile there was a bootmaker, a butcher shop, a store for ladies' clothes, and even a place that sold pretty much nothing beyond hats—and darn good ones, at that. There was a furniture maker and a mortician, as usual, under the same roof, and, as usual, the same man. The largest hotel was the Belvedere, a three-story structure that hulked on a corner, right alongside a barbershop. I put up my horse at the livery stable with instructions to replace his shoes, grain him good, and keep him on good hay.

I was a mess and I'm sure I didn't smell like the first flower of springtime, so I went into the barbershop. There were three chairs and three barbers, something I'd never seen before. The chairs were full so I sat in a comfortable stuffed chair and looked at the newspaper on the small table next to me, along with some racy "gentlemen's journals," which featured lurid, huge-breasted, seminude women. It's a good thing that paper was there: the four of us were depicted with full beards, long hair, and what appeared to be ruddy complexions. Our prices had gone up: Davey and I were worth $7500 each and Randall and Howard $5000.

The barber was an overly talkative fellow who followed everything he said with a forced and phony laugh. I could envision him saying to a close relative, "Your sister Rose is dead," and following the words with his laugh.

I told him I wanted a clean shave, a haircut, and a

bath afterward—and some silence. The silence part didn't please him but he did shut the hell up as he worked.

The shop had three tubs the size of stock troughs, portioned off from one another by hanging tarps. There was a healthy fire going just outside the back door, and a sweating black man hustled to keep the tubs full of water almost too hot to stand. I gave him a dollar afterward, and he beamed delightedly and thanked me profusely. I gave the barber a dollar, too, and told him my name was Sam Coleridge and that I'd be staying at the Belvedere.

I picked up some new pants and a shirt at the mercantile, as well as a box of cheroots. As I strolled from the mercantile to the Belvedere, I noticed that about 80 percent of the men on the street—perhaps a few more than that—carried holstered pistols. Many of the men were wealthy looking—bankers and lawyers and so forth—but there was a good mix of cattlehands, most of who were obviously drunk, and farmers and various sorts of laborers. Traffic on the street was as thick as fleas on an ol' hound—not only freighters, wagons, carriages, and carts, but men on horseback.

The freighters were quick with their tongues and their language was quite foul.

It was a bustling town with all sorts of business being transacted in the various shops and stores, and reminded me of photographs I'd seen of Chicago, except the men in Chicago weren't armed—or at least, not obviously so.

I registered for a first-floor room in the Belvedere under the Coleridge name. There was a fifty-cent-a-night premium for first-floor rooms, the reason being that they were easy to get out of in case of fire. The room was simple but nice enough. I sat on the bed and was pleased not to hear the crunching created by corn shucks; the mattress was stuffed with some sort of fabric.

I changed into my new clothes, gave my boots a swipe with my old shirt, and went out to see what I could see. The sheriff's office was about a half block away from the Belvedere and looked to be of good construction—block and stone. At the far end of the street was the Traders Trust Company. Almost directly across the street from the sheriff's office was the El Paso Savings & Loan. The Traders Trust was the obvious choice because of the proximity of the other bank to the lawman's office, but as I thought about it, I realized that fact didn't make much of a difference. The two banks were but a hundred or so yards apart.

I eased open the batwings to the Cattleman Saloon and stood at the bar. I ordered a schooner of beer and was delighted to find that the beverage was almost ice-cold, and tasted like real, aged beer as opposed to the swill most saloon owners made themselves.

There was a mixed group in the Cattleman, but it was a workingman's bar rather than a restaurant. There were ten or so men at the long, nicely polished bar. A few card games were going on at the five tables scattered around the floor.

I'm a good listener, particularly to conversations in which I'm not involved. I've always thought I could learn more listening than I could flapping my gums, and that principle has always held true for me.

I heard talk of what a skinflint the old Jewish fellow who owned the mercantile was, the wonders of the body of a Miss Thronson who worked in the dress shop, the qualities of various horses up for sale or trade, and so on. I considered moving on, but instead ordered another beer. As it turned out, I'm glad that I did.

A couple of fellows down the bar a bit from me were discussing what had taken place in Sweetwater not too many days ago. "What they done," one man explained, "is raped Twisted Foot's wife, shot his son, and then rode over both mother and son laughin' and yellin' all the while."

"Awful," the other answered. "Jus' plain awful. I seen Twisted Foot's squaw one time an' I'd rather rape a beer barrel, but there wasn't no reason to shoot the kid or to ride over the both of them."

"Don't much matter now, I guess. All four are dead men. They jus' ain't realized it yet. That Twisted Foot is one crazy sumbitch, for true."

"You heard the game he played back a few years, not too far from San Antone?"

"Game?"

"Yeah. Him an' that buncha loons he travels with raided a settler's Conestoga—seven people in it, including three wee kids. What Twisted Foot done was had each of them buried so's only their heads was aboveground. Then them savages busted the spokes offa a couple wheels an' rode by, swingin' at the people. I hear tell it was a god-awful mess. Some of the heads was torn right offa the necks."

"Damn."

"Yeah. That's why I say them bank robbers is already dead, 'cept they're still movin' around. They ain't got the chance of a block of ice in hell. An' that Twisted Foot, he'll never give up the chase—never."

"I don't know for sure that this is true, but a fella told me he seen Twisted Foot. . . ."

I'd heard enough and didn't care to hear anymore. Both the speakers were slugging down beer fast, and they'd obviously been in the Cattleman for a good bit of time before I arrived. Nevertheless, rumors and stories don't begin on their own. There's always a shred of truth behind them that generates them, and in Twisted Foot's case that shred of truth seemed to be very large and very substantial.

I was a bit bored and really had nothing to do until I hooked up with Davey. Then, Davey and I had nothing to do, either. I decided to stroll down the street to the Traders Trust just to look the place over, check out the guard, and see how the possibilities of getting in and out fast might be. I had folded a fifty into my pants pocket before I left the Belvedere, just in case a contingency such as this one arose.

There was a lot of marble walls and ceilings in the bank and it was maybe fifteen degrees cooler in there than it was outside. It was quiet, just as banks almost always are, except when they're being robbed. Maybe it's about all that money being there or maybe folks just plain preferred to keep their financial matters to themselves, but banks always seem solemn and subdued.

There were four tellers, all men of about middle age, and all dressed in white shirts that were so clean they almost sparkled. Each wore a dark vest and one of those long ties that were becoming stylish and popular in the big cities. Two or three people waited patiently at each teller's window, papers or bills clutched in their hands.

The guard that was posted just inside the door,

had some years on him but he stood at attention as straight as General Lee always had. A holstered Smith & Wesson with worn grips was at his right side. I doubted that the wear on those grips came from using that pistol for anything but its intended purpose. Next to the guard a double-barreled shotgun leaned against the wall, its posture as good as the guard's. He eyed me as I walked by and I nodded affably at him. He didn't return the nod, nor did his face change an iota. The message that he was there to guard the bank and not to visit with customers was abundantly clear.

I got in a teller line and looked over the rest of the bank. The president's desk was the prominent one, and this case rested on a pedestal maybe two inches high. Behind him were six desks in two lines of three. The vault was located a few feet behind the first teller, and it was closed. The steel it was made from was brightly polished, and the wheel that worked the combination was made from brass and was also well polished.

When I reached the teller I presented the fifty and asked if I might have two twenties and two fives in exchange for it. That's how I phrased it too: "I wonder if I might exchange this . . ."

The teller looked at the bill briefly and smiled at me. His teeth were pretty bad. I suspected he was a tobacco chewer outside business hours. He said, "Certainly, sir," made the change from his drawer, handed it over, and asked if he could be of further service. "Our custom savings plan pays a full 5 percent per annum, and—"

"Not just now, thank you," I said. I folded the bills, put them in my pocket and went back out into the heat. I had nothing better to do, and I didn't want to cash another bill at the second bank the same day as the first, so I headed back to the hotel.

I lit a cheroot and got it drawing just right as I walked down the hall—and then stopped abruptly. There was a quarter inch of light showing from inside my room, and I'd locked the door when I left. I crushed out my cigar on the floor, drew my Colt, and crouched low. I figured whoever was inside would expect me to come in high, pistol blazing, but I saw no sense to that. Whoever was in my room would more than likely be aiming at mid-door and it would take him the tiniest part of a second to lower his muzzle. In that speck of time I could probably nail him.

I took a long, deep breath and dove through the door, leading with my Colt, finger tight and sweaty on the trigger.

"Well, damn," Davey laughed from the bed, where he'd been leaning against the backboard looking through a newspaper, "ain't you the twitchy one, though?"

"You cretin," I sputtered, "I could have blown your brains out!"

"Yeah, but you didn't," he grinned. I noticed he'd gotten a shave and a haircut and bought new pants and a new shirt, just as I had. He held out the page of the news sheet to me. "Don't look much like us, does it?"

I holstered my pistol. "No," I admitted, "not much." I stood there looking at Davey for a few moments, my every instinct yelling to me to give the kid a massive ass-chewing, but I didn't say anything quite yet.

Davey focused on my eyes and the smile disappeared from his face. "What?" he asked.

"I could have plugged you, Davey, before I could stop my natural reflexes. You—we—got lucky this time. You're still alive. But, dammit . . ."

He put the paper aside. "OK. Fine. I see what you mean, Pound. I screwed the pooch just now and I might have—maybe should have—ended up dying or dead. I know that we're not just hick bank robbers. We got all the law in Texas after us, and the most savage Injun anyone's ever heard of lookin' for us 'cause we killed his woman an' his kid." He paused for a moment as if he expected a response from me. When I didn't say anything, he went on. "No more jokes and no more screwin' around, Pound—at least not for a long, long time. I . . . uh . . . apologize. What I done was dumb."

I held my hand out to him. "I don't think there's a person on earth who hasn't screwed up big in one way or another. Thanks for saying what you just said."

We shook hands. I was surprised that his palm was sweaty, clammy. I took that as a good sign. What'd we'd said had sunk in deeply enough for Davey to realize how close to death he'd come, simply by leaving a door open a crack. He learned that afternoon that a man doesn't get many mistakes in the robbery and murder business until it's all over for him.

I sat on the hard-backed chair and lit another cheroot. When it was firing nicely I told Davey about my trip to the Traders Trust, mentioning everything I'd seen from the guard's posture to the teller's teeth. I told him about the layout, the president's pedestal for his desk—everything I'd observed. Davey listened without questions, taking in what I was saying, visualizing it in his mind.

"While you were doin' that I wasn't just snoozin' here on the bed, Pound," he said. "I went on over to the El Paso Savings & Loan, right after I got trimmed and had a bath and got into my new pants an' shirt. I'll tell you what: that sumbitch sure didn't look like any bank I ever seen. Looked like a French whorehouse, fer godsake."

I laughed. "How much do you know about French whorehouses?" I asked.

That got him a little huffy. "I seen one in a book," he said. "I know how to read, you know."

"Fine," I said. "But tell me about the bank."

"There's a guard to the left of the front doors. He had that look about him that tells a man this fella might not know how to handle the weapons he carried. He had a couple of them single-action Colts strapped on, but the butts was facing forward, like he'd have to do a cross-draw to get at them. He had long, red hair, too, that musta reached halfway down his back. There was a twelve-gauge leaning against the wall next to him. One thing I noticed is that his eyes never stayed still; they was always sweeping around the bank."

"How was he dressed?" I asked.

"He was all fresh an' sharp-lookin', an' there was a gold watch chain 'cross his gut. He was wearin' Mex silver spurs, although he probably wouldn't be on a horse 'til the end of his workday."

I told Davey he did real well and then took some time to think things over. I'd seen the butt-forward thing a couple of times, both times on dandies who couldn't draw the goddamn things if they had a day and a night to do it. It sounded a lot to me like this guard was one of those dandy-types who liked to play that they were tough and ready, but were pushovers to any real gunman. Fact is, I saw one get half a dozen slugs in his chest before his pistols came close to clearing leather. I wondered whether we might better risk that fancy guard across from the sheriff's office rather than the hard man I saw at the Traders Trust.

A clatter and some horse noise drew us to the grimy window looking out onto the street. There were driverless carts and freighters stopped every which way, like the drivers had simply run off. As it turned out, that's precisely what had happened.

An Indian man, who was every bit of six and a half feet tall, stood in the center of the street. He had his bow in his hand and an arrow notched, but the arrowhead was pointed to the ground. His body looked flint-hard and his skin was that tan-red that the Lakotas seem to have. The muscles in his arms pushed against his flesh, and even from where we were it was easy to see the veins in them. His hair was in two greased braids, one of which hung down his chest on either side of his head. He had scars across his chest that stood out red against the color of his skin; the scars were either from battle or part of a ritual. He stood as still and at ease as a statue, yet there was a tension, an intensity about him that was precisely the opposite sensation of peace a statue can convey. The Indian wore a breechcloth and moccasins. His legs were as muscular and as taut as the rest of his body. His left moccasin was turned at a sharp angle so that the toes of that foot faced his right ankle.

"Jesus," Davey whispered. "It's Twisted Foot."

Down the street about thirty paces a tall man with a star on his black vest stood, right hand hovering near the grips of the holstered .45 that was tied to his leg. He had his hat tipped way down—the setting sun was behind the Indian.

The street—the town—was so quiet we could hear the words they said.

"You got no choice and you got no chance, Twisted Foot. You're goin' into my cell." The sheriff's voice was deep, confident, unhurried. If he was at all scared, his voice didn't reveal it. "Drop the bow, take the knife from your belt and drop it too, and we'll be all set. Otherwise, you're goin' to die in El Paso."

The faintest glimmer of a grin appeared on the Indian's face. "You seem awful sure of yourself, lawman. Better men than you have tried to kill me and they're all dead now." Twisted Foot's voice was slightly hoarse but his pronunciation was distinct and correct—and I'd know. I'd been a schoolteacher.

"They couldn't have been better than me, Twisted Foot. If they were, you'd be rotting in a hole in the ground somewhere."

"Do you talk or do you fight, lawman?" The question itself was an insult, and so was the way it was delivered—like a white man asking a boy to shine his boots.

The grin on Twisted Foot's face got a bit larger. His teeth were white against the muted bronze of his skin.

It's impossible to say exactly what happened first. It may have been the sheriff beginning his draw, or it may have been Twisted Foot raising his bow. There was no question about the outcome of the duel, though. About four inches of arrow was buried into the lawman's left eye.

His body fell straight back, twitched once, and that was it. Another brave rode around the corner and halted next to Twisted Foot, leading a finely muscled bay horse. Twisted Foot swung up, took the rein from his friend, and they both rode off, picking their way through the abandoned carts and freighters, in no particular hurry.

"Anybody with a rifle or even a good man with a pistol could have taken that goddamn Injun down," Davey said. "Anybody at all."

I pointed to my 30.06 that was leaning against the wall near the bed. "Why didn't you, then? Why didn't I?"

"I . . . well . . . damn. I guess I . . . I dunno, Pound. I knew the rifle was there but I couldn't take a step and make myself pick it up."

"That's Twisted Foot's medicine," I said, "or at least part of it. Like you said, it would've been an easy shot and we'd be all finished with the sumbitch. Neither of us picked up the rifle."

"I don't believe in that Injun medicine horseshit, Pound."

"Maybe you should," I said.

We drank a little whiskey that night and quite a bit of beer. We each had a steak at a restaurant, and shared a pot of chicory coffee. Some whores came to talk to us in the saloon, but neither of us was interested. We listened to the stories of what had happened that afternoon out on the street—by the time we left the saloon, the tale had become Twisted Foot had put half a dozen arrows into the sheriff's head, cut out his heart, and eaten it. There was talk of bolts of lightning and of Twisted Foot and the other brave's horses having red eyes that could start a fire with a quick glance. One fellow guaranteed that the brave had a forked tail, and that small, goatlike horns sprouted atop his head.

We grew tired of the ever-escalating rumors and went back to the Belvedere to make plans. Davey had taken a room just down the hall from mine. I slept well and Davey said he did too.

The next morning we ate a good breakfast in the Belvedere's restaurant and walked to the livery stable to get our horses. We rode to the front of the El Paso Savings & Loan until a kid of about thirteen came strolling by.

"You want to earn an easy dollar, son?" I asked the boy.

"You betcha."

"Good. All you need to do is to stand out here and hold our reins. I'll even give you your dollar now."

It didn't go well in the bank, but we got the job done. The fancy dude with the crossed pistols actually banged his hands together as he attempted his draw after I'd shouted, "This is a robbery. Stay still and you won't get hurt." I put a bullet in his chest and he went down, but he was alive and reaching for the shotgun. I put another bullet into the side of his head.

The president was dumb enough to pull a hideout derringer out of his desk drawer and Davey shot him. We wouldn't know until later if he died or not. We cleaned out the tellers' drawers with no particular problems, but didn't get into the safe because of the bank president being shot.

The boy outside, white-faced and trembling, handed over our reins. We mounted up and rode out of El Paso.

"I didn't have no choice but to gun that president," Davey said.

"Yeah," I said. "I know how that goes."

Chapter Seven

We rode off in pretty much the direction we'd come from, not pushing terribly hard. The lawman was dead and Davey'd heard that his deputy had quit a few weeks ago to escape a very angry and very dangerous husband.

There was a tall stake in the ground near where we'd camped. My impulse was to tell Davey to stay back, that he didn't need to see this. But that would have been a major insult—like telling a school kid he'd gotten a zero on a test he'd studied for all night.

Atop the stake was Howard's head. He'd been scalped, his eyes plucked out, and his lips cut off. His nose was split—a sign of cowardice among many of the tribes. About halfway down the pole, there was a penis and scrotum tacked, presumable Howard's.

"I never seen anything like that before," Davey said quietly.

Both horses were a bit fractious because of the smell of death around the post, but we were able to hold them in check without too much trouble.

"I have," I said. "Once. It was back before the war."

"What would they have done with the rest of him?" Davey asked.

"I don't know. Probably left him for the coyotes and the buzzards. But look, I've had an idea in my mind that's been poking away at me for a few days. You ever been on a train, Davey?"

"I rode a flatbed once for a mile or so, but that's all. Me an' a pal was jus' screwin' around."

"Well," I said, "here's what I'm thinking. We head back down the tracks we followed getting here, to a depot. Then we load on our horses, look out the windows, and ride with our asses in nice, soft chairs."

"Going where?"

"It doesn't matter. When we want to get off, we will."

"But the law—"

"Look," I explained patiently. "The law is looking for four bearded men riding together, not for a pair of dandies riding on a train. We'll put some miles between us and this part of Texas, and see what we can find."

"Don't we need to buy tickets or something? I don't think we can just climb on a train an' get on off wherever we care to, Pound."

"That's the beauty of it. We just keep buying tickets until we get to where we're going."

"Where's that?"

"I don't know. We could get off at Odessa, or go on to Abilene or Fort Worth, or even Dallas."

Davey thought for a minute. "Them places is a long haul from the Rio Grande an' Mexico, though. You said—"

"I know what I said, dammit! Have you even counted your share of the money yet?"

"I . . . uhhh . . . I ain't had time."

"Well, Davey, I found the time. Each of our shares is a bit over eight thousand dollars after Randall and Howard and Zeke's cut, and what we sent to Agnes Stone."

"That's a basketful of money, Pound."

"It is, but it's a long way from the twenty-five thousand dollars I'm after. We're getting notorious out this way. And another thing about using the railroad is that Twisted Foot will have a hell of a time finding us. After all, he can't use the system the way we can."

"'Less he hops a flatcar like me an' my pal done."

There are times when Davey is a whole hell of a lot brighter than one might think. This was one of them.

"That's possible," I said, "but trains go all over the place. How does he know which one to ride?"

Davey grinned. "Good point. Thing is, I'd sure like to spend some of this money I'm haulin' in my saddlebags."

"You will," I said. "First decent-sized town we come to we're going to buy us real gentlemen's clothes so we look like exactly what we're going to be: traveling businessmen."

"What's our business?"

"Land speculation."

"What's that?"

"It's when one party buys a piece of land somewhere and then sells it to somebody else for a good profit."

"Well, hell, Pound, there's free land all over the place for farms an' ranches an' so forth. Who'd pay money for somethin' what's free?"

"I'll tell you what: when it comes to the business part, you let me do the talking, OK?"

"Fine with me. But payin' for free land jus' don't make no sense."

Within a few hours our horses began to get antsy, dancing a bit, shying away from the railroad tracks. "Train coming," I said.

"Look," Davey pointed out, there's no depot around here. That sumbitch'll roll by us like a hurricane 'less we stop it."

"Yeah, you're probably right. But we got a good bunch of train-stopping equipment."

Davey smiled. "Money?"

"Right. You ride on down the track and then dismount and wave a good fistful of bills at the engineer. Then, point down the line toward me. Those things can't stop on a dime from high speed, so you ride back up here, where the train should be stopped. Then, all we need do is load our horses into a stock carrier, give the engineer a bit of cash, and sit back and enjoy the scenery."

Davey spun his horse and took off down the tracks. The train itself came into sight when it was about a mile away, and the engineer blasted his horn. It's a funny thing about train horns. During the day they always sound angry, but at night they sound mournful.

That damned fool Davey, instead of standing next to the tracks put himself between them, and began waving bills long before the engineer could make out what he was holding. When he did catch on the drive wheels dragged, spewing sparks, screeching in a piercing note humans rarely hear. The locomotive stopped a few yards before where I stood, waving cash.

I explained to the engineer that we'd been misled by a faulty map and ended up out there, in nowhere. I said we were more than happy to line the old boy's pocket for picking us up. The quart of booze I slipped him didn't hurt negotiations.

Getting our horses up the ramp to the dark stock car from the bright sun took considerable pushing, pulling, and cursing. But, we got it done.

The engineer explained to his few disinterested passengers that a spliven housing on the pistachio had busted, but that he'd fixed it up. If anyone wondered where Davey and I came from, they didn't mention it. One rumpled-looking fellow eyed us pretty closely, but didn't say anything to us. The train chugged into motion and we were off to wherever the hell we were going.

There's a strange thing about Texas scenery. If one falls asleep for an hour or so and then opens his eyes, essentially nothing has changed. Scrub growth and dry land and prairie dog villages aren't what one would call scintillating viewing.

Davey and I sat on one seat together with an empty one directly in front of us. The rocking motion of the train fascinated Davey. He seemed to like it a great deal, while it made me vaguely nauseous.

The rumpled fellow had a large suitcase in his lap. I noticed that every so often he'd pull the cork on a flask, give it substantial use, and then cork it and put it back in his jacket pocket.

Davey was excited about our travels. "I heard that most big cities have zoos where a fella can see a elephant and other critters," he said. "I'm gonna see me a elephant this trip, I can tell you that much!"

The fellow with the suitcase stood and lumbered over to the empty seat facing us.

"You gents wouldn't mind me settin' here and talking with you a spell, would you?" he asked. He smelled like a whiskey barrel.

"Frankly, we would," I said. "We're conducting business here and—"

"Good, good. Because that's jus' what I'll talk about is business." He pronounced it "bidness." He patted his suitcase and said, "The product I have in here will change the entire West," he said.

I began to say, "We're not interested," when Davey said over my protests, "That right? Jus' what's in your case?"

The salesman said, "My name is Cyrus Aaron Steadyworth. I represent the most reputable weapon manufacturer in the entire world. Here," he said, handing me a business card that was stained with something—sweat or food or whatever. He worked the latches on his suitcase and spun it in his lap so that the open area faced us.

There were a couple dozen small pistols—derringers, they're usually called—each held in its own place by leather brackets.

Davey laughed. "Ladies' guns is gonna change the West?" He slapped his knee. "That's a good one, Cyrus!"

"Ladies' guns?" The salesman responded as if Davey had just told him his mother was a syphilitic whore. "No, my young friends, these are not guns for women—they're guns for men who occasionally need to defend themselves in tight situations." He carefully removed a pearl-handled two-shot and handed it to Davey.

"This baby is a .40 caliber and it's available in .38 caliber, as well." He leaned forward as if sharing an important secret. "Either of these will kill a man with a single shot—kill him just as dead as the irons you boys are carrying."

"No," Davey said incredulously. "That little gun?"

"Absolutely," Cyrus said.

"It seems to me," I said, "that there's no advantage to a pistol that holds but one or two cartridges."

He pulled another from his suitcase. "This wonder of the world of weaponry is a four-shot unit, my friend. If a man needs more than four rounds to kill someone, there's something wrong with him, not with this pistol."

"But what's the point?" Davey asked. "These here Colts my friend and me carry for sure get the job done. We're used to them."

"Well," the salesman said, "I'm not saying that you should throw your Colt .45s away—not at all. But, gentlemen, being businessmen such as you are, you'll find that the larger cities have stringent laws about carrying weapons. Those Colts of yours—no slur intended—are as big as a horse's ass. Whereas this"—he held out the four-shot—"fits easily and comfortably in a man's pocket or waistband, or even in a small holster under his arm." He sat back, uncorked his flask, and hit it hard.

Davey was leaning forward, admiring the tiny pistols. "Looks like they's made good," he said.

"Oh, indeed they are. That's the finest German steel in the world. With care, all of these weapons will last a lifetime."

I have to admit that this drunken huckster made some good points. We'd draw attention to ourselves in most places with our .45s at our sides, while one of these derringers was all but invisible. I doubted that the accuracy of such short-barreled pistols would amount to much, but in close, they'd be pretty much as deadly as our Colts.

I reached over and took a wooden-gripped two-shot .38 from the suitcase. The finish on the wood was excellent, and the pistol smelled slightly of both furniture polish and gun oil. I cracked it open. Both bores were perfectly clean and without burrs. I closed it and pulled the trigger. The snap was smooth, sharp, and satisfying to the ear.

"That, sir," Cyrus said, "is one of my finest pieces."

Davey was still examining the first pistol he'd picked up, turning it in his hands, aiming it out the window, dry-firing it.

The salesman laughed. "It's clear you gentlemen know and appreciate fine weapons. You've picked out the best I have to offer."

I handed the wooden-gripped gun to the huckster. "Suppose," I said, "I was interested in buying these two guns. What would you need to get for them?"

"Look," Cyrus said in a confidential tone of voice, "we've become friends here, enjoying one another's company, discussing firearms. For those two units—well, I shouldn't do this but I will—I'd charge you sixty-five dollars. I'd see no profit on the transaction, but I'd have the satisfaction of knowing that two friends of mine are adequately armed."

"Bullshit," I said. "I'll give you forty."

Davey started to protest, but I elbowed him into silence.

"Oh, no—that's completely impossible," Cyrus said.

"Fine," I said, handing the pistol back. "Nice talking with you."

"But," Cyrus said, "I could be coerced into taking fifty-five."

I thought for a long moment, watching the salesman's eyes. He wasn't about to go any lower.

"Agreed at fifty-five dollars," I said. I took a few bills out of my pocket, paid the man, and dropped the pistol into my pocket. It was amazingly light. Davey was near ecstatic. "Hot damn," he said, "ain't this little gun somethin'? Ain't it, Pound?"

The salesman gave me a handful of .38s and a few .40s to Davey, which I thought may have been a mistake, since he was like a kid with a new toy on Christmas morning. Cyrus closed his suitcase, set the latches, and said he was going up a few seats to catch some sleep. I watched him as he sat down. His ass had hardly touched fabric before he was sucking at his flask.

When Davey began struggling to open the grimy, soot-encrusted window, I *knew* giving him the cartridges had been a mistake.

"See that cactus comin' up—the big tall one?" he asked.

"Shit," I said.

The report was tremendous within the confines of the railroad car. My ears rang and buzzed for a good long time afterward.

"See that?" Davey asked excitedly. "I took a hunk as big as a bucket outta that segura!" He looked at me, questioningly. "Ain't you gonna try yours out?"

I suppose it was stupid and childish, but I have to admit that I did have a hankering to fire that little pistol, to see how it performed. I aimed at a rock and squeezed the trigger. An eruption of dirt, sand, and stone spit up from the ground a few feet short of my target. Davey fired again, hitting the rock. I fired again and missed it again.

We were reloading when the conductor stormed down the car aisle. "You can't shoot no goddamn guns in here!" he bellowed, red-faced. "You wanna shoot you go out on the coupling platform between the cars. An' now, I gotta report to my boss that a couple of knuckleheads was shooting guns inside my passenger car!" Another quart of whiskey calmed the man right down. He walked back toward the locomotive grumbling, "Goddamn fools . . ."

I looked around at the few other passengers. All were studiously avoiding looking at Davey or me. Nobody said a word.

A couple of hours later I felt the train begin to slow and the cadence of the wheels on the track change. I walked up to the front of the car and went to the locomotive door.

"You stopping for some reason?" I asked.

"Jus' a few minutes to take on water and pick up any freight they might be holdin'."

"Is it a town?"

"More of a couple buildings near a water tower an' depot. Ain't a real town—I don't think it even has a name."

"Is there a store there?"

"A mercantile, but it ain't big."

"My friend and I are getting out for a few minutes. You wait on us, you hear?"

"I ain't in no hurry." He took his first quart of booze from a tall oil can where he'd stashed it, and took several glugs.

Davey and I climbed down when the train stopped and walked over to a small structure that had the word STORE painted over its door. It was the rattiest mercantile I'd ever been in. Davey sneezed from the dust and then grumbled, "Jesus, what a shithouse."

The men's clothing department consisted of four suits, all in the same grayish-brown color and fabric. We each bought a suit and then Davey and I traded pants, since mine were too long and his too short. The coats fit tolerably well. We also picked up some shirts and a pair of cheap suitcases. I was looking around the store when Davey nudged me. "Lookit, Pound, that sumbitch has a wart on his nose the size of a watermelon!"

Davey wasn't exaggerating by a whole lot. I've seen some warts in my time, but never one like this.

"I'm kinda proud of 'er," the old clerk told us. "Folks around here, they hardly notice it no more, but newcomers, they damned near shit!"

We changed into our new suits and shirts in the back of the store and put them and our gun belts and Colts into the suitcases. We bought some ammunition for our new pistols. I picked up a cheroot to smell it, and the damned thing was so old and so dry it almost came apart in my fingers.

"I'm goin' down an' check on the horses," Davey said. "I'll probably scare hell outta them in this fancy-ass suit."

I saw a few newspapers on the store counter. I handed over a nickel and picked one up. The headline was bold and striking: BANK PRESIDENT & GUARD MURDERED BY ROBBERS. I read the article on my way back to the train. The story was much like the others that'd been written about us: We were bloodthirsty animals who barged into banks firing and cursing, killing anyone in our way. The article mentioned that there were only two of us this time, but the reporter had "good information from a reliable source" that the absent two members were involved in a major robbery elsewhere. The artist's renderings of us still showed us with beards and long hair.

Davey had brought back a bottle from his saddlebags in the stock car. I didn't feel much like drinking, but after a couple of belts I cheered up a bit. I don't know why it was that the newspaper article had bothered me so much. I knew I was a bank robber and I knew that I'd killed when I had no other choice, but to be referred to as a "bloodthirsty animal" hurt me.

I look at it this way: I'm a thief. If I need to kill to defend myself, I do. Robbing banks is pretty much like any other job, except more dangerous. There are good days and bad days. I'd tried other professions. Schoolteaching didn't work out; neither did clerking in a mercantile. So, what was left for me to do?

At that point I laughed at the utter stupidity of my last thoughts and took another slug from the bottle. Before long, I was asleep. Davey was too, but the engineer was shaking his shoulder. "Mister," he said, quite a bit too loud. "Mister?"

"What?" Davey mumbled groggily.

"See, I can't allow you gents to sleep in this car. We got sleeper cars to sleep in, but they're a dollar more. That ain't much for a good night's sleep, now is it?"

"Go away."

"I got rules to follow just like anybody else," the engineer said. "I don't even get a goddamn porter on this run—gotta do everything myself. Now, you boys get up an' I'll take you through to the—"

Davey reached up with his right hand, grabbed the engineer's shirt, and slammed his face against the metal rail at the top of the opposite seat. Davey was prepared to do it again but I put my hand on his arm to stop him.

"You drunken' ol' tub of shit," Davey snarled. "We paid you five times or more than you'd get for haulin' us an' our horses. Now you want more?"

The engineer stood there, dazed, blood running freely from his nose. "I . . . uhhh . . ." he mumbled.

"'I . . . uh . . .' my ass," Davey mocked. "Get the hell back up front an' drive the train an' don't bother us again. You hear?"

Whatever the old boy said was more of a grunt than anything else, but he nodded his head. He turned from us and weaved his way forward.

"Dumb sumbitch," Davey said.

"Seems like you're a tad feisty when someone wakes you up for no good reason," I said.

"Damn right."

If there is any charm to riding on a train, it dissipates very rapidly. The never-ending *clunk-clunk* of the wheels on the tracks doesn't seem to fade into the background as most constant sounds do—the rustling and mooing of cattle, for instance. Cowhands have told me that they don't even hear it, much less respond to it, after the first few days of a drive.

Trains are dirty too. The cinders and ash from the locomotive find their way to everything until one can't even blink without feeling the abrasive grit. Don't get me wrong: trains are the way to travel these days, but that doesn't make riding on them much more palatable.

We got off at a little place called Hunt, which had a large factory where chairs were built, and little else. There was no bank. "Can you imagine putting in your whole life in a factory that makes chairs?" Davey asked.

"No," I said.

We unloaded our horses and found them to be none the worse for the trip. We rode them down to the livery and ordered up good hay and two rations a day of crimped oats mixed with molasses. There was a depot in Hunt, so we could resume our train trip whenever we cared to do so. We left our tack with the liveryman and carried our suitcases down the street to the Sunrise Hotel & Restaurant. There were several horses standing at the hitching rail outside the saloon, heads hanging in the heat, tails swishing at flies.

We were both hungry so we went into the restaurant side of the Sunrise. The bar ran through the middle of the place, and the only difference I could see between the restaurant and the saloon was the fact that there were no cardplayers in the restaurant. Davy opted for a steak; I selected a half dozen eggs, scrambled, with a a double helping of strip bacon. The waitress, an Indian woman, brought us a pot of coffee without being asked.

When we finished eating, Davey decided he needed a drink in order to calm down all that good beef. It sounded like a good idea to me. After all, we had nothing to do and nowhere we had to go. We were traveling businessmen.

We stood at the bar rather than taking one of the

tables not occupied by poker games. The bartender was a gregarious old fellow who liked to talk. He told us Hunt had started thirty, forty years ago as a gold town—a miner had come upon a good stream with a strong yield. Of course, word got around and tents and shacks sprang up from the ground like mushrooms. Then came the saloon, the whores, the gamblers, and the gunfights. The stream had long since run out, although every so often a kid would find a pea-sized nugget. When the gold played out just about everyone else left, there not being much business for the saloon and even less for the whores. The only reason the place still existed was the railroad depot, which shipped some beef to the eastern markets.

"Ain't no land to speculate around here," Davey said, dumping down a shot of whiskey.

"I don't care. I just wanted to get off that train for a couple of days, is all."

"Me too. My ass is surely achin' to have my horse under me."

"Well, we just put ours up. How about this: we take a couple rooms here and then go down and rent a couple of nags and take a look at whatever there is to see?"

"That sounds real good, Pound. Here," he said, filling my glass and his own, "let's tip these down and then go for a look-see."

The livery rental stock—as we knew it would be—were a dozen or better examples of underfed, overaged, barely broke buzzard bait.

"You can see," the liveryman said, "I keep only prime stock for rentals. Now, businessmen like yourselves might not know horses real good, so how's about I pick out a couple of—"

"Cut the bullshit, you ol' bastard," Davey said. "There ain't a horse in the bunch that's worth the bullet it'd take to kill him. We ain't goin' out to race or cut cattle—jus' to take a little ride. Saddle up that black mare an' that bay, over there, by the fence."

We walked into the barn to get out of the sun. Davey reached into an oat barrel and took out a handful. The grain seemed to clump together, not in a big mass but in smaller, half-palm-sized gobs. He held the mixture to his nose and sniffed deeply. "That ol' fella might be a thief when it comes to rentin' horses, but this is the finest mix of crimped oats an' molasses I seen in a long time."

Davey rode the black and I got the bay. It wouldn't have made any difference; neither horse was any damned good for anything. One had to damn near tear a jaw off the jughead's head with a rein to get the horse to turn, and their fastest speed was a shambling, clumsy, semilope.

We rode away from Hunt for no particular reason. "Ain't much to see out here," Davey said.

"It's better than pouring down that rotgut whiskey all day, though."

"Maybe. Maybe not. Hey—look," he said, pointing at the sky far behind us.

A narrow tendril of smoke rose in the hot air, slowly broke up, and was followed by a larger, thicker puff. When that one came apart, another wavery, narrow line appeared.

"Shit," I said.

"Yeah," Davey agreed. "But look: it could be a bunch of Injuns came on a few buffalo, or one of their chiefs croaked, or any damn thing."

"It could be Twisted Foot's outriders, telling him they're on our trail," I said. "I think my idea is more logical than yours."

"How the hell'd they get onto us, then? They sure don't let no Injuns ride on trains."

"But there's nothing to stop an Indian from watching who gets on or off a train, Davey. We'd best get back to Hunt, figure out what we're going to do." I looked over at Davey and I noticed that the fingers of his right hand were reaching for his Colt—which, of course, wasn't there. "These popguns that drunk sold us don't look so good now."

We rode back to the livery at the most speed we could get out of our half-dead mounts. As I was saddling up my horse, I asked the liveryhand what time the next train came through.

"'Bout a hour—mebbe two. Depends on how much water they gotta take on down the line."

We went back to the hotel, picked up our suitcases, and rode to the depot. When Davey climbed down from his roan I noticed a substantial lump in the right pocket of his suit coat. "Davey," I said, "Why not make up a sign that you can wear around your neck that says, 'I've got a Colt .45 in my right front pocket'?"

He looked over at me. "Ya know, Pound, all that good food an' beer an' easy livin' and such, well, I do believe you've put on some weight."

I grinned. "Only here, at my waist," I said. I rapped lightly on the grips of my .45 that was riding behind my belt, covered by my buttoned suit coat.

We sat on a bench in front of the depot awaiting the train. A yellow dog meandered over for a scratch, which I gave him. He grunted happily and then went off about his business, whatever business a yellow dog in Hunt, Texas, might have.

There was a young man who doubled as a ticket agent and a freight handler. I looked at the map on the wall and tapped on a city. Davey nodded. "Fine with me," he said. I bought a pair of tickets to Abilene and made arrangements for our horses.

"Will the tickets be for sleepers, sir?" the agent asked.

"Please. And look—is there any decent food to be had on the train?"

The clerk smiled as broadly and proudly as he would if he owned the train. "It jus' so happens the train comin' in afore long is the Silver Streak—with a full bar an' dining car. You'll find the food quite acceptable. Hell, you'll . . ." He clapped his hand to his mouth. "One of the rules of my job is no cussin'," he said. "You gents wouldn't up an' blow me in, would you?"

We assured the man we wouldn't.

I sure didn't know anything about trains, but I can say this: that Silver Streak was one of the very best. Its locomotive was huge, massive, but didn't have the clunky, boxy look of most locomotives. We soon found that a sleeper was a little room onto itself with a good-sized—and clean—window and pair of over-and-under bunks. The porter—an elderly black man—told us he'd fetch anything we wanted from the kitchen or bar, but that we might want to try the dining car in person. "It's better'n the finest restaurant you've ever saw, gentlemen."

We thanked him for the advice and then the three of us stood, looking self-consciously at one another.

After a long moment I asked, "Is there something else?"

"Well," the black man said, "no sir, there ain't. Not officially, anyway. See, on the Streak it's the custom of the passengers in the sleepers to slip the porter maybe some spare change."

I was reaching into my pocket when Davey handed the man a ten-dollar bill. "This ought to do her," he said, "but we might need some help from you. For instance, if anyone should come looking for anybody who looks anything like us, why, you've never seen us. Right? And if you come across an Injun pokin' around, you let us know right away."

"Injuns ain't allowed on the Streak, sir." He looked at the ten-dollar bill for a moment, folded it tightly, put it in his breast pocket, thanked us again, and went out the little door.

There was a little fold-down table between the seats. The seats themselves were plush and soft. There were even drapelike affairs that we could close to avoid looking at the nothingness outside. We sat for maybe a half hour, luxuriating, speaking very little.

Eventually, Davey stood up. "I'm itchin' to see that dinin' car the fella spoke of—and I'm hungry as a bear too. What say we go down an' give her a look and get some grub?"

I stood. "Let's go, pard."

There were two other cars lined with sleepers and the final one opened into a room that opened into a bar. On the other side of the bar was the dining area. Each table was set with crystal that picked up the late-day sun and glinted it back, sparkling like polished diamonds. Each table had a tablecloth, too, and they were starched and brilliantly white. On either side of each plate was a covey of silver knives and forks and spoons. In the very center of each table a red rose rested in a glass vase.

"What're all the forks an' shit for?" Davey asked.

"I don't know," I said.

"And them tiny water bowls at each place—hell, there isn't enough in them to drown a cockroach."

There were tall stools arranged along the bar. I didn't see any spittoons. A couple of gents were sitting side by side on stools, talking quietly. The scent of a good cigar wafted about the room.

The 'tender was a black man, dressed in black pants, a white shirt, and a red vest. "What can I get you gentlemen this afternoon?" he asked.

"Hell, a beer an' a shot of red-eye'll do me," Davey said. "The beer cold?" The two men down the bar turned to us for a moment and then went back to their conversation.

"Oh, yes, sir—it's Milwaukee beer, too, which is the best beer in the world. What's your pleasure in terms of whiskey?"

Davey scratched his jaw, thinking. "I like to take on jus' so much rotgut that the whores start to look good. Then, I might have a couple of glugs just afore I pass out. That's my pleasure with whiskey, I reckon."

The bartender—very much to his credit—didn't crack a smile. He turned to me. "And you, sir?"

"A beer and a shot of good bourbon—the best you have. And tell me, how are those cigars you have back there?"

"Purely excellent, sir. They come all the way from Cuba."

"Good. Give us each one of those with our drinks."

The bourbon had that smoky richness—the very faintest taste of the barrel—and went down as smoothly as fresh-churned cream. The beer, as the man had said, was arctic-cold and tasted wonderful. Comparing the local swill to it would have been like comparing a fifty-cent whore to the queen of England.

We each had another drink, finished our cigars, and decided to have an early dinner. The same two fellows were at the bar when we left. Davey stiffened as we walked by them, but didn't say anything.

In the restaurant a gent with a white towel over his arm led us to a table. "All you needed to do was point us at it," Davey said to him. "Coulda saved you some shoe leather." The waiter—or whatever he was—forced a grin. He began to pull a chair out for Davey, but Davey said, "I got her," and pulled the chair out for himself.

I let the waiter present my chair and sat down. I watched Davey inspecting the array of silverware on the table. As he looked, he picked up the tiny bowl and drank the water from it.

"Will the gentlemen be having a beverage before dinner?" the waiter asked.

"I should damn well hope so," Davey said. "There wasn't enough water in that little sumbitch to wet my tongue."

The waiter coughed discretely. "That was the finger bowl, sir," he said.

"Dumb idea," Davey said. "Bring us a coupla them beers and a couple shots of that good bourbon my friend likes. An' what's good on the griddle?"

"The . . . griddle?"

"Yeah. What ya got that's good tonight?"

The waiter listed a series of dishes he memorized, with many words in foreign languages.

"I'll have a steak, blood-rare, and mashed potatoes," I said. "And bring a pot of coffee."

"Sounds right for me too. I'll take the same."

When the waiter had scurried off, shaking his head, Davey's face became hard and serious.

"Somethin' ain't right here," he said. "I . . . I know somethin's wrong but I'm not sure what it is."

"What could be wrong, Davey? We're on the classiest train in the world, it's moving with no problems, we have bunks to sleep in, and all the bourbon and beer we can drink."

Davey didn't say anything for a long moment. Then he pushed his chair back and stood. "I'm going back out to the bar for a second. Be right back."

"Why? You ordered beer, and the waiter—"

"Be back in a minute," he repeated.

Actually, it wasn't much longer than a minute before he returned. "Let me lay somethin' out for you, Pound. See what you think."

"Fine," I said.

"OK. When we come in the bar them two fellers were settin' there drinkin' and talkin', no?"

"Sure. Probably business travelers, just like—"

He held up his hand to stop me. "They was dressed good—nice suits, white shirts, all that. I noticed that every so often one or the other would glance at us, but I didn't think much about it. Here's the thing: when I was out in the bar just now them two had moved down six stools so's they could still see us."

"That is a little odd." My stomach began to clutch up.

"Also, with those fancy suits, those two men are wearin' boots that're worse'n the ones we're wearin'. I got a little look the first time we left and a closer look the second time. Those boys are bad news for us."

"Scouting us out for Twisted Foot," I said. "There'd be no way an Indian could board this train, no matter what kind of clothes he had. So Twisted Foot sent a couple of watchdogs."

"Gotta be. They're playin' a goddamn game with them clothes the same we are with ours."

The waiter brought our food and drinks and we didn't say anything until he left.

"What do you think, Pound?"

"It all makes sense. At first I didn't think it did, but those men watching us so closely and their boots—and there's another thing I noticed. Both of them had pink faces, like they'd just had a beard shaved off. Remember how it took a few days before we stopped looking like scalded pigs?"

"So, whadda we do?"

"We can't stay on the train, and that might take some doing, because we have to stop it in order to get our horses. I think this might work: one of us goes up to the locomotive and makes the engineer slow and then stop the train. Then, the other of us takes care of those two spies, we unload our horses, and we haul ass."

"An' then?"

"Jesus, Davey, how would I know? Whatever we need to do, we'll do it."

"Yeah. But look: I'm the one who takes out the spies."

"No—that's my job."

"Bullshit."

I took a coin out of my pocket and flipped it into the air. "Call it," I said.

"Heads."

It came up tails.

"I meant two outta three, Pound!"

"Your ass. Just make sure you get the train stopped."

Davey settled back in his chair, selected a knife and fork, and hacked into his steak. "No sense wastin' all this food," he said.

I looked down at my steak. It smelled awfully good.

"Right," I said.

Chapter Eight

I enjoyed my steak as I watched Davey consume his. Watching Davey eat was much like watching one of those newfangled threshers at work. The thresher's blades, much like Davey's hands, never stopped. The machine cut grain and pushed it onto the flatbed behind it; Davey's hands cut off chunks of meat and deposited them into his mouth even as he was cutting a new mouthful.

I was having some second thoughts. "I wonder if we haven't let that insane Indian spook us—after what he did to Randall and Howard."

"You seen Twisted Foot put a arrow into the lawman's eye, Pound."

"I did. But I think I could beat Twisted Foot and I *know* you could."

"So?" Davey asked.

"I don't know. Maybe those two fellows saved up some money and got all gussied up to head down the line to buy themselves one of those expensive ladies, have a few drinks, and take the next train home."

"Nah," Davey said, not breaking his eating process at all. "I know trouble when I see it, Pound. Those boys'll set us up for sure—you watch and see."

"Look, Davey," I said, "this big Indian isn't anything but a crazy damned fool with a bow. Like I said, I'd face him and kill him and so would you."

"Not if he put an arrow through your back from a hundred yards away. An' if that happens, you damn well better hope that it kills you right then and there, because if it doesn't you're in for a lot of pain. I'll tell you this, too: I don't fancy looking over my shoulder all the time, waiting to be taken down. That ain't no way to live. Seems to me the only thing we can do right now is stop them two on the other side of the bar and head out."

"I don't know, Davey . . ."

"Pound," Davey said, "I've been letting you call all the shots: what we rob and what we don't, where we go, all this train shit. You gotta trust me on this one."

I exhaled. "OK," I finally said. "You go on back and get the horses tacked up and then go up front and make the engineer slow and stop the train. I'll take care of these men up here and meet you at the stock car."

"Good, Pound. Right good. Let's get this done."

I nodded. The whole damned thing smelled funny, is all.

I sipped at my coffee while I waited. It probably wasn't more than twenty minutes, but it seemed like a century. When the train began to slow I let out a breath I didn't realize that I'd been holding. I stood, put down a five-dollar bill on the table, and walked around the bar where the two men sat. I noticed that the bartender was rubbing furniture oil into the bar where the two had been sitting earlier.

I stood behind them. "Howdy, gents," I said. The one on my left turned to me first. I hit him on the top of his head with the butt of my Colt hard enough to kill him. He toppled toward his partner, who directed a kick at me that missed my eggs by a frog's hair.

"What the hell is this?" he yelled. He tried to stand up from his stool but tripped over a valise on the floor with some gold-leaf printing on it. His right hand was in his coat pocket and he had a pistol about halfway out of it. I put two rounds in his chest. The thunderous voice of my Colt was stunningly loud. The other one—the one I'd whacked—had a derringer in his hand and was bringing it to me. I put a bullet in the side of his head.

There aren't many black men in Texas who'd even catch a white man's eye, much less pull a weapon on him. This fellow on the Silver Streak was the exception. He brought a cut-off shotgun up from behind the bar. My shot caught him just a bit left of his nose.

There were few others in the bar and dining car, but all of them dove for the floor, women screaming. I backed away and almost tripped over that damned valise. The lettering on it said, EVERGROW SEED COMPANY.

I ran through the cars to the stock carrier where Davey had the horses saddled and the ramp down. His face looked unusually pale. "I had to gun the engineer and the fireman," he said. We led our mounts down the ramp, climbed on, and rode away from the railroad tracks.

We didn't stop until full dark, except to let our horses drink whatever water we crossed. We didn't build a fire; we had nothing to cook. I leaned back against a desert pine and Davey sat, Indian style, facing me.

"I didn't like killing those men, Pound," Davey said. "But I had no choice. The engineer, he drew down on me and the fireman came at me with a shovel. If I didn't shoot him, he'd have stove my head in." He paused a bit. "What about your two?"

"Both dead," I said, "and the bartender too."

Davey whistled a long, low note.

"They were a pair of seed salesmen, Davey—that accounts for their boots. They trek out to the fields with the farmers. And, the reason they moved down the bar wasn't to watch us—it was because the 'tender asked them to so he could polish that part of the bar." My voice trembled a bit as I said, "We killed five men for absolutely nothing, Davey. Nothing at all."

Davey was quiet for a long time. Eventually he said, "Twisted Foot killed them five men, Pound. It wasn't us."

I looked at him.

"If it hadn't of been for that crazy sumbitch, none of this would have happened. He killed them—we didn't."

I pushed myself to my feet and faced Davey. "That's the stupidest, most ass-backward thing I've ever heard in my life." I walked out into the dark. I sat there in the dirt, listening to the night sounds—the whirring of wings, the occasional song of a coyote, the quiet rustling of rodents in the scrub.

I recalled when I graduated normal college. It seemed like I'd leaped a barrier in my life, and that now everything would be different. I'd speak differently, I'd be respected, I'd have students who loved me, I'd find a wife to hold onto at night.

Just now I felt that same shifting of cosmic gears. Before today I'd been a bank robber and a killer.

Now I was a murderer and there's one hell of a lot of difference between the two. I'd taken the lives of three completely innocent men—a pair of seed drummers and a bartender.

I got up and went back to where Davey was sitting and leaned, once again, against the tree. The piney bark smelled fresh and alive. "We gotta get provisions and keep on moving," I said. "The railroad will have the Pinkertons after us as sure as you're born. The law wants us real bad too. The newspapers both out here and back east are going to be all over us. Bounty hunters will be doggin' us, and . . ."

"And there's Twisted Foot circling around like a goddamn buzzard."

I didn't respond.

After a long moment, Davey said, "This is strange: the five men back in that train aren't no deader than the bank people we killed, but there's a terrible different feel to it."

I glanced over at Davey just as a cloud passed the moon. Lines of tears on his face made tiny silver trails. "Was my idea," he said quietly, "about them men in the bar. I figured they was—"

"I know what you figured, Davey. You were wrong—dead wrong."

"Maybe could be you don't want to ride with me no more," Davey said.

"That isn't the way it works," I said, hotly. "That isn't what being partners is all about. One pard doesn't ride off and leave the other twisting in the wind. You wouldn't do that to me and I'm not about to do it to you."

"Damn straight I wouldn't do it to you, Pound."

"That's what I just said."

"Yeah. Where are we goin' now, Pound? Maybe head east for a bit? We have money to live on."

"We don't have many other options, Davey. We're too well known around here, now. I thought maybe go on over into Louisiana or even deeper into Rebel country—Mississippi or Alabama."

"We need provisions. All we got now is ammunition, whiskey, and a few scraps of jerky. And coffee—we got coffee."

"I suppose we'd best let our beards grow back in. Thing is, I never been to the deep South and I don't know a thing about it."

"I never been there either, but Ma, she was born in Krotz Springs, Louisiana, and she always talked good about it. I got people up there too. Fact my Uncle Caspar was—maybe still is—the biggest 'shine operation for jus' miles an' miles aron'."

"You think these folks would put us up without gettin' the law on us?"

Davey laughed. "Law? Shit, Pound, more lawmen get shot there every year than pheasants do. Anyways, it ain't likely they'd ever heard of us or what we done. Most ain't big on readin' or news or such things."

"How do we get there?"

"That ain't as hard as you might think. There are all kinds of hollers and settlements and half-assed towns scattered around Louisiana. All we gotta do is stop anywhere an' ask where the Weatherhog family is at."

"So," I said, "I guess we ride due east startin' tomorrow and keep moving until we run into a Weatherhog."

"That's about it. Funny—the story what always comes to my mind is what Ma told me. Once, she seen a cottonmouth hangin' in a tree after a flood an' the sumbitch was six feet long an' as thick as your arm. Her pa blew his head off an' they took him home an' measured him out. With his head, he'da been even longer."

"Wonderful," I said sarcastically.

"You ain't got no fear of snakes, have you, Pound?"

"It's not that I'm afraid of them—I simply don't like them. They always seem to surprise a man, slinking and sliding along and spooking his horse or biting his leg if he's on foot."

"Well, hell, Pound—a snake's gotta make a livin', jus' like anybody else."

I doubted that I'd sleep that night, but eventually, I did. Images of the Evergrow valise flitted through my mind, as did that bartender going for a gun to protect what wasn't even his. I felt the thud of my pistol's butt slamming into the salesman's head, and I kept on hearing how loud my shots were in that closed railroad car. I drifted off, I guess, but I woke up before first light.

I decided to make a little fire and brew up some coffee. Perhaps that wasn't too bright of a thing to do, but I thought it unlikely a posse could have been gotten together to track us—in fact, I didn't know what town we were near. The railroad would get the Pinkertons out in force almost immediately, and bounty hunters would be real interested, since the prices on our heads would no doubt escalate.

I was gathering some dried branches when I heard the distinctive *click* of the hammer on a pistol being drawn back. It's a sound that's unique. I don't think it could be mistaken for anything else. "Davey," I said. "It's me. Put up that gun, for godsake!"

"You coulda tol' me you'd be out wanderin' around, Pound."

"Look," I said. "It was your idea that got us right where we are now. You gotta calm down a tad, boy, or you're going to get us in yet more deep shit." I arranged the kindling and branches and lit the fire before Davey spoke.

"I'm sorry, Pound. I might be wound kinda tight lately. But I didn't fire, did I? I was jus' playin' it safe."

"No, you didn't fire. I gotta give you that. But I still need you to calm down some. Now come on—the coffee's almost ready."

Game wasn't what you'd call plentiful as we traveled, but we generally managed to shoot down a prairie hen or two, and, more frequently, hares. We didn't drink much of the whiskey we'd taken from the raiders, because it was a good commodity for trade.

After a bit I couldn't have told you what day it was, nor could Davey. It made no difference at all—a day was simply a bunch of hours during which we rode east. Sometimes, if the moon was generous, we'd ride at night to beat the suffocating heat of the day.

Terrain changes slowly, but it does change. I didn't expect a sign saying HERE'S LOUISIANA, but when we added up the differences—the small, swampy areas, the Spanish moss on the trees, finding water daily—we knew we'd left Texas and entered Louisiana.

The swampy areas got bigger—much bigger, until

we had to pick our way around them rather than riding on through. The mosquitoes were the size of barn owls and just as mean. We plastered reddish mud on our faces and hands, and covered our horses with it as well as we could. It helped some, but not a lot, particularly for the horses. They'd sweat off the mud quickly and be open, again, to the bloodsucking sonsabitches.

An old cowboy told me that if you add a cup of vinegar to your horse's trough every morning through the winter, their sweat would smell of it and keep the mosquitoes at bay. Knowing that, of course, did us no good whatsoever.

We came to a clearing as we edged our way around a large patch of swamp. The place was a shack more than a home. The fellow who lived there was sitting on a little dock fishing, watching his bobber and taking the occasional glug from his jug of corn whiskey.

Davey got down from his horse and talked to the fisherman. "Gettin' anythin'?"

"Yeah. Drunk an' sunburned."

Davey laughed more than the joke called for. "Say," he said, "you wouldn't know where I could find any Weatherhogs, now, would you?"

"I might—and I might not. See, around here we don't jus' pass out information on folks. Who be you, boy?"

"I'm Davey Weatherhog," he said. He nodded toward me, still sitting in my saddle. "My partner is Pound Taylor."

"Zat right? You wouldn't happen to know who Rose of Sharon Weatherhog up an' married, would you?"

Davey smiled. "I for sure would. She was my pa's cousin and she married him."

"Hmmm," the old guy said. "Any special reason why they married up?"

"My ma, she was way up a stump—'bout four or five months' worth—an' her pa threatened to kill my pa 'less he married my ma."

"You have any brothers or sisters, boy?"

"Nope. Ma messed up her plumbin' birthin' me, an' she couldn't have no more little ones."

The old man took a long drink from his jug. After a moment, he said, "I remember your ma right good. No disrespect meant, mind you, but she had the purtiest ass God ever hooked onto a woman. Good tits, too, now that I recollect. Harley an' her, they took off 'fore their kid was born."

"She put on some weight, I guess," Davey said. "I remember her havin' an ass the size of a mule's."

"Well, anyways, you follow the edge of this here swamp eight, ten miles, you'll come to a little cluster of shacks like mine. Them's the Weatherhogs. Tell 'em Thesalonious Buckram give you the directions. Stick close to the edge of the swamp or one of them Weaterhogs'll shoot you right off your horse, thinkin' you're come to raid their still."

"I do thank you," Davey said. "We're much obliged."

"One more thing," the fisherman said. "Goddamn cottonmouths are as thick as mosquitoes this year for some goddamn reason. Watch your horses an' watch where you step. Kill as many as you can, even though it won't make no difference."

"Yessir," Davey said, and we rode away from the dock and the shack.

There was no way we could ride the edge of the swamp without riding under those huge old trees with the Spanish moss draped over them like shrouds over a corpse. We went on for a bit and then Davey asked, "What's wrong, Pound? Yer as nervous as a whore in church. Every time a bird moves in a tree, you damn near draw on it. You want a slug of whiskey, calm you down some?"

I started to say no, but then changed my mind. "Hand me the bottle," I said. He did and I pulled the cork and took a long swig. I recorked the bottle and handed it back to Davey, who took a glug and then returned the bottle to his saddlebag.

It took a couple of minutes for the whiskey to end the spastic trembling of my hands and to calm my jangled nerves a bit. "Those snakes," I said. "It's the damned snakes that got me so spooked." I cleared my throat and then went on. "I've had a problem with the goddamn things ever since I was a kid—and not only rattlers and cottonmouths and so forth, but all of them: blacksnakes, water snakes, racers—all of them."

"Why, was you ever bit?"

"No. It's not that. It's . . . well . . . you know how some folks are afraid of high places? Like being up on a barn or looking over a cliff or something? That's how it is with snakes and me. I guess there's not much I can do about it—if there was, I would have done it already."

Davey untied the shotgun from behind his saddle and handed it over to me. "This here'll do just fine on any snakes in the trees, or on the ground, too. You can't miss. If you see somethin' you just cut loose an' blow it to bits."

I accepted the shotgun and positioned it across my lap, in front of the rise of my saddle. "Thanks,

Davey," I said. "I feel better knowing if I see one of the damned things, I can kill it without doing anything but pointing the muzzle somewhere near the right direction."

The eight or ten miles Mr. Buckram mentioned must have been calculated in a straight line, as-the-crow-flies manner. Following the berm along the swamp probably tripled that distance.

We camped that first night just before dark. Davey shot a beaver, which I'd never eaten before. If my life holds straight, I never will again, either. The meat—if one cares to call it meat—is a semisolid glob of viscous grease that tastes of sewage and rot. I watched as Davey ate a good part of the creature and hurled the carcass out into the swamp. He belched loudly. "Damn," he said, "he was a nice fat one, wasn't he? I'd wager he weighed ten, twelve pounds, which ain't huge for a beaver, but it's a good eatin' size."

The couple bites I'd taken stirred my gut like a witch's cauldron, but I'd have used a cork for my bung before I'd move out of the light from our fire. I kept feeding that fire all night long, and when I did manage to drift off, I had dreams about snakes entwining themselves around me, hissing and spitting, their eyes brilliant red jewels.

Long about first light I couldn't hold it any longer. I tore several pages out of the Monkey-Ward catalog we'd brought along for sanitary purposes and moved twenty paces or so from the fire. I took the shotgun with me and I was clutching the stock so hard my knuckles were white.

I found what I considered a likely spot in a rough V formed from rocks and small boulders, dropped my trousers, and got to it. The release was, in a sense, a thing of beauty, the ridding of my body of noxious materials.

That's when I heard it, or, more exactly, when I saw it.

Cottonmouths, Davey had told me, would shake their tails exactly in the manner of a rattlesnake, but there's no noise emitted by the motion. Strangely, the lack of a warning sound made the cottonmouth, in my mind, anyway, more malevolent, more purely evil.

I'd just used the second page I'd brought from the catalog. I dropped it and the paper drifted to the ground, which the snake must have perceived in its primordial little brain as a threat to it. The snake was, at the most, six feet away from me. It was coiled tightly with its Satan's fork of a tongue tasting the air and it slowly raised a third of its body length into the air, leaning backward to a good degree, and opened its mouth wider than I'd believed the creature could do. The reason for the naming of the snake became immediately apparent: its gaping maw was a pure, fluffy white, much like clean cotton, and its fangs were every bit of two inches long.

My drawers were, of course, at my boots, the shotgun at my side. It was a life-or-death standoff for both the snake and for me: if I made the wrong move the snake would strike me, and if the snake moved a bit out of range I'd blow hell out of it with the twelve-gauge.

Nothing seemed to be happening. The only movement in the world was that bloodred tongue. There were no bird sounds, no tickling breeze—nothing but a rushing waterlike sound I heard in my head.

Remember, I was squatting for all of this time. My calf muscles began to fire jabs of pain, and although my boots were a good ways apart I was beginning to feel a lack of balance. If I toppled I knew that'd be it for me. On the other hand, I couldn't stay here forever. If I didn't fall over, it's likely Davey would come looking for me and spook the cottonmouth.

Little red spots began to float in and out of my vision, and the spots were becoming increasingly larger. The water sound was louder too. I had no choice. I sure as hell had to do something—so I did.

My boots had good purchase on the ground. I tensed myself, took in a long, slow breath, and hurled myself backward, grabbing up the shotgun as I did so. The snake came over my shoulder, close enough for its dry scales to sluff against my shirt. I rolled to the side and fired just as the cottonmouth was pulling its body into a striking coil. I splattered the damned thing over a good piece of country. Before I pulled up my drawers I ejected the fired cartridge from the shotgun and replaced it with a fresh one from my pocket.

Davey had the coffeepot on the coals of the fire when I got back to camp.

"Snake?" he asked.

"Yes." I didn't yet have enough saliva in my mouth to say anything else.

"What you wanna look out for is when a cottonmouth kinda stands up with its mouth way wide open. That means you better kill the sumbitch, 'cause he's going to attack, and if he gits them two fangs in you, it won't be long before you're tellin' your friends in hell the whole story."

He poured us each some coffee. It was strong and good. "What I can't understand is how anyone in his right mind would want to live in this . . . this viper pit."

"I guess folks can get used to about anything 'cept a cheatin' wife. Hell, Pound, don't we just naturally shake out our boots if we take them off an' set them aside an' our bedrolls an' saddle blankets, too, 'cause of scorpions? A scorpion ain't no prettier'n a cottonmouth."

"That's different."

"How?" Davey asked. "How is it different?"

He had me there for a moment. *How is it different?*

"Here's how it's different, Davey. I've been stung by lots of scorpions and I can't say I enjoyed the experience, but it didn't kill me. But if that cottonmouth had gotten his fangs into me I'd be dead."

"You know somethin', Pound? There's times you're a complete pain in the ass. Come on—let's get saddled up an' make it to the Weatherhog place in time for a good dinner."

As I was pulling the cinch on my bay, I asked, "What kind of name is Weatherhog? I've never heard anything like it before. Is it—I dunno—Polish or something?"

"I dunno what it is, actually. See, Pa knocked up Ma but they never talked about their families much. I don't think Pa was born in the U. S. of A. An' even before I killed him he never told me nothin' about the Weatherhogs, 'cept this is right about where they live. See, kin is real important to these folks—anybody else they'd jus' as soon waste a bullet on as not."

"The Weatherhogs must have gone outside the family to marry, no?"

Some time passed before Davey asked, "You know what incinderous is, Pound?"

"I don't think so."

"What incinderous is, is when maybe a brother marries an' takes up with his own brother's daughter. Ma tol' me they had some real strange-lookin' babies, but most of 'em croaked."

Meeting these swamp rats will be just splendid, I thought. To Davey, I said, "Incest is bad news, Davey. You've seen horses bred back to their mothers, and the get is no damn good. I think the same thing applies to people."

"It's our way, I guess."

"Jesus Christ," I said to myself.

The Weatherhog homes were situated in an almost grown-over clearing that was quite small, very near the shore of the swamp. Like the old fisherman, the Weatherhogs had a rickety dock built out onto the swamp to fish from. As we rode up, two things happened simultaneously: a kid about ten shot a cottonmouth that had crawled up on the dock, and a gaunt, hard-faced, bearded man stepped out from behind a clump of scrub with a pistol in each hand, one leveled at Davey and one at me. He looked like a scarecrow.

"Hold it right there," the scarecrow said. "You got business here?"

"I'd say we have," Davey said quite happily. "I'm Davey Weatherhog an' this fella's my pardner, Pound. We come a good distance to visit with you folks."

"We don't need no visitors," the scarecrow said. He thumbed back the hammers on the two pistols.

An elderly woman in a homemade dress stepped out from behind a tree, a shotgun at port arms. Her face was so wrinkled it resembled a dried apple. "You hol' on there, Aaron," she told the scarecrow. She peered at Davey and then at me. Her eyes were a brilliant, piercing blue—eyes one would expect to see on a beautiful society lady.

She shifted her eyes back to my partner. "You Rose of Sharon's boy, Davey?"

"I sure am," Davey said.

"Tell me somethin' about your pa, boy," she said.

"Well," Davey said, "he was the meanest ol' sumbitch I ever seen. He was drunk most of the time an' when he wasn't, he was hittin' me or Ma."

"He still livin'?"

"No, ma'am. I killed him a ways back."

The woman's old face brightened and she smiled, or showed her gums, actually, because she had no teeth. "Why, praise Jesus!" she exclaimed. "We heard all 'bout that. Aaron, you put them pistols away. This boy here is our blood kin."

"The partner ain't kin," Aaron said.

"You let the partner be," the woman told him. "If he's ridin' with Davey, he's good people. Don't you go shootin' him."

I took a bit of time to look around the clearing. There were nine or ten shacks, each one more disreputable and flimsy than its neighbor. They were placed in a rough circle, facing a well in the center. A couple of naked kids peeked out from behind a shack, gawking at us. The little girl's head looked way too big for her body.

"You boys come on inside, have some coffee or corn, an' we'll talk about family some. Round—we'll bore your ass off, but a taste of corn will help you out."

"It's Pound, ma'am, not Round."

"I'll beggin' yer pardon. Yer name's a bit strange."

Weatherhog isn't a strange name?

"Why don' you," she said, "go out in back an' put your horses up in the corral? There's some shade, a little grazing, an' water too."

The corral looked as if it'd been constructed by a drunken four-year-old. In theory, it was post and rail: in actuality it was warped, splintered junk-wood boards and rotting posts that hadn't been treated with creosote to give them a life span of more than a season. It was maybe an eighth of an acre in size and did offer some buffalo grass, some shade, and a tiny watering hole. I stripped the saddles and blankets off our horses and rested them on the fence. I hobbled both Davey's horse and mine.

The Weatherhog horses were pathetic creatures—bowlegged, ribby, chestless animals with scruffy, mange-infested coats. I closed the gate as well as I could, given the fact that it hung from only one hinge. I walked back to the old woman's house, stepping very carefully through the long grass and weeds.

Davey and the woman were sitting across from one another at a table that had once been a door. It was supported by sawhorses. There was a jug on the table but no sign of a coffeepot or coffee. There was a small herd of shifty-eyed miscreants and future prison cell inhabitants wandering about the room and in and out of the door.

The woman was speaking as I walked in. ". . . 'course, he died early. Got rat-bit in his crib an' got a infection. He's planted right out by the corral."

"Auntie Bess," Davey asked, "what about them twins used to beat up on my pa all the time?"

"They're both in prison in Yuma. A meaner pair you couldn't find in hell or on earth."

Auntie Bess pointed me to a chair and shoved it out a bit for me. She moved the jug to my place. "Have a sip or two," she said.

I'd had corn whiskey before and found it to be a vile drink with a strange, oily texture to it. Nevertheless, I took a quick glug of the corn and was pleasantly surprised. The Weatherhog corn whiskey was as good as store-bought bourbon—strong, smoky, and went down easily.

The woman grinned. "Best corn you ever had, no? We're proud people an' we take pride in our 'shine."

"Excellent," I said.

The conversation rattled on back and forth between Davey and his aunt for quite some time and I drifted comfortably in my mind, paying no attention at all. Auntie Bess's question, "So what are you fellas doin' out this way?" brought me back to the conversation, but Davey answered before I could.

"Truth to tell, Auntie, me an' Pound is on the run from the law an' from a crazy Injun."

"Seems like them lawmen can't leave a soul alone," Auntie Bess said. "What's this Injun thing all about? We don't much take to 'em 'round here."

Davey ran through the entire story of the robbery, the mother and child we ran down, and the fight between the sheriff and the Indian.

"That same Injun—Twisted Foot—killed your great uncle Abimilech. Put a arrow right through Abe's heart."

"Where was this?" I asked.

"Out toward New Orleans, is what we heard." She swept a hand vaguely toward where New Orleans was. "Far as I know, Twisted Foot ain't ever been down here."

"So anyway," Davey went on, "we was hopin' you could put us up for a bit. See, we got in some trouble on a train an' had to kill five men."

"I never been on no train," Auntie Bess said. "I'd sure like to take a ride on one sometime, though."

"Well, about puttin' us up . . ."

"You're in luck there, Davey," Auntie Bess said. "Yer uncle Nelson choked to death on a catfish bone not three weeks ago. His place is open an' you boys are welcome to it. It's right on across from here—the place with the busted-in door." For a moment, Auntie Bessie drifted away from her squalid little shack and Davey and Davey's unsavory pard, into a warm and pleasant world of her own. She was silent. Davey and I both stared at her. Eventually, she shook her head as if to relieve a slight dizziness.

"I've fished these waters all my goddamn life," she said. "I've hauled big cats outta here, an' I've filled my buckets with bluegills an' perch. I've been out in the morning when the sun ain't nearly showin', an' I've fished at night even while the sonsabitches skeeters were drinkin' me dry." She sighed. "An' a walkin' pus-wart like Uncle Nelson hauls that huge cat outta the water. Why, the man ain't fished a whole hour in his useless life. It jus' ain't right."

"No, ma'am, it don't sound right to me, neither."

Auntie Bess took a long drink from her jug, wiped her mouth with the back of her hand, and smiled. "No sense in holdin' a grudge against a dead man, I guess," she said. "Maybe you boys want to go over to

Uncle Nelson's place and clean her up a bit. Watch for cottonmouths. I never seen a year when we had so many. You might want to look under Nelson's cot an' in the cupboards an' such."

"We'll sure do that, ma'am," I said, meaning every word of it.

Auntie Bess touched the jug, turned it around on the table, but didn't pick it up.

"I got quite a surprise for you two," she grinned. "We're goin' to have a couple more visitors who'll hang around a bit."

"Who would they be?" Davey asked.

"I figure we'll put them in with you two in Uncle Nelson's place. There's plenty of room for four fellas."

I looked through the glassless window. Nelson's shack was about eight feet by ten feet—barely the size of a good box stall. I sighed. It's not like we had a lot of places we could go.

"These fellas comin' in are right famous, an' they're good, honest men who believe in the Confederate cause. Now, I ain't sayin' they're angels. They've robbed a few banks an' a train, an' they've gunned lots of men—men who needed to be kilt. Thing is, a teller got killed over in Russellville, Kentucky, an' the law got all riled up an' put the Pinkertons on them. They got a message to us askin' us could they come by for a visit 'til things cool down some."

I was very curious by now. These two desperados—no matter who they were—followed the same career path Davey and I did. Even though the four of us would be jammed together in a space smaller than a prison cell, I thought that perhaps these boys may be interesting to talk to, particularly after listening to Davey and his Auntie Bess.

"They's brothers, these two are," Bess said.

"Oh?" Davey asked.

Auntie Bess smiled toothlessly as she made her announcement. "Yessir. Their names are Jesse and Frank . . ." She paused for a moment, apparently to build tension and intensity, and then said, "James!"

"Whoooo-hooo!" Davey exclaimed. "I've always wanted to meet them. They say anythin' about the Youngers bein' with them?"

"No—just Jesse an' Frank. I guess Cole an' Bob found hidey-holes of their own. They've got a passel of family around."

I'd followed much of Jesse and Frank James's career in crime through the newspapers. Then, some addled writer of dime novels started making heroes out of them, saving maidens and killing Indians and so forth. If nothing else, I thought, meeting these men would be interesting.

Later that day Davey went into Uncle Nelson's place with a shovel, me a step behind him with the shotgun loaded, cocked, and ready to fire.

"Careful 'bout shootin' me in the back," Davey warned me as we shoved the broken door out of the way.

"I will," I promised.

My hands were sweating and for a moment I felt dizzy and disoriented.

"Ready?" Davey asked.

"Ready," I said.

Davey whacked hell out of everthing in that

shack—the ratty cot, the small pile of clothes in one corner, the cupboards inside and out, and the holes in the floorboards. He flushed a couple of rats and one snake of some kind—a bullnose, he called it. It was long—maybe six feet—and thick, and kind of reddish with a white spot on top of its head. I blew it to bits.

"Them bullnose snakes, they're good for keepin' down rats an' mice," Davey said. "No reason to shoot that fella."

"I'll deal with the rats and mice," I said. "I don't want any snakes around."

Davey shook his head, but didn't say anything else.

Jesse and Frank James rode in about sunset of the next day. It'd been ungodly hot and they'd obviously ridden all day. Their horses were frothed with sweat and the men's shirts stuck to their bodies as if they were glued on.

The Weatherhogs gathered around the James brothers, shaking hands with them, talking all at once, asking questions, setting up a clamor around these two fatigued outlaws.

It wasn't too hard to see that Frank had had enough of being greeted. The smile he'd forced earlier was gone, and now his face was in a grimace, a mockery of a smile. He handed his reins to one of the young boys and told him, "You walk him out 'til he's dry an' then rub him down good. Give him some water but not a lot at one time. Grain him up good too."

"We got no grain," Auntie Bess pointed out. "Pasture ain't too bad, though."

"It'll have to do, I guess," Frank said. I got a good look at Frank James as the boy led his horse away. Frank stood at five-foot-ten or so, and was average build. He looked like he could use some weight, though. His arms were awfully thin and his face somewhat gaunt.

Jesse was a little taller, and his body was fuller than his brother's. He had an engaging smile that didn't, however, reach his eyes. Jesse moved easily, almost catlike, which isn't easy to do after more than a full day in the saddle.

Auntie Bess introduced Davey and me to the James. "You know," Frank said, "seems to me I read about you two shooting hell out of a bank, killed . . . what? Two? Three men?"

"Three it was," I said. "The job just kinda fell apart on us."

Frank nodded. "That'll happen, no matter how good the job is laid out aforehand." He shook his head, as if in disgust. "I could never figure out why the hell some teller who's making maybe a couple of dollars a week would risk getting killed for the bank's money. It doesn't make no sense."

"No. No, it doesn't."

Auntie Bess had a cauldron of possum stew that'd been cooking all the day. The scent of the wild onions she found, and the spices and whatall, hung around the fire like a cloud.

After the stew was ladled out by Auntie Bess, we all sat around the fire to eat. I'd not yet gotten a close look at the members of the Weatherhog family. If nothing else, seeing the whole group together further established in my mind that incest wasn't a good way to increase a family. There were more slack-jawed, dull-eyed children and adults than I'd ever seen in one place before. Larger than normal-sized heads were the rule rather than the exception. Several children sat, rocking gently back and forth, humming, totally lost in their own worlds.

The women were almost, without exception, as fat as autumn heifers. Most of the Weatherhogs used their fingers to take pieces out of their stew, although Jesse, Frank, Davey, and I used our pocket knives. The stew was amazingly good. One of the women had baked a loaf of bread. Unfortunately, she didn't bake it nearly long enough. The outside was a thick black crust, but the inside was a doughy, gelatinous mass.

There was still some light when Davey and I showed the James brothers the shack they'd be staying in. Frank looked disgusted; Jesse laughed. "Shit," he said, "I know hogs that'd be too proud to sleep in here."

Nevertheless, they spread their bedrolls on the floor. I'd been sleeping on the cot and Davey against one of the walls.

"These people are something, aren't they? I've never seen anything quite like them," Jesse said.

"They're strange, all right, but they took Davey and me in when we didn't have anywhere else to go."

"The law an' the Pinkertons hounding you?" Jesse asked.

"Yeah. Plus we ran down an Indian's wife and child and he's out for our blood."

"Well, hell," Jesse said. "An Indian isn't going to cause you much trouble."

"This one's name is Twisted Foot," I said.

There was a long, deep silence. Finally, Jesse said, "Holy shit."

Frank didn't say anything but I could see in the moonlight that he'd moved his Colt from under his bedroll to right next to his head.

Chapter Nine

Neither of the James brothers were what you'd call gregarious—they pretty much kept to themselves. The days got awfully long around the Weatherhog shacks and there was next to nothing to do, unless one cared to sit on the shady side of a shack and drink oneself into oblivion. That gets old in a hurry, although I'd developed a taste for Weatherhog 'shine. There was some fishing to be done in the swamp, but the intensity of the sun reflecting off the stagnant water took the fun out of that.

Frank was a reclusive sort. Although he ate with the Weatherhogs, Davey, and me, he'd often wander off during the day and we wouldn't see him for a few hours. Quite often we heard gunshots resounding across the swamp, and they sent the rest of us scrambling for our weapons. Jesse told us not to worry; it was merely Frank keeping his shooting eye trained. Apparently, Frank had some sort of fear that he'd lose his skills if he didn't keep practicing.

Jesse admitted candidly that Frank was the better shot of the two of them, but there was an addendum to that statement: Frank was tighter on targets, but

Jesse was more accurate where it really counted—against other men with guns.

Jesse and I got to be friendly, although it's doubtful that Jesse ever really had friends. He had men he was fond of, but his heart was in total allegiance to his family.

Fairly frequently, Jesse and I would go out walking. My purpose was to kill cottonmouths; Jesse's was to get away from the clamor of the Weatherhogs. On one occasion as we were walking, Jesse maybe a half step ahead of me, he gave me a fine exhibition of his speed and accuracy. I saw his right hand move, but it actually moved too fast for me to follow it and the three shots he fired rang out almost as one, they were so rapid. I stepped up next to him and saw his target. It was a cottonmouth—a big one—and the stalk of its body was still elevated in its slightly backward position. Its head, however, was gone.

Jesse was interesting enough to talk with, but there was a feel about the man—an aura—that made me uncomfortable. It was like talking to an undertaker, is about as close as I can come to the sensation. Jesse said he had no doubt in his mind that he'd take a bullet and die; it was simply a matter of where and when. He said he'd killed thirty-six men and that he planned on killing many more before he was finished.

The dime novels portrayed Jesse, Frank, and the Youngers as modern-day Robin Hoods, stealing from the rich and giving to the poor. Jesse got a good laugh out of that when I told him about it. "Robin Hood, my ass," he laughed. "Me an' Frank have more goddamn money stashed away than we can count. Hell, if a man with a shovel did some digging around our ma's house, he'd walk away a very rich man."

"If you have all that money," I asked, "why keep at it? Why not buy a spread somewhere and settle down?"

He didn't answer for a while as we continued walking. Then, he said, "It's like this, Pound. There are some folks who collect whalebone carvings, or books, or whatever the hell. But it's not having the carving or the book that gives them the thrill: it's the collecting of it. It gets in a man's blood. Me an' Frank don't need no money. Our ma is set up good and I got a half brother who won't want for much of anything. But Frank and me, we keep at it."

Davey had been palling around with two of the Weatherhog boys—two of the more normal ones—named Abraham and Moses. Many, if not most, of the Weatherhogs had biblical names. They'd go out into the swamp in a flat-bottomed skiff and shoot snakes out of trees. Davey used his rifle and the Weatherhogs used shotguns. Even with their scatterguns, Davey confided in me, neither one of the boys could shoot worth a damn.

A month—possibly six weeks—had gone by with us as guests of the Weatherhogs. I'd had more than enough. So had Frank and Jesse. One day, as we walked, Jesse said, "You know, me an' Frank might could find a place for you an' Davey in the gang we're bringin' back together. There's a god-awful lot of money to be made. Hell, we stole the strong box of army pay—cash, not script—from a stagecoach not long ago. Taking a stagecoach is about as hard as grabbing a peppermint stick from a baby."

I'll admit that I gave it a lot of thought, but I simply

couldn't see Davey and me riding with such a band of cutthroats. Like I said, I kind of liked Jesse James, but he was a man who loved to see blood flow a bit more than I was comfortable with. So, I told him Davey and I weren't cut out to ride with gangs and preferred to work alone. Jesse accepted that with no problems.

Davey and I talked quite a bit about where we'd go when we left Louisiana. I didn't think going back West was a good idea, but I wasn't real set on going deeper into the South, either. So, our discussions went on and on without resolution.

We hadn't seen a newspaper in all the time we'd been with the Weatherhogs, so I didn't know if we were still hot items or if we'd been pushed off the front page. And, of course, we'd heard nothing of Twisted Foot. It's not that we expected to: he and his killings weren't the sort of thing most easterners cared to read about. In the end we decided to ride up into Arkansas and then perhaps over to Kansas, if we decided that's what we wanted to do. I wanted to eventually work my way back to the Mississippi with enough money so that I wouldn't need to steal anymore, and cross into Mexico, just as I'd planned for some time.

I was so damned weary of snakes and Weatherhog food and the Weatherhogs themselves, that going to hell would have been a nice vacation. Nevertheless, I wanted to make a good decision. I think I did. A couple days later Davey and I set off for Arkansas.

Saying good-bye to the Weatherhogs wasn't difficult, and was made even easier by the fact that a number of them didn't seem to know who we were or that we'd been there at all. We shook hands formally with Jesse and Frank James, and we wished one another well.

Our horses had done amazingly well in the corral. We checked them over daily and rode at least once every couple of days. Their shoes looked good but we planned to stop at the first blacksmith shop we came to and have them reset.

The one thing we didn't leave behind when we left the Weatherhog family was the sun. It continued to flex its muscles daily, and it wasn't the sort of heat a man could get used to—it was sapping, enervating, and constant.

Our conversations were desultory, for the most part. My ears pricked up a bit when Davey told me that Frank James told him there was a judge named Roy Bean somewhere in Arkansas who strung up better than eighty men. Davey said a saloon served as the courtroom and there was a sign over the batwings saying LAW WEST OF THE PECOS. I reached into my watch packet to make sure the one bullet I was saving for myself in case of imminent capture was still there. I was never going to face an executioner with his black hood and noose.

The first town we came to in Arkansas was Allensville. It was small, but it had a barbershop, a livery, a saloon with rooms to rent, and a mercantile. I didn't see that we needed anything else.

I wouldn't have stepped into that goddamn swamp to clean up a tad, no matter how bad I smelled—and I did smell, I can tell you that. So, Davey and I had both parted with a quarter for a hot bath. We decided to leave our beards and hair alone. While I soaked I picked up a couple of newspapers from the chairs for waiting customers. We weren't front-page news any longer, but we were still news. The murders of the railroad personnel had stirred up a hell of a hornet's nest. The Pinkertons were out, as we expected, but the railroad had raised the ante on Davey and me to $20,000 each, dead or alive. Randall and Howard were said to have left our gang and were suspected to be riding with the James and Younger brothers. There was no mention of Twisted Foot or any other Indian, for that matter.

The blacksmith was a giant of a man, as many in his profession are, and he suggested new shoes all the way around each of our horses. He wasn't trying to drum up sales—he showed me the wear on the shoes wasn't bad yet, but would get worse shortly. I told him to go ahead and shoe them both, and to grain them.

There were three cowponies tied to the rail in front of the saloon. We headed over from the 'smith's to the saloon and took places at the bar. Allensville had ice, which surprised me. I guess I was a bit behind the times: I could recall when a man couldn't get a cold beer to save his life, and now, in the modern world, it was available almost everywhere. It was piss-poor beer, but it was better than no beer at all.

We'd just ordered our second schooners when a heavy, big-gutted man to Davey's right said to him, "You wear that Colt awful low, boy."

"I wear it like that so my children can pull it out an' play with it without botherin' me as I read my Bible," Davey said.

The fat man's face reddened. "You mouthin' off to me, boy?"

"Yeah, as a matter of fact," Davey said.

The fat man looked closer at Davey. "You a shootist,

boy, one of them gunslingers cause trouble wherever they go?"

I stepped over to the man. "Look," I said, "my friend and I stopped in for a couple of beers. He's not looking for any trouble and neither am I. So how about—"

"You clam up, mister. I'm talkin' to the gunman here, not you."

I put my hand lightly on Davey's arm. "We don't need this," I said. "Let's just leave."

Davey thought it over and then nodded. We turned and took a couple of steps toward the batwings, me a step ahead of my partner. Davey slammed into my back with enough power to shove me on through the batwings and fall on my ass in the street. Davey managed to keep his balance, but I'm not sure how. The fat man was standing now, face more crimson than ever, laughing.

"Thought I'd give you a little help findin' the door," he said.

I looked at his waist. He had a Smith & Wesson .38 in a Mexican, fancy-tooled holster.

I got to my feet quickly and grabbed Davey. "Come on!" I urged him. "Let's fetch our horses. We don't need any trouble." I again put my hand on Davey's arm. This time it felt as hard as a steel beam.

Shit, I thought.

Davey backed out to the middle of the street and stood there, hands loose at his sides, the fingers on his right hand curled slightly inward.

The big man pushed through the batwings and stood, gazing at Davey, who was perhaps thirty paces from him. "I'm damned if this boy isn't challengin' me to draw agin him," he said. He grinned, showing yellowed teeth. "I got notches on my grips, boy," he said. "Lots of them."

I began to walk between them when Davey said, "Pound—no. Let's let this play out."

"You're going to have another notch—right between your eyes. You'd best go back inside an' drink your beer," I told the big man.

He took a step farther and then stood, legs far apart, body making a target as big as a barn.

"Make your move, lardass," Davey said.

"By an' by I just might do that, boy, you keep on insultin' me." As he spoke his hand moved to his pistol and he began pulling it from its fancy holster, when he suddenly lurched backward like he'd been blown off his feet by a tornado wind. He landed on the grit and dirt of the street, raising a cloud of dust with the impact. He didn't move. There was a neat, ten-cent-piece hole squarely between his eyes.

Davey holstered his pistol. "Let's get our horses," he said.

Our mounts were in stalls, their shoeing completed, their coats shining from the brushing down the 'smith had given them. The oat bins in front of each were just about empty. The blacksmith said, "That'll be $3.45 . . ."

I handed him a ten-dollar bill. "Keep it," I said. "We're in kind of a hurry."

We saddled up and rode out of Allensville, leaving yet another corpse behind us.

I can't say I blamed Davey a hundred percent. A man can only be pushed so far before he does something about it. We were doing absolutely nothing that could rile anyone, but the fat man had to get rid of some meanness, and he decided to spit it into Davey's face.

We were on our way out of the bar when the big man shoved Davey, and our backs to the big oaf. Then his talk about his notches was nothing but a pure challenge to Davey. Still, what the hell? If we'd gotten our horses and ridden out, we wouldn't have added to our problems. What about the law in Allenstown? I didn't see a sheriff or marshall's office, but lots of these villages and burgs didn't have a lawman—they depended on the army. I'd seen lots of army peacekeepers in my day—usually passed-out drunk at tables in saloons.

"Dumb sumbitch," Davey mumbled, when we slowed to a walk. "He damned near forced me to draw on him."

"It might not be too big a deal, Davey. He was haulin' at his pistol when you nailed him—that looks like self-defense to me. Could be he was just another saddletramp."

"Like us?" Davey asked.

"Hell, no! We're businessmen."

Davey laughed. "Have you looked at yourself or me lately? These fancy clothes look like we found them in a ditch somewheres."

Of course, Davey was right. It would have worked out a lot better for us if we'd visited the general store in Allensville before we went into the saloon. "Next time we head directly for a mercantile, and then do whatever needs to be done, OK?"

"Sure."

"A decent meal wouldn't hurt at all, either," Davey said. "I'm right grateful to the Weatherhogs for takin' us in' an' puttin' us up all that time, but Jesus God, that ol' woman couldn't boil water in hell. First place we come to, I'm goin' to have me a steak 'bout the size of a wagon wheel."

"That sounds good, Davey. But the food isn't what bothered me so much. It was those goddamned snakes. You notice as soon as we were a day or so out from the swamp we didn't see a single one?"

"All we need to watch out here abouts is rattlers an' scorpions," Davey said.

"At least a rattlesnake has the common decency to make some noise, let folks know he's around. I swear I'll have nightmares about those cottonmouths for the rest of my life."

We rode on.

Riding a good-striding horse at a walk has an almost hypnotic effect to it. There's next to no motion in the saddle and a rider's legs can be relaxed, and his rein hand—his left, if he's right-handed—can come to rest on the saddle horn. The rider's eyes will lose their motion and will fix on something—a cactus, a rock, whatever. When that milestone is passed the rider will pick out another—without necessarily knowing he's doing it—and focus his eyes on it.

A good-stepping horse is one whose back hoofprints fit precisely into his front prints at a walk. The shifting of the saddle is so subtle because the motion is so uniform, so precise, step after step, that it's difficult to realize for the horseman that it's happening at all. But, it is.

Both Davey and I were baking like a couple of apple pies in an oven. The moon was small at night, and there was cloud cover, as well, which precluded our riding during the night and sleeping during the day.

It's not an unpleasant ride at all, except for the heat. I had a medical doctor tell me once that the reason it felt good to a cowboy is that it reminds him of his ride in his mother's womb—the sloshing around and so forth in the woman's plumbing brought back memories the man never knew he had. The thing is, the doc was drunk enough for any three men, and also told us about some goddamn bugs or blogs that are carried in a man's blood and could get into another man's blood if the doc didn't wash his hands real good between treating people who'd gotten shot up.

Well, hell. Blood is blood. If some is spilled from one man and is carried on a surgeon's hands to another, it doesn't make a lick of difference.

What about the tents both sides set up around major battle sites? First and Second Bull Run, Gettysburg, Shiloh, Fredericksburg, all those? Those tents were called the "amp" tents, short for the word "amputate." The docs used the same goddamn saw hacking off an arm as they did hacking off the next man's leg, and you can bet there sure was no time to wash that sawblade between operations. They used to pile arms and legs out behind the amp tents, and sometimes the piles would be as tall as the tent—like at Gettysburg, for instance.

None of that has anything to do with this story.

About the fourth day we were walking along when Davey pushed at my shoulder. "Pound," he said. "Lookit that. You think it's that Injun?"

There was a narrow stripe of dust a few miles ahead of us. It stood out brown against a blue sky without a cloud in it. It was steady, and we could see that it was moving slowly.

"I doubt that it's Twisted Foot," I told Davey, "but I don't know what it is. How about this? We swing way the hell over to the south and come straight at it. If we see it's more trouble than we can handle, we haul ass."

"Makes some sense," Davey said. "It sure ain't a posse. There ain't enough riders. The Pinkertons, they'd be coming in from two sides, not leavin' us a path to trail. Might could be a couple army riders; they couldn't track a man through a new-plowed field if they had signs in the ground every so often sayin', 'Go this way.' "

"Well," I said, "no matter what or who it is, we need to find out if it's any danger to us." We did as we planned—swung over to the south a good distance, putting us ahead of the line of dust in the sky, and then came more or less directly at it, using the low hills as cover.

It was a drummer's wagon, and a great big one at that. We didn't see any danger in it so we rode up and "helloed" the drummer. He was a man of fifty or so, of average build and average height. His graying hair was carefully cut and his beard looked like he trimmed it and evened it up daily. He wore thick glasses that magnified the size of his brown eyes.

What was interesting was the way he was dressed. He wore a full suit in that insufferable heat, with a white shirt and tie. His boots were well polished enough to reflect light and images just as a mirror would. On the side of the freighter were the words, FAIRNESS TO ALL ROLLING MERCANTILE ESTABLISHMENT: WILLIAM "BILL" BURNS, PROP.

He reined his matched bays to a halt and smiled at the pair of us. "Good day, gents," he said. "I'll admit I'm happy to see another human being—it seems like I've been traveling for weeks without seeing a living soul. But, please excuse my lack of manners: I'm Bill Burns, owner and operator of this operation."

Davey and I introduced ourselves as Joe Goodnight and Tom Smith—the names that came to our minds the quickest. Burns looked at me. "Joe," he said, "you wouldn't be a relative of the famous Charles Goodnight, now would you?"

"Only in my dreams," I said. "Seems like Mr. Goodnight owns all the cattle and most of the money on earth. Nope—no relation."

"And Tom," Burns said. "Where do you hail from, lad?"

"Well, I'll tell you, Bill—I don't have no regular home. I kinda drift, if you know what I mean."

"Certainly," Burns said. He stood in his driver's seat and stretched a bit. "I insist you gents sit down with me and have a cup of the finest coffee in the world. It comes to the States from Brazil."

He set the wagon's brake, took a wrap with his reins around it, and stepped down to the ground, looking up at us expectantly.

"That's a fine offer, Bill," I said, "and one we'll take you up on."

The back of the wagon dropped down to make a ramp to the inside. Wooden struts and shelves had been constructed in the wagon, each holding stock of almost any kind. A small table extended from the gate and a coffeepot and a sack of coffee rested just inside the wagon. Burns scurried about like an old hen, starting a little fire, putting out cups, filling the pot's basket with coarse ground coffee. There was a central aisle the length of the wagon, which allowed customers to pass on through, inspecting the goods for sale. Davey and I walked through—just looking, mind you—and came out with our arms loaded with stock. We each purchased denim pants and a shirt, a sack of Arbuckle's ground coffee, ammunition for our weapons, and some luxuries too: we bought four cans of peaches in sweet syrup. Davey picked up a couple of scarves, which he liked to wear around his neck to sop up sweat, and a few packages of Bull Durham and rolling papers. Davey wasn't much of a smoker, but every so often he enjoyed one. He bought a set of underwear, a couple of tin cups, and some teat balm to work into his saddle. I came out with a box of cheroots, underwear, a farrier's file, and a deck of playing cards. I considered a new hat. Burns had some nice ones, but they weren't Stetsons, so I decided to keep the lid I was wearing.

By the time we'd finished our shopping, the Brazilian coffee was perking. It had a wonderful aroma to it. Actually, all coffee smells good, but this potful was yet more savory.

We sat on the shaded side of the wagon and sipped at our coffee. Burns offered to add a drop of bourbon in our cups but we declined—the coffee tasted great just as it was. Burns was kind enough to give each of our horses a bucket of water from the three barrels of it strapped to the side of his wagon.

I lit a cheroot. Davey rolled a cigarette. Bill stoked up a pipe that issued very pleasant-smelling smoke.

"You must do an awful lot of traveling, Bill," I said.

"Oh, yes—that I do. Nothing much goes on around

here that I don't know about. I make it a point to be as observant as possible."

"Have you ever heard of an Injun named Twisted Foot?" Davey asked.

"I have indeed. He's a very bad man—the devil incarnate, in my mind."

"Why do you say that?" I asked.

"Because I've seen the aftermath of a few of his attacks. I won't go into details."

"No need to," I said. "We've seen his work too."

We were all quiet for a moment. Then, Bill changed the subject. "Were you gents aware that the army is constructing a new fort over near Livonia? If you have special skills, the army is hiring on civilians."

"Where's this Livonia?" I asked.

"About thirty-five miles off to the east," Bill said. "Nice little town with a stockyard that draws some decent herds. I hear tell the army is going to use the new fort as a training facility for soldiers and also as their horse and mule procurement center."

"Must be lots of soldiers there by now," I said.

"Not really," Bill said. "Maybe fifty or a hundred, at the outside. Not much for them to do except grunt labor and wait on the paymaster to pull in."

I tried to keep my voice casual. "How often does that happen?"

"Once a month," Bill said. "I know that because I make it a point to be around then—there are stores in Livonia, but lots of the boys stay loyal to me."

There was a comfortable silence, each thinking our own thoughts. "I was wondering, Bill, why you dress so spiffy. Seems like it'd be awful hard to keep your clothes clean."

Burns exhaled a cloud of bluish-white smoke.

"I'm in business, my friend," he said. "I feel like I owe it to my customers—no matter who they are—to present a businesslike appearance. And, I guess I'm just clean by nature."

We finished the coffee and the three of us stood. I put my hand out to Burns. "Many thanks for the coffee, Bill," I said. "I hope to see you again."

Davey shook with him too. "Thanks, Bill," he said. "Best coffee I ever drank."

"Say," Burns said, "I never got around to asking where you gentlemen are headed."

"That's a little hard to say just now," I said. "Could be we'll pick up some cattle work before long. Right now, we're just drifting a bit to see what we can see."

Burns returned to his driver's seat and we swung onto our horses. We watched Burns drive away. We looked at one another and grinned. "Livonia?" Davey said.

"Livonia," I answered.

It took us almost three days to cover the thirty-five miles Bill Burns had told us about. It wasn't that the terrain was rough or that there were a lot of steep grades. Rather, it was the heat. The sky was always cloudless, a breeze almost never stirred, and the pounding, debilitating heat tired both man and horse to the point of exhaustion daily.

We'd bought a canned ham from Burns and we had jerky and our peaches, and it wasn't difficult to shoot a rabbit or two to roast. We'd pretty much forgotten about the sow Davey gunned down outside the saloon at Allenstown, figuring there were a slew of witnesses to what we considered a clear case of self-defense.

I wasn't even terribly worried about the Pinkertons. They're good, but it'd take even them a while to locate us, and I hoped that by the time they did I'd be in Mexico and out of their jurisdiction. The sheriffs and marshals in the villages and towns didn't have time to try to track men like Davey and me. They'd be most pleased to gun us in a second if we rode into their towns, but other than that, we weren't a main concern.

Twisted Foot, however, remained on my mind almost constantly. Running to Mexico wouldn't slow him down—he didn't give a damn about any national borders or jurisdictions. From what we'd heard about him, he never gave up. He'd track us down for the rest of our lives if we let him. The only way to get him off our backs was to kill him, and that's what I planned to do. How, when, and where I didn't know, but I believed I'd somehow get it done, because if I didn't I'd be looking over my shoulder for the rest of my life.

We heard the fort—to be called Fort Chamberlaine—long before we saw it. The rapping of hammers and the screech of saws carry real well across the prairie. We came upon it as we topped a rise and it was spread out below us. It was a normal-sized fort with half-completed barracks and other buildings. The stockade around it was perhaps half completed. There was a large, well-fenced corral with hay feeders and water troughs placed here and there in it. There were maybe twenty horses in it, but it could easily accommodate five or six times that many.

There were dozens of one- and two-man tents set up in a sort of helter-skelter non-pattern. The men, stripped to their waists and glistening with sweat, worked away with their hammers and hacked tree-length pieces to proper length with either two-man saws or a huge circular saw set on a pedestal with a track next to it for the horses that supplied the power to keep it going.

Livonia was another three miles beyond the fort. There was nothing different or special about Livonia—as I've said before these little burgs are pretty much the same. The only difference was that more than half of the horses tied in front of the saloon and the other stores were strapped into flat, military saddles rather than the stock saddles working cowboys and most other riders use.

The saloon was long and fairly narrow, and the bar extended almost the full length of the structure. There were a few tables out on the floor. At one larger table in the rear of the place sat a fat man puffing on a cigar. A line of men, most of them in military clothing, although not full uniforms, stood in line waiting to reach the table and drinking from large mugs of beer.

Davey and I got as close to the table as we could without being conspicuous.

The fat man was the jolly type, as many heavy folks are, and he had a cigar box in front of him on the table. When a man approached the table, the heavy fellow would take some money from him and then hand over a small slip of paper to the man in line.

"Borrow four an' pay back seven ain't much of a deal, Mr. Blanchard," mumbled one man as he handed over his money and got his slip of paper.

Mr. Blanchard laughed heartily. "You didn't think it was all that bad when you borrowed the money,

Alton. You know how it works—you pay me off within twenty-four hours of the paymaster hitting town. You don't like the way I do business, go somewheres else."

"I don't get it," Davey said to me.

"This Blanchard," I said, keeping my voice low, "is a money-lender. He gives the boys a few bucks and gets more than a few bucks back on payday. It's a crooked business with outrageous interest rates, but if a man runs clean out of money he goes to someone like Blanchard."

"Damn," Davey said. "That means we just missed payday."

"That's OK. We'll get settled in and nose around until we have all the information we need—the route the stage with the pay uses, the number of guards and outriders, all that. It's possible this is too big for us, Davey. If that's the case, we move on."

We finished our beers and went over to the two-story hotel and took a pair of rooms on the first floor. I picked up a newspaper in the lobby, and there was no mention of the gunfight in Allenstown or anything about our past work.

The hotel had a restaurant. The prices were pretty stiff, but that made little difference to us. My steak, potatoes, and coffee were $1.20. Davey complained a bit but ordered the same thing.

It made us both a little nervous to see so many uniforms around, but I figured we'd get used to that. Livonia treated the soldiers well, even though I suspected that many of the townspeople held Confederate beliefs. Soldiers, however, spend freely and often, and the proprietors liked that about them just fine.

Davey had a way about him that allowed him to

talk to just about anyone, and he made friends easily. I'm more reclusive, I guess, kind of a loner, actually, and Davey and I decided that he'd be the chief information gatherer for the plan that was beginning to take form in our minds.

My plan was a simple one. The payroll wagon would have a good deal of cash in its strongboxes as it made its way to Livonia. If I—we—could rob that stagecoach and get away alive, I'd head straight to Mexico with my share. I hear land is very cheap across the river. Granted, the land is more like sand than anything else, but I don't plan to farm it or run cattle on it—I just want to have it.

Davey came staggering in midnight or after each night, often bringing a bottle and at least one soldier. At the end of the first week we were in Livonia, he brought a pair of sloshed soldiers, a bottle of whiskey, and a bucket of beer. I'd been sleeping, clothed, on top of my bed. Davey shook my shoulder to awaken me. The two soldiers, both kids of about twenty or so, were passing the beer bucket back and forth without bothering with mugs or schooners. The bottle was getting some hard use, as well.

"We got us some kinda famous men right here, Pound," Davey said. "These two have been outriders for the paymaster's coach a couple of times. Ain't that somethin' for fellas this young?"

"They must be awful good soldiers," I said. "And awful good with their guns."

"Nah, hell," one of the boys slurred. "It's just a day of ridin', is all. Ain't nobody ever tried to hold up the U.S. Army."

Davey and the other soldier found the comment terribly funny. I forced a laugh too.

"I've been wondering," I said, "how much money that wagon brings in. Must be a lot to pay suppliers and so forth."

One of the boys looked around the room as if to check if anyone was lurking there, listening. "Now, you didn't hear this from us, but the next wagon in will be haulin' over one hundred and fifty thousand dollars in good ol' American money."

Davey shook his head and said, "Damn."

I whistled.

"Yessir," the soldier said. "That's God's own truth. I seen the books when I was cleanin' out the commander's office. See, the stock contractors and the lumber suppliers and all of them gotta be paid this time."

I lit a cheroot and leaned against the headboard. The conversation went on around me, drifting from the paymaster to a whore named Lucretia to the fastest horse in the regiment. I took a glug from the bottle.

"You gents ever hear of an Indian name of Twisted Foot?" I asked.

"Oh, hell yeah," a soldier answered. His friend nodded solemnly in agreement. "Sumbitch is pure insane," he said. "Only way to take him down is from a couple hundred yards away with a Sharps—and then burn his body to make sure he's daid."

My eyes met Davey's. I could see from the clarity that a good deal of his drunkenness was a ploy, a device to keep the young soldiers running their mouths.

"I'd imagine there's some damn good riflemen in that paymaster wagon," I said.

The soldiers laughed. "Bullshit! Ain't nobody but the driver an' his shotgun rider. Like I said, who's got the balls to try to rob the U.S. Army?"

I stubbed out my cheroot and closed my eyes. The conversation between the soldiers and Davey was becoming increasingly incoherent. Lucretia was the main topic when I drifted off to a light sleep. Every so often a raucous laugh would awaken me, but I always was able to drift back to sleep.

I had no idea what time it was when the soldiers left, but I woke to morning light and went on down to Davey's room. He was sitting on his bed pulling on his boots, which surprised me. I figured he'd still be dead asleep.

"Ain't that somethin'?" Davey asked. "The damned fools all but handed over the reins to that coach to us."

"You think it's good information?"

"Yeah. I do. They was both drunker'n hoot owls and it's the rare man who can lie when he's in a booze fog."

I thought that over for a while and decided that what Davey said made good sense. "A hundred and fifty thousand dollars," I said. "One robbery and we ride off with more money than a dozen bank jobs would bring in. Sounds good to me, Davey—too good to let go by."

"It does. 'Course we'd have the whole damned army after us."

"Not after we crossed into Mexico, we wouldn't. Much as they'd like to hunt us down and string us up, they can't do it."

"That jurisdiction is a beautiful thing, ain't it?" Davey said.

"Indeed. We're still lacking some vital information, though—where the wagon is coming from and when it's due in."

"Somethin' else is botherin' me too, Pound. I'm afraid I ain't got it in me to gun those two clowns, the outriders. They're jus' kids, for godsake."

"That's something we need to work out," I said. "I don't have any stomach for killing young boys, either. But there's a good deal of plannin' to do, Davey. Let's find out a little more about the operation. Those two still on leave tonight?"

"Yeah. Yesterday was their first day—they got today and tomorra."

"Good. You'll hook up with them tonight, right?"

"I'll be as tight to those boys as a tick is on a dog's ass." Davey grinned.

"The most important thing is which way the wagon comes into town. The rest we can figure out, but where they're coming from is crucial."

"I'm not sure my pals know that, Pound. I hope to find out tonight after I get them liquored up an' ready to flap their gums."

Davey and I ate in the hotel restaurant again. We were becoming regulars both there and at the saloon, and I was becoming a fixture, sitting out in front of the hotel reading, smoking, or merely sitting there watching what went on around me.

The day after Davey brought the two young soldiers back to the hotel with him I walked down to the livery to check on our horses. They were looking good: the rest and the grain and the sweet hay had put the shine back into their coats. Their shoes were tight. I went all the way around to make sure. Then, I saddled up my bay and headed out of the prairie. The horse was feeling good—that was easy enough to see. He bucked a couple of times when I mounted, but he didn't mean anything serious and I knew that.

I rode out four or five miles and then made a big, wide circle all the way around Livonia and the fort being built. The main road—if one could call it that—was the one Davey and I rode into town on. But, I noticed, there were wagon ruts pretty much everywhere, coming and going in all directions.

I'm not much of a tracker, but eventually I found what I was looking for: tracks showing the same-size wagon or coach had followed the same path a number of times.

I followed the tracks away from Livonia, poking along on my horse. There was a slight rise ahead of me and the slope was studded with rocks, boulders, scrub and desert pines. I dismounted and tied my horse to a tree and did some exploring on foot. At one point a few large boulders created a sort of jagged funnel—it was either ride between the rocks or go way the hell around either side. Both sides sloped and wagon drivers avoided such slopes as much as they possibly could.

I walked the distance between two of the largest boulders in the funnel and found it to be about fifty feet, maybe a tad more. Those rocks radiated heat like a bonfire, it seemed, but I poked around them on all sides, kind of checking things out. I liked what I saw.

I rode on a couple of miles and made another circle around Livonia. There were some places similar to what I'd found, but there weren't enough ruts in them to indicate frequent coach travel.

Satisfied, I rode back into Livonia, sucking on a cheroot, looking for all the world like a gent out taking a little ride on a good horse.

I returned my horse to the livery and walked to the mercantile. The store was almost empty except for a few clerks. They descended on me like a horde of vultures, but when I said I was just looking around, they went about their other duties, which seemed to consist of leaning on counters.

There was an open case of dynamite in the farming equipment area—farmers used the stuff to blow stumps and rocks out of their fields. I took two sticks and eased them into my shirt, next to my skin.

I was looking at the various grades of rope, when I saw a coil of unbarbed wire. I waved a clerk over. "How long is this coil?" I asked. He crouched down and looked at a little tag. "This one is ninety feet. I got some longer ones in back, should you care to look them over."

"No, the length is OK. But, tell me this: if I set up a little temporary corral will this wire keep a couple of horses where they belong?"

"Why shore it would. That wire is thin, but it's plenty stout."

I thought for a moment, scratching my chin. There were a couple of other items I needed, but I didn't want to buy them all at once. Davey and I were going to cover our faces with bandannas for this robbery; it's possible we wouldn't be identified. If we were, well, what the hell. But it'd be better if we weren't.

I purchased the wire, several licorice straps, and a Cuban cigar and took everything back to my room. Then, I took my place in front of the hotel, smoking, tipping my hat to the ladies, and doing nothing—or, at least, appearing to do nothing. What I was doing was planning.

Chapter Ten

A kid came by the front of the hotel, barefoot, kicking a stone in front of him, a sizable dog at his side. The dog looked like it might have some collie in it, but it had spaniel feet, and it stood as tall as any fighting pit bull I've ever seen. I called out, "Hey, kid—need a couple of extra dollars?"

The boy's father probably didn't clear two dollars a week trying to gouge a crop off the arid and unfertile ground, so the boy was immediately interested.

"I reckon I would, mister," he said. "Whatcha need done?"

I pulled my pocket book out of my side pocket and counted out four dollars. "What I need, boy, is three throwin' ropes—and none of that Mexican shit. I want rope made in Texas. Hear?"

"Yeah," the kid said, "but the mercantile ain't but down the road a short walk. You could go yourself an'—"

"All right," I said. "Forget it. Get lost."

"No! Wait! I'll run down an' get you yer ropes. I was just sayin' . . ."

"The least you say is the better," I told the boy. I

handed over the money. "Now you go on and take care of my business."

"Yessir!" the boy exclaimed, and he set off at a run to the mercantile with his dog loping next to him. The transaction didn't take him five minutes when he ran back with the three coils of rope, each probably thirty-five feet long, which is about standard for working cowhands.

I checked the ropes: they had that tight, waxy feel to them that told me they were Texas products. "What'd they cost?" I asked.

"'Bout a buck apiece," the boy said.

"You lyin' little bastard!" I yelled. "I try to give you a piece of work and you gotta come back and lie to me. I oughtta come down there and dust you good!"

The dog stepped up next to his master, the change in the tone and texture of the voices making him nervous.

"You go right ahead an' do that, mister—but you'll have to get through Buster first. An' from looking at you, you ain't got the chance of a skinny goddamn hen against a timber wolf. Up to you, though. You ain't carryin' just now, mister. You don't have a chance."

I took my derringer from my pocket. "I figure it'd take one good shot to kill that dog—maybe two. But this weapon will drop him sure's you're born."

Much of the smirk left the kid's face, but he didn't back up at all. "You kill my Buster," he said slowly and distinctly, "you better never close your eyes agin, 'cause when you do I'm gonna cut your goddamn throat."

I had to laugh. "You're a pistol, boy—that you are.

You keep the rest of the money. But you remember—this whole thing never happened, right?"

"Yessir. Right."

"I mean it, kid—anybody ever ask you if you talked to the fella in front of the hotel, you tell them 'no.' You was buying ropes for some drunken cowboys you figured you could screw out of some change."

"Yessir," the boy said. He scratched his dog's neck and set off down the street.

I hadn't seen Davey all day, but assumed he was boozing it up with his army pals. There'd been a fight in the saloon about midafternoon and I was certain Davey was in there, swinging. When I went up to my room to fetch an old paper I'd been reading, there was a note on a piece of brown butcher paper. "Toosday nexxt," it said. "Same 2 outraders." Davey never was real big on spelling. I tore the note up and let the pieces flutter out the window.

After a bit more time out in front of the hotel I went inside the restaurant and had a meal and then went to my room and took a nap. It must have been close to midnight when I woke up and walked over to the saloon. Davey was standing between his two friends. There was a mass of empty schooners and shot glasses in front of the three men.

Davey turned to greet me, a sloppy, drunken grin on his face. I punched him as hard as I could, my fist taking him at the bridge of his nose, which immediately began pumping out blood.

"You drunken son of a bitch!" I bellowed at him. "You just lost me thousands of dollars 'cause you couldn't keep your nose out of a jug long enough to do business!"

He hadn't gone down when I hit him—the punch

had shoved him back against the bar, and it was the only thing keeping him on his feet. "From this very goddamn second forward there is no partnership, no Ace Land Speculation Company, no nothing. I'm completely finished with you."

I slugged him in the gut and he folded. As his face came down, I caught it with my knee. He fell back, slid down the bar, and ended up on his side, on the floor. "Drunken turd," I said loud enough for all to hear.

The soldiers had moved in to defend Davey. I stood glaring at them for a long moment, then spun on my heel, slammed my way through the batwings, and stomped over to the hotel.

Bar fights were certainly nothing new in Livonia, but this one was special. For one thing it was between partners and business associates, and for another one of the men never got to get in a punch—in fact, he got his ass kicked without offering a bit of resistance.

I packed up what little I had—a carpetbag full of money, a shirt, some cigars, and a half bottle of bourbon. I paid at the desk and carried my truck down the street to the livery. I'd dropped the wire off there earlier, covered by the straw in my horse's stall. I paid the liveryman, tipped him generously, and saddled my horse. When the livery owner asked me about the bill on Davey's horse, I told him, "That's up to you and him. I have nothing to do with that drunken fool. How the hell I hired him in the first place is beyond me." I had enough anger in my voice that the man didn't question me any further.

I rode out of Livonia, never again to return—I sincerely hoped.

I set up a nice little camp a half mile from that rock funnel, found enough kindling and scrap branches, and got a nice little fire going. I brewed up a pot of Arbuckle's, put a drop or two of bourbon in it, and sat back, relaxing. My right knuckles hurt like a sumbitch, so I poured some whiskey over the abraded parts. It helped some, but not a lot. Davey, I imagined, was hurting a lot more than I was.

When I finished my coffee I added some more fuel to the fire. It was coming dark and I didn't want Davey to miss me.

I found a splendid anchoring point for one end of the wire. It was a lopsided boulder about six feet wide and four feet tall. It probably weighed more than Chicago. I took three wraps of wire around the base of the boulder, although I'm certain one would have been sufficient.

A man can't sling a knot in wire the way he can in a rope, but I did just fine. I wound my end to the coil, set the coil aside, and went back to the camp. I thought it'd be good to maybe have a touch more of bourbon. There was something that didn't set right with me about our whole operation, but for the life of me, I couldn't figure out what it was. It didn't *feel* right.

I need to admit this: it's the rare man or boy who'll take such a beating as I meted out to Davey and not only understand why it was done, but not come gunning for the man who slugged him. It made me proud of the boy, I'll tell you that.

A few minutes before full dark, Davey rode in. When he stood by the fire I could see he looked like hell. His lips were all swollen, his nose seemed to point to his right side—and it'd doubled its size—and there was a long, abraded rip across his forehead.

What I found to be so frighteningly bizarre was the fact that the damned fool was standing there grinning at me. I'm not sure if any teeth were missing; the fire didn't cast enough light for that.

"Lookit, Davey—there was no other way for us to show the army and the people in Livonia that we weren't pardners, wouldn't be riding together, wouldn't do our business together."

"Had I known what the hell was up, you'da had a fight on your hands, Pound. You'd best know that."

"Sure, Davey, but this is the way it needed to be done."

"I'm wonderin' if maybe you have a glug or so of booze."

"Davey," I said, "I got some bourbon that's sweeter than the finest nectar right in the midst of July. You sure deserve it."

"Damn right," Davey said. "I'd like to have at it right now, ya know? I'm kinda hurtin'—not that I ain't been banged around somewhat before, but not by my goddamn pardner."

"You ever had a partner, Davey?"

"That ain't a gooddamn bit of your business. Where's this bourbon at?"

I fetched up the bottle from behind my saddle roll and handed it to Davey.

"Thing is," I said, "I never had a partner before Zeb Stone. He was something, Davey. I saw him stick the barrel of his Colt so far up a buffalo hunter's nose that he bled like a stuck pig."

I stopped to draw some breath. "Then," I said, "there was this sheriff who was a fast gun. Zeb pulled—"

Davey waved the bottle toward me, pretty much telling me to shut up. "Pound, I don't care if you rode with the goddamn Archangel Michael in a fiery chariot pulled by them horses with the horns stickin' outta their heads. What I need to know is that we're real pards—real goddamn pards—an' . . ."

"And what, Davey?"

"That's about it, I guess. There's a good feelin' about havin' a partner, ya know?"

"Yeah," I said. "I do know."

The next day—Monday—there was some light rain that felt good, at least at first. After a bit, though, it gets tiresome to have everything—clothes, blankets, horses—damp. Nevertheless we got Davey's end of the wire wrapped around the base of a big rock, just like mine, and we pulled it taut. The wire was maybe ten inches above the ground. The wire was all but invisible, even when a man was looking for it, and Davey's outrider pals weren't going to look for it or expect it. The sloppiness of the ground helped us too. When the horses hit the wire, they'd go down—no doubt about it.

We were able to scrounge up enough dry wood to build a coffee fire. Davey looked worse that morning than he had the night before. The bruises on his face were turning that ghastly purple-yellow that bruises do, and his lips were still huge. While we drank our pot of coffee, we cut the throwing ropes I'd bought into pieces about six feet long.

The sky cleared in the late afternoon. We didn't have any special preparations to make, so we sat around drinking coffee and talking—or not talking, as the fancy struck us.

I was dozing just before dark when Davey shook my shoulder. "Pound," he said, "I think we got trouble." I sat up and directed my eyes to the far distance where Davey was pointing. Two puffs of white smoke rose until they dissipated, followed by a long strand of the same smoke.

"OK," I said. "Twisted Foot is either on us or about to be on us. It had to come to this and it did. I'm thinking this, Davey: we do our business here and ride on to a place where we figure we can either ambush the sumbitch or take him down in a square fight. He's just a man, Davey. There's no magic about him. He's a crazy Indian who needs to die. It's that simple. But, let's do one thing at a time. We got a coach to rob here, and worrying about Twisted Foot can wait."

Dawn was long in coming, probably because neither of us did a lot of sleeping that night. It was easy enough to see by first light that the day was going to be clear and hot. I smoked a cheroot—we didn't dare make a fire—and Davey rolled and smoked one cigarette after another.

Sound carries easily on the prairie, particularly when there's no wind, and this day was pure calm. We got behind the rocks and waited. The creaking of leather and the pounding of hooves came closer. We could tell by the cadence of the hoofbeats that the driver wasn't pushing his horses, but that he was moving along at a good clip.

Davey and I wrapped the bandannas around our faces and knotted them in the back. Then we each stuck a half-dozen strips of rope into our belts, dangling at our waists. We split up then, one of us on each side, behind the rocks. The sounds of the coach and the horses became louder, and then the two outriders, the ones Davey got drunk with, rode into the funnel at a slow lope.

The two horses hit the wire at just about the same time. There was a loud crack as one went down, which made me grimace. It wasn't our intent to cripple any of the horses.

Both riders were thrown violently forward, slamming into the ground, skidding a bit on their faces and bellies. Davey and I were over the rocks and had them tied by the time the wagon rolled up. The driver didn't have a chance to do anything—his horses panicked at the sight and sound of the squealing, frantic horses in front of them. The fellow riding shotgun brought his weapon to his shoulder. I put a slug in his leg. He dropped his weapon and grabbed at his leg with both hands. The driver had been knocked unconscious with the impact. Davey tied him securely and dragged him behind the rocks with the shotgun man.

The cash boxes were bolted to the wagon floor, with heavy locks at each corner of each box, which I'd expected. I jammed a stick of dynamite between the two of them, thought for a moment, and shoved the second stick in, as well.

I'd never had much of anything to do with dynamite, but I'd seen it used. It's pretty potent stuff. Davey and I crouched behind a boulder and I lit the fuses I'd intertwined with one another.

The roaring thunder shock of the explosion was like nothing I'd ever heard before. It was all-encompassing: it took everything away for some moments—the coach, the rocks, the prairie—as if it owned the entire world and made its own rules.

I had a good friend who fought for the Confederacy during the war. He was a sharpshooter, and a very good one. Anyhow, he got engaged in that goddamn fool Pickett's Charge, where the Rebs let go of all the cannon power they had—which was substantial. My friend said the blast of the cannons was more frightening than the Union bullets tearing men up from behind their nice, secure rock wall. He deserted after that goddamn mess.

Davey and I stepped out from behind our rocks and stood, awestruck.

"Damn," Davey said. "It's snowing money!" It was, actually. But, not as you'd expect. The money was wrapped and banded according to denomination into tight packets. Some of them broke open but most didn't.

Davey pulled a twenty out of the air as it drifted to the ground. "Kinda like a butterfly, ain't it?" he said.

There were still wrapped packets all over the place. Davey and I collected them—nothing smaller than tens—and loaded our grain sacks, saddlebags, and pockets.

We stood together in front of a scatter of packets. "Chickenshit," Davey said. "Nothin' but ones and fives."

I glanced over at my partner. Even with his swollen, grotesquely colored face, his grin was of a boy getting his first horse of his very own.

I was pawing through the packets when I heard a strange cough-gurgle from Davey. I looked up at him. His smile was gone and his face registered a look of both awe and confusion. That horrible rattle in his throat sounded again and he reached his hand out to me as if he were a supplicant.

Four inches of arrow and an arrowhead protruded from the middle of his chest, dripping blood. In a half heartbeat another couple of inches of arrow and arrowhead had pierced the back of his head and was sticking out of his mouth, like some sort of evil tongue. I rolled away from my partner's body and got into a clumsy crouch. Twisted Foot was not more than fifty feet from me. He was wearing the colors of mourning—blue and black—on his chest arms, and hands. I eased myself to my feet.

"You people—we have eaten you," he said. "We will gut you and spit you and eat you."

I'd learned a bit about gunfighting from my partner—partners, actually. Zeb Stone had shown me a good bit.

First, you stand sideways as much as you can, to make a smaller target. Second, you empty your gun into your opponent. As Zeb said, "I don't care if your first shot tears his goddamn head off, Pound—you empty out on him."

Twisted Foot was facing me, an arrow in place, its head pointing to the ground a yard ahead of him.

"You think you're faster?" he asked.

"I don't think it—I know it."

"We shall see," Twisted Foot said.

"You bet, you disgusting savage. We'll see."

Twisted Foot's arrow twitched a bit but didn't rise. "Savage?"

"Look—let's do this, and quit screwing around. I need to gather my money."

I was watching the tip of the arrow rather than Twisted Foot's movements or face.

It twitched again—moved forward a couple of inches and then came back to where it'd been.

"Like I said, I got things to do."

"Let me tell you a story—a legendary story—that many, many white men don't believe or respect. Nevertheless—"

I think Twisted Foot expected me to look at his eyes or at his face.

My first shot took him somewhere that didn't make a whole lot of difference, but the second caught him in the throat directly under his chin, and I put a pair into his chest. Then, as he was falling, I shot the back of his head off and put my final slug into his back.

I picked up Davey's grainsack—he sure had no use for it now.

I stood by him for some time. It was then that I promised myself I'd never have a partner again.

Then, I started the long ride to Mexico.

"When you think of the West, you think of Zane Grey." —*American Cowboy*

ZANE GREY

THE RESTORED, FULL-LENGTH NOVEL, IN PAPERBACK FOR THE FIRST TIME!

The Great Trek

Sterl Hazelton is no stranger to trouble. But the shooting that made him an outlaw was one he didn't do. Though it was his cousin who pulled the trigger, Sterl took the blame, and now he has to leave the country if he wants to stay healthy. Sterl and his loyal friend, Red Krehl, set out for the greatest adventure of their lives, signing on for a cattle drive across the vast northern desert of Australia to the gold fields of the Kimberley Mountains. But it seems no matter where Sterl goes, trouble is bound to follow!

"Grey stands alone in a class untouched by others." —*Tombstone Epitaph*

ISBN 13: 978-0-8439-6062-4

ROBERT J. CONLEY

FIRST TIME IN PRINT!

NO NEED FOR A GUNFIGHTER

"One of the most underrated and overlooked writers of our time, as well as the most skilled."
—Don Coldsmith, Author of the Spanish Bit Saga

BARJACK VS...EVERYBODY!

The town of Asininity didn't think they needed a tough-as-nails former gunfighter for a lawman anymore, so they tried—as nicely as they could—to fire Barjack. But Barjack likes the job, and he's not about to move on. With the dirt he knows about some pretty influential folks, there's no way he's leaving until he's damn good and ready. So it looks like it's the town versus the marshal in a fight to the finish... and neither side is going to play by the rules!

Conley is "in the ranks of N. Scott Momaday, Louise Erdrich, James Welch or W. P. Kinsella."
—*The Fort Worth Star-Telegram*

ISBN 13: 978-0-8439-6077-8

LOUIS L'AMOUR

For millions of readers, the name Louis L'Amour is synonymous with the excitement of the Old West. But for too long, many of these tales have only been available in revised, altered versions, often very different from their original form. Here, collected together in paperback for the first time, are four of L'Amour's finest stories, all carefully restored to their initial magazine publication versions.

BIG MEDICINE

This collection includes L'Amour's wonderful short novel *Showdown on the Hogback,* an unforgettable story of ranchers uniting to fight back against the company that's trying to drive them off their land. "Big Medicine" pits a lone prospector against a band of nine Apaches. In "Trail to Pie Town," a man has to get out of town fast after a gunfight leaves his opponent dead on a saloon floor. And the title character in "McQueen of the Tumbling K" is out for revenge after gunmen ambush him and leave him to die.

AVAILABLE JANUARY 2009!

ISBN 13: 978-0-8439-6068-6

RANDOM HOUSE WEBSTER'S

pocket american sign language

SECOND EDITION

RANDOM HOUSE REFERENCE

NEW YORK TORONTO LONDON SYDNEY AUCKLAND

 Published in the United States by Random House Reference, an imprint of The Random House Information Group, a division of Random House, Inc., New York, and simultaneously in Canada by Random House of Canada Limited, Toronto.

This is a revised and updated work based on the *Random House American Sign Language Dictionary* originally published in hardcover in 1994.

Illustration: Lois Lenderman, Paul M. Setzer, Linda C. Tom
Book design: Jan Ewing, Ewing Systems, New York, NY

Trademarks

A number of entered words that we have reason to believe constitute trademarks have been designated as such. However, no attempt has been made to designate as trademarks or service marks all terms or words in which proprietary rights might exist. The inclusion, exclusion, or definition of a word or term is not intended to affect, or to express a judgment on, the validity or legal status of the word or term as a trademark, service mark, or other proprietary term.

Please address inquiries about electronic licensing of any products for use on a network, in software, or on CD-ROM to the Subsidiary Rights Department, Random House Information Group, fax 212-572-6003.

This book is available at special discounts for bulk purchases for sales promotions or premiums. Special editions, including personalized covers, excerpts of existing books, and corporate imprints, can be created in large quantities for special needs. For more information, write to Random House, Inc., Special Markets/Premium Sales, 1745 Broadway, MD 6-2, New York, NY 10019, or e-mail specialmarkets@randomhouse.com.

Library of Congress Catalog Card Number: 99-66597

Printed in United States of America
10 9 8 7 6 5 4 3 2
ISBN: 978-0-375-72278-3

Contents

Guide

How to use this dictionary

How to Find a Sign

Complete Entries

All entries are presented in large boldface type in a single alphabetical listing, following a strict letter-by-letter order.

Cross References

A cross-reference entry, at its own alphabetical listing, sends the reader to one or more complete entries, where signs will be found.

How to Make a Sign

Illustrations

Formation of the sign is illustrated at every complete entry.

In a sequence of pictures, the illustrations in a circle focus on some significant portion of the movement, often the final position of the hands. The reader should execute the signs in the order shown, from left to right.

Descriptions

Each illustration is supplemented by a description in terms of the four component parts of a sign: (1) handshape, (2) location in relation to the body, (3) movement of the hands, and (4) orientation of the palms.

Within the description, italicized terms such as *A hand* and *C hand* refer to handshapes shown in the chart of the Manual Alphabet (p. x). Terms such as *1 hand* or *10 hand* refer to handshapes for numbers. Other special handshapes, such as *bent hand*, *open hand*, and *flattened C hand*, are shown on page ix.

Hints

Beginning most descriptions is a bracketed memory aid, or *hint*. These hints help the reader understand the nature of the sign and better remember how it is made.

An *initialized sign* is formed with the handshape for the relevant letter in the English term, taken from the American Manual Alphabet (see chart on p. x).

Fingerspelled signs use the Manual Alphabet to spell out a short word or abbreviation.

An occasional reference is made to "the finger used for feelings." Signs made with the bent middle finger often refer to concepts of sensitivity, feelings, or personal contact. Allusions to the "male" and "female" areas of the head indicate that signs referring to men, such as **father** and **uncle**, begin at or are made near the forehead, whereas signs referring to women, such as **mother** and **aunt**, begin at or are made near the chin.

Abbreviations Used in This Dictionary

adj.	adjective
adv.	adverb
conj.	conjunction
interj.	interjection
n.	noun
n. phrase	noun phrase
pl. n.	plural noun
pl. pron.	plural pronoun
prep.	preposition
pron.	pronoun
v.	verb
v. phrase	verb phrase

Handshapes Used in This Dictionary

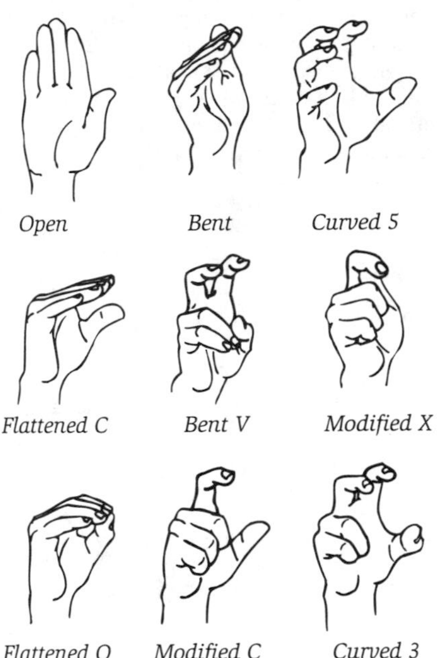

Manual Alphabet

The American Manual Alphabet is a series of handshapes used to represent each letter of the English alphabet. Many countries have their own manual alphabets, just as they have their own sign languages. It is important to note that although English is spoken in the United States and in England, the English Manual Alphabet, which is formed by using two hands, is very different from the American Manual Alphabet.

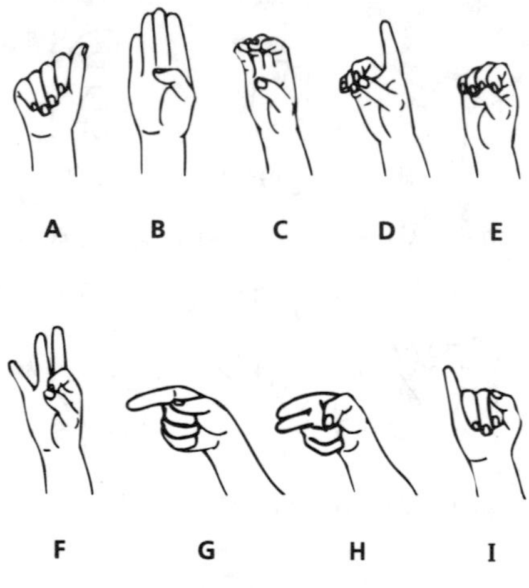

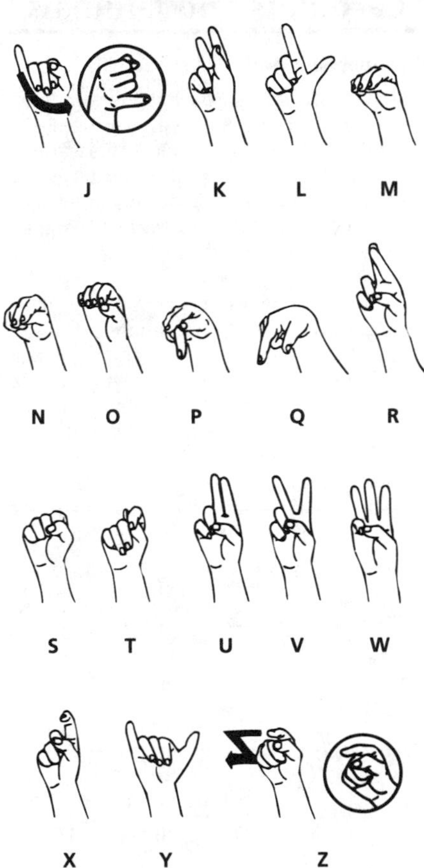
J
K
L
M
N
O
P
Q
R
S
T
U
V
W
X
Y
Z

Numbers: Cardinals and Ordinals

Cardinal Numbers

Numbers are formed by holding the dominant hand comfortably in front of the shoulder with the palm either forward or in, depending on the context for using the number. When counting objects up to five, the palm should face in toward the signer. However, when expressing age or time, the palm should face forward.

The following are the signs for numbers from zero to 30. From the numbers from 31 to 99, the signs follow a regular pattern. For those numbers, sign each digit of the numeral moving the hand slightly to the right, such as for 34, sign *3* followed by *4*. For 60, sign *6* followed by *zero*. For numbers where both digits are the same (e.g., 44), bounce the hand slightly in place while holding the four handshape.

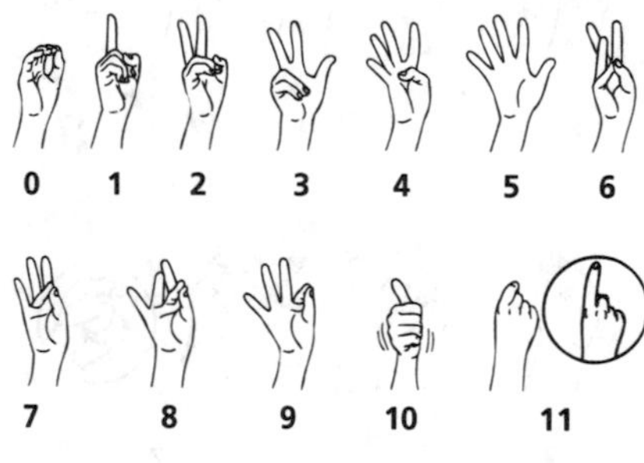

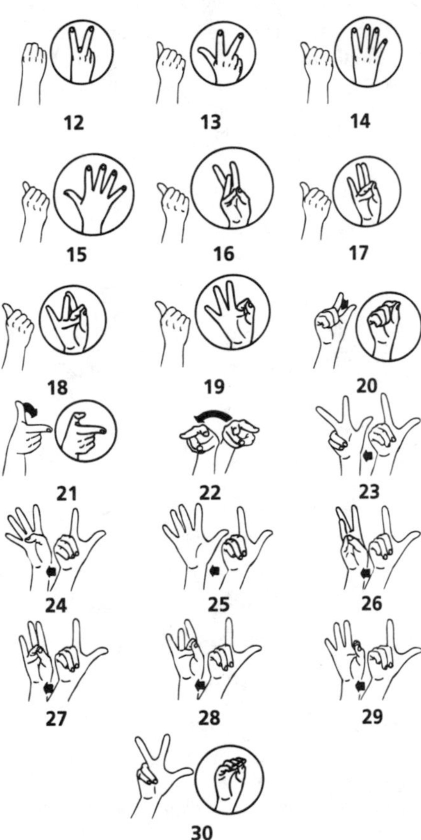
12
13
14
15
16
17
18
19
20
21
22
23
24
25
26
27
28
29
30

The following are signs for hundred, thousand, and million. When signing numbers over one hundred, the numbers are signed just as they are spoken. For example, 283 is signed *two-hundred* + *eighty* + *three*. Similarly, 5,690 is signed *five-thousand* + *six-hundred* + *ninety*.

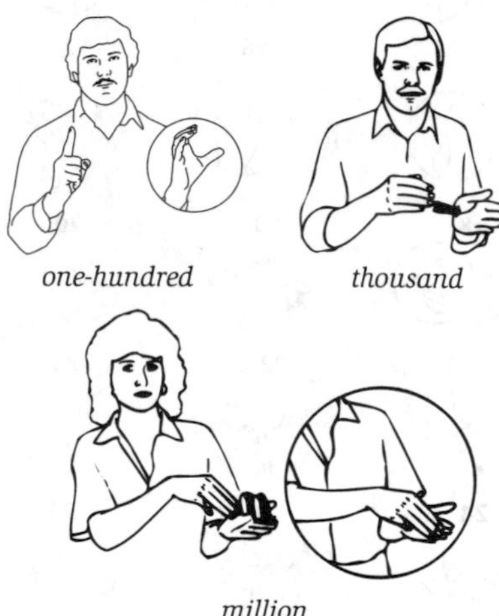

one-hundred *thousand*

million

When giving an address, sign the numbers in the manner in which an address is usually spoken. For example, 3812 Charles Avenue is signed *thirty-eight* + *twelve*.

Money is also signed in the same order that it is spoken, except for dollar amounts under ten dollars, which are signed by using the corresponding ordinal (see p. xvi). For example, "eight dollars" is signed with the sign used for *eighth*. For larger amounts, the sign *dollar* is used after the dollar amount, just as it is spoken. For example, \$86.17 is signed *eighty-six* + *dollar* + *seventeen*. For cents under a dollar, sign the cents sign followed by the amount. For example, 45¢ is signed *cents* + *forty-five*.

dollar

Fractions are formed by signing the top number of the fraction and then dropping the hand slightly to form the bottom number of the fraction. The following are two examples of fractions.

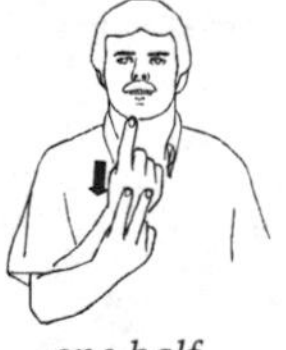

one-half

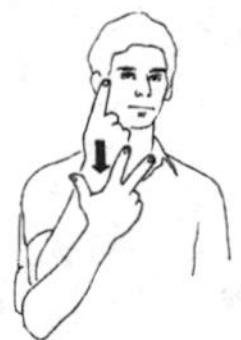

one-third

Ordinal Numbers

The following signs are used when expressing order or rank in a series. Hold the hand comfortably in front of the right shoulder, twisting the wrist when forming each sign. The same signs are used for dollar amounts under ten dollars.

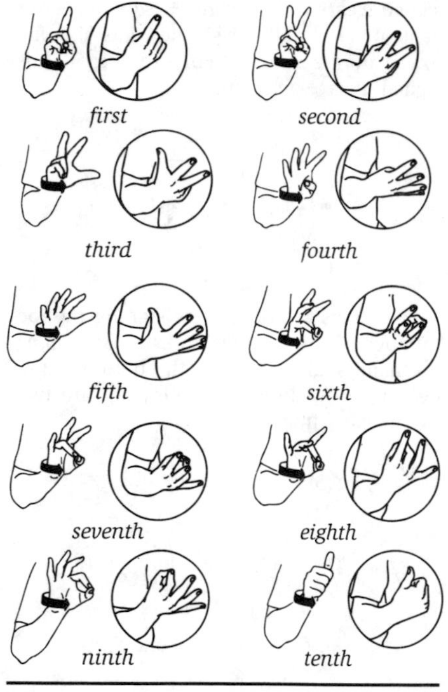

abandon *v.* Related form: **abandonment** *n.* Same sign used for: **discard, evict, expel, forsake, throw out.**

[Natural gesture of giving up hope] Beginning with both *S hands* in front of the chest, both palms facing in and the right hand above the left hand, quickly throw the hands upward to the right while opening into *5 hands* in front of the right shoulder, ending with the palms facing back and the fingers pointing up.

---

abbreviate *v.* See sign for BRIEF.

---

ability *n.* See sign for SKILL.

---

able *adj.* See sign for SKILL.

---

abolish[1] *v.* See sign for DAMAGE. Shared idea of destruction.

---

abolish[2] *v.* See signs for ELIMINATE[1], REMOVE[1].

---

abort *v.* See signs for ELIMINATE[1], REMOVE[1]. Related form: **abortion** *n.*

---

about *adv.* See signs for ALMOST, APPROXIMATELY.

---

above *prep., adv.* Same sign used for: **over.**

[Indicates area above] Beginning with the right *open hand* on the back of the left *open hand,* both palms facing down, bring the right hand upward in an arc, ending several inches above the left hand.

absent *adj., v.* Related form: **absence** *n.* Same sign used for: **drain, extinct, gone, miss, missing.**

[Something seems to go down the drain] Pull the right *flattened C hand,* palm facing in, downward through the left *C hand,* palm facing right, while closing the fingers and thumb of the right hand together.

absent-minded *adj.* See sign for BLANK[1].

accept *v.* Related form: **acceptance** *n.* Same sign used for: **adopt, adoption, approval, approve.**

[Bring something that is accepted toward oneself] Beginning with both *5 hands* in front of the chest, fingers pointing forward, bring both hands back toward the chest while pulling the fingers and thumbs of each hand together.

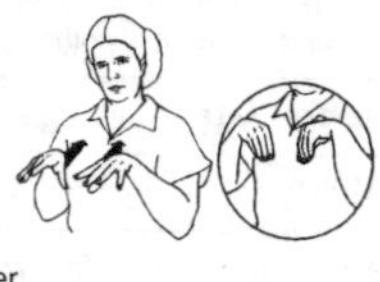

access code *n. phrase.* See sign for PASSWORD.

accident[1] *n.* Same sign used for: **collide, collision, crash.**

[Two things collide with each other] Move both *5 hands* from in front of each side of the chest, palms facing in and fingers pointing toward each other, while changing into *A hands,* ending with the knuckles of both *A hands* touching in front of the chest.

accident[2] *n.* See sign for HAPPEN.

accidentally *adv.* Alternate form: **by accident.** Related form: **accidental** *adj.* Same sign used for: **amiss.**

[Similar to sign for **mistake** except made with a twisting movement] Twist the knuckles of the right *Y hand,* palm facing in, on the chin from right to left.

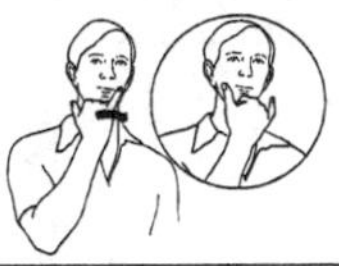

acclaim *v.* See sign for ANNOUNCE.

accomplish *v.* See sign for SUCCESSFUL. Related form: **accomplishment** *n.*

accumulate[1] *v.* Related form: **accumulation** *n.* Same sign used for: **amass.**

[More and more of something being piled up on top of other things] Beginning with the right *U hand,* palm facing left, beside the left *U hand,* palm facing down, flip the right hand over with a double movement, tapping the right fingers across the left fingers each time.

accumulate[2] *v.* See sign for COLLECT.

accurate *adj.* See signs for PERFECT, RIGHT[3].

accustomed to *v. phrase.* See sign for HABIT.

ache *v., n.* See signs for HURT, PAIN.

achieve *v.* Related form: **achievement** *n.* See also sign for SUCCESSFUL. Same sign used for: **chalk up, success.**

[An accumulation of something] Beginning with the left *bent hand* over the right *bent hand* in front of the chest, both palms facing down, move the hands with an alternating movement over each other to in front of the face.

acquaint *v.* See sign for ASSOCIATE.

acquire *v.* See signs for GET, TAKE.

across *prep., adv.* Same sign used for: **after, afterward, cross, over.**

[Movement across another thing] Push the little-finger side of the right *open hand,* palm facing left, across the back of the left *open hand,* palm facing down.

act[1] *v., n.* Related forms: **action** *n.*, **activity** *n.* Same sign used for: **deed.**

[The hands seem to be actively doing something] Move both *C hands,* palms facing down, simultaneously back and forth in front of the body with a swinging movement.

act[2] *v.* Same sign used for: **drama, perform, play, show, theater.**

[Initialized sign] Bring the thumbs of both *A hands,* palms facing each other, down each side of the chest with alternating circular movements.

active *adj.* See signs for AMBITIOUS[1], WORK.

actual *adj.* See signs for REAL, TRUE.

actually *adv.* See sign for TRUE.

adapt *v.* See sign for CHANGE[1].

add or **add to** *v.* Related forms: **addition** *n.* **additional** *adj.* Same sign used for: **amend, bonus, extra, supplement.**

[One hand brings an additional amount to the other hand] Swing the right *5 hand* upward from the right side of the body while changing into a *flattened O hand,* ending with the right index finger touching the little-finger side of the left *flattened O hand* in front of the chest, both palms facing in.

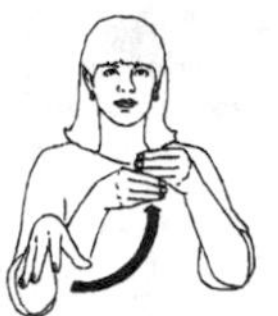

addicted *adj.*

[**become + habit**] With the palms of both *open hands* together, right hand on top of left hand, twist the wrists in opposite directions in order to reverse positions. Then with the heel of the right *S hand* across the wrist of the left *S hand,* both palms facing down, move the hands down simultaneously in front of the chest.

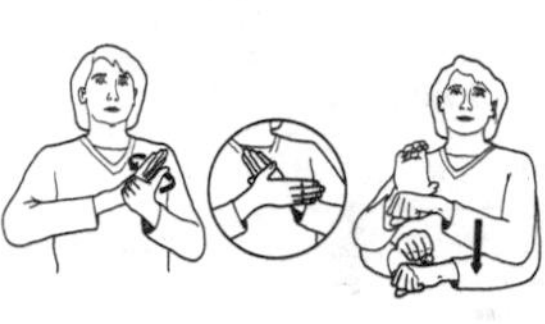

address[1] *n., v.*

[Initialized sign similar to sign for **live**] Move both *A hands,* palms facing in, upward on each side of the chest with a double movement.

address[2] *v.* See sign for SPEAK[2].

adequate *adj.* See sign for ENOUGH.

adhere *v.* See signs for APPLY[3], STICK[1].

adhesive *n., adj.* See sign for STICK[1].

adjust *v.* See sign for CHANGE[1].

administer *v.* See sign for MANAGE. Alternate form: **administrate.**

admit *v.* Related form: **admission** *n.* Same sign used for: **confess, confession, submit, willing.**

[Hand seems to bring a confession from the chest] Move the right *open hand,* palm facing in, from the chest forward in an arc while turning the palm slightly upward.

---

admonish *v.* See sign for SCOLD.

---

adopt *v.* See signs for ACCEPT, TAKE. Related form: **adoption** *n.*

---

adore *v.* See sign for WORSHIP.

---

adrift *adj.* See sign for ROAM.

---

adult *n., adj.*

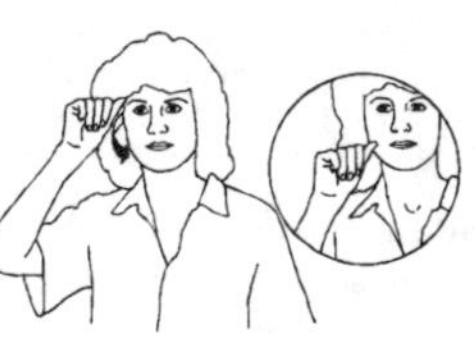

[Initialized sign formed in the traditional male and female positions; can be formed with an opposite movement] Move the thumb of the right *A hand,* palm facing forward, from the side of the forehead to the lower cheek.

---

advanced *adj.* Same sign used for: **elevate, elevated, elevation, exalt, exalted, exaltation, higher, prominent, promote, promotion, supreme.**

[Moving to a more advanced position] Move both *bent hands,* palms facing each other, from near each side of the head upward a short distance in a deliberate arc.

advantage[1] *n.* Same sign used for: **take advantage of.**

[Represents "an easy touch"] Flick the bent middle finger of the right *5 hand* upward off the heel of the left *open hand.*

advantage[2] *n.* See sign for BENEFIT.

advertise *v.* Related form: **advertisement** *n.* Same sign used for: **broadcast, commercial, propaganda, publicity, publicize.**

[Suggests "blowing one's own horn" in order to advertise] Beginning with the thumb side of the right *S hand,* palm facing left, against the little-finger side of the left *S hand,* palm facing right, move the right hand forward and back with a double movement.

advice *n.* Same sign used for: **effect.**

[Sending information to another] Beginning with the fingertips of the right *flattened O hand* on the back of the left *open hand,* palm facing down, move the right hand forward while spreading the fingers into a *5 hand.*

advocate *v.* See sign for SUPPORT.

affect *v.* See sign for INFLUENCE.

affection *n.* See sign for HUG. Related form: **affectionate** *adj.*

affiliation *n.* See sign for COOPERATION.

affix *v.* See sign for APPLY[3].

afford *v.* Same sign used for: **debt, due, owe.**

[Indicates that money should be deposited in the palm] Tap the extended right index finger on the palm of the left *open hand* with a double movement.

affront *v.* See sign for INSULT.

afraid *adj.* Same sign used for: **fright, frightened, panic, scared, timid.**

[Hands put up a protective barrier] Beginning with both *A hands* in front of each side of the chest, spread the fingers open with a quick movement, forming *5 hands,* palms facing in and fingers pointing toward each other.

after[1] *prep., conj., adv.* Same sign used for: **afterward, beyond, from now on, rest of.**

[A time frame occurring after another thing] Beginning with the palm of the right *bent hand* touching the back of the fingers of the left *open hand,* both palms facing in, move the right hand forward a short distance.

after[2] *prep.* See sign for ACROSS.

after a while *prep., adv.* See sign for LATER.

afternoon *n.* Same sign used for: **matinee.**

[The sun going down in the afternoon] With the bottom of the right forearm resting on the back of the left *open hand,* palm facing down, move the right *open hand* downward with a double movement.

afterward *adv.* See signs for ACROSS, AFTER[1], LATER.

again *adv.* Same sign used for: **reiterate, repeat.**

[The movement indicates wanting something to be repeated] Beginning with the right *bent hand* beside the left *curved hand,* both palms facing up, bring the right hand up while turning it over, ending with the fingertips of the right hand touching the palm of the left hand.

against *prep.* Same sign used for: **anti-** [prefix], **opposed to, prejudice.**

[Demonstrates making contact with a barrier] Hit the fingertips of the right *bent hand* into the left *open hand,* palm facing right.

age *n.*

[An old man's beard] Move the right *O hand,* palm facing left, downward a short distance from the chin while changing into an *S hand.*

aggressive *adj.* See sign for AMBITIOUS[1].

agile *adj.* See sign for SKILL.

ago *adj.* Same sign used for: **last, past, was, were.**

[Indicates a time in the past] Move the right *bent hand* back over the right shoulder, palm facing back.

agree *v.* Same sign used for: **compromise, in accord, in agreement.**

[**think**[1] + lining up two things to show they agree with each other] Move the extended right index finger from touching the right side of the forehead downward to beside the extended left index finger, ending with both fingers pointing forward in front of the body, palms facing down.

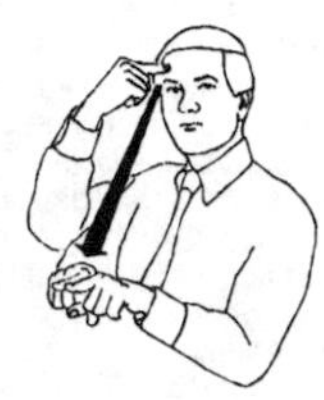

aid *n.* See sign for HELP.

aide *n.* See sign for ASSISTANT.

aim *v.* See sign for GOAL.

airplane *n.* Same sign used for: **airport, jet, plane.**

[Shape and movement of an airplane] Move the right hand with the thumb, index finger, and little finger extended, palm facing down, forward with a short repeated movement in front of the right shoulder.

airport *n.* See sign for AIRPLANE.

alarm *n.* Same sign used for: **alert, drill.**

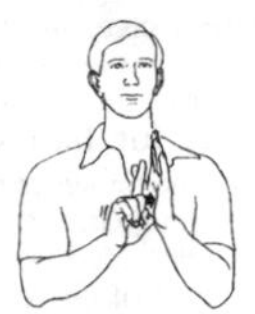

[Action of clapper on alarm bell] Tap the extended index finger of the right hand, palm facing forward, against the left *open hand,* palm facing right, with a repeated movement.

alert *n.* See sign for ALARM.

align *v.* See sign for LINE UP.

alike *adj., adv.* Same sign used for: **identical, look alike, same, similar.**

[Sign moves between two people or things that are similar] Move the right *Y hand,* palm facing down, from side to side with a short repeated movement in front of the body.

alive *adj.* See sign for LIVE.

all *pron.* Same sign used for: **entire, whole.**

[The hand encompasses the whole thing] Move the right *open hand* from near the left shoulder in a large circle in front of the chest, ending with the back of the right hand in the left *open hand* held in front of the body, palms facing in.

all along *adv.* See sign for GO ON.

all gone *adj.* See sign for RUN OUT OF.

all right *adv.* See sign for RIGHT².

allegiance *n.* See sign for SUPPORT.

allow *v.* See sign for LET.

allowance *n.* See sign for PENSION.

ally *n.* See sign for RELATIONSHIP.

almost *adv.* Same sign used for: **about, barely, nearly.**

[The fingers almost touch the other hand] Brush the fingertips of the right *open hand* upward off the back of the left fingers, both palms facing up.

alone *adv., adj.* Same sign used for: **isolated, lone, only, solely.**

[Shows one thing alone] With the right index finger extended up, move the right hand, palm facing back, in a small repeated circle in front of the right shoulder.

a lot *adv.* See signs for MANY, MUCH.

aloud *adv.* See sign for NOISE.

already *adv.* See sign for FINISH[1].

alter *v.* See sign for CHANGE[1].

alternate *v.* See sign for TURN[1].

alternative *n.* See sign for EITHER[1].

altitude *n.* See sign for HIGH.

always *adv.* Same sign used for: **ever.**

[A continuous circle signifying duration] Move the extended right index finger, palm facing in and finger angled up, in a repeated circle in front of the right side of the chest.

amass *v.* See sign for ACCUMULATE[1].

amaze *v.* See signs for SURPRISE, WONDERFUL. Related form: **amazement** *adj.*

ambiguous *adj.* See sign for VAGUE.

ambitious[1] *adj.* Related form: **ambition** *n.* Same sign used for: **active, aggressive.**

[Initialized sign] Move both *A hands,* palms facing in, in large alternating circles upward on each side of the chest.

ambitious[2] *adj.* See sign for GOAL.

amen *interj.* Same sign used for: **pray, prayer.**

[Natural gesture for folding one's hands to pray] Bring the palms of both *open hands* together, fingers angled upward, while moving the hands down and in toward the chest.

amend *v.* See sign for ADD.

America *n.* Related form: **American** *adj., n.*

[The rail fences built by settlers] With the fingers of both hands loosely entwined, palms facing in, move the hands in circle in front of the chest.

amid or **amidst** *prep.* See sign for AMONG.

amiss *adj.* See sign for ACCIDENTALLY.

among *prep.* Same sign used for: **amid, amidst, midst.**
[Shows one moving among others] Move the extended right index finger in and out between the fingers of the left *5 hand,* both palms facing in.

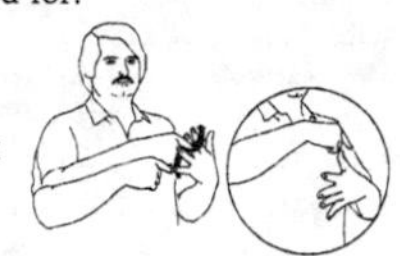

amount *n.* Same sign used for: **heap, lump, pile.**
[Shows a small amount in a pile] Move the extended right index finger, palm facing down, in an arc from near the heel to the fingers of the upturned left *open hand,* ending with the right palm facing in toward the chest.

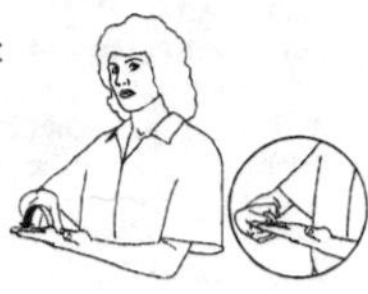

amuse *adj.* See sign for FUNNY.

analyze *v.* Related form: **analysis** *n.* Same sign used for: **diagnose, diagnosis.**
[Taking something apart to analyze it] With both *bent V hands* near each other in front of the chest, palms facing down, move the fingers apart from each other with a downward double movement.

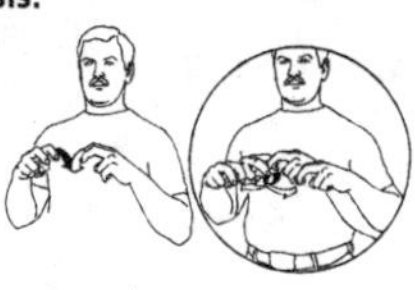

ancient *adj.* See sign for LONG AGO.

and *conj.*
[Stretching one part of a sentence to connect it to the rest] Move the right *curved 5 hand,* palm facing left, to the right in front of the body while closing the fingers to the thumb, ending in a *flattened O hand.*

and so forth *conj.* See sign for VARIETY.

anger *n.* Related form: **angry** *adj.* See also sign for CROSS[1]. Same sign used for: **enrage, fury, mad, outrage, rage.**

[Hands bring up feeling of anger in the body] Beginning with the fingertips of both *curved 5 hands* on the lower chest, bring the hands upward and apart, ending in front of each shoulder.

angry *adj.* See sign for CROSS[1].

animal *n.* Same sign used for: **beast.**

[Shows an animal breathing] Beginning with the fingertips of both *curved 5 hands* on the chest near each shoulder, roll the fingers toward each other on their knuckles with a double movement while keeping the fingers in place.

annex *v.* See sign for BELONG.

announce *v.* Related form: **announcement** *n.* Same sign used for: **acclaim, declaration, declare, proclaim, proclamation, reveal, tell.**

[**tell**[1] with a movement that shows a general announcement] Beginning with the extended index fingers of both hands pointing to each side of the mouth, palms facing in, twist the wrists and move the fingers forward and apart from each other, ending with the palms facing forward and the index fingers pointing outward in opposite directions.

annoy *v.* Same sign used for: **bother, disturb, interfere, interrupt, irritate.**

[A gesture showing something interfering with something else] Sharply tap the little-finger side of the right *open hand,* palm facing in at an angle, at the base of the thumb and index finger of the left *open hand* with a double movement.

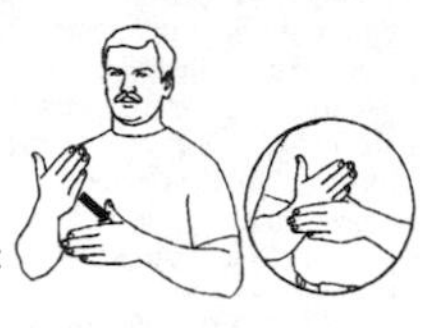

another *adj., pron.* Same sign used for: **other**.

[Points away to another] Beginning with the right *10 hand* in front of the body, palm facing down and thumb pointing left, flip the hand over to the right, ending with the palm facing up and the thumb pointing right.

answer *n., v.* Same sign used for: **react, reply, response.**

[Indicates directing words of response to another] Beginning with both extended index fingers pointing up in front of the mouth, right hand nearer the mouth than the left and both palms facing forward, bend the wrists down simultaneously, ending with fingers pointing forward and the palms facing down.

antagonism *n.* See sign for STRUGGLE.

anti- *prefix.* See signs for AGAINST, RESIST.

anxiety *n.* See sign for NERVOUS.

anxious *adj.* See signs for NERVOUS, TROUBLE[1].

any *adj., pron.*

[Initialized sign pointing to a selection of things] Beginning with the right *10 hand* in front of the chest, palm facing left, twist the wrist and move the hand down and to the right, ending with the palm facing down.

anyway *adv.* Same sign used for: **despite, doesn't matter, even though, hardly, however, nevertheless, whatever.**

[Flexible hands signify no firm position] Beginning with both *open hands* in front of the body, fingers pointing toward each other and palms facing in, move the hands forward and back from the body with a repeated alternating movement, striking and bending the fingers of each hand as they pass.

apologize *v.* See sign for SORRY. Related form: **apology** *n.*

apparently *adv.* See sign for SEEM.

appeal *v.* See sign for SUGGEST.

appear *v.* See signs for SEEM, SHOW UP.

appetite *n.* See sign for HUNGRY.

applaud *v.* Related form: **applause** *n.* Same sign used for: **clap.**

[Natural gesture for clapping] Pat the palm of the right *open hand* across the palm of the left *open hand* with a double movement.

apple *n.*

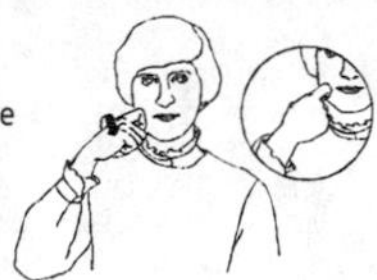

[Shows action of chewing an apple] With the knuckle of the right *X hand* near the right side of the mouth, twist the wrist downward with a double movement.

apply[1] *v.* Related form: **applicable** *adj.* Same sign used for: **charge, file, install, post.**

[Put messages on a spindle] Move the fingers of the right *V hand,* palm facing forward, downward on each side of the extended left index finger, pointing up in front of the chest.

apply[2] *v.* Related form: **application** *n.* Same sign used for: **candidate, eligible, nominate, volunteer.**

[Seems to pull oneself forward to apply for something] Pinch a small amount of clothing on the right side of the chest with the fingers of the right *F hand* and pull forward with a short double movement.

apply[3] *v.* Same sign used for: **adhere, affix.**

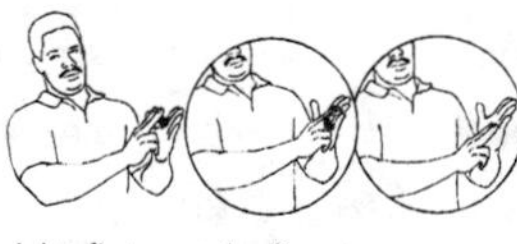

[Mime applying tape or a label] Tap the fingers of the right *H hand,* palm facing left, against the palm of the left *open hand,* palm facing right, first near the fingers and then near the heel.

apply[4] *v.* See sign for LABEL.

appoint *v.* Same sign used for: **choose, elect, select.**

[Fingers seem to pick someone] Beginning with the thumb side of the right *G hand,* palm facing down and fingers pointing forward, against the left *open hand,* palm facing right and fingers pointing up, pull the right hand in toward the chest while pinching the index finger and thumb together.

appointment *n.* Same sign used for: **assignment, book, reservation.**

[The hands are bound by a commitment] Move the right *S hand,* palm facing down, in a small circle and then down to the back of the left *A hand,* palm facing down in front of the chest.

appreciate *v.* See sign for ENJOY. Related form: **appreciation** *n.*

apprehend *v.* See sign for UNDERSTAND.

approach *v.* See sign for CLOSE.

approve *v.* See sign for ACCEPT. Related form: **approval** *n.*

approximate *adj.* See sign for ROUGH.

approximately *adv.* Related form: **approximate** *adj.* Same sign used for: **about, around.**

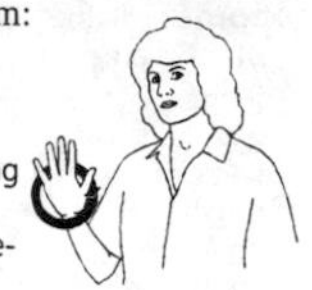

[Natural gesture of vagueness] Move the right *5 hand,* palm facing forward, in a circle in front of the right shoulder with a double movement.

---

area *n.* Same sign used for: **place, space.**

[Indicates an area] Move the right *5 hand,* palm facing down and fingers pointing forward, in a flat forward arc in front of the right side of the body.

---

argue *v.* Related form: **argument** *n.* Same sign used for: **fight, quarrel, squabble.**

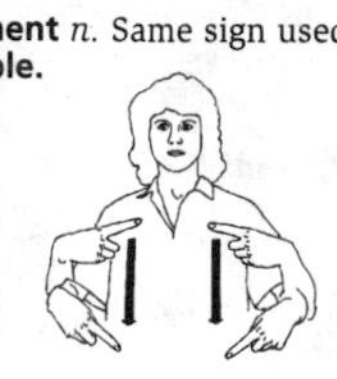

[Represents opposing points of view] Beginning with both extended index fingers pointing toward each other in front of the chest, palms facing in, shake the hands up and down with a repeated movement by bending the wrists.

---

argument *n.* See sign for DISCUSS.

---

arithmetic *n.* Same sign used for: **estimate, figure, figure out, multiplication.**

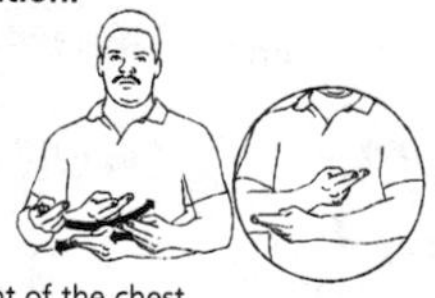

[Movement suggests combining things] Brush the back of the right *V hand* across the palm side of the left *V hand,* both palms facing up, as the hands cross with a double movement in front of the chest.

---

around *prep.* See sign for APPROXIMATELY.

---

arouse *v.* See sign for AWAKE.

arrange *v.* See signs for PLAN, PREPARE.

arrest *v.* See signs for CAPTURE, CATCH[1].

arrive *v.* Same sign used for: **reach.**

[Hand moves to arrive in other hand] Move the right *bent hand* from in front of the right shoulder, palm facing left, downward, landing the back of the right hand in the upturned left *curved hand.*

arrogant *adj.* See signs for CONCEITED, PROUD.

art *n.* Same sign used for: **drawing, illustration, sketch.**

[Demonstrates drawing something] Move the extended right little finger with a wiggly movement down the palm of the left *open hand* from the fingers to the heel.

artificial *adj.* See sign for FAKE.

ascend *v.* See sign for CLIMB.

ashamed *adj.* Same sign used for: **shame, shameful, shy.**

[Blood rising in the cheeks when ashamed] Beginning with the back of the fingers of both *curved hands* against each cheek, palms facing down, twist the hands forward, ending with the palms facing back.

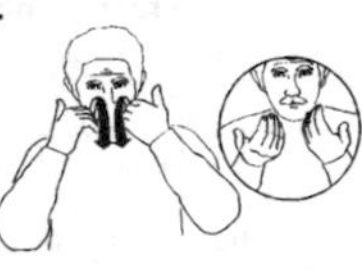

ask *v.* Same sign used for: **pray, request.**
[Natural gesture used for asking] Bring the palms of both *open hands* together, fingers angled upward, while moving the hands down and in toward the chest.

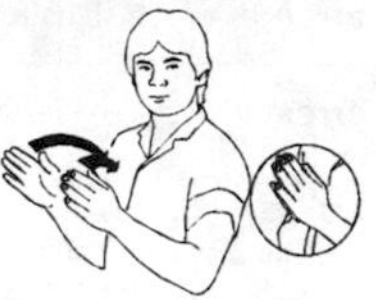

asleep *adv.* See sign for FALL ASLEEP.

aspire *v.* See sign for ZEAL. Related form: **aspiration** *n.*

assemble *v.* See signs for GATHER[1].

assembly *n.* See sign for MEETING.

assign *v.* See signs for APPOINT, CHOOSE[1].

assignment *n.* See sign for APPOINTMENT.

assist *v.* See sign for HELP.

assistant *n., adj.* Same sign used for: **aide.**
[Initialized hand showing giving a boost or aid to another] Use the thumb of the right *A hand* under the little-finger side of the left *A hand* to push the left hand upward in front of the chest.

associate *v., n.* Same sign used for: **acquaint, brotherhood, each other, fellowship, fraternity, interact, mingle, one another, socialize.**
[Represents mingling with each other] With the thumb of the left *A hand* pointing up and the thumb of the right *A hand* pointing down, circle the thumbs around each other while moving the hands from left to right in front of the chest.

assume *v.* See signs for GUESS, TAKE. Related form: **assumption** *n.*

astound *v.* See sign for SURPRISE.

at fault *adj.* See sign for BLAME.

at last *adv. phrase.* See sign for FINALLY.

at odds *adj.* See sign for STRUGGLE.

attach *v.* See sign for BELONG.

attack *v.* See sign for HIT.

attain *v.* See sign for GET.

attempt *v.* See sign for TRY.

attend *v.* See also sign for GATHER[1]. Same sign used for: **go to.**

[**go** formed with a directed movement] Beginning with both extended index fingers pointing up in front of the chest, right hand closer to the chest than the left and both palms facing forward, move both hands forward simultaneously while bending the wrists so the fingers point forward.

attention *n.* Related form: **attend** *v.* Same sign used for: **concentrate, concentration, focus on, pay attention, watch.**

[Forms blinkers to direct one's attention] Move both *open hands* from near each cheek, palms facing each other, straight forward simultaneously.

attitude *n.*

[Initialized sign similar to sign for **character**] Move the thumb of the right *A hand* in a circular movement around the heart, palm facing left, ending with the thumb against the chest.

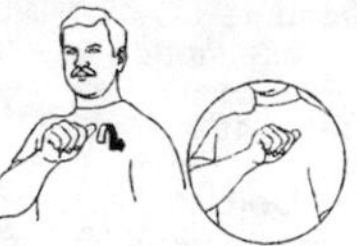

audience *n.* Same sign used for: **crowd, horde.**

[**people** + movement indicating large crowd of people] Move both *P hands,* palms facing down, in alternating forward circular movements in front of each side of the body. Then move both *curved 5 hands,* palms facing down, from in front of each side of the body forward with a simultaneous movement.

aunt *n.*

[Initialized sign formed near the right cheek] Shake the right *A hand*, palm facing forward, near the right cheek.

authority *n.*

[Shows muscle in arm symbolizing strength and authority] Beginning with the extended right thumb of *A hand,* palm facing left, near the left shoulder, move the hand down in an arc while twisting the right wrist, ending with the little-finger side of the right hand in the crook of the left arm, bent across the body.

automatic *adj.* See sign for FAST.

automobile *n.* See sign for CAR.

autumn *n.* See sign for FALL[2].

available *adj.* See sign for EMPTY.

avenge *v.* See sign for REVENGE.

average *adj.*

[Shows split down the middle] Beginning with the little-finger side of the right *open hand* across the index-finger side of the left *open hand,* palms angled down, twist the wrists down, bringing the hands apart a short distance with a double movement, palms facing down.

avoid *v., adj.* Same sign used for: **back out, elude, evade, fall behind, get away, shirk.**

[One hand moves away from the other to avoid it] Beginning with the knuckles of the right *A hand,* palm facing left, near the base of the thumb of the left *A hand,* palm facing right, bring the right hand back toward the body with a wiggly movement.

awake *v.* Related form: **awaken** *v.* Same sign used for: **arouse, wake up.**

[Indicates eyes opening when becoming awake] Beginning with the *modified X hands* near each eye, palms facing each other, quickly flick the fingers apart while widening the eyes.

award *n.* See signs for GIFT.

aware[1] *adj.* Same sign used for: **familiar, knowledge.**

[Shows location of awareness] Tap the fingertips of the right *bent hand,* palm facing in, against the right side of the forehead with a double movement.

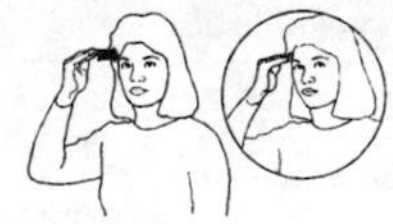

aware[2] *adj.* See sign for NOTICE[1].

awful *adj.* Same sign used for: **disastrous, dreadful, fierce, horrible, sordid, terrible.**

[Natural gesture used when indicating something terrible] Beginning with both *8 hands* near each side of the head, palms facing each other, flip the fingers open to *5 hands* while twisting the palms forward.

awkward *adj.* Same sign used for: **clumsy.**

[Represents walking awkwardly] Beginning with both *3 hands* in front of the body, right hand higher than the left and both palms facing down, raise the left and then the right hand in alternating movements.

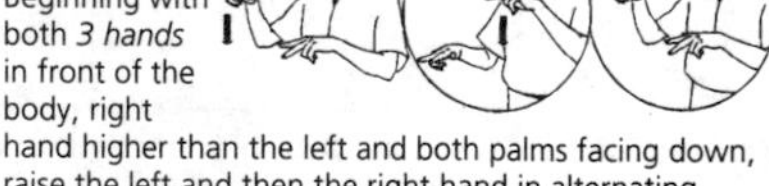

babble *v.* See sign for BLAB.

baby *n.* Same sign used for: **infant.**

[Action of rocking a baby in one's arms] With the bent right arm cradled on the bent left arm, both palms facing up, swing the arms to the right and the left in front of the body with a double movement.

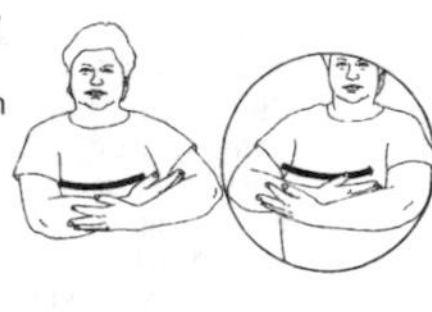

back *n.* Same sign used for: **rear.**

[Natural gesture indicating location] Pat the fingertips of the right *open hand* behind the right shoulder with a repeated movement.

back and forth *adv.* See sign for COMMUTE.

back out *v. phrase.* See signs for AVOID, RESIGN.

backslide *v.* See sign for BEHIND.

backup *n.* See sign for SUPPORT.

bacon *n.*

[The hands show the wavy shape of fried bacon] With the thumbs of both hands pointing up and fingers of both *U hands* touching in front of the chest, palms facing in, bring the hands apart while bending the fingers back into each palm with a double movement.

bad *adj.* Related form: **badly** *adv.* Same sign used for: **evil, nasty, naughty, wicked.**

[Gesture tosses away something that tastes bad] Move the fingers of the right *open hand* from the mouth, palm facing in, downward while flipping the palm quickly down as the hand moves.

badge *n.* See sign for POLICE.

baggage *n.* Same sign used for: **luggage.**

[Shows carrying a bag in each hand] Shake both *S hands,* palms facing in, up and down with a short movement near each side of the waist with the elbows bent.

bake *v.* See sign for COOK.

balance *v., n.*

[Action shows trying to balance something] With a simultaneous movement bring the right *open hand* and the left *open hand,* both palms facing down, up and down in front of each side of the chest, shifting the entire torso slightly with each movement.

bald *adj.* Related form: **baldness** *n.* Same sign used for: **bareheaded, scalp.**

[Indicates bare area of head] Move the bent middle finger of the right *5 hand,* palm facing down, in a circle around the top of the head.

ball *n.*

[The shape of a ball] Touch the fingertips of both *curved 5 hands* together in front of the chest, palms facing each other.

balloon *n.* Same sign used for: **expand.**

[Shows shape of balloon as it expands] Beginning with the left fingers cupped over the back of the right *S hand* held in front of the mouth, move the hands apart while opening the fingers, ending with both *curved 5 hands* near each side of the face, palms facing each other.

ban *v.* See signs for FORBID, PREVENT.

banana *n.*

[Mime peeling a banana] With the extended left index finger pointing up in front of the chest, palm facing forward, bring the fingertips of the right *curved 5 hand* downward, first on the back and then on the front of the index finger, while closing the right fingers to the thumb each time.

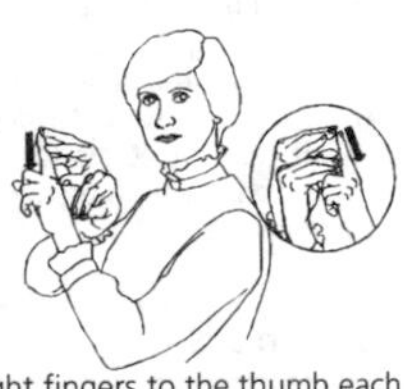

bandage *n.* Same sign used for: **Band-Aid** (*trademark*).

[Mime putting on a bandage] Pull the right *H fingers*, palm facing down, across the back of the left *open hand*, palm facing down.

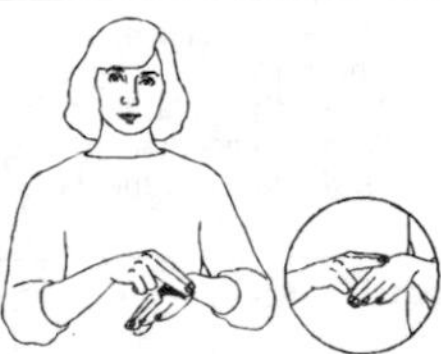

banter *v.*, *n.* See sign for STRUGGLE.

bare *adj.* See signs for EMPTY, NUDE.

bareheaded *adj.* See sign for BALD.

barely *adv.* See sign for ALMOST.

barrier *n.* See sign for PREVENT.

base *n.* Related forms: **basic** *adj.*, **basis** *n.*
[Initialized sign] Move the right *B hand,* palm facing left, in a flat circle under the left *open hand,* palm facing down.

baseball *n.* Same sign used for: **softball.**
[Natural gesture of swinging a baseball bat] With the little finger of the right *S hand* on the index finger of the left *S hand,* palms facing in opposite directions, move the hands from near the right shoulder downward in an arc across the front of the body with a double movement.

based on *v.* See sign for ESTABLISH.

basement *n.* Same sign used for: **beneath, cellar.**
[Indicates an area beneath a house] Move the right *10 hand,* palm facing in, in a flat circle under the left *open hand* held across the chest, palm facing down.

batch *n.* See sign for PILE[1].

bath *n.* Related form: **bathe** *v.*

[Washing oneself when bathing] Rub the knuckles of both *10 hands,* palms facing in, up and down on each side of the chest with a repeated movement.

bathroom *n.* See sign for TOILET.

batter *n.* See sign for BEAT[1].

battery *n.* See sign for ELECTRIC.

battle *n., v.* Same sign used for: **war.**

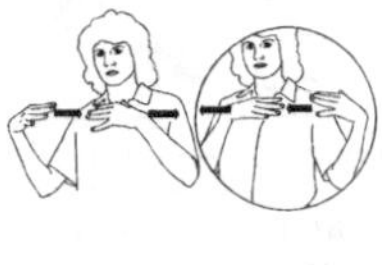

[Indicates opponents in warlike maneuvers] Beginning with both *5 hands* in front of the right shoulder, palms facing down and fingers pointing toward each other, move the hands toward the left shoulder and then back toward the right shoulder.

bawl out *v. phrase.* Same sign used for: **burst, burst out.**

[Represents a sudden burst of words] Beginning with the little finger of the right *S hand* on the top of the index-finger side of the left *S hand,* flick the hands forward with a deliberate double movement while opening the fingers into *5 hands* each time.

beads *pl. n.* Same sign used for: **necklace.**

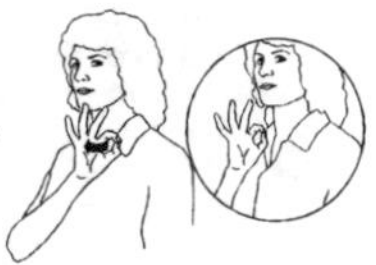

[Location and shape of a necklace of beads] Move the index-finger side of the right *F hand,* palm facing left, from the left side of the neck smoothly around to the right side of the neck.

bean *n.*

[Shape of a string bean] Beginning with the extended left index finger, palm facing in and finger pointing right, held between the index finger and thumb of the right *G hand,* palm facing left, pull the right hand outward to the right with a double movement.

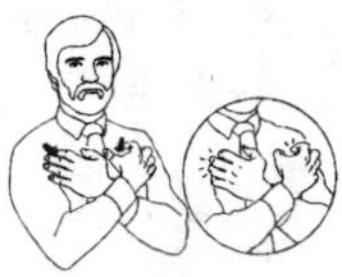

bear[1] *n.*

[Action of a bear scratching itself] With the arms crossed at the wrist on the chest, scratch the fingers of both *curved hands* up and down near each shoulder with a repeated movement.

bear[2] *v.* See signs for BURDEN, PATIENT[1].

bear up *v. phrase.* See sign for ENCOURAGE.

beard *n.*

[Location and shape of beard] Beginning with the right *C hand* around the chin, palm facing in, bring the hand downward while closing the fingers to the thumb with a double movement.

beast *n.* See sign for ANIMAL.

beat[1] *v.* Same sign used for: **batter, mix, stir.**

[Mime beating using a spoon in a bowl] Move the right *A hand,* palm facing the chest, in a quick repeated circular movement near the palm side of the left *C hand,* palm facing right.

beat[2] *v.*

[Indicates beating something] Hit the back of the right *S hand,* palm facing in, against the palm of the left *open hand,* palm facing right, with a double movement.

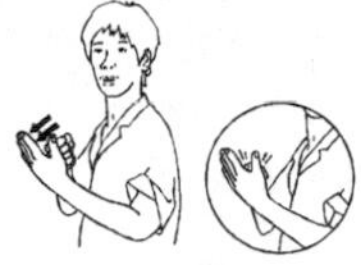

beat[3] *v.* See also sign for DEFEAT.

[Directing a single blow] Beginning with the right *S hand* in front of the right shoulder, palm facing left, move the hand quickly forward while opening the fingers to form a *H hand.*

beau *n.* See sign for SWEETHEART.

beautiful *adj.* Related form: **beauty** *n.* See also sign for PRETTY. Same sign used for: **lovely.**

[Hand encircles a beautiful face] Move the right *5 hand* in a large circular movement in front of the face while closing the fingers to the thumb, forming a *flattened O hand.* Then move the hand forward while spreading the fingers quickly into a *5 hand.*

because *conj.* Same sign used for: **since.**

Bring the index finger of the right *L hand* with a sweeping movement across the forehead from left to right, changing to a *10 hand* near the right side of the head.

become *v.* Same sign used for: **turn into.**

[Hands reverse positions as if to change one thing into another] Beginning with the palm of the right *open hand* laying across the upturned palm of the left *open hand,* rotate the hands, exchanging positions while keeping the palms together.

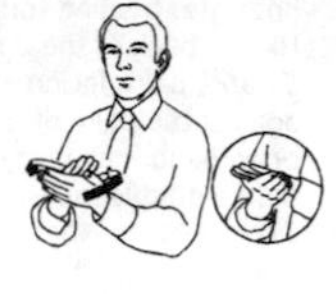

bed *n.*

[Mime laying the head against a pillow] Rest the right cheek at an angle on the palm of the right *open hand.*

been *v.* See sign for SINCE[1].

been (there) *v.* Same sign used for: **finish.**

[Similar to sign for **touch** except made more quickly] Bring the bent middle finger of the right *5 hand* downward to tap quickly the back of the left *open hand* held across the chest, both palms facing down.

beer *n.*

[Initialized sign] Slide the index-finger side of the right *B hand,* palm facing forward, downward on the right cheek with a double movement.

before *adv.* Same sign used for: **last, past, previous, prior.**

[Indicates a time or place in the past] Move the fingertips of the right *open hand,* palm facing back, from near the right cheek back and down to touch the right shoulder.

beg[1] *v.* Same sign used for: **implore, plead.**

[Mime extending a hand while begging] While holding the wrist of the upturned right *curved 5 hand* in the left palm, constrict the right fingers with double movement.

beg[2] *v.* See sign for WORSHIP.

beginning *n.* See sign for START.

behind *prep.* Same sign used for: **backslide.**

[Indicates a position behind another] Move the right *10 hand,* palm facing left, from in front of the left *10 hand,* palm facing right, back toward the chest in a large arc.

believe *v.* Related form: **belief** *n.*

[**mind** + clasping one's beliefs close] Move the extended right index finger from touching the right side of the forehead downward while opening the hand, ending with the right hand clasping the left *open hand,* palm facing up, in front of the body.

bell *n.* Same sign used for: **reverberate, ring.**

[Indicates the striking of a bell's clapper and the sound reverberating] Hit the thumb side of the right *S hand,* palm facing down, against the palm of the left *open hand.* Then move the right hand to the right while opening the fingers into a *5 hand,* wiggling the fingers as the hand moves.

belong *v.* Same sign used for: **annex, attach, combine, connect, fasten, hook up, join, joint, link, unite.**

[Two things coming together] Beginning with both *curved 5 hands* in front of each side of the body, palms facing each other, bring the hands together while touching the thumb and index fingertips of each hand and intersecting with each other.

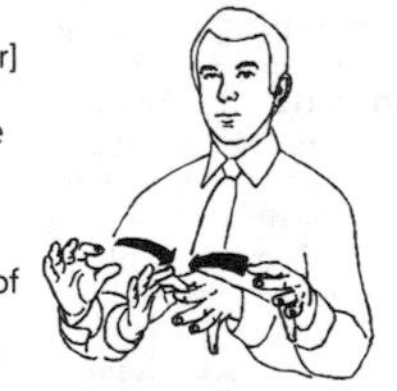

below *prep., adv.* Same sign used for: **beneath, bottom.**

[Indicates a position below] Beginning with the left *open hand* on the back of the right *open hand,* both palms facing down, bring the right hand downward in an arc, ending several inches below the left hand.

belt *n.*

[Location of a belt] Move both *H hands* from each side of the waist around toward each other until the fingers overlap in front of the waist.

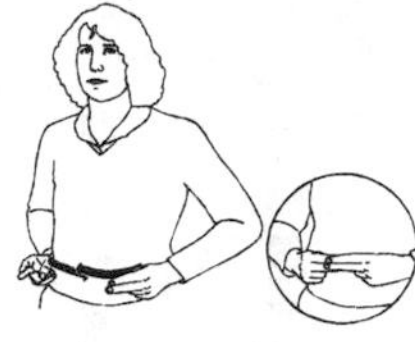

bend[1] *v.* Related form: **bent** *adj.*

[Indicates the ability to bend] Grasp the fingers of the left *open hand,* palm facing right, with the fingers of the right *flattened O hand,* and then bend the left fingers downward until both palms are facing down and hands are bent.

bend[2] *v.* See sign for BOW[1].

beneath *prep., adv.* See signs for BASEMENT, BELOW.

benefit *n.* Same sign used for: **advantage.**

[Pocketing a beneficial item] Push the thumb side of the right *F hand* downward on the right side of the chest, palm facing down, with a short double movement.

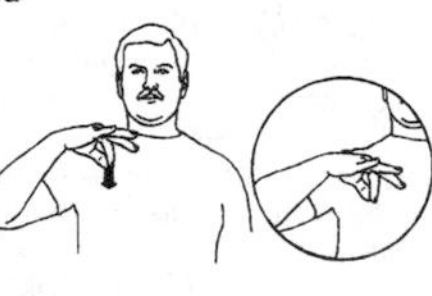

bent *adj.* See sign for DENT.

berry *n.*

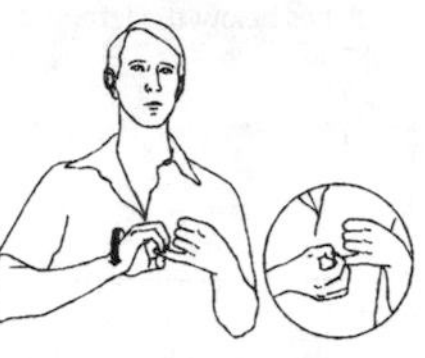

[Twisting a berry to pick it from the vine] Grasp the extended little finger of the left hand, palm facing in, with the fingertips of the right *O hand* and twist the right hand outward with a double movement.

beside *prep.* Same sign used for: **next to.**

[Indicates a location beside another] Beginning with the palm of the right *bent hand,* palm facing in and fingers pointing left, touching the back of the left *bent hand,* palm facing in and fingers pointing right, move the right hand forward in a small arc.

best *adj., adv.*

[Modification of **good,** moving the sign upward to form the superlative degree] Bring the right *open hand,* palm facing in and fingers pointing left, from in front of the mouth upward in a large arc to the right side of the head, changing to a *10 hand* as the hand moves.

bet *n., v.* Same sign used for: **bid, gamble, wager.**

[Initialized sign showing the turning of dice] Beginning with both *B hands* in front of each side of the body, palms facing each other and fingers pointing forward, turn the hands toward each other, ending with the palms facing down.

better *adj., adv.*

[Modification of **good,** moving the sign upward to form the comparative degree] Bring the right *open hand,* palm facing in and fingers pointing left, from in front of the mouth upward in an arc to the right side of the head, changing to a *10 hand* as the hand moves.

between *prep.* Same sign used for: **gap, lapse.**

[Indicates space between two things] Brush the little-finger side of the right *open hand,* palm facing left, back and forth with a short repeated movement on the index-finger side of the left *open hand,* palm angled right.

beverage *n.* See sign for DRINK[1].

bewilder *v.* See sign for SURPRISE.

bewildered *adj.* See sign for PUZZLED.

beyond *prep., adv.* See sign for AFTER[1].

bicycle *n.*

[Shows action of pedaling a bicycle] Move both *S hands* in alternating forward circles, palms facing down, in front of each side of the body.

bid *n., v.* See signs for BET, SUGGEST.

big *adj.* See also sign for LARGE. Same sign used for: **enlarge.**

[Shows big size] Move both *L hands* from in front of the body, palms facing each other and index fingers pointing forward, apart to each side in large arcs.

big-headed *adj.* See sign for CONCEITED.

big shot *n.* See sign for CONCEITED.

bill *n.* See sign for DOLLAR.

bird *n.* Same sign used for: **chicken, coward, fowl.**

[Mime the action of a bird's beak] Close the index finger and thumb of the right *G hand,* palm facing forward, with a repeated movement in front of the mouth.

birth *n.* Same sign used for: **born.**

[Indicates the birth of a baby] Bring the right *open hand,* palm facing in, from the chest forward and down, ending with the back of the right hand in the upturned palm of the left *open hand.*

birthday *n.*

[**birth** + **day**] Bring the right *open hand,* palm facing in, from the chest forward and down, ending with the back of the right hand in the upturned palm of the left

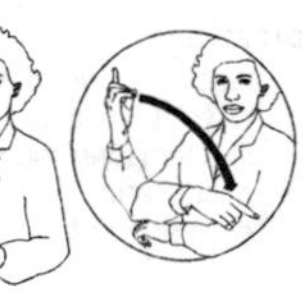

open hand. Then, with the right elbow resting on the back of the left hand held across the body, palm down, bring the extended right index finger downward toward the left elbow in a large sweeping arc.

biscuit *n.* See sign for COOKIE.

bitter *adj.* See sign for SOUR.

bizarre *adj.* See sign for STRANGE.

blab *v.* Same sign used for: **babble, chat, chatter, gab, gossip, talk, talkative.**

[Action of the mouth opening and closing] Beginning with both *flattened C hands* near each side of the face, palms facing each other, close the fingers and thumbs together simultaneously with a double movement.

black *adj., n.*

[Shows a black eyebrow] Pull the side of the extended right index finger, palm facing down and finger pointing left, from left to right across the forehead.

blah *slang.* See sign for NEVERMIND.

blame *v.* Same sign used for: **at fault.**

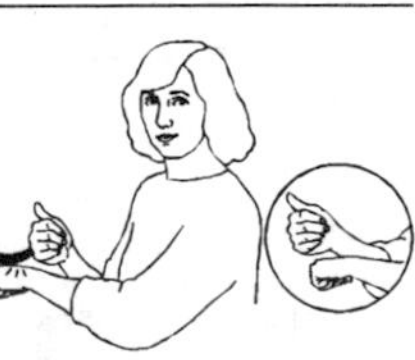

[Shoves blame at someone] Push the little-finger side of the right *A hand,* palm facing left, forward across the back of the left *A hand,* palm facing down.

blank[1] *adj.* Same sign used for: **absent-minded.**

[Indicates a blank mind] Bring the bent middle finger of the right *5 hand,* palm facing in, from left to right across the forehead.

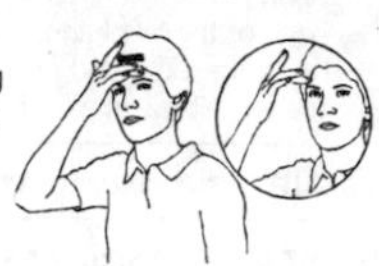

blank[2] *adj.* See sign for EMPTY.

blanket *n.*

[Initialized sign miming pulling up a blanket to the chest] Move both *B hands* from in front of the body, palms facing down and fingers pointing toward each other, upward, ending with both index fingers against the upper chest.

blaze *n.* See sign for FIRE[1].

blend *v.* See signs for CIRCULATE, MESH, MIX[1].

block *v.* See sign for PREVENT. Related form: **blockage** *n.*

blood *n.* Related form: **bloody** *adj.* Same sign used for: **shed.**

[**red** + a gesture representing the flow of blood from a wound] Brush the extended right index finger, palm facing in, downward on the lips. Then open the right hand into a *5 hand* and bring it downward while wiggling the fingers, palm facing in, past the open left hand held across the chest, palm facing in and fingers pointing right.

blouse *n.*

[Location and shape of woman's blouse] Touch the bent middle fingers of both *5 hands* on each side of the upper chest, and then bring the hands down in an arc, ending with the little fingers of both hands touching the waist, palms facing up and fingers pointing toward each other.

blow *v.*

[Indicates the flow of air through the mouth] Beginning with the back of the *flattened O hand* at the mouth, palm facing forward and fingers pointing forward, move the hand forward a short distance while opening the fingers into a *5 hand.*

blue *adj.*

[Initialized sign] Move the right *B hand,* fingers angled up, back and forth by twisting the wrist in front of the right side of the chest.

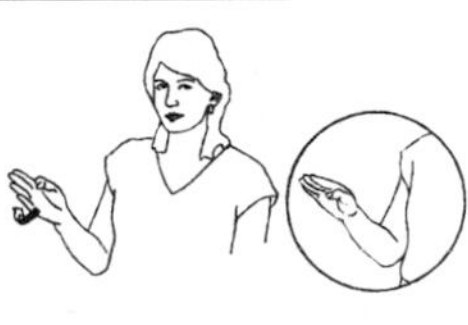

blurry *adj.* See sign for VAGUE.

board *n.*

[Initialized sign formed similar to sign for **member**] Touch the index-finger side of the right *B hand,* palm facing left, first to the left side of the chest and then to the right side of the chest.

boast *v.* See sign for BRAG.

boat *n.* Same sign used for: **cruise, sail, sailing, ship.**

[Shows the shape of a boat's hull] With the little-finger sides of both *curved hands* together, palms facing up, move the hands forward in a bouncing double arc.

body *n.*

[Location of the body] Touch the fingers of both *open hands,* palms facing in and fingers pointing toward each other, first on each side of the chest and then on each side of the waist.

bold *adj.* See signs for BRAVE, CONFIDENT, STRICT, WELL[1].

bone *n.*

[**rock**[1] + **skeleton**] Tap the palm side of the right *A hand,* palm facing down, against the back of the wrist of the left *A hand.* Then, with the hands crossed at the wrists, tap the fingers of both *bent V hands* on the opposite side of the chest, palms facing in.

bonus *n.* See sign for ADD.

book[1] *n.*

[Represents opening a book] Beginning with the palms of both *open hands* together in front of the chest, fingers angled forward, bring the hands apart at the top while keeping the little fingers together.

book[2] *v.* See sign for APPOINTMENT.

boost *n.* See sign for SUPPORT.

boring[1] *adj.* Related forms: **bore** *v.*, **bored** *adj.* Same sign used for: **dull.**

[Boring a hole on the side of the nose] With the tip of the extended right index finger touching the side of the nose, palm facing down, twist the hand forward.

boring[2] *adj.* See sign for DRY.

born *adj.* See sign for BIRTH.

borrow *v.* Same sign used for: **lend me.**

[Bring borrowed thing toward oneself; opposite of movement for **lend**] With the little-finger side of the right *V hand* across the index-finger side of the left *V hand,* bring the hands back, ending with the right index finger against the chest.

boss *n.* See signs for CAPTAIN, CHIEF[1].

both *adj., pron.* Same sign used for: **pair.**

[Two things pulled together to form a pair] Bring the right *2 hand,* palm facing in, downward in front of the chest through the left *C hand,* palm facing in and fingers pointing right, closing the left hand around the right fingers as they pass through and pulling the right fingers together.

bother *v.* See sign for ANNOY.

bottle *n.* Same sign used for: **glass.**

[Shape of a bottle] Beginning with the little-finger side of the right *C hand,* palm facing left, on the upturned left *open hand,* raise the right hand.

bottom *n.* See sign for BELOW.

bow[1] *v.* Same sign used for: **bend, nod.**

[Represents bowing one's head] Beginning with the forearm of the right *S hand,* palm facing forward, against the thumb side of the left *B hand,* palm facing down and fingers pointing right, bend the right arm downward while bending the body forward.

bow[2] *n.* Same sign used for: **ribbon.**

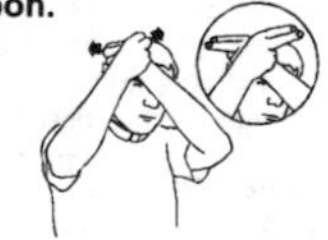

[The shape of a hair bow] With both *S hands* crossed on the right side of the head, palms facing in, flip the *H fingers* of both hands outward with a deliberate movement.

bowl *n.* Same sign used for: **pot.**

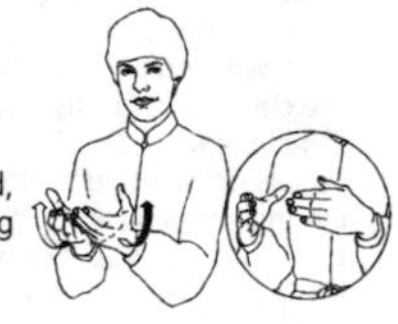

[The shape of a bowl] Beginning with the little fingers of both *C hands* touching, palms facing up, bring the hands apart and upward, ending with the palms facing each other.

box *n.* See also sign for ROOM. Same sign used for: **package, present.**

[Shape of a box] Beginning with both *open hands* in front of each side of the chest, palms facing each other and fingers pointing forward, move the hands deliberately in opposite directions, ending with the left hand near the chest and the right hand several inches forward of the left hand, both palms facing in. (This sign may also be formed with the hands beginning in the final position and then changing to the first position.)

boy *n.* Same sign used for: **male.**

[Grasping the visor of a baseball cap] Beginning with the index-finger side of the right *flattened C hand* near the right side of the forehead, palm facing left, close the fingers to the thumb with a repeated movement.

boycott *v.* See sign for COMPLAIN.

bracelet *n.*

[The location of a bracelet] With the right thumb and middle finger encircling the left wrist, twist the right hand forward with a double movement.

bracket *n.* See sign for CLASS.

brag *v.* Same sign used for: **boast, show off.**

[Natural gesture while bragging] Tap the thumbs of both *10 hands,* palms facing down, against each side of the waist with a double movement.

brain *n.* See sign for MIND.

brand *n.* See signs for LABEL, STAMP[2].

brat *n.* See sign for CONCEITED.

brave *adj.* Same sign used for: **bold, courage.**

[Hands seem to take strength from the body] Beginning with the fingertips of both *5 hands* on each shoulder, palms facing in and fingers pointing back, bring the hands deliberately forward while closing into *S hands*.

bread *n.*

[Slicing a loaf of bread] Move the fingertips of the right *bent hand* downward on the back of the left *open hand* with a repeated movement, both palms facing in.

break[1] *v.* Same sign used for: **tear apart.**

[Mime breaking something] Beginning with both *S hands* in front of the body, index fingers touching and palms facing down, move the hands away from each other while twisting the wrists with a deliberate movement, ending with the palms facing each other.

break[2] *n., v.* See sign for FRACTURE. Related form: **broken** *adj.*

break down *v.* Same sign used for: **collapse, destruction, fall through, tear down.**

[Indicates things crumbing down] Beginning with the fingertips of both *curved 5 hands* touching in front of the chest, palms facing each other, allow the fingers to loosely drop, ending with the palms facing down.

breakfast *n.*

[**eat** + **morning**] Bring the fingertips of the right *flattened O hand* to the lips. Then, with the left *open hand* in the crook of the bent right arm, bring the right *open hand* upward, palm facing in.

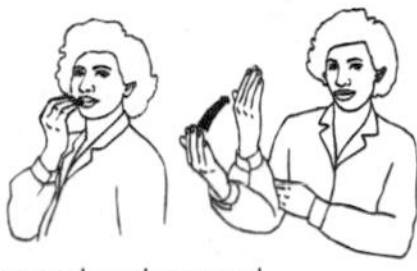

breath *n.* Related form: **breathe** *v.* Same sign used for: **expel, inhale, pant, respiration.**

[Indicates the movement of the lungs when breathing] With the right *5 hand* in front of the chest above the left *5 hand,* fingers pointing in

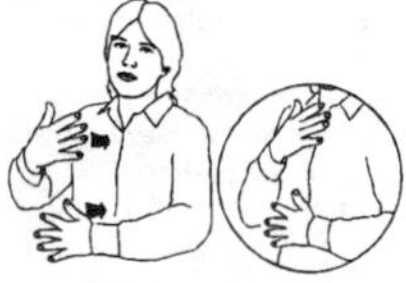

opposite directions and palms in, move both hands forward and back toward the chest with a double movement.

breed *v.* See signs for CONFLICT[1], PREGNANT[1].

bride *n.* Same sign used for: **bridesmaid.**

[Mime walking with a bride's bouquet] With the little-finger side of the right *S hand* on the thumbside of the left *S hand,* move the hands forward a short distance and then forward again.

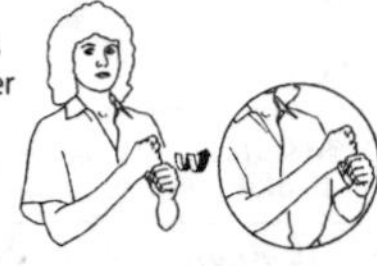

bridesmaid *n.* See sign for BRIDE.

bridge *n.*

[Shows the structure of supports for a bridge] Touch the fingertips of the right *V hand,* palm facing left, first to the bottom of the wrist and then near the elbow of the left arm held in front of the chest, palm facing down.

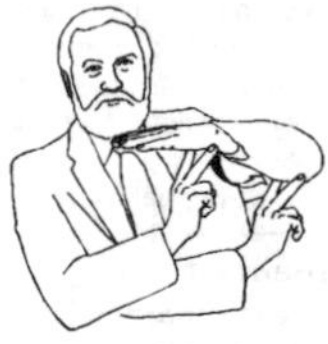

brief *adj.* See also sign for SHORT[1]. Same sign used for: **abbreviate, condense, reduce, squeeze, summarize.**

[Squeeze information together as if to condense] Beginning with both *5 hands* in front of the chest, right hand above the left hand and fingers pointing in opposite directions, bring the hands toward each other while squeezing the fingers together, ending with the little-finger side of the right *S hand* on top of the thumb side of the left *S hand.*

bright *adj.* Same sign used for: **clarify, clear, light, radiant.**

[Hands spread to reveal brightness] Beginning with the fingertips of both *flattened O hands* touching in front of the chest, palms facing each other, move the hands quickly upward in arcs to above each shoulder while opening to *5 hands*.

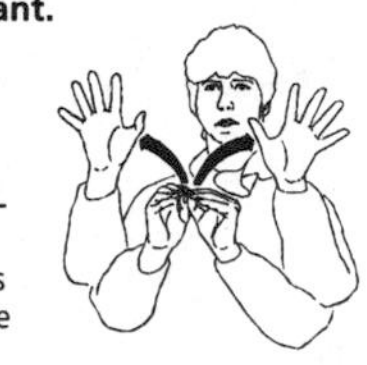

brilliant *adj.* See sign for SMART.

bring *v.* Same sign used for: **deliver, return, transport.**

[Moving an object from one location to another] Move both *open hands,* palms facing up, from in front of the left side of the body in large arcs to the right side of the body. (This sign may be formed in the direction of the referent or its proposed new location.)

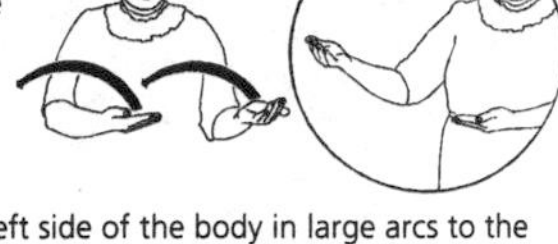

broad *adj.* See signs for GENERAL[1], WIDE.

broadcast *v., n.* See sign for ADVERTISE.

brochure *n.* See sign for MAGAZINE.

broke *adj. Informal.* See sign for PENNILESS.

broom *n.* Same sign used for: **sweep.**

[Mime sweeping] Beginning with both *S hands* in front of the right side of the body, right hand above the left hand and palms facing in, move the hands to the right with a double swinging movement.

brother *n.*

[The male area of the head plus a sign similar to **same**[1] indicating a boy in the same family] Beginning with the thumb of the right *L hand* touching the right side of the forehead, palm facing left, move the right hand downward, landing across the thumb side of the left *L hand,* palm facing right.

brotherhood *n.* See sign for ASSOCIATE.

brown *adj.*

[Initialized sign] Slide the index-finger side of the right *B hand,* palm facing left, down the right cheek.

browse *v.* See sign for LOOK OVER.

brush[1] *n., v.*

[Mime brushing one's hair] Move the palm of the right *A hand* down the right side of the head with a repeated movement.

brush[2] *n.* See sign for PAINT.

budget *n.* See sign for TRADE.

bug *n.* Same sign used for: **insect.**

[Represents a bug's antennas] With the extended thumb of the right *3 hand* on the nose, palm facing left, bend the extended index and middle fingers with a repeated movement.

build *v.* Related form: **building** *n.* Same sign used for: **construct, construction.**

[Shows putting one thing upon another to build something] Beginning with the fingers of the right *bent hand* overlapping the fingers of the left *bent hand* in front of the chest, palms facing down, reverse the position of the hands with a repeated movement as the hands move upward.

bulk *n.* See sign for PILE[1].

bully *n.* See sign for CONCEITED.

bump *n.* See sign for LUMP[1].

bunch *n.* See sign for CLASS.

burden *n.* Same sign used for: **bear, fault, liability, obligation, responsible, responsibility.**

[The weight of responsibility on the shoulder] With the fingertips of both *bent hands* on the right shoulder, push the shoulder down slightly.

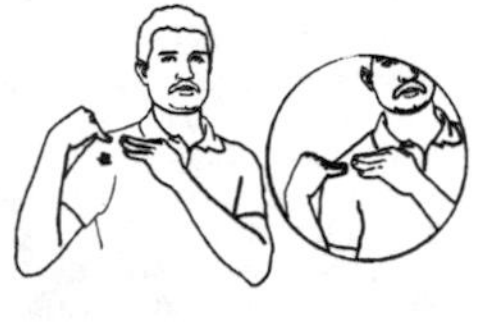

burglary *n.* See signs for ROB, STEAL.

burst *v.* See sign for BAWL OUT.

burst out *v. phrase.* See sign for BAWL OUT.

bury *v.* Same sign used for: **grave.**

[Shape of a mound of dirt on a grave] Move both *curved hands,* palms facing down and fingers pointing down, back toward the body in double arcs.

bus *n.*

[Initialized sign] Beginning with the little-finger side of the right *B hand* touching the index-finger side of the left *B hand,* palms facing in opposite directions, move the right hand back toward the right shoulder.

bust *v.* See sign for MEAN[1].

busy *adj.*

[Initialized sign] Brush the base of the right *B hand,* palm facing forward, with a repeated rocking movement on the back of the left *open hand,* palm facing down.

but *conj.* Same sign used for: **however.**

[Indicates opinions moving in opposite directions] Beginning with both extended index fingers crossed in front of the chest, palms facing forward, bring the hands apart with a deliberate movement.

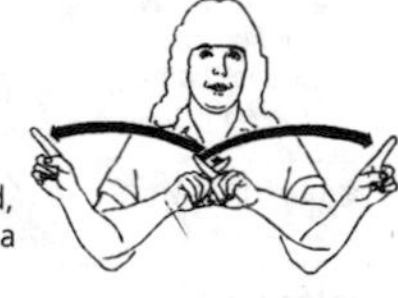

butt in *v.* See sign for NOSY.

butter *n.* Same sign used for: **margarine.**

[Mime spreading butter] Wipe the extended fingers of the right *U hand,* palm facing down and thumb extended, across the palm of the left *open hand* with a repeated movement, drawing the right fingers back into the palm each time.

button *n.*

[Shape and location of buttons] Touch the index-finger side of the right *F hand,* palm facing left, first in the center of the chest, and then lower on the chest.

buy *v.* Same sign used for: **purchase.**

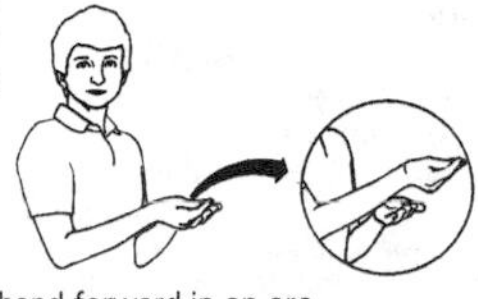

[Shows taking money from the hand to buy something] Beginning with the back of the right *flattened O hand,* palm facing up, in the upturned palm of left *open hand,* move the right hand forward in an arc.

bye *interj.* See sign for GOOD-BYE.

cab *n.* Same sign used for: **taxi.**

[Represents the lighted dome on top of a taxi] Tap the fingertips of the right *C hand,* palm facing down, on the top of the head with a double movement.

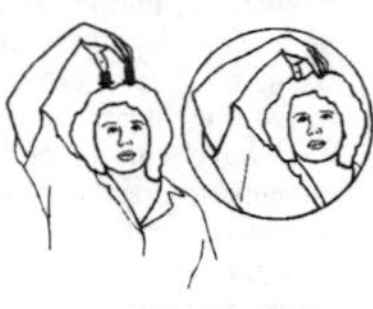

cable *n.* See sign for WIRE.

cafeteria *n.* Alternate form: **café.**

[Initialized sign similar to sign for **restaurant**] Touch the index-finger side of the right *C hand,* palm facing left, first on the right side of the chin and then on the left side.

cage *n.*

[Shape of a wire cage] Beginning with the fingertips of both *4 hands* touching in front of the chest, palms facing in, bring the hands away from each other in a circular movement back toward the chest, ending with the palms facing forward.

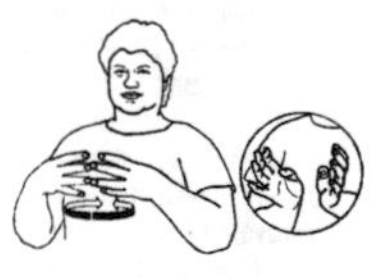

cake *n.*

[Represents a cake rising] Beginning with the fingertips of the right *curved 5 hand* on the palm of the left *open hand,* raise the right hand upward in front of the chest.

calculator *n.*

[Mime using a calculator] Alternately tap each fingertip of the right *5 hand* while moving up and down the upturned left *open hand* held in front of the body.

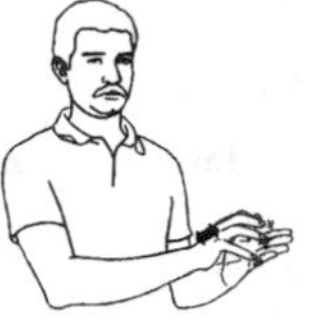

calendar *n.*

[Initialized sign indicating turning pages on a calendar] Move the little-finger side of the right *C hand,* palm facing left, from the heel upward in an arc over the fingertips of the left *open hand,* palm facing in and fingers pointing up.

call[1] *v.* Same sign used for: **summon.**

[Tap on the hand to get one's attention] Slap the fingers of the right *open hand* on the back of the left *open hand,* palm facing down, dragging the right fingers upward and closing them into an *A hand* in front of the right shoulder.

call[2] *v.* Same sign used for: **name.**

[Similar to sign for **name**[1]] With the middle-finger side of the right *H hand* across the index-finger side of the left *H hand,* move the hands forward in an arc in front of the body.

call[3] *v.* See sign for TELEPHONE.

calm *adj., v.* See signs for QUIET, SETTLE, SILENT.

calm down *v. phrase.* See signs for QUIET, SETTLE, SILENT.

camera *n.*
[Mime taking a picture with a camera] Beginning with the *modified C hands* near the outside of each eye, palms facing each other, bend the right index finger up and down with a repeated movement.

can[1] *auxiliary v.* Same sign used for **may.**
[Both hands sign **yes**, indicating ability to do something] Move both *S hands*, palms facing down, downward simultaneously with a short double movement in front of each side of the body.

can[2] *n.* See sign for CUP.

cancel *v.* Same sign used for: **condemn, correct.**
[Finger crosses out something to cancel it] With the extended right index finger, draw a large X across the upturned left *open hand.*

candidate *n.* See sign for APPLY[2].

candle *n.* Same sign used for: **flame, glow.**
[Represents the flame on a candle] With the extended

right index finger touching the heel of the left *5 hand,* palm facing right, wiggle the left fingers.

candy *n.* Same sign used for: **sugar.**

[Similar to sign for **sweet**] Bring the fingers of the right *U hand* downward on the chin with a repeated movement, bending the fingers each time.

can't *contraction.* Alternate form: **cannot.**

[One finger is unable to move the other finger] Bring the extended right index finger downward in front of the chest, striking the extended left index finger as it moves, both palms facing down.

cap *n.*

[Mime tipping a cap with a visor] Bring the right modified *X hand* from in front of the head, palm facing left, back to the top of the head.

capable *adj.* See sign for SKILL.

capital *n.*

[Initialized sign] Tap the thumb of the right *C hand,* palm facing left, on the right shoulder with a double movement.

captain *n.* Same sign used for: **boss, chief, general, officer.**

[Location of epaulets on captain's uniform] Tap the fingertips of the right *curved 5 hand* on the right shoulder with a repeated movement.

capture *v.* Same sign used for: **arrest, catch, claim, conquer, nab, occupy, possess, repossess, seize, takeover.**

[Mime grabbing at something to capture it] Beginning with both *curved 5 hands* in front of each shoulder, palms facing forward, move the hands downward while closing into *S hands.*

car *n.* Same sign used for: **automobile.**

[Mime driving] Beginning with both *S hands* in front of the chest, palms facing in and the left hand higher than the right hand, move the hands in an up-and-down motion with a repeated alternating movement.

card *n.* Same sign used for: **check, envelope.**

[Shows shape of a rectangular card] Beginning with the fingertips of both *L hands* touching in front of the chest, palms facing forward, bring the hands apart to in front of each shoulder, and then pinch each thumb and index finger together.

cards *n.* Same sign used for: **play cards.**

[Mime dealing cards] Beginning with both *A hands* in front of the body, palms facing each other, flick the right hand to the right with a repeated movement off the left thumb.

care[1] *n.* Same sign used for: **monitor, patrol, supervise, take care of.**

[Represents eyes watching out in different directions] With the little finger side of the right *K hand* across the index finger side of the left *K hand,* palms facing in opposite directions, move the hands in a repeated flat circle in front of the body.

care[2] *v.* See sign for TROUBLE[1].

careful *adj.* Same sign used for: **cautious.**

[Eyes looking attentively] Tap the little-finger side of the right *K hand* with a double movement across the index-finger side of the left *K hand,* palms facing in opposite directions.

carefully *adv.* Same sign used for: **cautiously.**

[Eyes looking in all directions] With the little-finger side of the right *K hand* across the index finger side of the left *K hand,* palms facing in opposite directions, move the hands upward and forward in large double circles.

careless *adj.* Related form: **carelessly** *adv.* Same sign used for: **reckless.**

[Misdirected eyes] Move the right *V hand* from near the right side of the head, palm facing left and fingers pointing up, down to the left in front of the eyes with a double movement.

carry *v.* Alternate forms: **carry on** or **onto.**

[Having something in one's hands to transfer to another place] Beginning with both *curved hands* in front of the right side of the body, move the hands in a series of simultaneous arcs to the left, ending in front of the left side of the body.

cast *v.* See sign for THROW.

casual *adj.* See sign for DAILY.

cat *n.*

[Cat's whiskers] Move the fingertips of both *F hands,* palms facing each other, from each side of the mouth outward with a repeated movement.

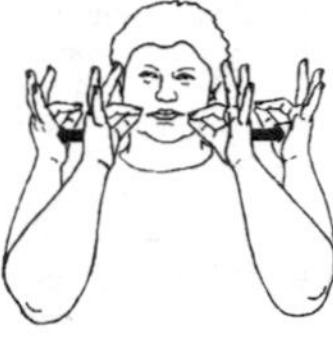

catch[1] *v.* Same sign used for **arrest, convict, nab.**

[Hand moves to "catch" the finger on the other hand] Move the right *C hand* from in front of the right shoulder, palm facing left, forward to meet the extended left index finger, palm facing right and finger pointing up, while changing into an *A hand*.

catch[2] *v.* Same sign used for: **prone.**

[One's fingers receive something and bring it to oneself] With an alternating movement, move first the right *curved 5 hand* and then the left *curved 5 hand* from in front of the chest, palms facing down and fingers pointing forward, back to the chest while changing into *flattened O hands*.

catch[3] *v.* See sign for CAPTURE.

catch up *v. phrase.*
[One hand catches up with the other hand] Bring the right *A hand* from near the right side of the chest, palm facing left, forward to the heel of the left *A hand,* palm facing right, held in front of the body.

category *n.* See sign for CLASS.

catsup *n.* See sign for KETCHUP.

cattle *n.* See sign for COW.

cause *v.*
[Something moving out from the body to affect others] Beginning with both *S hands* near the body, palms facing up and left hand nearer the body than the right hand, move both hands forward in an arc while opening into *5 hands.*

caution *v.* See sign for WARN.

cautious *adj.* See sign for CAREFUL.

cease *v.* See sign for STOP[1].

celebrate *v.* Related form: **celebration** *n.* Same sign used for: **festival, gala, rejoice.**
[Waving flags in celebration] With *modified X hands* in front of each shoulder, move both hands in large repeated outward movements, palms angled up.

cell phone or **cellular phone** *n.*
[Holding a cell phone] Hold the right *curved hand* near the right ear.

cellar *n.* See sign for BASEMENT.

cent *n.* Same sign used for: **penny.**
[Symbolizes the head on a penny] With a double movement, move the extended right index finger forward at an outward angle from touching the right side of the forehead, palm facing down.

center *n.* See sign for MIDDLE.

cereal *n.*
[Action of scooping cereal from bowl to mouth] Move the right curved hand, palm facing up, from the palm of the left *open hand,* palm facing up, upward to the mouth with a double movement.

certain *adj.* See signs for SURE[1], TRUE.

certainly *adv.* See sign for TRUE.

certificate *n.* Related forms: **certify** *v.* **certification** *n.*
[Initialized sign showing shape of certificate] Tap the thumbs of both *C hands* together in front of the chest with a repeated movement, palms facing each other.

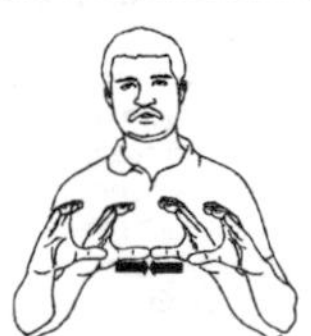

chair *n.* Same sign used for: **seat.**

[Fingers represent legs hanging down when sitting] With a double movement, tap the fingers of the right *curved U hand* across the fingers of the left *U hand,* both palms facing down.

chalk up *v. phrase.* See sign for ACHIEVE.

challenge *v., n.* Same sign used for: **versus.**

[Hands seem to confront each other] Swing both *10 hands,* palms facing in, from in front of each side of the chest toward each other, ending with the knuckles touching in front of the chest, thumbs pointing up.

champagne *n.* See sign for COCKTAIL.

chance *n.*

[Initialized sign formed like turning over dice] Beginning with both *C hands* in front of each side of the body, palms facing up, flip the hands over, ending with the palms facing down.

change[1] *v.* See also sign for TURN. Same sign used for: **adapt, adjust, alter, justify, modify, shift, switch.**

[Hands seem to twist something as if to change it] With the palm sides of both *A hands* together, right hand above left, twist the wrists in opposite directions in order to reverse positions.

change[2] *n.* See sign for SHARE. Shared idea of dividing an amount of money to be shared.

chant *n.* See sign for MUSIC.

chaos *n.* See sign for MESSY.

chapel *n.* See sign for CHURCH.

character *n.* Related form: **characteristic** *n.*
[Initialized sign similar to sign for **personality**] Move the right *C hand,* palm facing left, in a small circle and then back against the left side of the chest.

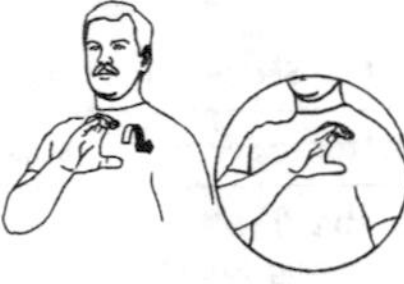

charge[1] *v.* Same sign used for: **credit card.**
[Represents getting impression of credit card charge] Rub the little-finger side of the right *S hand,* palm facing in, back and forth on the upturned left *open hand.*

charge[2] *v.* See signs for APPLY[1], COST.

charity *n.* See sign for GIFT.

chart *n.* See sign for SCHEDULE[1].

chase *v.* Same sign used for: **pursue**.
[One hand seems to pursue the other hand] Move the right *A hand,* palm facing left, in a spiraling movement from in front of the chest forward, to behind the left *A hand* held somewhat forward of the body.

chat[1] *v.* Same sign used for: **talk.**

[Exchanging dialogue between two people] Move both *5 hands,* palms angled up, from in front of each shoulder downward at an angle toward each other with a repeated movement.

chat[2] *v.* See sign for BLAB.

chatter *v.* See sign for BLAB.

cheap *adj.*

[Pushing down the cost] Brush the index-finger side of the right *B hand* downward on the palm of the left *open hand,* bending the right wrist as it moves down.

check[1] *v.* Same sign used for: **examine, inspect.**

[Bringing one's attention to something to inspect it] Move the extended right index finger from the nose down to strike sharply off the upturned palm of the left *open hand,* and then upward again.

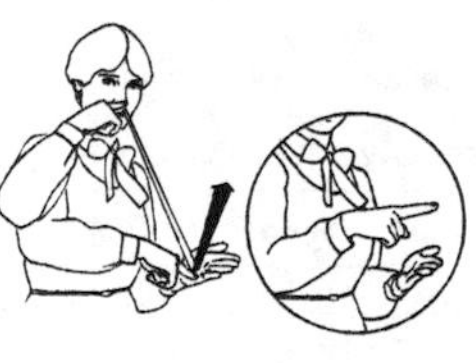

check[2] *n.* See sign for CARD.

check for *v. phrase.* See sign for LOOK FOR.

cheer *n.* See sign for HAPPY.

cheerful *adj.* See signs for FRIENDLY, HAPPY.

cheese *n.*

[Pressing cheese in a cheese press] With the heel of the right *open hand* pressed on the heel of the upturned left *open hand,* palms facing each other and perpendicular to each other, twist the right hand forward and back slightly with a repeated movement.

chew *v.* Same sign used for: **grind.**

[Represents grinding motion of teeth when chewing] With the palm sides of both *A hands* together, right hand on top of the left hand, move the hands in small repeated circles in opposite directions, causing the knuckles of the two hands to rub together.

chewing gum *n.* Same sign used for: **gum.**

[Action of jaw when chewing gum] With the fingertips of the right *V hand* against the right side of the chin, palm facing down, move the hand toward the face with a double movement by bending the fingers.

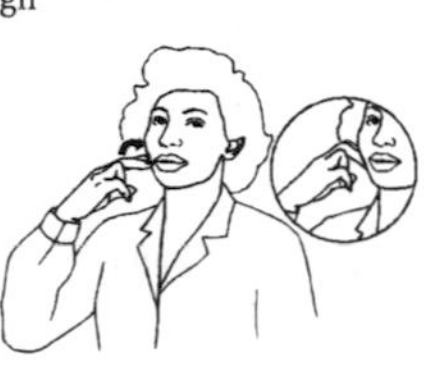

chicken *n.* See sign for BIRD.

chief[1] *n., adj.* Same sign used for: **boss, officer, prominent, superior.**

[Shows higher location] Move the right *10 hand* upward from in front of the right side of the chest, palm facing in and thumb pointing up.

chief[2] *n.* See sign for CAPTAIN.

child *n.*

[Patting child on the head] Pat the right *bent hand* downward with a short repeated movement in front of the right side of the body, palm facing down.

children *pl. n.*

[Patting a number of children on their heads] Pat the right *open hand,* palm facing down, in front of the right side of the body and then to the right with a double arc.

chilly *adj.* See sign for COLD[2].

chocolate *n., adj.*

[Initialized sign] Move the thumb side of the right *C hand,* palm facing forward, in a repeated circle on the back of the left *open hand* held in front of the chest, palm facing down.

choice *n.* See sign for EITHER[1].

choose[1] *v.* Related form: **choice** *n.* See also sign for SELECT. Same sign used for: **assign, draw, pick.**

[Hand picks from alternatives] Beginning with the bent thumb and index finger of the right *5 hand* touching the index finger of the left *5 hand,* palms facing each other, pull the right hand back toward the right shoulder while pinching the thumb and index finger together.

choose[2] *v.* See sign for APPOINT.

Christmas *n.*

[Initialized sign showing the shape of a wreath] Move the right *C hand,* palm facing forward, in a large arc from in front of the left shoulder to in front of the right shoulder.

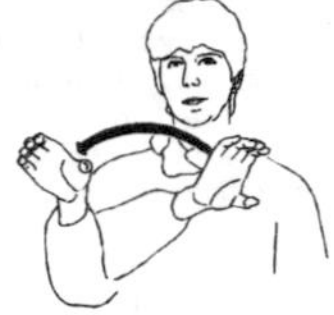

church *n.* Same sign used for: **chapel.**

[Initialized sign similar to sign for **rock**[1]] Tap the thumb of the right *C hand,* palm facing forward, on the back of the left *S hand,* palm facing down.

cigarette *n.*

[Tapping a cigarette to settle the tobacco] Tap the extended index finger and little finger of the right hand with a double movement on the extended left index finger, both palms facing down.

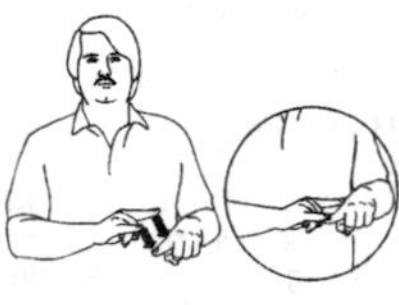

circle[1] *n.* Same sign used for: **cycle, round.**

[Shape of circle] Draw a circle in the air in front of the right side of the chest with the extended right index finger, palm facing down and finger pointing forward.

circle[2] *n.*

[Represents a number of people sitting in a circular pattern] Beginning with both *4 hands* in front of the chest, palms facing forward, bring the hands away from each other in outward arcs while turning the palms in, ending with the little fingers together.

circulate *v.* Related form: **circulation** *n.* Same sign used for: **blend, merge, mix, random.**

[Movement of circulating similar to sign for **mix**] Beginning with the right *5 hand* hanging down in front of the chest, palm facing in and fingers pointing down, and the left *5 hand* below the right hand, palm facing up and fingers pointing up, move the hands in circles around each other.

circumstance *n.* See sign for CONDITION.

city *n.* Same sign used for: **community.**

[Multiple housetops] With the palms of both *bent hands* facing in opposite directions and the fingertips touching, separate the fingertips, twist the wrists, and touch the fingertips again with a double movement.

claim *v.* See sign for CAPTURE.

clap *v.* See sign for APPLAUD.

clarify *v.* See sign for BRIGHT.

class *n.* Same sign used for: **bracket, bunch, category, group, mass, section, series.**

[Initialized sign showing an identifiable group] Beginning with both *C hands* in front of the chest, palms facing each other, bring the hands away from each other in outward arcs while turning the palms in, ending with the little fingers near each other.

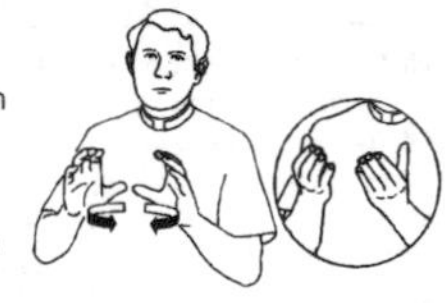

classical *adj.* See sign for FANCY.

classified *adj.* See sign for SECRET.

clean *v.* Alternate form: **clean up.**

[Wiping dirt off something to clean it] Slide the palm of the right *open hand* from the heel to the fingers of the upturned palm of the left *open hand* with a repeated movement. For the adjective, the same sign is used, but made with a double movement.

clear *adj.* See sign for BRIGHT.

clever *adj.* See sign for SMART.

climb *v.* Same sign used for: **ascend, ladder.**

[Mime climbing a ladder] Beginning with both *curved 5 hands* in front of the chest, palms facing forward and right hand higher than the left, move the hands upward one at a time with an alternating movement.

cling to *v. phrase.* See sign for DEPEND.

clock *n.*

[**time** + round shape of a clock's face] Tap the curved right index finger on the back of the left wrist. Then hold both *modified C hands* in front of each side of the face, palms facing each other.

close *adv.* Same sign used for: **approach, near.**

[Moves one hand close to the other] Bring the back of the right *bent hand* from the chest forward toward the left *bent hand,* both palms facing in and fingers pointing in opposite directions.

closet *n.*

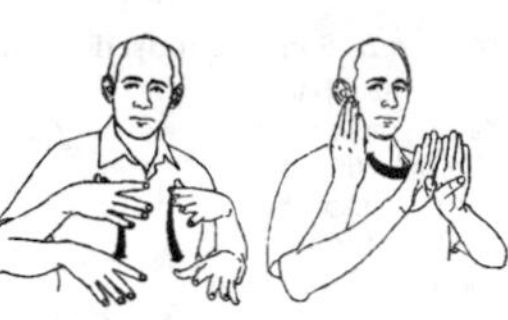

[**clothes** + **door**] Brush the thumbs of both *5 hands* downward on each side of the chest with a double movement. Then, beginning with the index-finger side of both *B hands* touching in front of the chest, palms facing forward and fingers pointing up, swing the right hand back toward the right shoulder with a double movement by twisting the wrist.

close up *adv.*

[Location of something close up to the face] Move the right *open hand,* palm facing in and fingers pointing up, back toward the face.

clothes *pl. n.* Same sign used for: **costume, dress, suit.**

[Location of clothes on body] Brush the thumbs of both *5 hands* downward on each side of the chest with a double movement.

cloud *n.*

[Shape and location of clouds] Beginning with both *C hands* near the left side of the head, palms facing each other, bring the hands away from each other in outward arcs while turning the palms in, ending with the little fingers close together. Repeat the movement near the right side of the head.

clumsy[1] *adj.* Same sign used for: **inexperienced.**

[Being held back, causing one to be clumsy] While holding the thumb of the right *5 hand* tightly in the left *S hand,* twist the right hand forward and down.

clumsy[2] *adj.* See sign for AWKWARD.

coach *n.*

[Initialized sign similar to sign for **captain**] Tap the thumb of the right *C hand,* palm facing left, against the right shoulder with a double movement.

coarse *adj.* See sign for ROUGH.

coat *n.* Same sign used for: **jacket.**

[A coat's lapels] Bring the thumbs of both *A hands* from near each shoulder, palms facing in, downward and toward each other, ending near the waist.

cocktail *n.* Same sign used for: **champagne, drink.**

[Mime drinking from a small glass] Beginning with the thumb of the right *modified C hand* near the mouth, palm facing left, tip the index finger back toward the face.

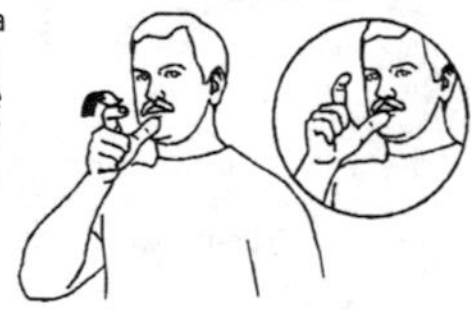

coffee *n.*
[Grind coffee beans] Move the little-finger side of the right *S hand* with a circular movement on the index-finger side of the left *S hand,* palms facing in opposite directions.

cogitate *v.* See sign for MULL.

coin *n.*
[Shape of coin held in the hand] Move the extended right index finger, palm facing in and finger pointing down, in a double circular movement on the left *open hand,* palm facing up.

Coke *n. Trademark.* Alternate form: **Coca-Cola** (*trademark*).
[Mime injecting a drug] With the index finger of the right *L hand,* palm facing in, touching the upper left arm, move the right thumb up and down with a double movement.

cold[1] *n.*
[Mime blowing one's nose] Grasp the nose with the thumb and index finger of the right *A hand,* palm facing in, and pull the hand forward off the nose with a double movement.

cold[2] *adj.* Same sign used for: **chilly, frigid, shiver, winter.**
[Natural gesture when shivering from cold] Shake both *S hands* with a slight movement in front of each side of

the chest, palms facing each other.

collapse *n.* See sign for BREAK DOWN.

collect *v.* Related form: **collection** *n.* Same sign used for: **accumulate, gather.**

[Pulling money to oneself] With a double movement, bring the little-finger side of the right *curved hand,* palm facing left, across the palm of the left *open hand,* palm facing up, from its fingertips to the heel while changing into an *S hand.*

college *n.*

[Similar to sign for **school** but moves upward to a higher level] Beginning with the palm of the right *open hand* across the palm of the left *open hand* in front of the chest, move the right hand upward in an arc, ending in front of the upper chest, palm angled forward and fingers angled upward toward the left.

collide *v.* See sign for ACCIDENT[1]. Related form: **collision** *n.*

color *n.*

[The fingers represent the colors of the rainbow] Wiggle the fingers of the right *5 hand* in front of the mouth, fingers pointing up and palm facing in.

comb *n.*

[Mime combing hair] Drag the fingertips of the right *curved 5 hand* through the hair on the right side of the head with a short double movement. The verb is the same sign as the noun, but made with a longer double movement.

combine *v.* See signs for BELONG, MATCH, MESH.

come *v.*

[Indicates direction for another to come toward oneself] Beginning with both extended index fingers pointing up in front of the body, palms facing in, bring the fingers back to each side of the chest.

come back *v. phrase.* See sign for REFUND.

come on or **come in** *v. phrase.*

[Natural gesture beckoning someone] Move the right *open hand,* palm angled up, back toward the right shoulder.

come up *v. phrase.* See sign for SHOW UP.

command *n., v.* See sign for ORDER.

comment *v.* See sign for SAY.

commercial *n.* See sign for ADVERTISE.

commit *v.* See signs for DO, PROMISE.

committee *n.*

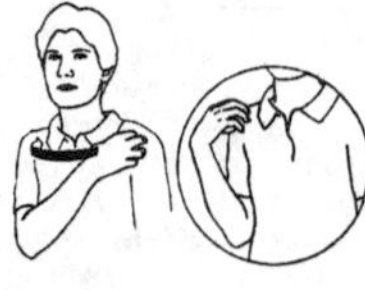

[Initialized sign similar to sign for **us**] Touch the fingertips of the right *curved 5 hand* first to the left side of the chest and then to the right side of the chest, palm facing in.

common *n, adj.* See sign for STANDARD.

communication *n.* Related form: **communicate** *v.* Same sign used for: **conversation, converse.**

[Initialized sign indicating words moving both to and from a person] Move both *C hands,* palms facing each other, forward and back from the chin with an alternating movement.

community *n.* See signs for CITY, TOWN.

commute *v.* Same sign used for: **back and forth.**

[Demonstrates movement to and from] Move the right *10 hand,* palm facing left, from in front of the right side of the body to in front of the left side of the body with a double movement.

compare *v.* Related form: **comparison** *n.*

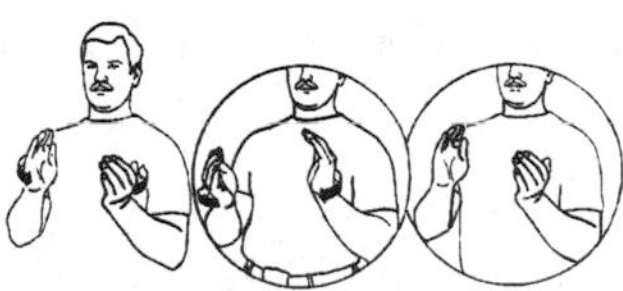

[Holding something in one hand and comparing it with something in the other hand] With both *curved hands* in front of each side of the chest, palms facing, alternately turn one hand and then the other toward the face while turning the other hand in the opposite direction, keeping the palms facing each other and the fingers pointing up.

---

complain *v.* Same sign used for: **boycott, gripe, grumble, object, protest, riot, strike.**

[Natural gesture used when complaining] Tap the fingertips of the right *curved 5 hand* against the center of the chest.

---

complaint *n.* See sign for PROTEST[1].

---

complete *v., adj.* See signs for END[1], FINISH[1], FULL[2].

---

complex[1] *adj.* Same sign used for: **complicated.**

[Thoughts moving through the brain in opposite directions] Beginning with both extended index fingers point toward each other in front of each side of the face, both palms facing down, continuously bend the fingers up and down as the hands move past each other in front of the face.

---

complex[2] *adj.* See sign for MIX[1].

comprehend *v.* See sign for UNDERSTAND.

compromise *n.* See sign for AGREE.

computer *n.*
[Initialized sign] Move the thumb side of the right *C hand,* palm facing left, from touching the lower part of extended left arm upward to touch the upper arm.

comrade *n.* See sign for FRIEND.

conceal *v.* See sign for HIDE.

conceited *adj.* Same sign used for: **arrogant, big-headed, big shot, brat, bully.**
[**big** formed near the head, signifying a person with a "big head"] Beginning with both *L hands* in front of each side of the forehead, index fingers pointing toward each other and palms facing in, bring the hands outward away from each other a short distance.

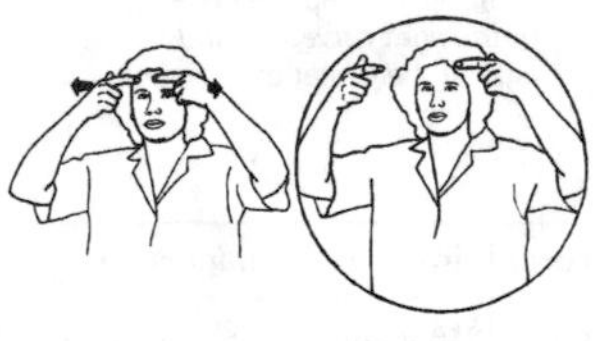

conceive *v.* See sign for PREGNANT[1].

concentrate *v.* See sign for ATTENTION. Related form: **concentration** *n.*

concept *n.* Same sign used for: **creative.**
[Initialized sign similar to sign for **invent**] Move the right *C hand,* palm facing left, from the right

side of the forehead forward and slightly upward in a double arc.

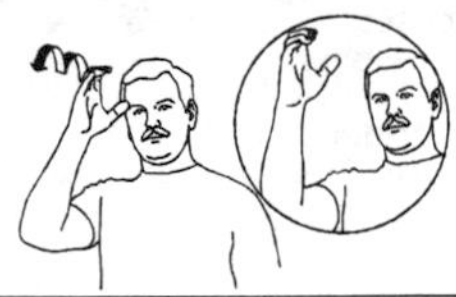

concern[1] *v.* Same sign used for: **consider, think.**

[Thoughts moving through the brain] Beginning with both extended index fingers in front of each side of the forehead, palms facing in and fingers angled up, move the fingers in repeated alternating circular movements toward each other in front of the face.

concern[2] *n.* See sign for TROUBLE[1].

concise *adj.* See sign for PRECISE.

conclude *v.* See sign for END[1].

condemn *v.* See signs for CANCEL, CURSE.

condense *v.* See sign for BRIEF.

condition *n.* Same sign used for: **circumstance, culture.**

[Initialized sign showing area around a thing] Beginning with the right *C hand,* palm facing left, near the extended left index finger, palm facing right, move the right hand in a circle forward and around the left finger.

conduct *v.* See signs for DO, LEAD.

conference *n.* See sign for MEETING.

confess *v.* See sign for ADMIT. Related form: **confession** *n.*

confident *adj.* Related form: **confidence** *n.* Same sign used for: **bold, trust.**

[Holding firmly to one's beliefs] Beginning with both *curved 5 hands* in front of the chest, right hand above the left and palms facing in, bring both hands downward a short distance with a deliberate movement while closing into *S hands.*

confidential *adj.* See sign for SECRET.

confined *adj.* See sign for STUCK.

conflict[1] *n., v.* Same sign used for: **breed, cross-purposes, fertilize.**

[Represents a crossing of opinions] Beginning with both extended index fingers in front of each side of the body, palms facing in and fingers angled toward each other, move the hands toward each other, ending with the fingers crossed.

conflict[2] *v., n.* See sign for STRUGGLE.

confuse[1] *v.* Related form: **confusion** *n.* Same sign used for: **mixed up.**

[**think** + **mix**[1]] Bring the extended right index finger from touching the right side of the forehead, palm facing in, down to in front of the chest, changing into a *curved 5 hand.* Then, with the right *curved 5 hand* over the left *curved 5 hand,* palms facing each other, move the hands simultaneously in repeated circles going in opposite directions.

confuse[2] *v.* See sign for MIX[1].

connect *v.* See sign for BELONG.

connection *n.* See sign for RELATIONSHIP.

conquer *v.* See signs for CAPTURE, DEFEAT.

consider *v.* See signs for CONCERN[1], WONDER.

constant *adj.* Same sign used for: **continual, persistent, steadfast, steady.**

[Indicates continuing movement] Beginning with the thumb of the right *10 hand* on the thumbnail of the left *10 hand*, both palms facing down in front of the chest, move the hands downward and forward in a series of small arcs.

construct *v.* See sign for BUILD. Related form: **construction** *n.*

contact *n., v.* Same sign used for: **in touch with.**

[Indicates two things coming into contact with each other] With the right hand above the left hand in front of the chest, touch the bent middle finger of the right *5 hand* to the bent middle finger of the left *5 hand* with a double movement, palms facing each other.

contained in *adv.* See sign for INCLUDE.

contemplate *v.* See sign for WONDER.

continual *adj.* See sign for CONSTANT.

continue[1] *v.* Same sign used for: **last, remain.**

[Indicates continuous movement] Beginning with the thumb of the right *10 hand* on the thumbnail of the left *10 hand,* both palms facing down in front of the chest, move the hands downward and forward in an arc.

continue[2] *v.* See sign for GO ON.

contrary *adj.* See sign for OPPOSITE.

contrast *v.* See signs for DISAGREE, OPPOSITE.

contribute *v.* See signs for GIFT, GIVE. Related form: **contribution** *n.*

control[1] *v.* Same sign used for: **restrain, suppress, tolerate.**

[The hands seem to suppress one's feelings] Beginning with the fingertips of both *curved 5 hands* against the chest, palms facing in, bring the hands downward while forming *S hands,* palms facing up.

control[2] *v.* See sign for MANAGE.

controversy *n.* See sign for STRUGGLE.

convenient *adj.* See sign for EASY.

convention *n.* See sign for MEETING.

converse *v.* See sign for COMMUNICATION. Related form: **conversation** *n.*

convey *v.* See sign for NARROW DOWN.

convict *v.* See sign for CATCH[1].

convince *v.*

[The hands come from both sides to influence someone] Beginning with both *open hands* in front of each shoulder, palms angled upward, bring the hands down sharply at an angle toward each other.

convocation *n.* See sign for MEETING.

cook *v.* Same sign used for: **bake, flip, fry, turn over.**

[As if turning food in a frying pan] Beginning with the fingers of the right *open hand,* palm facing down, across the palm of the left *open hand,* flip the right hand over, ending with the back of the right hand on the left palm.

cookie *n.* Same sign used for: **biscuit.**

[Mime using a cookie cutter] Touch the fingertips of the right *C hand,* palm facing down, on the upturned palm of the left *open hand.* Then twist the right hand and touch the left palm again.

cool *adj.* Same sign used for: **pleasant, refresh.**

[As if fanning oneself] With both open hands above each shoulder, palms facing back and fingers pointing up, bend the fingers up and down with a repeated movement.

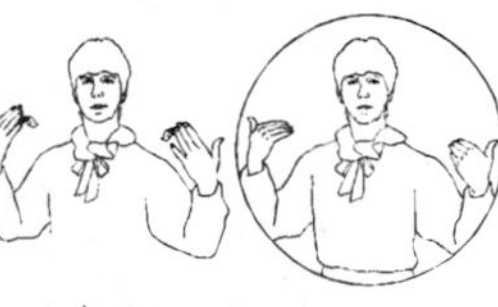

cooperate *v.* Related form: **cooperation** *n.* Same sign used for: **affiliation, union, unity, universal.**

[One thing is linked to another] With the thumbs and index fingers of both *F hands* intersecting, move the hands in a flat circle in front of the chest.

coordinate *v.* Same sign used for: **relate.**

With the thumbs and index fingers of both *F hands* intersecting, move the hands forward and back with a double movement.

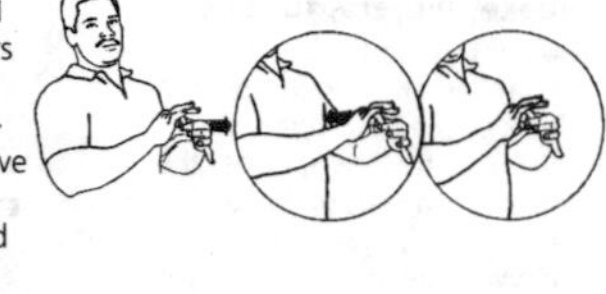

cop *n.* See sign for POLICE.

copy *v.* Same sign used for: **duplicate, imitate, impose.**

[Represents taking information and recording it on paper] Move the right *curved hand* in front of the chest, palm facing forward, down to touch the palm of the left *open hand* while closing the right fingers and thumb into a *flattened O hand.* The noun is formed in the same way except with a double movement.

cord *n.* Same sign used for: **thread, wire.**

[Shape of a coiled cord] Beginning with both extended little fingers pointing toward each other in front of the chest, palms facing in, move the fingers in circular movements while moving the hands away from each other.

correct *v.* See signs for CANCEL, RIGHT[3].

corridor *n.* See sign for HALL.

cosmetics *pl. n.* See sign for MAKE-UP.

cost *n., v.* Same sign used for: **charge, fare, fee, fine, price, tax.**

[Making a dent in one's finances] Strike the knuckle of the right *X hand,* palm facing in, down the palm of the left *open hand,* palm facing right and fingers pointing forward.

costly *adj.* See sign for EXPENSIVE.

costume *n.* See sign for CLOTHES.

cough *v., n.*

[Location of the origin of a cough in the chest] With the fingertips of the right *curved 5 hand* on the chest, palm facing in, lower the wrist with a repeated movement while keeping the fingertips in place.

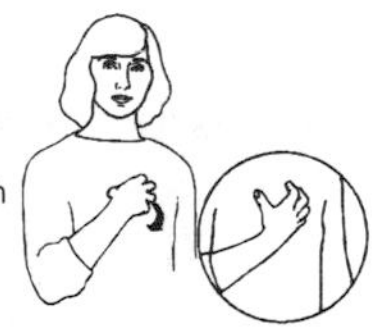

council *n.* See sign for MEETING.

count *v.*

[Counting beads on an abacus] Move the fingertips of the right *F hand*, palm facing down, across the upturned palm of the left *open hand* from the heel to the fingers.

counter *adj.* See sign for OPPOSITE.

counterfeit *n.* See sign for FAKE.

country[1] *n.*

[Similar to sign for **country**[2] but formed with a *Y hand*] Rub the bent fingers of the right *Y hand,* palm facing in, in a circle near the elbow of the bent left arm with a repeated movement.

country[2] *n.*

[The tattered elbows of a farm worker] Rub the palm of the right *open hand* in a circle near the elbow of the bent left arm with a repeated movement.

couple *n.* Same sign used for: **pair.**

[Pointing to two people making up a couple] Move the right *V fingers,* palm facing up and fingers pointing forward, from side to side in front of the right side of the body with a repeated movement.

courage *n.* See sign for BRAVE.

course *n.* Same sign used for: **lesson.**

[Initialized sign similar to sign for **list**] Move the little-finger side of the right *C hand,* palm facing in, in an arc, touching first on the fingers and then near the heel of the upturned left hand.

court *n.* See sign for JUDGE.

courteous *adj.* See sign for POLITE. Related form: **courtesy** *n.*

cousin *n.*

male

female

[Male cousin: Initialized sign formed near the male area of the head] Move the right *C hand,* palm facing left, with a shaking movement near the right side of the forehead.

[Female cousin: Initialized sign near the female area of the head] Move the right *C hand,* palm facing left, with a shaking movement near the right side of the chin.

cover *n.* See signs for LID.

covetous *adj.* See sign for GREEDY.

cow *n.* Same sign used for: **cattle.**

[A cow's horns] With the thumbs of both *Y hands* on

both sides of the forehead, palms facing forward, twist the hands forward.

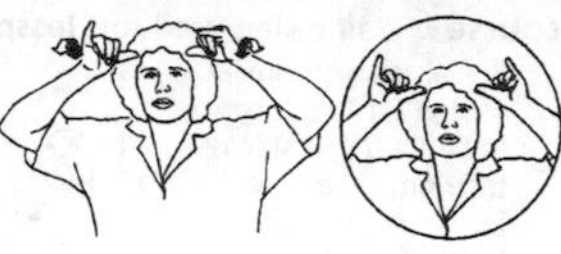

coward *n.* See signs for BIRD, FEAR.

cracker *n.*

[The old-world custom of breaking a cracker with the elbow] Strike the palm side of the right *A hand* near the elbow of the bent left arm with a repeated movement.

cramped *adj.* See sign for CROWDED.

crash[1] *n., v.*

[Shows impact of a crash] Beginning with the right *5 hand* near the right side of the chest, palm facing down and fingers angled forward, move the hand deliberately to hit against the palm of the left *open hand,* bending the right fingers as it hits.

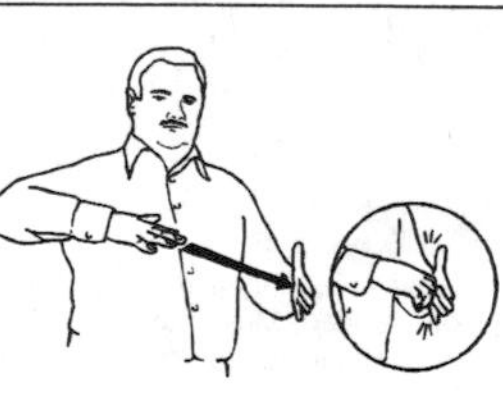

crash[2] *n.* See sign for ACCIDENT[1].

crave *v.* See sign for HUNGRY.

crazy *adj.* Same sign used for: **wacky** (*slang*).

[Indicates that things are confused in one's head] Twist the *curved 5 hand,* palm facing in, forward with a repeated movement near the right side of the head.

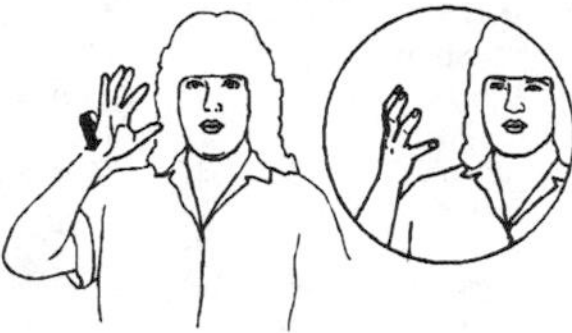

cream *n.*
[Initialized sign representing skimming cream from the top of milk] Bring the little-finger side of the right *C hand,* palm facing left, back toward the chest in a circular movement across the palm of the left *open hand.*

create *v.* See signs for INVENT, MAKE.

creative *adj.* See sign for CONCEPT.

credit card *n.* See sign for CHARGE[1].

cross[1] *adj.* See also sign for ANGER. Same sign used for: **angry, mad.**
[Hand seems to pull the face down into a scowl] With the palm of the right *5 hand* in front of the face, fingers pointing up, bring the hand slightly forward while constricting the fingers into a *curved 5 hand.*

cross[2] *prep., adv.* See sign for ACROSS.

cross-purposes *n.* See sign for CONFLICT[1].

crowd *n.* See sign for AUDIENCE.

crowded *adj.* Same sign used for: **cramped, crushed.**

[The hands are crushed tightly together] Beginning with the palms of both *A hands* together in front of the chest, twist the hands in opposite directions.

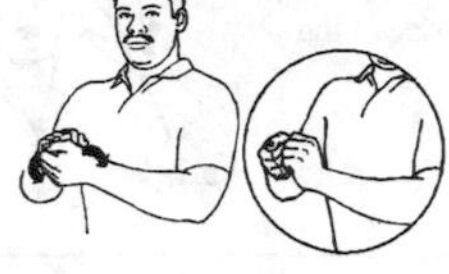

cruel *adj.* See sign for MEAN[1].

cruise *n.* See sign for BOAT.

crushed *adj.* See sign for CROWDED.

cry[1] *v.* Same sign used for: **weep.**

[Tears flowing down the cheeks] Bring both extended index fingers, palms facing in and fingers pointing up, downward from each eye with an alternating movement.

cry[2] *v.* See sign for SCREAM.

culture *n.* See sign for CONDITION.

cup *n.* Same sign used for: **can.**

[Shape of a cup] Bring the little-finger side of the right *C hand,* palm facing left, down to the upturned left *open hand* with a double movement.

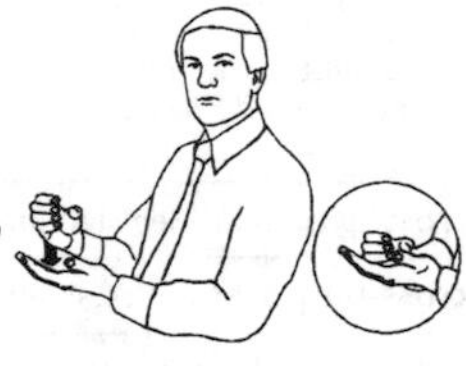

cure *n., v.* See sign for WELL[1].

curious *adj.* Related form: **curiosity** *n.*

[Pulling the neck forward out of curiosity] With the fingertips of the right *F hand* against the neck, palm facing left, twist the hand downward with a double movement.

current *adj.* See sign for NOW.

curse *n., v.* Same sign used for: **condemn, swear.**

[Threatening words are directed toward God] Beginning with the right *curved 5 hand* near the mouth, palm facing in, bring the hand upward with a deliberate movement while closing into an *S hand.*

cut[1] *v.* Same sign used for: **haircut.**

[Mime cutting hair] Move both *V hands,* palms facing down, back over each shoulder while opening and closing the fingers of the *V hands* repeatedly as the hands move.

cut[2] *v.*

[Represents cutting across a piece of paper] Move the right *V hand,* fingers pointing left, across the fingertips of the left *open hand,* palm facing down, with a deliberate movement while closing the *V fingers* together.

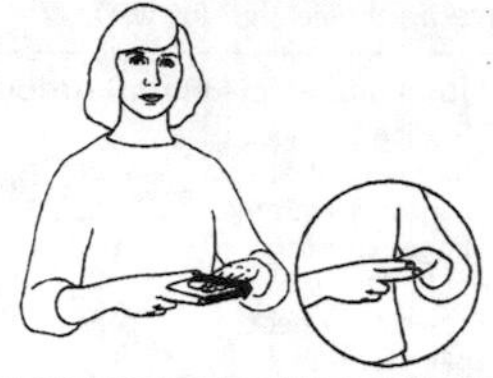

cute *adj.*

[Similar to the sign for **sweet** but formed with a *U hand*] With the right thumb extended, brush the fingers of the right *U hand,* palm facing down, downward on the chin while changing into a *10 hand.*

cycle *n.* See sign for CIRCLE[1].

dad *n.* See sign for FATHER. Related form: **daddy** *n.*

daily *adj., adv.* Same sign used for: **casual, domestic, everyday, every day, ordinary, routine, usual.**

[Similar to sign for **tomorrow,** only repeated to indicated recurrence] Move the palm side of the right *A hand* forward on the right side of the chin with a repeated movement.

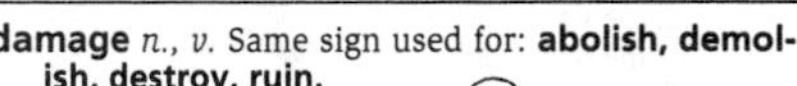

damage *n., v.* Same sign used for: **abolish, demolish, destroy, ruin.**

[Hands seem to take something and pull it apart] Beginning with both *curved 5 hands* in front of the chest, right hand over the left, right palm facing down and left palm facing up, bring the right hand in a circular movement over the left. Then close both hands into *A hands* and bring the knuckles of the right hand forward past the left knuckles with a deliberate movement.

damp *adj.* See sign for WET.

dance *v., n.* Same sign used for: **disco, gala.**

[Represents legs moving in rhythm to dance music] Swing the fingers of the right *V hand,* palm facing in and fingers pointing down, back and forth over the upturned left *open hand* with a double movement.

danger *n.* Related form: **dangerous** *adj.* Same sign used for: **endanger, harassment, harm, hazard, risk, threat.**

[Represents hidden danger coming at a person] Move the thumb of the right *10 hand,* palm facing left, upward on the back of the left *A hand,* palm facing in, with a repeated movement.

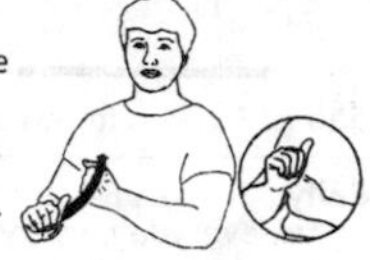

dark *adj.* Related form: **darkness** *n.* Same sign used for: **dim, dusk.**

[Hands shade the eyes from light] Beginning with both *open hands* in front of each shoulder, palms facing back and fingers pointing up, bring the hands past each other in front of the face, ending with the wrists crossed and the fingers pointing in opposite directions at an angle.

daughter *n.*

[Begins at the female area of the head + **baby**] Beginning with the index-finger side of the right *B hand,* palm facing left, touching the right side of the chin, swing the right hand downward, with the bent right arm cradled in the bent left arm held across the body.

dawn *n.* See sign for SUNRISE.

day *n.*

[Symbolizes the movement of the sun across the sky] Beginning with the bent right elbow resting on the back of the left hand held across the body, palm facing down, bring the extended right index

finger from pointing up in front of the right shoulder, palm facing left, downward toward the left elbow.

daydream *v., n.* See sign for DREAM.

dead *adj.* See sign for DIE.

deaf *adj.*

[Points to the ear and mouth to indicate that a person cannot hear or talk] Touch the extended right index finger first to near the right ear and then to near the right side of the mouth.

deal *v.* See sign for PASS AROUND.

death *n.* See sign for DIE.

debt *n.* See sign for AFFORD.

decal *n.* See sign for LABEL.

decay *v.* See sign for WEAR OUT.

decide *v.* Related form: **decision** *n.* Same sign used for: **determine, make up your mind, officially.**

[**think**[1] + laying one's thoughts down decisively] Move the extended right index finger from the right side of the forehead, palm facing left, down in front of the chest while changing into an *F hand,* ending with both *F hands* in front of the body, palms facing each other.

decimal or **decimal point** *n.* See sign for PERIOD.

declare *v.* See sign for ANNOUNCE. Related form: **declaration** *n.*

decline *v., n.* Same sign used for: **deteriorate.**

[Hands move downward in location] Beginning with both *10 hands* in front of each shoulder, palms facing in and thumbs pointing up, move both hands down in front of each side of the chest.

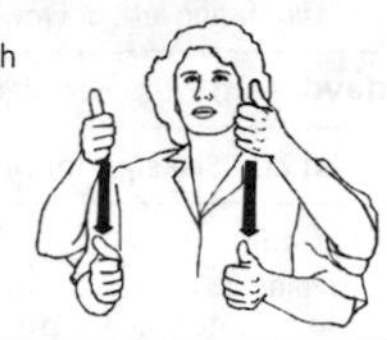

decorate *v.* Related form: **decoration** *n.*

[Hands seem to arrange ornamental items] Beginning with both *flattened O hands* in front of each side of the chest, palms facing forward, move them in alternating circles with a repeated movement.

decrease *n., v.* Same sign used for: **lessen, lose, reduce, reduction.**

[Taking some off to decrease it] Beginning with the fingers of the right *U hand* across the fingers of the left *U hand,* both palms facing down, take the right fingers off by flipping the right hand over.

deduct *v.* See sign for SUBTRACT.

deed *n.* See sign for ACT[1].

deep *adj.* Same sign used for: **depth, detail.**

[Indicates direction of bottom of something deep] Move the extended right index finger, palm facing down, downward near the fingertips of the left *5 hand,* palm facing down.

defeat *v.* See also sign for BEAT[3]. Same sign used for: **conquer, overcome, subdue, vanquish.**

[Represents forcing another down in defeat] Move the right *S hand* from in front of the right shoulder, palm facing forward, downward and forward, ending with the right wrist across the wrist of the left *S hand,* both palms facing down.

defend *v.* Related forms: **defense** *n.*, **defensive** *adj.* Same sign used for: **protect, security, shield.**

[Blocking oneself from harm] With the wrists of both *S hands* crossed in front of the chest, palms facing in opposite directions, move the hands forward with a short double movement.

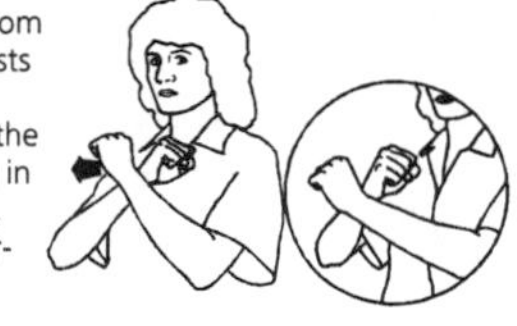

defensive *adj.* See sign for RESIST.

defer[1] *v.* Same sign used for **delay, procrastinate, put off.**

[Represents taking something and putting it off several times] Beginning with both *F hands* in front of the body, palms facing each other and the left hand nearer to the body than the right hand, move both hands forward in a series of small arcs.

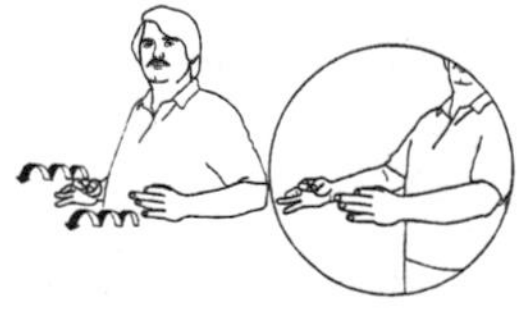

defer[2] *v.* See sign for POSTPONE.

define *v.* See sign for DESCRIBE. Related form: **definition** *n.*

delay *n., v.* See signs for DEFER, LATE, POSTPONE.

delete *v.* See sign for ELIMINATE[1].

deliberate *v.* See sign for MULL.

delicious *adj.* Same sign used for: **tasty.**

[Something is tasted appreciatively] Touch the bent middle finger of the right *5 hand* to the lips, palm facing in, and then twist the right hand quickly forward.

delighted *adj.* See sign for HAPPY.

deliver *v.* See sign for BRING.

deluxe *adj.* See sign for FANCY.

demand *v.* Same sign used for: **insist, require.**

[Something is dragged in on a hook] With the extended right index finger, palm facing in, touching the palm of the left *open hand* bring both hands back toward the chest.

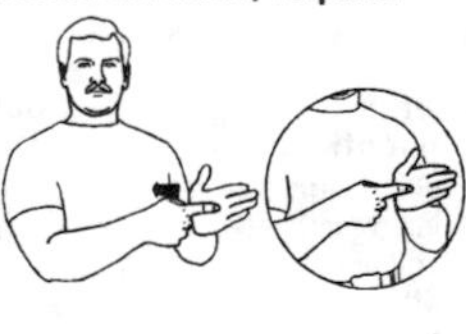

demolish *v.* See sign for DAMAGE.

demonstrate *v.* See sign for SHOW[1]. Related form: **demonstration** *n.*

demote *v.* See sign for LOW.

dentist *n.*

[Initialized sign showing locaton of teeth] Tap the fingers of the right *D hand,* palm facing in and index finger pointing up, against the right side of the teeth with a repeated movement.

deny *v.*

[**not** with a repeated movement] Beginning with the thumb of the right *A hand* under the chin, palm facing left, and the left *A hand* held somewhat forward, palm facing right, move the right hand forward while moving the left hand back. Repeat the movement with the left hand.

depart *v.* See signs for GO, LEAVE[1]. Related form: **departure** *n.*

department *n.*

[Initialized sign similar to sign for **class**] Beginning with the fingertips of both *D hands* touching in front of the chest, palms facing each other, bring the hands away from each other in outward arcs while turning the palms in, ending with the little fingers together.

depend or **depend on** *v.* Related forms: **dependency** *n.*, **dependent** *adj.* Same sign used for: **cling to, rely.**

[Represents resting on another] With the extended right index finger across the extended left index finger, palms facing down, move both fingers down slightly with a double movement.

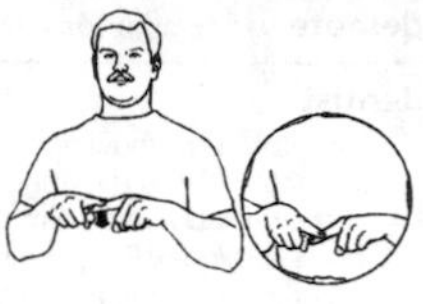

deplete *v.* See sign for RUN OUT OF.

deposit[1] *v., n.*

[Sealing a deposit envelope with the thumbs] Beginning with the thumbs of both *10 hands* touching in front of the chest, both palms facing down, bring the hands downward and apart by twisting the wrists.

deposit[2] *n., v.* See sign for INVEST.

depressed *adj.* Related forms: **depressing** *adj.*, **depression** *n.* Same sign used for: **despair, discouraged.**

[Feelings moving downward in the body] Beginning with the bent middle fingers of both *5 hands* on each side of the chest, palms facing in and fingers pointing toward each other, move the hands downward with a simultaneous movement.

depth *n.* See sign for DEEP.

describe *v.* Related form: **description** *n.* Same sign used for: **define, definition, direct, direction, explain, explanation, instruct, instruction.**

[Bringing something before one's eyes to describe it]

Beginning with both *F hands* in front of the chest, palms facing each other and index fingers pointing forward, move the hands forward and back with an alternating movement.

desert *v.* See sign for LEAVE[1].

deserve *v.* See sign for EARN.

design *v.* Same sign used for: **draw, drawing, draft.**

[Initialized sign similar to sign for **art**] Move the fingertips of the right *D hand,* palm facing left, down the palm of the left *open hand* with a wavy movement.

desire *v.* See signs for WANT, WISH.

desist *v.* Same sign used for: **stop.**

[Natural gesture used when asking another to stop doing something] Beginning with the fingers of both *5 hands* in front of each side of the chest, palms facing in, twist the wrists to flip the hands in a quick movement, ending with the palms facing down.

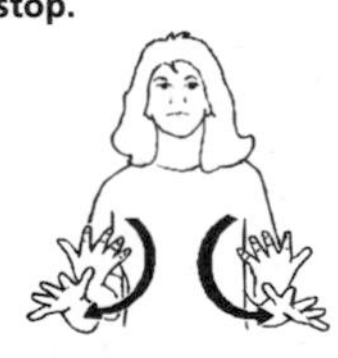

desk *n.* Same sign used for: **table.**

[**table**[1] + shape of a desk] Pat the forearm of the bent right arm with a double movement on the bent left arm held across the chest. Then, beginning with the fingers of both *open hands* together in front of the chest, palms facing down, move the hands apart to in front of each shoulder and then straight down, ending with the palms facing each other.

despair *n., v.* See sign for DEPRESSED.

despise *v.* See sign for HATE.

despite *prep.* See sign for ANYWAY.

dessert *n.*

[Initialized sign] Tap the fingertips of both *D hands,* palms facing each other, together with a repeated movement in front of the chest.

destroy *v.* See sign for DAMAGE.

destruction *n.* See sign for BREAK DOWN.

detach *v.* See sign for DISCONNECT.

detail *n.* See sign for DEEP. Shared idea of careful attention to important matters.

deteriorate *v.* See sign for DECLINE.

determine *v.* See sign for DECIDE.

detest *v.* See sign for HATE.

develop *v.*

[Initialized sign moving upward to represent growth or development] Move the fingertips of the right *D hand,* palm facing

left, upward from the heel to the fingers of the left *open hand,* fingers pointing up and palm facing right.

device *n.* See sign for EQUIPMENT.

dew *n.* See sign for WET.

diagnose *v.* See sign for ANALYZE. Related form: **diagnosis** *n.*

dictionary *n.* See sign for PAGE.

die *v.* Same sign used for: **dead, death, perish.**

[Represents a body turning over in death] Beginning with both *open hands* in front of the body, right palm facing down and left palm facing up, flip the hands to the right, turning the right palm up and the left palm down.

diet *n.* Same sign used for: **lean, shrink, slim, thin.**

[Shows slimmer body] Beginning with both *L hands* in front of each side of the chest, palms facing in, swing the hands downward by twisting the wrists, ending with the hands in front of each side of the waist, both palms facing down.

different *adj.* Related form: **difference** *n.*

[Moving things apart that are not the same] Beginning with both extended index fingers crossed in front of the chest, palms facing forward, bring the hands apart from each other with a deliberate movement.

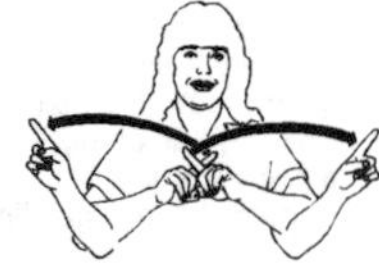

difficult *adj.* Same sign used for: **hard, problem, trouble.**

[The bent fingers impede each other, making movement difficult] Beginning with both *bent V hands* in front of the chest, right hand higher than the left hand, palms facing in, move the right hand down and the left hand upward with an alternating movement, brushing the knuckles of each hand as the hands move in the opposite direction.

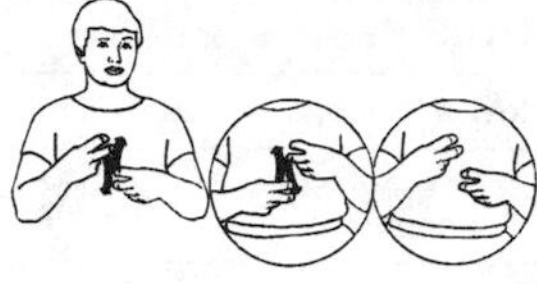

dim *adj.* See sign for DARK.

dime *n.* Same sign used for: **ten cents.**

[**cent** + **ten**] Beginning with the extended right index finger touching the right side of the forehead, palm facing down, bring the right hand forward while changing into a *10 hand.* Then slightly twist the right *10 hand* with a repeated movement, palm facing in and thumb pointing up.

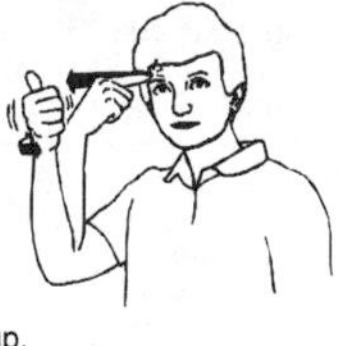

direct *v., adj.* See signs for DESCRIBE, MANAGE, ORDER, STRAIGHT[1]. Related form: **direction** *n.*

dirt *n.* Same sign used for: **ground, land, soil**

[Feeling the texture of dirt] Beginning with both *flattened O hands* in front of each side of the body, palms facing up, move the thumb of each hand smoothly across each fingertip, starting with the little fingers and ending as *A hands.*

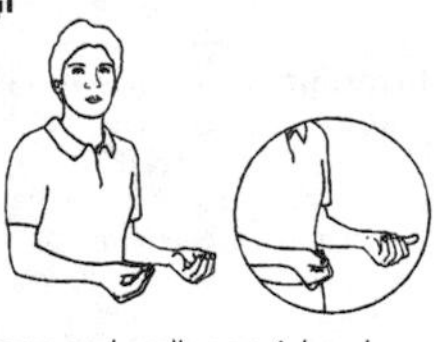

dirty *adj.* Same sign used for: **filthy, nasty, pollution, soiled.**

[Represents a pig's snout groveling in a trough] With the back of the right *curved 5 hand* under the chin, palm facing down, wiggle the fingers.

disability *n.* Same sign used for: **handicap.**

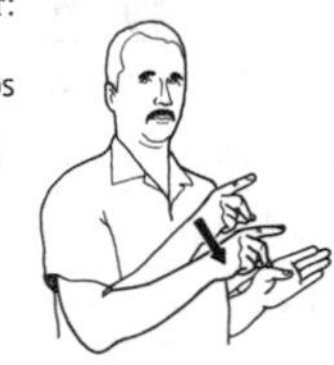

[Initialized sign] Tap the fingertips of the right *D hand*, palm down, on the base of the thumb of the left *B hand*, palm down.

disagree *v.* Same sign used for: **contrast, object.**

[**think**[1] + **opposite**] Move the extended right index finger from touching the right side of the forehead downward to meet the extended left index finger held in front of the chest. Then, beginning with both index fingers pointing toward each other, palms facing in, bring the hands apart to each side of the chest.

disappear[1] *v.* Related form: **disappearance** *n.* Same sign used for: **vanish.**

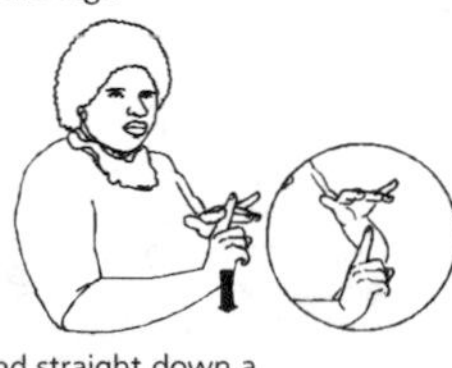

[Moving out of sight] Beginning with the extended right index finger, palm facing left, pointing up between the index and middle fingers of the left *5 hand,* palm facing down, pull the right hand straight down a short distance.

disappear[2] *v.* See sign for DISSOLVE.

disappointed *adj.* Related form: **disappointment** *n.* Same sign used for: **miss.**

[Symbolizes "Take it on the chin," a result of disappointment] Touch the extended right index finger to the chin, palm facing down.

disastrous *adj.* See sign for AWFUL.

discard *v.* See sign for ABANDON.

discharge *v.* See sign for DISMISS.

disco *n.* See sign for DANCE.

disconnect *v.* Same sign used for: **detach, loose, part from, withdraw.**

[Demonstrates releasing of a connection] Beginning with the thumb and index fingertips of each hand intersecting with each other, palms facing each other and right hand nearer the chest than the left hand, release the fingers and pull the left hand forward and the right hand back toward the right shoulder.

discount[1] *n.*

[Initialized sign showing reduction] Beginning with both *D hands* in front of the chest, right hand above the left hand, palms facing each other, and index fingers pointing forward, bring the hands toward each other.

discount[2] *v.* See sign for SUBTRACT.

discouraged *adj.* See sign for DEPRESSED[1].

discover *v.* See sign for FIND.

discuss *v.* Related form: **discussion** *n.* Same sign used for: **argument, dispute.**

[Natural gesture used when making a point] Tap the side of the extended right index finger, palm facing in, on the upturned left *open hand* with a double movement.

dish *n.*

[Shape of a dish] Beginning with the fingertips of both *curved hands* touching in front of the chest, palms facing in, move the hands away from each other in a circle, ending with the heels together close to the chest.

dismiss[1] *v.* Related form: **dismissal** *n.* Same sign used for: **discharge, lay off, pardon, parole, waive.**

[Movement seems to wipe person away] Wipe the right *open hand,* palm down, deliberately across the upturned left *open hand* from the heel off the fingertips.

dismiss[2] *v.* See sign for FIRE[2].

disorder *n.* See signs for MESSY, MIX[1].

dispute *v.* See sign for DISCUSS.

disseminate *v.* See sign for SPREAD.

dissolve *v.* Same sign used for: **disappear, evaporate, fade away, melt, perish.**

[Something in the hands seems to melt away to nothing] Beginning with both *flattened O hands* in front of the body, palms facing up, move the thumb of each hand smoothly across each fingertip, starting with the little fingers and ending as *10 hands* while moving the hands outward to each side.

distance *n.* See sign for FAR. Related form: **distant** *adj.*

distribute *v.* See signs for SELL, SPREAD.

disturb *v.* See sign for ANNOY.

divide *v.* Same sign used for: **split, split up.**

[Split something as if to divide it] Beginning with the little-finger side of the right *B hand* at an angle across the index-finger side of the left *B hand,* palms angled in opposite directions, move the hands downward and apart, ending with the hands in front of each side of the body, palms facing down.

divorce *v., n.*

[Initialized sign representing two people moving apart] Beginning with the fingertips of both the *D hands* touching in front of chest, palms facing each other and index fingers pointing up, swing the hands away from each other by

twisting the wrists, ending with the hands in front of each side of the body, palms facing forward.

do *v.* Related form: **done** *adj.* Same sign used for: **commit, conduct.**

[Hands seem to be actively doing something] Move both *C hands,* palms facing down, from side to side in front of the body with a repeated movement.

doctor *n.* Same sign used for: **medical, physician.**

[Formed at the location where one's pulse is taken] Tap the fingertips of the right *M hand,* palm facing left, on the wrist of the upturned left *open hand* with a double movement.

document *v.* See sign for PUT DOWN.

doesn't or **does not** See sign for DON'T[1].

doesn't matter See sign for ANYWAY.

dog *n.*

[Natural gesture for signaling or calling a dog] With a double movement, snap the right thumb gently off the right middle finger, palm facing up, in front of the right side of the chest.

dollar *n.* Same sign used for: **bill.**

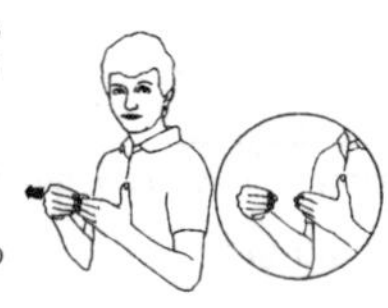

Beginning with the fingertips of the right *flattened C hand* holding the fingertips of the left *open hand,* both palms facing in, pull the right hand to the right with a double movement while changing to a *flattened O hand.*

domestic *adj.* See sign for DAILY.

dominoes *n.*
[Represents moving two dominoes end to end with each other] Bring the fingertips of both *H hands,* palms facing in, together in front of the body with a double movement.

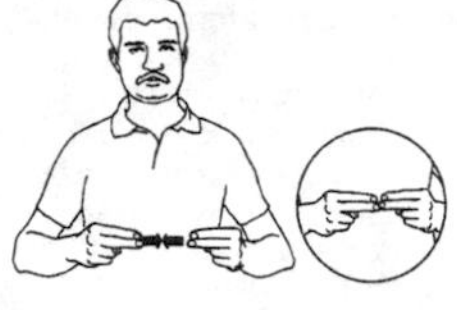

donate *v.* See signs for GIFT, GIVE. Related form: **donation** *n.*

done *adj.* See sign for FINISH[1].

donkey *n.* Same sign used for: **mule, stubborn.**
[Represents a donkey's ears] With the thumb side of the right *B hand* against the right side of the forehead, palm facing forward, bend the fingers up and down with a repeated movement.

don't[1] *contraction.* Same sign used for: **doesn't, does not.**
[Natural gesture of denial] Beginning with both *open hands* crossed in front of the chest, palms angled in opposite directions, swing the hands downward away from each other, ending at each side of the body, palms facing down.

don't[2] *contraction.* See sign for NOT.

don't believe See sign for DOUBT.

don't care Same sign used for: **don't mind, indifferent, nonchalant.**

[Outward movement indicates the negative] Beginning with the extended right index finger touching the nose, palm facing down, swing the hand forward by twisting the wrist, ending with the index finger pointing forward in front of the right shoulder.

don't know Same sign used for: **unaware, unconscious, unknown.**

[**know** + an outward gesture indicating the negative] Beginning with the fingers of the right *open hand* touching the right side of the forehead, palm facing in, swing the hand forward by twisting the wrist, ending with the fingers pointing forward in front of the right shoulder.

don't mind See sign for DON'T CARE.

door *n.*

[Shows movement of a door being opened] Beginning with the index-finger sides of both *B hands* touching in front of the chest, palms facing forward, swing the right hand back toward the right shoulder with a double movement by twisting the wrist.

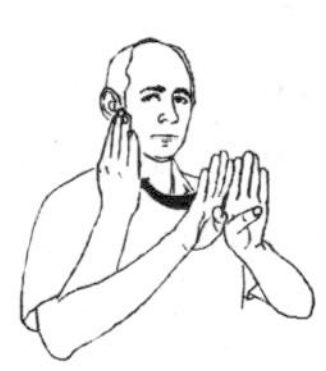

dot *n.* See sign for PERIOD.

doubt *v., n.* Same sign used for: **don't believe.**

[As if one is blind to what is doubted] Beginning with the fingers right *bent V hand* in front of the eyes, palm facing in, pull the hand downward a short distance while constricting the fingers with a single movement.

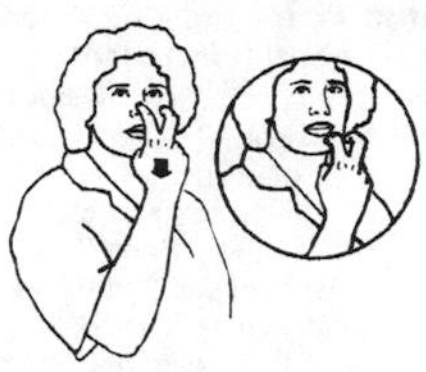

doubtful *adj.* Same sign as for DOUBT but made with a double movement.

down *adv., prep.*
[Shows direction] Move the extended right index finger downward in front of the right side of the body.

downstairs *adv.* Same sign as for DOWN but made with a double movement. Same sign used for: **downward.**

doze *v.* See signs for FALL ASLEEP, SLEEP.

draft[1] *v.* See sign for DESIGN.

draft[2] *n.* See sign for ROUGH.

drag *v.* Same sign used for: **draw, haul, pull, tow.**
[Mime pulling something] Beginning with the right *curved hand* in front of the body and the left *curved hand* somewhat forward, both palms facing up, bring the hands back toward the right side of the body while closing them into *A hands.*

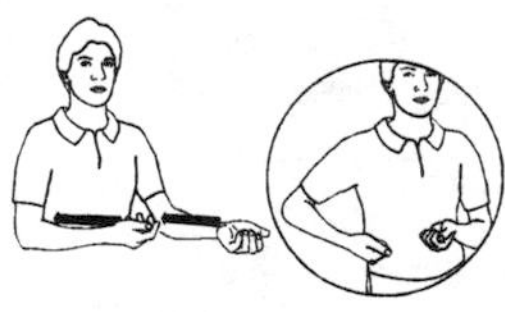

drain *adj.* See signs for ABSENT, LEAK.

drama *n.* See sign for ACT[2].

draw *v.* See signs for CHOOSE, DESIGN, DRAG, FIND.

draw back *v. phrase.* See sign for RESIGN.

drawing *n.* See signs for ART, DESIGN.

dreadful *adj.* See sign for AWFUL.

dream *v., n.* Same sign used for: **daydream.**

[Represents an image coming from the mind] Move the extended right index finger from touching the right side of the forehead, palm facing down, outward to the right while bending the finger up and down.

dress[1] *v.*

[Location of dress] Brush the thumbs of both *5 hands* downward on each side of the chest.

dress[2] *n.* See sign for CLOTHES.

dribble *v.* See sign for DRIP.

drill *n.* See sign for ALARM.

drink[1] *n., v.* Same sign used for: **beverage.**

[Mime drinking from a glass] Beginning with the thumb of the right *C hand* near the chin, palm facing left, tip the hand up toward the face, with a single movement for the noun and a double movement for the verb.

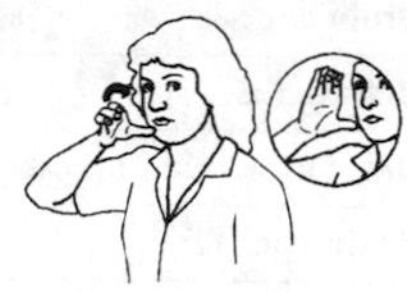

drink[2] *n.* See sign for COCKTAIL.

drip *n., v.* Same sign used for: **dribble, drop, leak.**

[Represents action of water dripping] Beginning with the right *S hand,* palm facing down, near the fingertips of the left *open hand,* palm facing down and fingers pointing right, flick the right index finger downward with a repeated movement.

drive to *v. phrase.*

[Represents continuous driving] Beginning with both *S hands* in front of the chest, palms facing in, move the hands forward with a deliberate movement.

drop[1] *v.*

[Represents dropping something held in the hands] Beginning with both *flattened O hands* in front of the body, palms facing in and fingers pointing toward each other, drop the fingers of both hands downward while opening into *5 hands,* ending with both palms facing in and fingers pointing down.

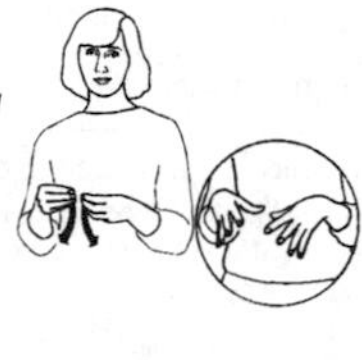

drop[2] *n.* See sign for DRIP.

drop out *v. phrase.* See sign for RESIGN.

drug *n.*
[Represents injecting a drug] Pound the little-finger side of the right *S hand,* palm facing up, with a double movement near the crook of the extended left arm.

dry *adj.* Related form: **dried** *adj.* Same sign used for: **boring.**
[Wiping the chin dry] Drag the index-finger side of the right *X hand,* palm facing down, from left to right across the chin.

due *adj.* See sign for AFFORD.

dull *adj.* See sign for BORING[1].

dumb *adj.* Same sign used for: **stupid.**
[Natural gesture] Hit the palm side of the right *A hand* against the forehead.

dump *v.* See sign for THROW.

duplicate *v., n.* See sign for COPY.

during *prep.* Same sign used for: **meanwhile, while.**
[Shows two events occurring simultaneously] Beginning with both extended index fingers in front of each side

of the body, palms facing down, move them forward in parallel arcs, ending with the index fingers angled upward.

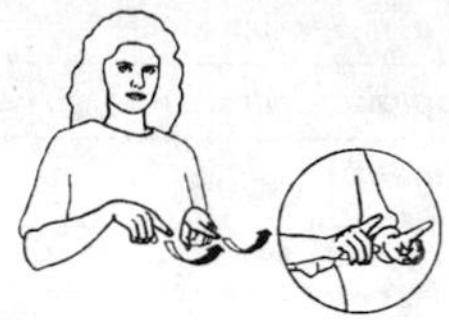

dusk *n.* See sign for DARK.

dwell *v.* See sign for LIVE.

each *adj., pron., adv.* Same sign used for: **per.**

[Emphasizes one] Bring the knuckle side of the right *10 hand* down the knuckles of the left *10 hand,* palms facing each other and thumbs pointing up.

each other *pron.* See sign for ASSOCIATE.

eager *adj.* See sign for ZEAL.

ear *n.*

[Location of an ear] Wiggle the right earlobe with the thumb and index finger of the closed right hand.

earbuds *pl. n.*

[Placing earbuds in ears] Beginning with both *G hands* in front of the body, fingers pointing toward each other, bring the hands upward to each ear.

early *adv., adj.*
[Represents a bird hopping around looking for the early worm] Push the bent middle finger of the right *5 hand* across the back of the left *open hand,* both palms facing down.

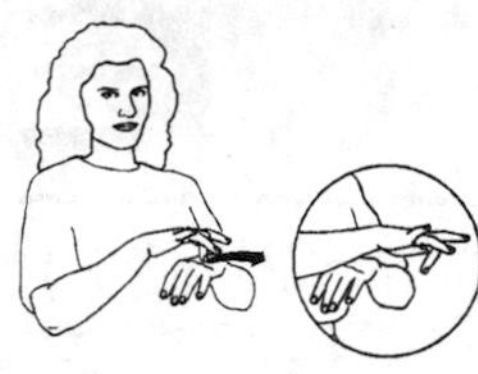

earn *v.* Same sign used for: **deserve, income, salary, wages.**
[Bringing earned money toward oneself] Bring the little-finger side of the right *curved hand,* palm facing left, across the upturned left *open hand* from fingertips to heel while changing into an *S hand.*

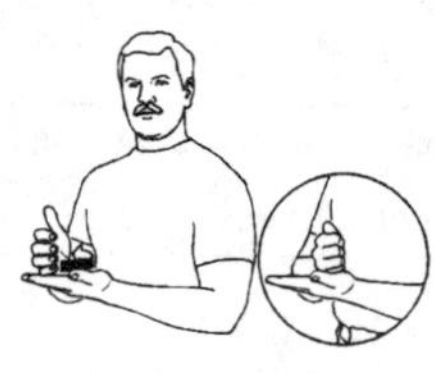

earphones *pl. n.*
[Putting on earphones] Tap the fingertips of both *curved 5 hands,* palms facing in, on each side of the head around each ear with a repeated movement.

earring *n.*
[Location of earring] Shake the right earlobe with the index finger and thumb of the right *F hand* with a repeated movement. For the plural, use the same sign but made with both hands, one at each ear.

earth *n.* Same sign used for: **geography.**

[The earth rotating on its axis] Grasp each side of the left *S hand,* palm facing down, with the bent thumb and middle finger of the right *5 hand,* palm facing down. Then rock the right hand from side to side with a double movement.

east *n., adj., adv.*

[Initialized sign showing an easterly direction on a map] Move the right *E hand*, palm facing forward, a short distance to the right in front of the right shoulder.

easy *adj.* Same sign used for: **convenient, simple.**

[The fingers are moved easily] Brush the fingertips of the right *curved hand* upward on the back of the fingertips of the left *curved hand* with a double movement, both palms facing up.

eat *v.*

[Putting food in the mouth] Bring the fingertips of the right *flattened O hand,* palm facing in, to the lips with a repeated movement.

eavesdrop *v.* See sign for LISTEN.

edit *v.* See sign for WRITE.

educate *v.* See signs for LEARN, TEACH. Related form: **education** *n.*

education *n.* Related form: **educate** *v.*

[Initialized sign **e-d** similar to sign for **teach**] Beginning with both *E hands* near each side of the head, palms facing each other, move the hands forward a short distance while changing into *D hands.*

effect *n.* See signs for ADVICE, INFLUENCE.

efficient *adj.* See sign for SKILL.

effort *n.*

[Initialized sign similar to sign for **try**] Move both *E hands* from in front of each side of the body, palms facing each other, downward and forward simultaneously in an arc.

egg *n.*

[Represents cracking eggs] Beginning with the middle-finger side of the right *H hand* across the index-finger side of the left *H hand,* palms angled toward each other, bring the hands downward and away from each other with a double movement by twisting the wrists each time.

either[1] *adj., pron., conj.* See also sign for OR. Same sign used for: **alternative, choice.**

[Shows alternative choices] Tap the fingertips of the right *V hand* with a repeated alternating movement on the fingertips of the left *V hand*, palms facing each other.

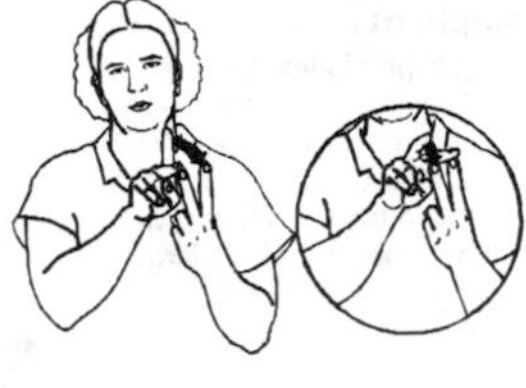

either[2] *adj., pron., conj.* See sign for WHICH.

elastic *adj.* See sign for STRETCH[1].

elect *v.* See sign for APPOINT. Related form: **election** *n.*

electric or **electrical** *adj.* Related form: **electricity** *n.* Same sign used for: **battery.**

[An electrical connection] Tap the knuckles of the index fingers of both *X hands* together, palms facing in, with a double movement.

elegant *adj.* See sign for FANCY.

elementary *adj.*

[Initialized sign similar to sign for **base**] Move the right *E hand,* palm facing forward, from side to side with a repeated movement below the left *open hand,* palm facing down and fingers pointing right, in front of the chest.

elephant *n.*

[Shape of elephant's trunk] Beginning with the back of the right *bent B hand* against the nose, palm facing down, move the hand downward and forward with a large wavy movement.

elevate *v.* See sign for ADVANCED. Related forms: **elevated** *adj.*, **elevation** *n.*

elevator *n.*

[Initialized sign showing movement of elevator] Move the index-finger side of the right *E hand,* palm facing forward, up and down with a repeated movement against the left *open hand,* palm facing right and fingers pointing up.

eligible *adj.* See sign for APPLY².

eliminate¹ *v.* Same sign used for: **abolish, abort, delete, omit, remove, repel, rid, terminate.**

[Natural gesture] Beginning with the back of the right *modified X hand,* palm facing in, touching the extended left index finger, palm facing in and finger pointing right, bring the right hand upward and outward to the right while flicking the thumb upward, forming a *10 hand.*

eliminate² *v.* See sign for SUBTRACT.

else *adj., adv.* See sign for OTHER¹.

elude *v.* See sign for AVOID.

email[1] or **e-mail** *n., v.* Same sign used for: **mail.**

[Initialized sign similar to **mail**[1]] Hold the index-finger side of the left *B hand,* palm down and fingers pointing right, against the wrist of the right *E hand* held in front of the right shoulder, palm forward. Then flick the fingers of the right *bent hand* forward across the back of the left *open hand*, both palms facing down, with a quick movement, straightening the right fingers as the right hand moves forward.

email[2] or **e-mail** *n., v.* Same sign used for: **mail.**

[Email being sent] Move the extended right index finger from pointing left in front of the chest past the palm side of the left *C hand,* palm right, ending with the right index finger pointing forward.

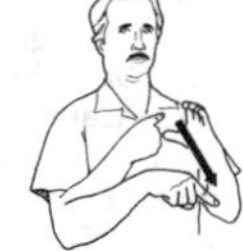

embarrass *v.* Related form: **embarrassed** *adj.*

[Indicates blood rising in the face when embarrassed] Move both *5 hands,* palms facing each other, in repeated alternating circles near each cheek.

embrace *v.* See sign for HUG.

emergency *n.*

[Initialized sign] Move the right *E hand,* palm facing forward, back and forth with a double movement in front of the right shoulder.

emotional *adj.* Related form: **emotion** *n.*
[Initialized sign showing feeling welling up in the body] Move both *E hands,* palms facing in and knuckles pointing toward each other, in repeated alternating circles on each side of the chest.

emphasis *n.* See sign for IMPRESSION.

employ *v.* See sign for INVITE.

employment *n.* See sign for WORK.

empty *adj.* Same sign used for: **available, bare, blank, vacancy, vacant, void.**
[Indicates a vacant space] Move the bent middle fingertip of the right *5 hand* across the back of the left *open hand* from the wrist to off the fingertips, both palms facing down.

enable *v.* See sign for SKILL.

encourage *v.* Related form: **encouragement** *n.* Same sign used for: **bear up.**
[Hands seem to give someone a push of encouragement] Beginning with both *open hands* outside each side of the body, palms and fingers angled forward, move the hands toward each other and forward with a double pushing movement.

end[1] *v.* Same sign used for: **complete, conclude, finish, over, wind up.**

[Demonstrates going off the end] Beginning with the little-finger side of the right *open hand,* palm facing left, across the index-finger side of the left *open hand,* palm facing in, bring the right hand deliberately down off the left fingertips.

end[2] *n.* See sign for LAST[1].

endanger *v.* See sign for DANGER.

enemy *n.* Same sign used for: **foe, opponent, rival.**

[**opposite** + **person marker**] Beginning with both extended index fingers touching in front of the chest, palms facing down, pull the hands apart to in front of each side of the chest. Then move both *open hands,* palms facing each other, downward along each side of the body.

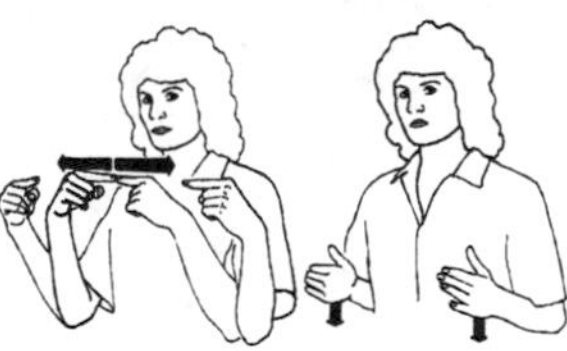

engaged *adj.* Related form: **engagement** *n.*

[Initialized sign showing the location of an engagement ring] Beginning with the right *E hand* over the left *open hand,* both palms facing down, move the right hand in a small circle and then straight down to land on the ring finger of the left hand.

enjoy *v.* Related form: **enjoyment** *n.* Same sign used for: **appreciate, leisure, like, please, pleasure.**

[Hands rub the body with pleasure] Rub the palms of both *open hands* on the chest, right hand above the left hand and fingers pointing in opposite directions, in repeated circles moving in opposite directions.

enlarge *v.* See sign for BIG.

enough *adj., pron., adv.* Same sign used for: **adequate, plenty, sufficient.**

[Represents leveling off a container filled to the top] Push the palm side of the right *open hand,* palm facing down, forward across the thumb side of the left *S hand,* palm facing in.

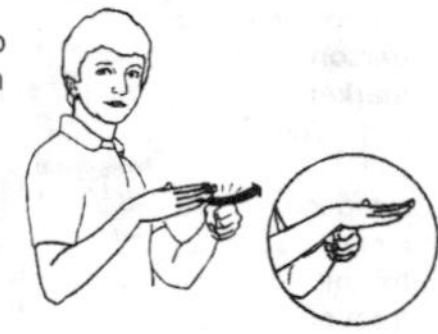

enrage *v.* See sign for ANGER.

enroll *v.* See sign for ENTER.

enter *v.* Related forms: **entrance** *n.*, **entry** *n.* Same sign used for: **enroll, immigrate, into.**

[Represents movement of entering] Move the back of the right *open hand* forward in a downward arc under the palm of the left *open hand,* both palms facing down.

enthusiastic *adj.* See sign for ZEAL.

entire *adj.* See sign for ALL.

entitle *v.* See sign for TITLE.

envelope *n.* See sign for CARD.

envy *n., v.* Related form: **envious** *adj.*

[Natural gesture used when a person envies another's possessions] Touch the teeth on the right side of the mouth with the right bent index fingertip.

equal *adj., v.* Same sign used for: **even, fair, get even.**

[Demonstrates equal level] Tap the fingertips of both bent hands, palms facing down, together in front of the chest with a double movement.

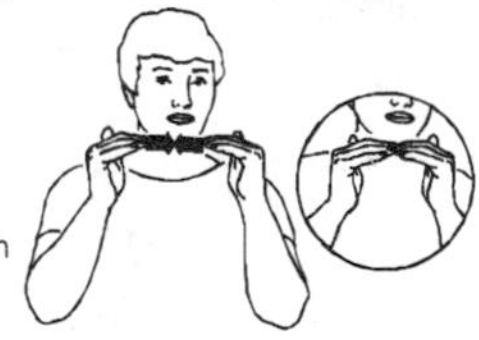

equipment *n.* Same sign used for: **device, hardware.**

[Initialized sign similar to sign for **thing**] Move the right *E hand,* palm facing up, from lying on the upturned palm of the left *open hand* to the right in a double arc.

erect *v.* See sign for SET UP.

escape *v.* See sign for RUN AWAY.

especially *adv.* See sign for SPECIAL.

essential *adj.* See sign for IMPORTANT.

establish *v.* Same sign used for: **based on, founded.**

[Represents setting something up firmly] Beginning with the right *10 hand* in front of the right shoulder, palm facing down, twist the wrist upward with a circular movement and then move the right hand straight down to land the little-finger side on the back of the left *open hand,* palm facing down.

estimate *n., v.* See signs for ARITHMETIC, GUESS, MULTIPLY, ROUGH.

eternal *adj.* See sign for FOREVER.

evade *v.* See sign for AVOID.

evaporate *v.* See sign for DISSOLVE.

even[1] *adj.* Same sign used for: **fair, level.**

[Shows things of equal level] Beginning with the fingertips of both bent hands touching in front of the chest, both palms facing down, bring the hands straight apart from each other to in front of each shoulder.

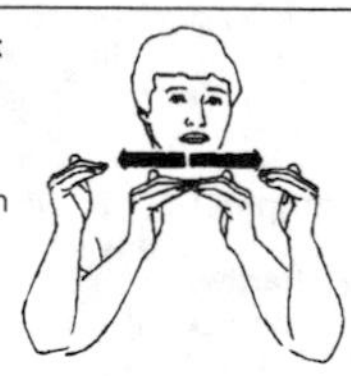

even[2] *adj., v.* See sign for EQUAL.

evening *n., adj.*

[Represents the sun low on the horizon] Tap the heel of the right *bent hand*, palm facing forward, with a double movement against the thumb side of the left *open hand* held across the chest, palm facing down.

event *n.* See sign for HAPPEN.

even though *conj.* See sign for ANYWAY.

ever *adv.* See sign for ALWAYS.

everlasting *adj.* See sign for FOREVER.

ever since *adv.* See sign for SINCE[1].

everyday *adj.* See sign for DAILY.

everything *pron.* See sign for INCLUDE.

evict *v.* See sign for ABANDON.

evidence *n.* See sign for PROOF.

evil *adj.* See sign for BAD.

exact *adj.* See sign for PRECISE.

exaggerate *v.* Same sign used for: **prolong, stretch.**
[Hands seem to stretch the truth] Beginning with the thumb side of the right *S hand,* palm facing left, against the little-finger side of the left *S hand,* palm facing right, move the right hand forward with a large wavy movement.

exalt *v.* See sign for ADVANCED. Related forms: **exalted** *adj.,* **exaltation** *n.*

examine *v.* See signs for CHECK[1], INVESTIGATE, LOOK FOR, TEST. Related form: **examination** *n.*

examination *n.* See signs for INVESTIGATE, TEST.

example *n.* See sign for SHOW[1].

exceed *v.* See signs for EXCESS, OVER.

excellent *adj.* See signs for SUPERB, WONDERFUL.

excess *n., adj.* Related form: **excessive** *adj.* Same sign used for: **exceed, massive, more than, too much.**

[Demonstrates an amount that is more than the base] Beginning with the right *bent hand* on the back of the left *bent hand,* both palms facing down, bring the right hand upward in an arc to the right.

exchange *n., v.* See sign for TRADE.

excite *v.* Related form: **excited** *adj.*, **exciting** *adj.*

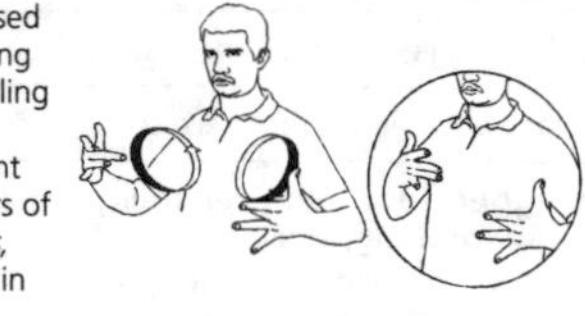

[The finger used to show feeling brings up feeling in the body] Move the bent middle fingers of both *5 hands,* palms facing in and fingers pointing toward each other, in repeated alternating circles on each side of the chest.

excuse[1] *n.*

[The hand seems to wipe away a mistake] Wipe the fingertips of the right *open hand* across the upturned left *open hand* from the heel off the fingertips.

excuse[2] *v.* See sign for FORGIVE.

excuse me Same sign as **excuse**[1] except made with a shorter double movement.

exempt *v.* See sign for SUBTRACT.

exercise[1] *n., v.* Same sign used for: **work out.**

[Mime exercising] Beginning with both *S hands* near each shoulder, palms facing each other, bring both arms up and down with a double movement.

exercise[2] *n., v.* See sign for PRACTICE.

exhausted *adj.* See sign for TIRED.

exhibit *n., v.* See sign for SHOW[2].

expand *v.* See sign for BALLOON.

expect *v.* See sign for HOPE. Related form: **expectation** *n.*

expel *v.* See signs for ABANDON, BREATH.

expensive *adj.* Same sign used for: **costly.**

[**money** + a gesture of throwing it away] Beginning with the back of the right *flattened O hand* on the upturned left *open hand,* bring the right hand upward to the right while opening into a *5 hand* in front of the right shoulder, palm facing down.

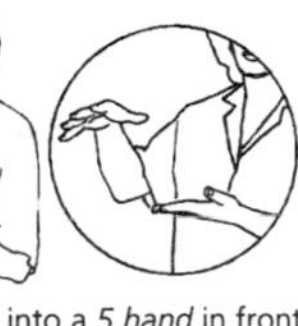

experience *n., v.* Same sign used for: **ordeal.**

[The grey sideburns of an experienced man] Beginning with the fingertips of the right *5 hand* on the right cheek, palm facing in, bring the hand outward to the right while closing the fingers into a *flattened O hand.*

expert *adj.* See signs for GOOD AT, SKILL.

explain *v.* See sign for DESCRIBE. Related form: **explanation** *n.*

expose *v.* See signs for SHOW[1], STICK[1].

expression *n.*
[Indicates the face's movement when changing expression] Move both *modified X hands,* palms facing forward, up and down with a repeated alternating movement in front of each side of the face.

external *n., adj.* See sign for OUTSIDE.

extinct *adj.* See sign for ABSENT.

extra *n.* See sign for ADD.

eye *n.*
[Location of the eye] Point the extended right index finger, palm facing in, toward the right eye with a double movement. For the plural, point to each eye.

eyeglasses *pl. n.* See sign for GLASSES.

face *n.*
[Location and shape of face] Draw a large circle around the face with the extended right index finger, palm facing in.

face to face *adj.* See sign for IN FRONT OF.

facing *adj., v.* (*pres. participle of* FACE) See sign for IN FRONT OF.

fact *n.* See sign for TRUTH.

factory *n.* See sign for MACHINE.

fade *v.* See sign for VAGUE.

fade away *v. phrase.* See sign for DISSOLVE.

fail *v.* Related form: **failure** *n.*
[Falling off the edge] Beginning with the back of the right *V hand* on the heel of the left *open hand,* palm facing up, move the right hand across the left palm and off the fingers.

fair[1] *adj.* Same sign used for: **sort of, so-so.**
[Natural gesture showing ambivalence] Rock the right *5 hand,* palm facing down, from side to side with a repeated movement in front of the right side of the body.

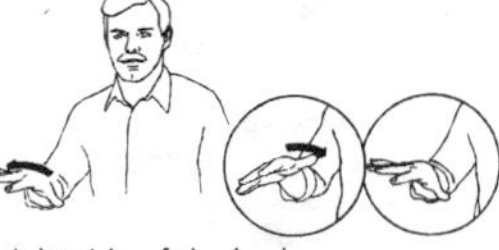

fair[2] *adj.* Related form: **fairly** *adv.*

[Initialized sign] Tap the middle finger of the right *F hand,* palm facing left, against the chin with a repeated movement.

fair[3] *adj.* See signs for EQUAL, EVEN[1].

faith *n.*

[**think** + initialized sign similar to sign for **confident**] Move the extended right index finger from touching the right side of the forehead downward while changing into an *F hand,* ending with the index finger of the right *F hand* on top of the index finger of the left *F hand* in front of the body, palms facing each other.

fake *adj.* Same sign used for: **artificial, counterfeit, pseudo, sham.**

[Indicates pushing the truth aside] Brush the extended right index finger, palm facing left, with a double movement across the tip of the nose from right to left by bending the wrist.

fall[1] *v., n.*

[Represents legs slipping out from under a person] Beginning with the fingertips of the right *V hand* pointing down, palm facing in, touching the upturned palm of the left *open hand,* flip the right hand over, ending with the back of the right *V hand* lying across the left palm.

fall[2] *n.* Same sign used for: **autumn.**

[Leaves falling from a tree] Brush the index-finger side of the right *B hand,* palm facing down, downward toward the elbow of the left forearm, held bent across the chest.

fall asleep *v. phrase.* Same sign used for: **asleep, doze.**

[Represents the head falling forward when dozing off] Beginning with the right *5 hand* in front of the face, palm facing in and fingers pointing up, bring the hand down while changing into an *A hand,* ending with the right hand, palm down, on top of the left *A hand,* palm up, in front of the body.

fall behind *v. phrase.* See sign for AVOID.

fall through *v. phrase.* See sign for BREAK DOWN.

familiar *adj.* See sign for AWARE[1].

family *n.*

[Initialized sign similar to sign for **class**] Beginning with the fingertips of both *F hands* touching in front of the chest, palms facing each other, bring the hands away from each other in outward arcs while turning the palms in, ending with the little fingers touching.

famished *adj.* See sign for HUNGRY.

famous *adj.* Related form: **fame** *n.* Same sign used for: **notorious.**

[Similar to sign for **tell**[1], except spreading the words far and wide] Beginning with both extended index fingers pointing to each side of the mouth, palms facing in, move the hands forward and outward in double arcs, ending with the index fingers pointing upward in front of each shoulder.

fancy *adj.* Same sign used for: **classical, deluxe, elegant, formal, grand, luxury.**

[The ruffles on an old-fashioned shirt] Move the thumb of the right *5 hand,* palm facing left, upward and forward in a double circular movement in the center of the chest.

fantastic *adj.* See signs for SUPERB, WONDERFUL.

far *adv., adj.* Related form: **farther** *adv., adj.* Same sign used for: **distance, distant, remote.**

[Moves to a location at a far distance] Beginning with the palm sides of both *A hands* together in front of the chest, move the right hand upward and forward in a large arc.

fare *n.* See sign for COST.

farewell *interj., n.* See sign for GOOD-BYE.

fascinating *adj.* See sign for INTEREST.

fast *adj., adv.* Same sign used for: **automatic, quick, sudden.**

[Demonstrates quickness] Beginning with both extended index fingers pointing forward in front of the body, palms facing each other, pull the hands quickly back toward the chest while constricting the index fingers into *X hands.*

fasten *v.* See signs for BELONG, STICK[1].

fat *adj.*

[Shows shape of fat body] Move both *curved 5 hands* from in front of each side of the chest, palms facing in and fingers pointing toward each other, outward in large arcs to each side of the body.

father *n.* Same sign used for: **dad, daddy, papa.**

[Formed in the male area of the head, indicating the head of the household] Tap the thumb of the right *5 hand,* palm facing left and fingers pointing up, against the middle of the forehead with a double movement.

fatigue *n.* See signs for TIRED, WEAK.

fault[1] *n.* Same sign used for: **accusation, blame.**

[Pushes blame toward another] Push the little-finger side of the right *10 hand,* palm facing left, forward and upward in an arc across the back of the left *S hand,* palm facing down.

fault[2] *n.* See sign for BURDEN.

favorite[1] *adj., n.* Related form: **favor** *v.* Same sign used for: **flavor, prefer, preference, rather, type, typical.**

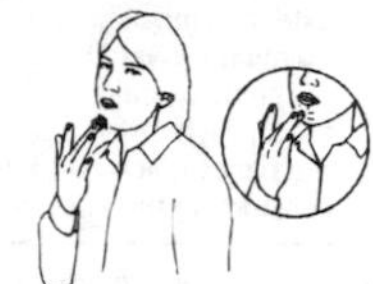

[Taste something on the finger] Touch the bent middle finger of the right *5 hand,* palm facing in, to the chin with a double movement.

favorite[2] *adj.* See sign for PARTIAL TO.

fear *n., v.* Related form: **fearful** *adj.* Same sign used for: **coward, frightened, scared.**

[Natural gesture of protecting the body from the unknown] Beginning with both *5 hands* in front of each side of the chest, palms facing in and fingers pointing toward each other, move the hands toward each other with a short double movement.

federal *adj. phrase.* See sign for GOVERNMENT.

fed up *adj. phrase.* See sign for FULL[1].

fee *n.* See sign for COST[1].

feeble *adj.* See sign for WEAK.

feed *v.* Same sign used for: **supply.**

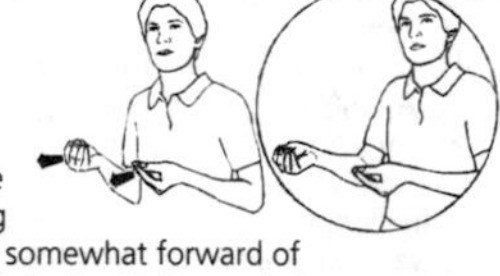

[Offering something to another] Beginning with both *flattened O hands* in front of each side of the body, palms facing up and right hand somewhat forward of the left hand, push the hands forward a short distance with a double movement.

feel *v.* Related form: **feeling** *n.* Same sign used for: **motive, sensation, sense.**

[Bent middle finger indicates feeling in sign language] Move the bent middle finger of the right *5 hand,* palm facing in, upward on the chest. Sometimes formed with a repeated movement.

fellowship *n.* See sign for ASSOCIATE.

female *n.* See sign for LADY.

fertilize *v.* See sign for CONFLICT[1].

festival *n.* See sign for CELEBRATE.

few *adj.* Same sign used for: **several.**

[A small number of items is revealed at a time] Beginning with the right *A hand* held in front of the right side of the chest, palm facing up, slowly spread out each finger from the index finger to the little finger, ending with an upturned *4 hand.*

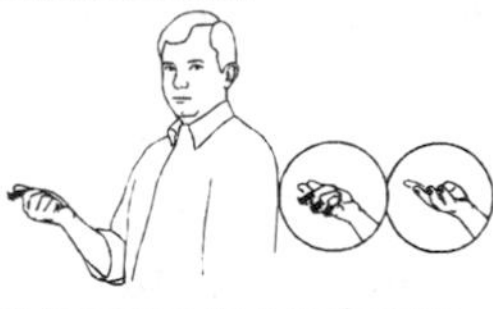

fib *v.* See sign for LIE.

field *n.* See sign for SPECIALIZE.

fierce *adj.* See sign for AWFUL.

fight[1] *n., v.* Related form: **fighting** *n.*

[Mime two people striking at each other] Beginning with both *S hands* in front of each shoulder, palms facing each other, move the hands deliberately toward each other, ending with the wrists crossed in front of the chest.

fight[2] *v.* See sign for ARGUE.

figure *n.*, *v.* See signs for ARITHMETIC, MULTIPLY.

figure out *v. phrase.* See signs for ARITHMETIC, MULTIPLY.

file[1] *v.* Same sign used for: **sort.**

[Insert something in order to file it] Slide the little-finger side of the right *B hand,* palm angled up, between the middle finger and ring finger of the left *B hand* held in front of the chest, palm facing in.

file[2] *v.* See signs for APPLY[1].

film *n.* Same sign used for: **movie, show.**

[Flicker of film on a screen] With the heel of the right *5 hand,* palm facing forward, on the heel of the left *open hand,* palm facing in, twist the right hand from side to side with a repeated movement.

filthy *adj.* See sign for DIRTY.

final *adj.* See sign for LAST[1]. Related form: **finally** *adv.*

finally *adv.* Same sign used for: **at last, succeed.**

[Moving to higher stages] Beginning with both extended index fingers pointing up near each cheek, palms facing in, twist the wrists forward, ending with the index fingers pointing up in front of each shoulder, palms facing forward.

find *v.* Same sign used for: **discover, draw.**

[Selecting something held out in the hand] Beginning with the right *curved 5 hand* inserted in palm side of the left *curved 5 hand,* palm facing right in front of the body, bring the right hand upward while closing the thumb and index finger, forming an *F hand.*

fine[1] *adj.*

[The ruffles on the front of a fine old-fashioned shirt] Beginning with the thumb of the right *5 hand* touching the chest, palm facing left, move the hand forward a short distance.

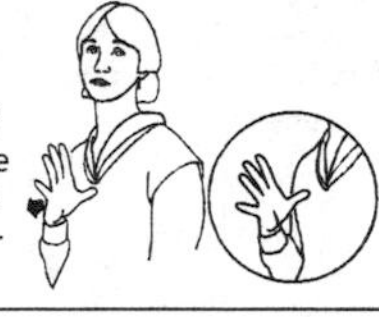

fine[2] *n.* See sign for COST.

finish[1] *v.* Same sign used for: **already, complete, done, over, then.**

[Something shaken off the hands when finished with it] Beginning with both *5 hands* in front of the chest, palms facing in and fingers pointing up, flip the hands over with a sudden movement, ending with both palms facing down and fingers pointing forward.

finish[2] *v.* See signs for BEEN THERE, END[1].

fire[1] *n.* Same sign used for: **blaze, flame.**

[Represents flames] Move both *5 hands,* palms facing up, from in front of the waist upward in front of the chest while wiggling the fingers.

fire[2] *v.* Same sign used for: **dismiss, terminate.**

[Indicates cutting a job short] Swing the back of the right *open hand,* palm facing up, across the index-finger side of the left *B hand,* palm facing in.

firm *adj.* See sign for STRICT.

first *adj., n., adv.* Same sign used for: **one dollar.**

[**one** formed with a twisting movement used for ordinal numbers] Beginning with the extended right index finger pointing up in front of the right side of the chest, palm facing forward, twist the hand, ending with the palm facing in.

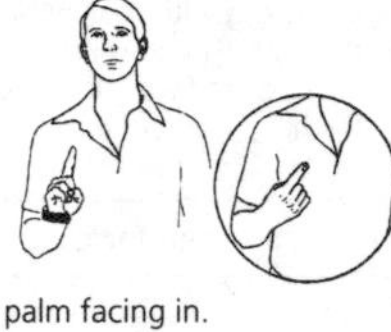

fish *n.*

[The movement of a fish in water] While touching the wrist of the right *open hand,* palm facing left, with the extended left index finger, swing the right hand back and forth with a double movement.

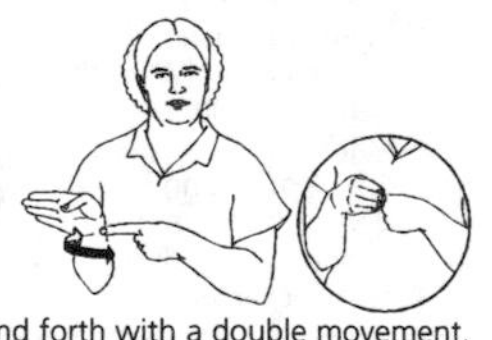

fit[1] *v.* Same sign used for: **suit.** *n.*

[Initialized sign showing that two things fit together] Beginning with the right *F hand* in front of the right shoulder, palm angled down, and the left *F hand* in front of the left side of the body, palm angled up, bring the fingertips together in front of the chest.

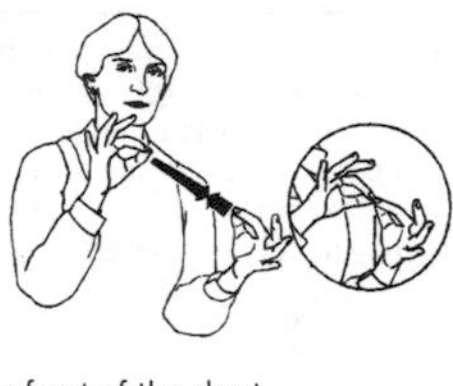

fit[2] *v., n.* See sign for MATCH.

five cents *pl. n.* See sign for NICKEL.

fix *v.* Same sign used for: **maintain, mend, repair.**

[The fingers seem to put things together] Brush the fingertips of both *flattened O hands* across each other repeatedly as the hands move up and down in opposite directions in a double movement.

flag *n.*

[Represents a waving flag] While holding the elbow of the raised right arm in the left palm, wave the right *open hand* back and forth with a repeated movement in front of the right shoulder.

flame *n.* See signs for CANDLE, FIRE.

flat *adj.*

[Shows flat surface] Beginning with the index-finger side of the right *bent hand* against the little-finger side of the left *bent hand,* both palms facing down, move the right hand forward a short distance.

flavor *n.* See sign for FAVORITE[1].

flesh *n.* See sign for SKIN.

flexible *adj.* Same sign used for: **floppy.**

[Shows something easily bent] With both *flattened O hands* in front of each side of the chest, palms facing in, bend the wrists to move the hands forward and back with an alternating repeated movement.

flip *v.* See sign for COOK.

flirt *v.* Same sign used for: **philander.**

[Represents batting one's eyelashes] Beginning with the thumbs of both *5 hands* touching in front of the chest, palms facing down and fingers pointing forward, wiggle the fingers up and down with an alternating movement.

floor *n.*

[Shows flatness of a floor's surface] Beginning with the index-finger side of both *B hands* touching in front of the waist, palms facing down and fingers pointing forward, move the hands apart to each side.

floppy *adj.* See sign for FLEXIBLE.

flower *n.*

[Holding a flower to the nose to smell it] Touch the fingertips of the right *flattened O hand,* palm facing in, first to the right side of the nose and then to the left side.

fluent *adj.* See sign for SMOOTH. Related form: **fluently** *adv.*

flunk *v. Informal.*
[Initialized sign] Strike the index-finger side of the right *F hand*, palm facing forward, against the palm of the left *open hand,* palm facing right and fingers pointing up.

fly *v.* Same sign used for: **wings.**
[Mime flapping wings to fly] Beginning with both *open hands* near each shoulder, and fingers angled outward in opposite directions, bend the wrists repeatedly, causing the hands to wave.

focus *v., n.*
[Directing one's attention] Beginning with both *B hands* near each side of the face, palms facing each other and fingers pointing up, bring the hands down while tipping the fingers downward and toward each other.

focus on *v. phrase.* See signs for ATTENTION, NARROW DOWN.

foe *n.* See sign for ENEMY.

folk *n.* See sign for PEOPLE.

follow *v.* Same sign used for: **trail.**

[One hand follows the other hand] With the knuckles of the right *10 hand,* palm facing left, near the wrist of the left *10 hand,* palm facing right, move both hands forward a short distance.

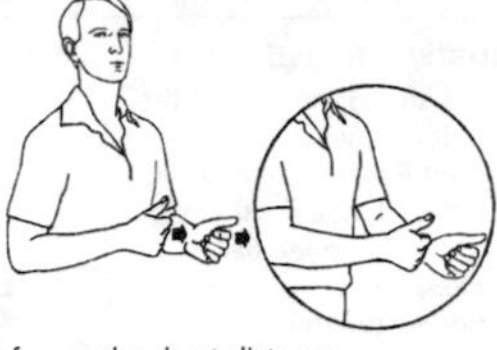

food *n.*

[Putting food in one's mouth] Bring the fingertips of the right *flattened O hand,* palm facing in, to the lips with a double movement.

fool around *v. phrase.* See sign for RUN AROUND.

foot *n.*

[Shows the length of a foot] Move the bent middle finger of the right *5 hand,* palm facing down, up and down the length of the left *open hand,* palm facing down, with a repeated movement.

football *n.*

[Represents scrimmage between two teams] Beginning with both *5 hands* in front of each side of the chest, palms facing in and fingers pointing toward each other, bring the hands together with a short double movement, interlocking the fingers of both hands each time.

for *prep.*

[Knowledge is directed for another's use] Beginning with the extended right index finger touching the right side of the forehead, palm facing down, twist the hand forward, ending with the index finger pointing forward.

forbid *v.* Same sign used for: **ban, illegal, prohibit.**

[Similar to sign for **against** to show an opposition to something] Bring the palm side of the right *L hand,* palm facing left, sharply against the palm of the left *open hand,* palm facing right and fingers pointing up.

fore *adj.* See sign for FRONT.

forecast *v.* See sign for PREDICT.

foreign *adj.*

[Initialized sign similar to sign for **country**] Move the thumb side of the right *F hand,* palm facing left, in a double circular movement near the bent left elbow.

foresee *v.* See sign for PREDICT.

forever *adv.* Same sign used for: **eternal, everlasting.**

[**always** + **still**[1]] Move the right *1 hand,* palm facing up, in a circle in front of the right side of the body. Then move the right

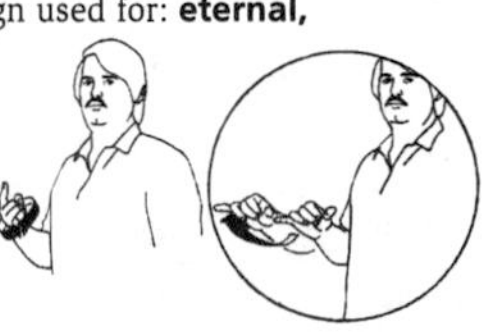

Y hand from in front of the right side of the body, palm facing down, forward and upward in an arc.

forget *v.*
[Wipes thoughts from one's memory] Wipe the fingers of the right *open hand,* fingers pointing left, across the forehead from left to right while closing into a *10 hand* near the right side of the forehead.

forgive *v.* Same sign used for: **excuse, pardon.**
[Wipes away mistake] Brush the fingertips of the right *open hand,* palm facing down, across the palm of the upturned left *open hand* from the heel off the fingertips with a double movement.

fork *n.*
[Tines of a fork] Touch the fingertips of the right *V hand,* palm facing down, on the palm of upturned left *open hand.* Then quickly turn the right hand so the palm faces the body and touch the left palm again.

form *n., v.* See sign for SHAPE.

formal *adj.* See sign for FANCY.

forsake *v.* See signs for ABANDON, IGNORE.

fortunate *adj.* See sign for LUCK.

forward *adv.* See sign for GO ON.

founded *adj.* See signs for ESTABLISH, SET UP.

fowl *n.* See sign for BIRD.

fracture *n.* Same sign used for: **break, broken.**

[**break + bone**] With a double movement, tap the back of the right bent *V hand,* palm facing up, on the back of the left *S hand*, palm facing down. Then, beginning with both *S hands* in front of the body, index fingers touching and palms facing down, move the hands away from each other while twisting the wrists with a deliberate movement, ending with the palms facing each other.

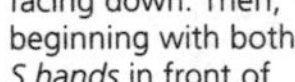

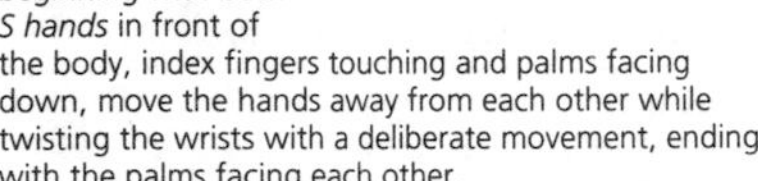

fragrance *n.* See sign for SMELL.

frank *adj.* See sign for HONEST. Related form: **frankly** *adv.*

fraternity *n.* See sign for ASSOCIATE.

freak *n., adj.* See sign for STRANGE.

free[1] *adj.* Related form: **freedom** *n.*

[Initialized sign similar to sign for **save**[1]] Beginning with both *F hands* crossed at the wrists in front of the chest, palms facing in opposite directions, twist the wrists to move the hands apart to in front of each shoulder, ending with the palms facing forward.

free[2] *adj.* See sign for SAVE[1]. Related form: **freedom** *n.*

freeway *n.* See sign for HIGHWAY.

freeze *v.* Same sign used for: **frost, frozen, ice, rigid, solidify.**

[Shows things hardening when frozen] Beginning with both *5 hands* in front of each side of the body, palms facing down and fingers pointing forward, pull the hands back toward the body while constricting the fingers.

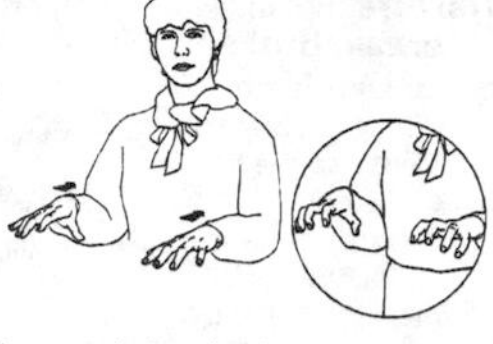

frequently *adv.* See sign for OFTEN.

Friday *n.*

[Initialized sign] Move the right *F hand,* palm facing in, in a repeated circle in front of the right shoulder.

friend *n.* Same sign used for: **comrade, pal.**

[Indicates the entwined lives of friends who have a close relationship] Hook the bent right index finger, palm facing down, over the bent left index finger, palm facing up. Then repeat, reversing the position of the hands.

friendly *adj.* Same sign used for: **cheerful, pleasant.**

[The face crinkling with smiles] With both *5 hands* near the cheeks, palms facing back, wiggle the fingers.

fright *n.* See sign for AFRAID. Related form: **frightened** *adj.*

frightened *adj.* See sign for FEAR.

frigid *adj.* See sign for COLD[2].

frog *n.*
Beginning with the index-finger side of the right *S hand* against the chin, palm facing left, flick the index and middle fingers outward to the left with a double movement.

from *prep.*
[Moving from another location] Beginning with the knuckle of the right *X hand,* palm facing in, touching the extended left index finger, palm facing right and finger pointing up, pull the right hand back toward the chest.

from now on *adv. phrase.* See sign for AFTER[1].

front *n., adj.* Same sign used for: **fore.**
[Location in front of the person] Move the right *open hand,* palm facing in and fingers pointing left, straight down from in front of the face to in front of the chest.

frost *v.* See sign for FREEZE.

frozen *adj.* See sign for FREEZE.

fruit *n.*

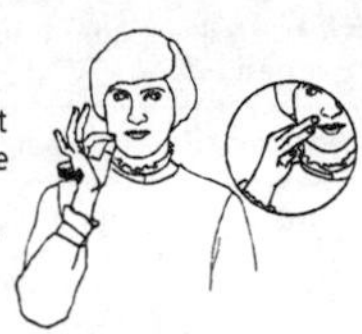

[Initialized sign] Beginning with the fingertips of the right *F hand* on the right side of the chin, palm facing left, twist the hand forward with a double movement, ending with the palm facing in.

frustrate *v.* Related form: **frustration** *n.*

[Facing a wall of opposition] Bring the back of the right *B hand,* palm facing forward, back against the mouth with a double movement or, sometimes, a single movement.

fry *v.* See sign for COOK.

fuel *n.* See sign for GAS.

full[1] *adj.* Same sign used for: **fed up, stuffed.**

[Represents feeling full] Move the right *B hand,* palm facing down, from the center of the chest upward with a deliberate movement, ending with back of the right fingers under the chin.

full[2] *adj.* Same sign used for: **complete.** Related form: **filled** *adj.*

[Leveling off something that is full] Slide the palm of the right *open hand,* palm facing down, from right to left across the index-finger side of the left *S hand,* palm facing right.

fume *n., v.* See sign for SMELL.

fun *n.*

[The nose wrinkles when laughing] Bring the fingers of the right *H hand* from near the nose downward, ending with the fingers of the right *H hand* across the fingers of the left *H hand* in front of the chest, both palms facing down.

fund *n.* See signs for MONEY, SUPPORT.

funeral *n.*

[Represents a procession following a casket] Beginning with both *V hands* in front of the chest, right hand closer to the chest than the left hand and both palms facing forward, move the hands forward simultaneously in a double arc.

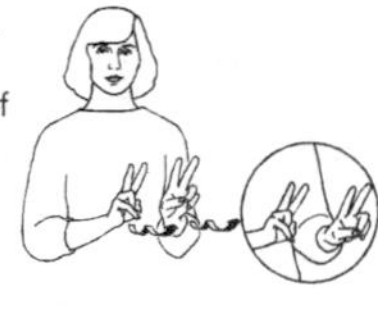

funny *adj.* Same sign used for: **amuse, humor.**

[The sign for **fun** moving toward something funny] With a double movement, brush the nose with the fingertips of the right *U hand,* palm facing in and thumb extended, bending the fingers of the *U hand* back toward the palm each time.

furniture *n.*

[Initialized sign] Move the right *F hand,* palm facing forward, from side to side in front of the right side of the chest with a repeated movement.

fury *adj.* See sign for ANGER.

future *n.*

[Hand moves forward into the future] Move the right *open hand,* palm facing left and fingers pointing up, from near the right cheek forward in a double arc.

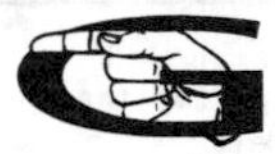

gab *v., n. Informal.* See sign for BLAB.

gain *v., n.* See sign for INCREASE.

gala *adj., n.* See signs for CELEBRATE, DANCE.

gamble *n., v.* See sign for BET.

game *n.*
[Represents opposing teams sparring] Bring the knuckles of both *10 hands,* palms facing in, against each other with a double movement in front of the chest.

gap *n.* See sign for BETWEEN.

garage *n.*
[Represents a car moving into a garage] Move the right *3 hand,* palm facing left, forward with a short repeated movement under the palm of the left *open hand,* palm facing down and fingers pointing right.

garbled *adj.* See sign for MESSY.

gas *n.* Alternate form: **gasoline.** Same sign used for: **fuel.**
[Mime pouring gas into the gas tank of a vehicle] Tap the extended thumb of the right *10 hand,* palm facing forward, downward with a repeated small movement into the thumb-side opening of the left *S hand.*

gather[1] *v.* See also sign for ATTEND. Same sign used for: **assemble, get together, go to.**

[Represents people coming together] Beginning with both *5 hands* in front of each shoulder, palms angled forward, bring the hands forward toward each other, ending with the palms facing down.

gather[2] *v.* See sign for COLLECT.

gay[1] *adj., n.* Same sign used for: **homosexual, queer** (*Slang, disparaging and offensive*).

[Initialized sign] Bring the fingertips of the right *G hand,* palm facing in, back to touch the chin with a double movement.

gay[2] *adj.* See sign for HAPPY.

general[1] *adj.* Same sign used for: **broad.**

[Hands open up broadly] Beginning with both *open hands* in front of the chest, fingers angled toward each other, swing the fingers away from each other, ending with the fingers angled outward in front of each side of the body.

general[2] *adj.* See sign for WIDE.

general[3] *n.* See sign for CAPTAIN.

generous *adj.* See sign for KIND[1].

gentle *adj.* See signs for KIND[1], POLITE, SOFT, SWEET.

genuine *adj.* See sign for REAL.

geography *n.* See sign for EARTH.

get *v.* Same sign used for: **acquire, attain, obtain, receive.**

[Reaching for something and bringing it to oneself] Beginning with both *curved 5 hands* in front of the chest, right hand above the left and palms facing in opposite directions, bring the hands back toward the chest while closing into *S hands,* ending with the little-finger side of the right hand on the index-finger side of the left hand.

get along *v. phrase.* See sign for GO ON.

get away *v. phrase.* See signs for AVOID, RUN AWAY.

get even *v. phrase.* See signs for EQUAL, REVENGE.

get together *v. phrase.* See sign for GATHER[1].

get up *v. phrase.* See sign for RAISE[1].

gift *n.* Same sign used for: **award, charity, contribution, donation, grant, present, reward, tribute.**

[Presenting something to another] Move both *X hands* from in front of the body, palms facing each other, forward in simultaneous arcs.

girl *n.*

[Formed in the female area of the head] Move the thumb of the right *A hand,* palm facing left, downward on the right cheek to the right side of the chin.

give *v.* Same sign used for: **contribute, donate, grant, present, provide.**

[Presenting something to another] Move the right *X hand* from in front of the right side of the chest, palm facing left, forward in a large arc.

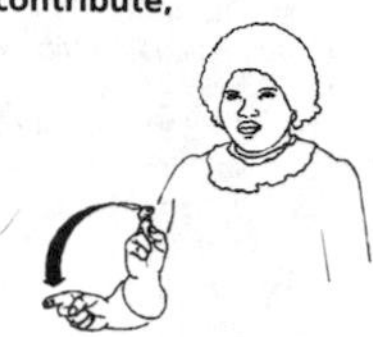

glad *adj.* See sign for HAPPY.

glass[1] *n.*

[Shows porcelain on teeth] Tap the fingertip of the right bent index finger against the front teeth with a repeated movement.

glass[2] *n.* See sign for BOTTLE.

glasses *n.* Same sign used for: **eyeglasses.**

[Shape and location of eyeglasses] Tap the thumbs of both *modified C hands,* palms facing each other, near the outside corner of each eye with a repeated movement.

glitter *v., n.* See sign for SHINY.

glossy *adj.* See sign for SHINY.

glove *n.*
[Represents pulling on a glove] Pull the right *5 hand,* palm facing down, from the fingers up the length of the back of the left *5 hand,* palm facing down. To indicate the plural, repeat with the other hand.

glow *v., n.* See signs for CANDLE, SHINY.

glue *n., v.*
[Initialized sign seeming to squeeze glue on paper] Move the fingertips of the right *G hand,* palm and fingers facing down, in a circular movement over the upturned left *open hand.*

go *v.* Same sign used for: **depart, go away, leave.**
[Represents something getting smaller as it disappears into the distance] Beginning with the *flattened C hand* in front of the right shoulder, fingers pointing left, move the hand quickly to the right while closing the fingers into a *flattened O hand.*

go ahead *v. phrase.* See sign for GO ON.

goal *n.* Same sign used for: **aim, ambitious, objective, target.**
[Indicates directing something toward something else] Move the extended right index finger from touching the right side of the forehead, palm facing down, forward

to point toward the extended left index finger held in front of the face, palm facing forward and finger angled up.

go by train *v. phrase.* See sign for TRAIN.

God *n.*

[Indicates the spirit of God moving down from above] Move the right *B hand,* palm facing left and fingers angled upward, from above the head downward in front of the face in an inward arc.

gold *n., adj.* Same sign used for: **golden.**

[Shows a gold earring + **yellow**] With the thumb, index finger, and little finger of the right hand extended, palm facing in, touch the index finger near the right ear. Then bring the right hand downward and forward with a shaking movement while turning the wrist forward and changing into a *Y hand.*

golden *adj.* See sign for GOLD. Shared idea of yellow color.

gone *v., adj.* See signs for ABSENT

good *adj.* Same sign used for: **well.**

[Presents something good for inspection] Beginning with the fingertips of the right *open hand* near the mouth, palm facing in and fingers pointing up, bring the hand downward, ending with the back of the right hand across the palm of the left *open hand,* both palms facing up.

good at Same sign used for: **expert, proficient.**

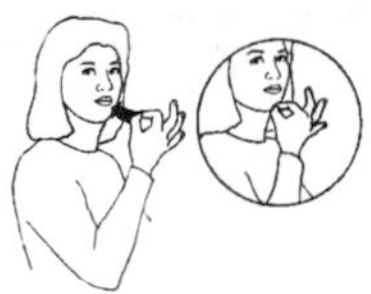

[Similar to sign for **adroit**] Bring the fingertips of the right *F hand,* palm facing in, back against the chin.

good-bye *interj., n.* Same sign used for: **bye, farewell.**

[Natural gesture for waving good-bye] Beginning with the right *open hand* in front of the right shoulder, palm facing forward and fingers pointing up, bend the fingers up and down with a repeated movement.

good-looking *adj.* See sign for LOOKS.

go on *v. phrase.* Same sign used for: **all along, continue, forward, get along, go ahead, onward, proceed.**

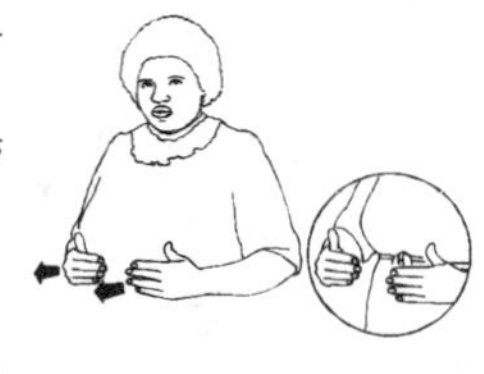

[Shows shoving something along ahead of oneself] Beginning with both *open hands* in front of the body, palms facing in and fingers pointing toward each other, move the hands forward a short distance simultaneously.

go out *v. phrase.* See sign for OUT.

go smoothly *v. phrase.* See sign for SMOOTH.

gossip[1] *n., v.* Same sign used for: **rumor.**

[Represents mouths opening and closing repeatedly] Move both *G hands,* palms facing each other, in a flat circular movement in front of the chest while pinching the index finger and thumb of each hand together with a repeated movement.

gossip[2] *n., v.* See sign for BLAB.

go to *v. phrase.* See signs for ATTEND, GATHER[1].

govern *v.* See sign for MANAGE.

government *n.* Same sign for: **federal**.

[Indicates the head, one in authority] Beginning with the extended right index finger pointing upward near the right side of the head, palm facing forward, twist the wrist to touch the finger to the right temple.

gracious *adj.* See sign for KIND[1].

grand *adj.* See signs for FANCY, LARGE.

grandfather *n.* Alternate form: **grandpa** (*informal*).

[**man** + moving forward one generation] Beginning with the thumb of the right *A hand* touching the forehead, palm facing left, bring the hand downward while opening into a *curved 5 hand* in front of the face, palm angled up.

grandma *n. Informal.* See sign for GRANDMOTHER.

grandmother *n.* Alternate form: **grandma** (*informal*).

[**girl** + moving forward one generation] Beginning with the thumb of the right *A hand* touching the chin, palm facing left, bring the hand downward while opening into a *curved 5 hand* in front of the chest, palm facing up.

grandpa *n. Informal.* See sign for GRANDFATHER.

grant *n., v.* See signs for GIFT, GIVE, LET.

graph *n.* See sign for SCHEDULE[1].

grass *n.*

[Blades of grass] Push the heel of the right *curved 5 hand,* palm facing up, upward a short distance on the chin.

grave *n., adj.* See signs for BURY, SAD.

gravy *n.* Same sign used for: **grease, syrup.**

[Represents dripping gravy] Beginning with the extended thumb and index finger of the right *G hand* grasping the little-finger side of the left *open hand,* both palms facing in, bring the right hand downward with a double movement while closing the index finger to the thumb each time.

gray *adj.*

[Suggests the blending of black and white] Beginning with both *5 hands* in front of the chest, fingers pointing toward each other and palms facing in, move the hands forward and back in opposite directions, lightly brushing fingertips as the hands pass each other.

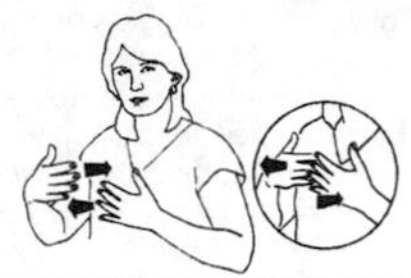

grease *n.* See sign for GRAVY. Related form: **greasy** *adj.*

great *adj.* See signs for LARGE, WONDERFUL.

greedy *adj.* Same sign used for: **covetous, niggardly, possess, selfish, thrifty, tight.**

[Clutching a prized possession] Beginning with the right *curved 5 hand* in front of the chin, palm facing in, bring the hand downward with either a single or double movement while closing the hand into an *S hand.*

green *adj.*

[Initialized sign] Twist the right *G hand,* palm facing left, back and forward with a small repeated movement in front of the right shoulder.

greet *v.* See signs for INVITE, MEET.

grievance *n.* See sign for PROTEST[1].

grin *v., n.* See sign for SMILE.

grind *v.* See sign for CHEW.

grip *n., v.* See sign for HOLD[1].

gripe *v.* See sign for COMPLAIN.

gross *adj.* See sign for PROFIT.

ground *n.* See sign for DIRT.

group[1] *n.*
[Initialized sign similar to sign for **class**] Beginning with both *G hands* in front of the chest, palms facing each other, bring the hands away from each other in outward arcs while turning the palms in, ending with the little fingers near each other.

group[2] *n.* See sign for CLASS.

grow *v.* Same sign used for: **sprout.**
[Represents a plant coming up through the soil] Bring the right *flattened O hand,* palm facing in, up through the left *C hand,* palm facing in and fingers pointing right, while spreading the right fingers into a *5 hand.*

grow up *v. phrase.* Same sign used for: **raise, rear.**
[Shows height as one grows] Bring the right *open hand,* palm facing down and fingers pointing left, from in front of the chest upward.

grumble *v.* See sign for COMPLAIN.

guarantee *n., v.* See sign for STAMP[2].

guess *v., n.* Same sign used for: **assume, estimate.**
[Hand seems to snatch at an idea as it passes the face] Move the right *C hand,* palm facing left, from near the

right side of the forehead in a quick downward arc in front of the face while closing into an *S hand,* ending with the palm facing down by the left side of the head.

guide *v.* See sign for LEAD.

guilt *n.* Related form: **guilty** *adj.*
[Initialized sign formed near the heart] Bring the thumb side of the right *G hand,* palm facing left, back against the left side of the chest.

gum *n.* See sign for CHEWING GUM.

gun *n.* Same sign used for: **pistol.**
[Demonstrates pulling back the hammer on a pointed gun] With the index finger of the right *L hand* pointing forward in front of the right side of the body, palm facing left, wiggle the thumb up and down with a repeated movement.

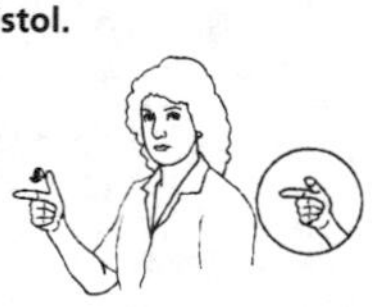

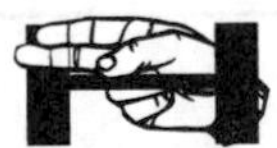

habit *n.* Same sign used for: **accustomed to.**

[Symbolizes being bound by tradition] With the heel of the right *S hand* across the wrist of the left *S hand,* both palms facing down, move the hands down simultaneously in front of the chest.

had *v.* See sign for HAVE.

hair *n.*

[Location of hair] Hold a strand of hair with the thumb and forefinger of the right *F hand,* palm facing left, and shake it with a repeated movement.

haircut[1] *n.*

[Mime cutting one's hair] Move the right *V hand,* palm facing left and fingers pointing up, from near the right cheek back to near the right ear while opening and closing the index and middle fingers with a double movement.

haircut[2] *n.* See sign for CUT[1].

half *adj.* See sign for ONE HALF.

hall *n.* Alternate form: **hallway.** Same sign used for: **corridor.**

[Shape of a hallway] Move both *open hands,* palms

facing each other and fingers pointing up, from in front of each shoulder straight forward.

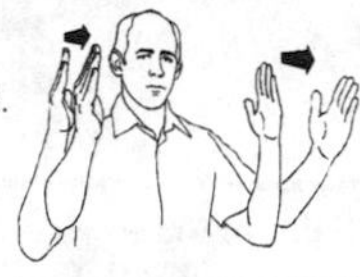

halt *v.* See signs for HOLD[2], STOP[1].

hamburger *n.*
[Mime making a hamburger patty] Clasp the right *curved hand,* palm facing down, across the upturned left *curved hand.* Then flip the hands over and repeat with the left hand on top.

handicap *n.* See sign for DISABILITY.

handle *v.* See signs for MANAGE, PIPE[1].

hands *pl. n.*
[Location of one's hands] Beginning with the little-finger side of the right *B hand* at an angle on the thumb side of the left *B hand,* palms facing in opposite directions, bring the right hand down and under the left hand in order to exchange positions. Repeat the movement with the left hand.

hands off *adj.* See sign for NOT RESPONSIBLE.

handsome *adj.* See sign for LOOKS.

handy *adj.* See sign for SKILL.

happen *v.* Same sign used for: **accident, event, incident, occur, occurrence.**
Beginning with both extended index fingers in front of the body, palms facing up and fingers pointing forward,

flip the hands over toward each other, ending with the palms facing down.

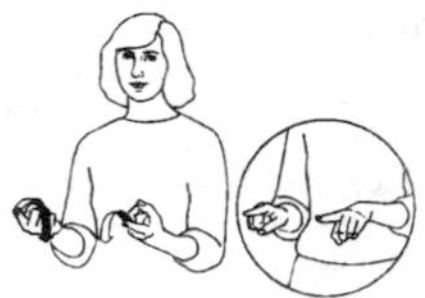

happy *adj.* Same sign used for: **cheer, cheerful, delighted, gay, glad, jolly, joy, merry.**

[Represents joy rising in the body] Brush the fingers of the right *open hand,* palm facing in and fingers pointing left, upward in a repeated circular movement on the chest.

harassment *n.* See sign for DANGER.

hard[1] *adj.* Same sign used for: **solid.**

[Indicates a hard surface] Strike the little-finger side of the right *bent V hand* sharply against the index-finger side of the left *bent V hand,* palms facing in opposite directions.

hard[2] *adj.* See sign for DIFFICULT.

hardly *adv.* See sign for ANYWAY.

hardware *n.* See sign for EQUIPMENT.

harm *v.* See signs for DANGER, HURT.

has *v.* See sign for HAVE.

hassle *v.* See sign for HURRY.

haste *n.* See sign for HURRY.

hat *n.*

[Location of a hat on one's head] Pat the top of the head with the fingers of the right *open hand,* palm facing down, with a double movement.

hate *v.* Same sign used for: **despise, detest.**

[The fingers flick away something distasteful] Beginning with both *8 hands* in front of the chest, palms facing each other, flick the middle fingers forward, changing into *5 hands.*

haul *v.* See sign for DRAG.

have *v.* Same sign used for: **had, has.**

[Brings something toward oneself] Bring the fingertips of both *bent hands,* palms facing in, back to touch each side of the chest.

have to *auxiliary.* See sign for MUST.

hazard *n.* See sign for DANGER.

hazy *adj.* See sign for VAGUE.

he *pron.* Same sign used for: **her, him, it, she.**

[Directional sign toward another] Point the extended right index finger, palm facing down, outward to the right or in the direction of the referent.

head[1] *n.*
[Location of the head] Touch the fingertips of the right *bent hand,* palm facing down, first to the right side of the forehead and then to the right side of the chin.

head[2] *v.* See sign for LEAD.

headache *n.* Same sign used for: **migraine.**
[Location of a headache] With both extended index fingers pointing toward each other in front of the forehead, palms facing down, jab them toward each other with a double movement.

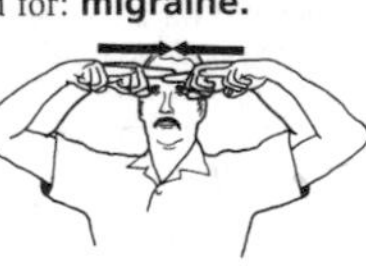

heal *v.* See sign for WELL[1].

healthy *adj.* See sign for WELL[1].

heap *n.* See sign for AMOUNT.

hear *v.* Related form: **hearing** *n.* Same sign used for: **sound.**
[Location of the organ of hearing] Bring the extended right index finger to the right ear.

heart *n.*

[Location and action of a heartbeat] Tap the bent middle finger of the right *5 hand,* palm facing in, with a repeated movement on the left side of the chest.

heat *adj.* See sign for HOT.

heaven *n.*

[Location of heaven] Beginning with both *open hands* in front of each shoulder, palms facing each other and fingers angled up, bring the hands upward toward each other, passing the right hand forward under the left *open hand,* both palms facing down, as the hands meet above the head.

heavy *adj.*

[The hands seem to be weighted down with something heavy] Beginning with both *curved 5 hands* in front of each side of the chest, palms facing up, move the hands downward a short distance.

height[1] *n.*

[Indicates the top of oneself] Tap the extended right index finger, palm facing up, on the top of the head with a double movement.

height[2] *n.* See sign for TALL[2].

hello *interj., n.*

[Natural gesture for a salute to greet someone] Beginning with the fingertips of the right *B hand* near the right side of the forehead, palm angled forward, bring the hand forward with a deliberate movement.

help *v., n.* Same sign used for: **aid, assist.**

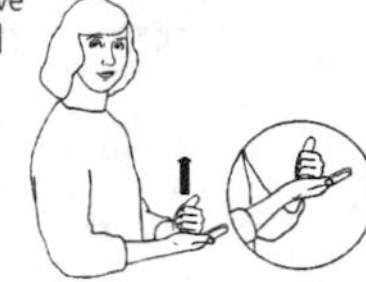

[The lower hand seems to give assistance to the other hand] With the little-finger side of the left *A hand* in the upturned right *open hand,* move both hands upward in front of the chest.

her or **hers** *pron.* See signs for HE, HIS.

here *adv., n.* Same sign used for: **present.**

[Indicates a location near oneself] Beginning with both *curved hands* in front of each side of the body, palms facing up, move the hands toward each other in repeated flat circles.

herself *pron.* See signs for HIMSELF, ITSELF.

hide *v.* Same sign used for: **conceal, mystery.**

[**secret** + a gesture putting something under the other hand as if to hide it] Move the thumb of the right *A hand,* palm facing left, from near the mouth downward in an arc to under the left *curved hand* held in front of the chest, palm facing down.

high *adj., adv.* Same sign used for: **altitude.**

[Initialized sign showing a location at a higher elevation] Move the right *H hand,* palm facing left and fingers pointing forward, from in front of the right side of the chest upward to near the right side of the head.

higher *adj.* See sign for ADVANCED.

highway *n.* Same sign used for: **freeway.**

[Initialized sign representing two streams of traffic going in opposite directions] Beginning with both *H hands* held in front of each side of the chest, palms facing down and fingers pointing toward each other, move the hands past each other toward the opposite sides of the chest with a repeated movement.

him *pron.* See sign for HE.

himself *pron.* See also sign for ITSELF. Same sign used for: **herself, itself.**

[Directional sign toward the person you are referring to] Push the extended thumb of the right *10 hand,* palm facing left, forward with a short double movement in front of the right side of the body.

hinder *v.* See sign for PREVENT.

hire *v.* See sign for INVITE.

his *pron.* Same sign used for: **her, hers, its.**

[Directional sign toward the person referred to] Push the right *open hand,* palm facing forward, at an angle forward in front of the right side of the body.

hit *v.* Same sign used for: **attack, impact, strike.**

[Demonstrates action of hitting] Strike the knuckles of the right *A hand,* palm facing in, against the extended left index finger held up in front of the chest, palm facing right.

hold[1] *v.* Same sign used for: **grip.**

[The hands seem to hold something securely] Beginning with the little-finger side of the right *C hand* on the index-finger side of the left *C hand,* both palms facing in, move the hands in toward the chest while closing the fingers of both hands into *S hands.*

hold[2] or **hold on** *v.* or *v. phrase.* Same sign used for: **halt, pause, stall, suspend.**

[One hand seems to suspend the other] With the index fingers of both *X hands* hooked together, palms facing down, pull both hands upward.

hold up *v. phrase.* See sign for ROB.

hole *n.*

[Shape of a hole] Move the extended right index finger, palm facing back and fingers pointing down, in a large circle around the index-finger side of the left *C hand,* palm facing down.

holiday *n.*

[Gesture often used when one is carefree] Tap the thumbs of both *5 hands* near each armpit, palms facing each other and fingers pointing forward, with a double movement.

home *n., adv.*

[A modification of the signs **eat** and **sleep** indicating that a home is a place where you eat and sleep] Touch the fingertips of the right *flattened O hand* first to the right side of the chin, palm facing down, and then to the right cheek.

homosexual *adj., n.* See sign for GAY[1].

honest *adj.* Related forms: **honestly** *adv.*, **honesty** *n.* Same sign used for: **frank, frankly, sure.**

[Initialized sign similar to sign for **clean**] Slide the extended fingers of the right *H hand,* palm facing left, forward from the heel to the fingers of the upturned left *open hand.*

hook up *v. phrase.* See sign for BELONG[1].

hope *v., n.* Same sign used for: **expect, expectation.**

[The hands seem to compare a thought with the anticipated future] Beginning with the right *open hand* near the right side of the head, palm angled left and fingers pointed up, and the left *open hand* in front of the chest, palm facing right and fingers pointing up, bend the fingers toward each other with a double movement.

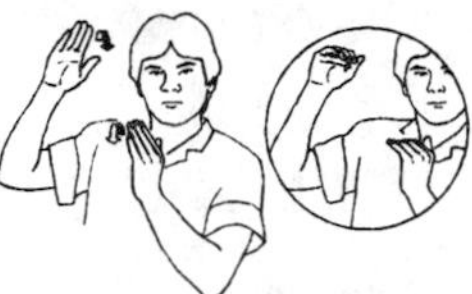

horde *n.* See sign for AUDIENCE.

horns *pl. n.* See sign for PRESIDENT.

horrible *adj.* See sign for AWFUL.

horse *n.*

[Represents a horse's ears] With the extended thumb of the right *U hand* against the right side of the forehead, palm facing forward, bend the fingers of the *U hand* up and down with a double movement.

hospital *n.*

[Initialized sign following the shape of a cross, symbolic of the American Red Cross, a health-care organization] Bring the fingertips of the right *H hand,* palm facing right, first downward a short distance on the upper left arm and then across from back to front.

host *v.* See signs for LEAD, SERVE.

hot *adj.* Same sign used for: **heat.**

[Hand seems to take something hot from the mouth and throw it away] Beginning with the right *curved 5 hand* in front of the mouth, palm facing in, twist the wrist forward with a deliberate movement while moving the hand downward a short distance.

hotel *n.*

[Initialized sign] Place the fingers of the right *H hand,* palm facing in and fingers pointing left, on the back of the extended left index finger, palm facing in and index finger pointing up in front of the chest.

hour *n.*

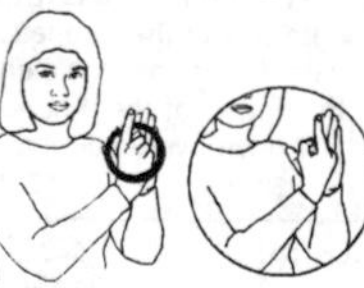

[Shows minute hand moving 60 minutes around a clock] With the right index finger extended, palm facing left, move the palm side of the right hand in a circle on the palm of the left *open hand,* palm facing right, while twisting the wrist, ending with the right palm facing in.

house *n.*

[Shape of house's roof and walls] Beginning with the fingertips of both *open hands* touching in front of the neck, palms angled toward each other, bring the hands at an downward angle outward to in front of each shoulder and then straight down, ending with the fingers pointing up and the palms facing each other.

how *adv., conj.*
[Similar to gesture used with a shrug to indicate not knowing something] Beginning with the knuckles of both *curved hands* touching in front of the chest, palms facing down, twist the hands upward and forward, ending with the fingers together pointing up and the palms facing up.

however *adv.* See signs for ANYWAY, BUT.

how many See sign for HOW MUCH.

how much Same sign used for: **how many.**
[An abbreviated form] Beginning with the right *S hand* in front of the right side of the chest, palm facing up, flick the fingers open quickly into a *5 hand.*

hug *v.* Same sign used for: **affection, affectionate, embrace.**
[Mime hugging someone] With the arms of both *S hands* crossed at the wrists, palms facing in, pull the arms back against the chest with a double movement.

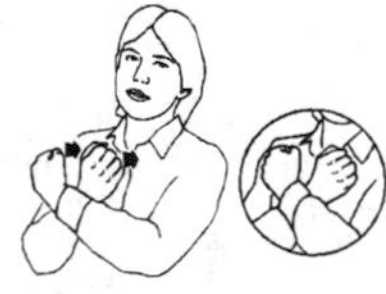

humid *adj.* See sign for WET.

humor *n.* See sign for FUNNY.

hungry *adj.* Same sign used for: **appetite, crave, famished, starved, yearn.** Related form: **hunger** *n.*

[Shows passage to an empty stomach] Beginning with the fingertips of the right *C hand* touching the center of the chest, palm facing in, move the hand downward a short distance.

hunt for *v. phrase.* See sign for LOOK FOR.

hurry *v., n.* Same sign used for: **hassle, haste, hustle, rush, urgent.**

[Initialized sign showing hurried movement] Beginning with both *H hands* in front of each side of the body, palms facing each other, move the hands up and down with a quick short repeated movement, moving the hands slightly forward each time.

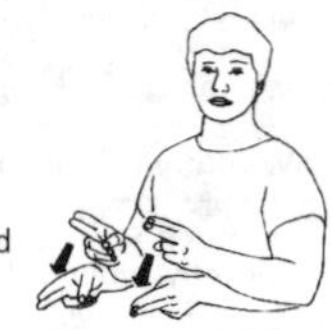

hurt *v., n.* See also signs for PAIN. Same sign used for: **ache, harm, wound.**

[Fingers indicate a stabbing pain] Beginning with both extended index fingers pointing toward each other in front of the chest, palms facing in, jab the fingers toward each other with a short repeated movement.

husband *n.*

[Hand moves from the male area of the head + **marry**] Move the right *C hand* from the right side of the forehead, palm facing left, down to clasp the left *curved hand* held in front of the chest, palm facing up.

hustle *v.* See sign for HURRY.

I *pron.* See sign for ME.

ice *n.* See sign for FREEZE.

ice cream *n.*

[Mime eating from an ice cream cone] Bring the index-finger side of the right *S hand,* palm facing left, back in an arc toward the mouth with a double movement.

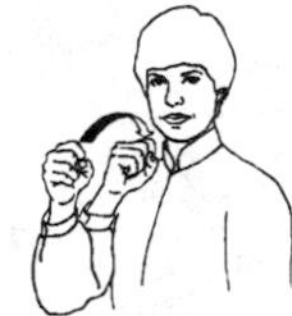

idea *n.*

[Initialized sign representing an idea coming from the head] Move the extended right little finger from near the right temple, palm facing down, upward in an arc.

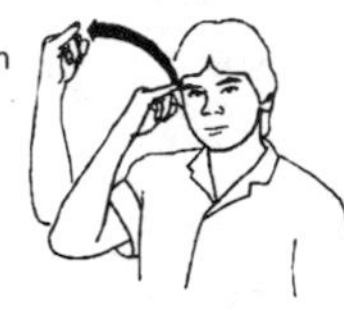

ideal *n., adj.* See sign for PERFECT.

identical *adj.* See sign for ALIKE.

identify *v.*

[Initialized sign similar to sign for **show**[1]] Tap the thumb side of the right *I hand,* palm facing left, with a double movement against the left open palm held in front of the chest, palm facing forward and fingers pointing up.

if *conj.* See sign for SUPPOSE.

ignore *v.* Same sign used for: **forsake, neglect.**

[Indicates attention moving away from object or person in view] While looking forward, place the index finger of the right *4 hand,* palm facing forward and fingers pointing up, near the right side of the face. Then move the hand outward to the right with a quick deliberate movement.

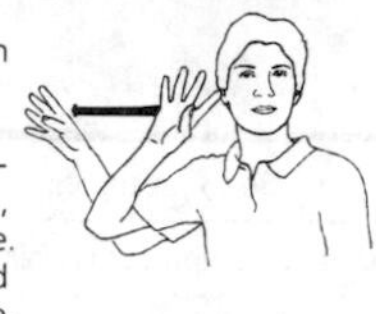

ill *adj.* See sign for SICK. Related form: **illness** *n.*

illegal *adj.* See sign for FORBID.

illegible *adj.* See sign for VAGUE.

illustration *n.* See sign for ART.

I love you (A special handshape in American Sign Language).

[Abbreviation **i-l-y** formed simultaneously in a single handshape] Hold up the right hand with the thumb, index finger, and little finger extended, palm facing forward, in front of the right shoulder.

image[1] *n.* Same sign used for: **indicate, indicator.**

[Initialized sign similar to sign for **show**[1]] Beginning with the index-finger side of the right *I hand* against the palm of the left *open hand,* palm facing right and fingers pointing up, move both hands forward simultaneously.

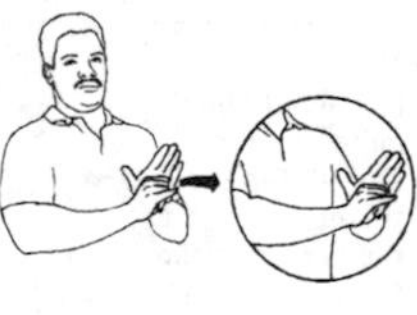

image[2] *n.* See sign for SHAPE.

imagine *v.* Same sign used for: **make believe.**

[Initialized sign similar to sign for **dream**] Move the

extended right little finger from near the right temple, palm facing down, upward in a double circular movement.

imitate *v.* See sign for COPY.

immigrate *v.* See sign for ENTER.

immune *adj.* See sign for RESIST.

impact *n.* See sign for HIT.

impair *v.* See sign for PREVENT.

implore *v.* See sign for BEG.

important *adj.* Same sign used for: **essential, main, significance, significant, value, worth.**

[The hands bring what is important to the top] Beginning with the little-finger sides of both *F hands* touching, palms facing up, bring the hands upward in a circular movement while turning the hands over, ending with the index-finger sides of the *F hands* touching in front of the chest.

impose *v.* See sign for COPY.

impression *n.* Same sign used for: **emphasis, stress.**

[Movement seems to press something in order to make an impression] With the extended thumb of the right *10 hand,* palm facing down, pressed into the palm of the left *open hand,* palm facing right, twist the right hand downward while keeping the thumb in place.

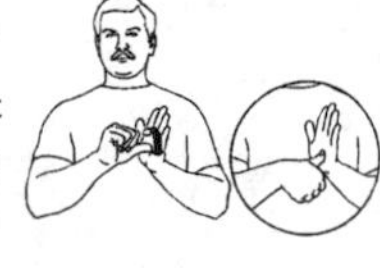

improve[1] *v.* Related form: **improvement** *n.*
[Hands seems to measure out an amount of improvement] Touch the little-finger side of the right *open hand,* palm facing back, first to the wrist and then near the crook of the extended left arm.

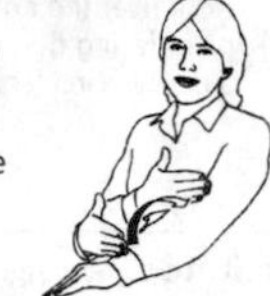

improve[2] *v.* Related form: **improvement** *n.*
Same sign used for: **remodel.** [**improve**[1] formed with a movement that indicates continued improvements] Brush the little-finger side of the right *open hand,* palm facing in and fingers pointing left, upward with a circular movement on the forearm of the bent left arm.

in *prep.* Related form: **inner** *adj.*
[Shows location in something] Insert the fingertips of the right *flattened O hand,* palm facing down, into the center of the thumb side of the left *O hand,* palm facing right in front of the chest.

in accord See sign for AGREE.

in agreement See sign for AGREE.

in behalf of See sign for SUPPORT.

incident *n.* See signs for HAPPEN, SHOW UP.

in case of See sign for SUPPOSE.

in charge of See sign for MANAGE.

include *v.* Same sign used for: **contained in, everything, involve, within.**

[The hand seems to encompass everything to gather it into one space] Swing the right *5 hand,* palm facing down, in a circular movement over the left *S hand,* palm facing in, while changing into a *flattened O hand,* ending with the fingertips of the right hand inserted in the center of the thumb side of the left hand.

income[1] *n.* Same sign used for: **revenue, salary, wages.**

[**money** + **earn**] Tap the back of the right *flattened O hand,* palm facing up, with a double movement against the left *open hand,* palm facing up. Then bring the little-finger side of the right *C hand,* palm facing left, with a double movement across the palm of the left *open hand,* closing the right hand into an *S hand* each time.

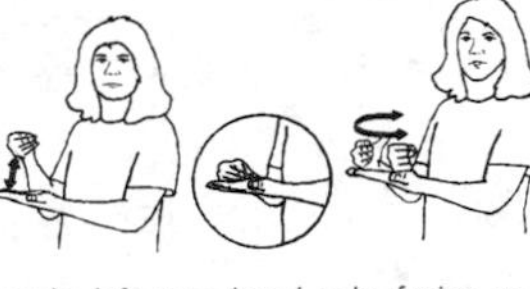

income[2] *n.* See sign for EARN.

incorrect *adj.* See sign for WRONG.

increase *n., v.* Same sign used for: **gain, raise.**

[Shows more and more things adding to a pile to increase it] Beginning with the right *U hand,* palm facing up, slightly lower than the left *U hand,* palm facing down, flip the right hand over, ending with the right fingers across the left fingers.

incredible *adj.* See sign for WONDERFUL.

indicate *v.* See signs for IMAGE, SHOW[1]. Related forms: **indicator** *n.,* **indication** *n.*

indifferent *adj.* See sign for DON'T CARE.

indoctrinate *v.* See sign for TEACH. Related form: **indoctrination** *n.*

industry *n.* See sign for MACHINE.

inexperienced *adj.* See sign for CLUMSY.

infant *n.* See sign for BABY.

in favor of See sign for SUPPORT.

infection *n.* See sign for INSURANCE.

influence *v., n.* Same sign used for: **affect, effect.**

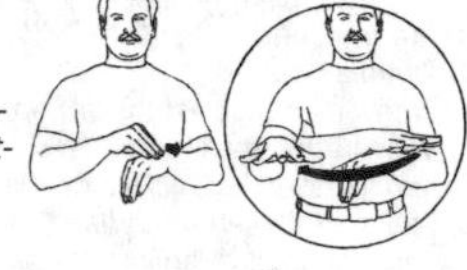

[Similar to sign for **advice** except spread outward to others] Beginning with the fingertips of the right *flattened O hand* on the back of the left *open hand,* palm facing down, move the right hand forward while opening into a *5 hand* and bringing the hand in a sweeping arc to in front of the right side of the body.

inform *v.* Same sign used for: **issue, let know, notice, notify.**

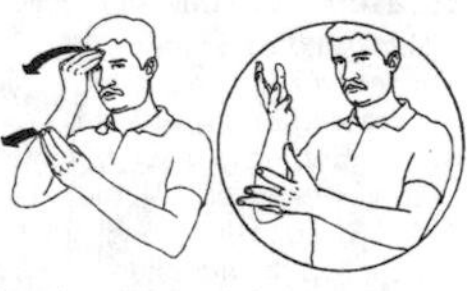

[Indicates taking information from one's head and giving it to others] Beginning with the fingertips of the right *flattened O hand* near the forehead and the left *flattened O hand* in front of the chest, move both hands forward while opening into *5 hands,* palms facing up.

information *n.* Similar to sign for **inform** except formed with a double movement.

information superhighway *n.* See sign for INTERNET.

in front of *adv.* Same sign used for: **face to face, facin**

[Shows two things facing each other] Beginning with both *open hands* in front of the chest, palms facing each other and fingers pointing up, move both hands forward simultaneously.

infuse *v.* See sign for MESH.

inhale *v.* See sign for BREATH.

injury *n.* See sign for PAIN.

inquire *v.* See sign for TEST.

insect *n.* See sign for BUG.

insert *v.*

[Action of inserting] Slide the little-finger side of the right *open hand,* palm angled up, between the index and middle fingers of the left *4 hand,* palm facing right.

inside *prep., adv., n., adj.* Same sign used for: **internal.**

[Shows location inside] Insert the fingertips of the right *flattened O hand,* palm facing down, into the center of the thumb side of the left *O hand,* palm facing right in front of the chest, with a repeated movement.

insist *v.* See sign for DEMAND.

inspect *v.* See signs for CHECK[1], INVESTIGATE. Related form: **inspection** *n.*

install *v.* See signs for APPLY[1], PUT.

instruct *v.* See signs for DESCRIBE, TEACH. Related form: **instruction** *n.*

insult *v., n.* Related form: **insulting** *adj.* Same sign used for: **affront.**

[Finger seems to direct an insult at another] Move the extended right index finger from in front of the right side of the body, palm facing left and finger pointing forward, forward and upward sharply in an arc.

insurance *n.* Related form: **insure** *v.* Same sign used for: **infection.**

[Initialized sign] Move the right *I hand,* palm facing forward, from side to side with a repeated movement near the right shoulder.

integrate *v.* See sign for MESH.

intelligent *adj.* See sign for SMART. Related form: **intelligence** *n.*

intend *v.* See sign for MEAN[2].

interact *v.* See sign for ASSOCIATE.

interest *n.* Related form: **interested** *adj.* Same sign used for: **fascinating.**

[The hands bring thoughts and feelings to the surface] Beginning with the right *modified C hand* in front of the face and the left *modified C hand* in front of the chest, both palms

facing in, move the hands forward simultaneously while closing into *A hands.*

interfere *v.* See sign for ANNOY.

internal *adj.* See sign for INSIDE.

international *adj.*

[Initialized sign similar to sign for **world**] Move both *I hands* in circles around each other, palms facing each other, ending with the little-finger side of the right hand on the index-finger side of the left hand in front of the chest.

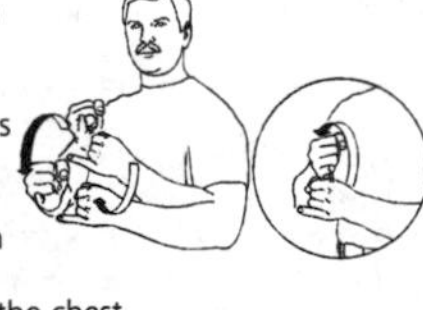

Internet or **the Net** *Informal. n.* Same sign used for: **information superhighway, network.**

[**connect** repeated to show network connections] Beginning with the bent middle fingers of both *5 hands* touching toward each other in front of the chest, twist both wrists to change positions.

interrupt *v.* See sign for ANNOY.

interview *v., n.*

[Initialized sign similar to sign for **communication**] Move both *I hands,* palms facing each other, forward and back toward the mouth with an alternating movement.

in touch with See sign for CONTACT.

into *prep.* See sign for ENTER.

introduce *v.* Related form: **introduction** *n.*

[The hands seem to bring two people together] Bring both *bent hands* from in front of each side of the body, palms facing up and fingers pointing toward each other, toward each other in front of the waist.

invent *v.* Same sign used for: **create, make up, originate.**

[The hand seems to take ideas from the head] Move the index-finger side of the right *4 hand,* palm facing left, from the forehead upward in a forward arc.

invest *v.* Related form: **investment** *n.* Same sign used for: **deposit, stocks.**

[Represents depositing money in a bank] Insert the fingertips of the right *flattened O hand,* palm facing left, into the center of the thumb side of the left *O hand,* palm angled forward.

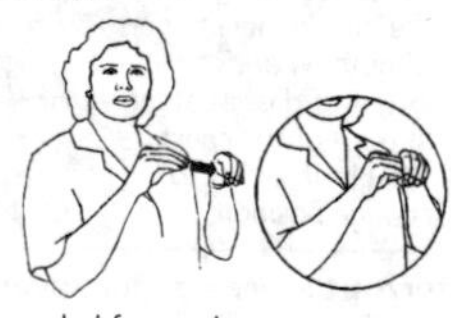

investigate *v.* Related form: **investigation** *n.* Same sign used for: **examination, examine, inspect, inspection.**

[The finger seems to be paging through pages of documents] Brush the extended right index finger with a repeated movement from the heel to the fingertips of the upturned palm of the left *open hand.*

invite *v.* Related form: **invitation** *n.* Same sign used for: **employ, greet, hire, welcome.**

[The hand brings another to oneself] Bring the upturned right *curved hand* from in front of the right side of the body in toward the center of the waist.

involve *v.* See sign for INCLUDE.

irritate *v.* See signs for ANNOY, ITCH.

isolated *adj.* See sign for ALONE.

issue *v.* See signs for INFORM, NEWSPAPER.

it or **its** *pron.* See signs for HE, HIS.

itch *n., v.* Related form: **itchy** *adj.* Same sign used for: **irritate.**

[Mime scratching an itchy place] Move the fingertips of the right *curved 5 hand,* palm facing in, back and forth with a double movement on the back of the left *open hand,* palm facing in and fingers pointing right.

itself[1] *pron.* Same sign used for: **herself.**

[Uses the handshape used for reflexive pronouns to emphasize another thing not in view] Bring the knuckles of the right *10 hand,* palm facing left, firmly against the side of the extended left index finger, palm facing right and finger pointing up in front of the chest.

itself[2] *pron.* See sign for HIMSELF.

jacket *n.* See sign for COAT.

jail *n.*

[Represents jail bars] Bring the back of the right *4 hand* from near the chest forward with a double movement while bringing the left *4 hand* in to meet the right hand, ending with the fingers crossed at an angle, both palms facing in.

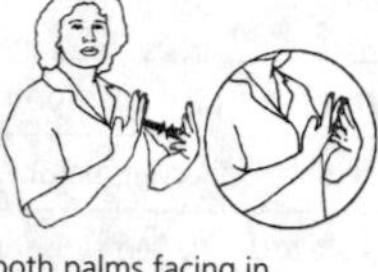

jam *n.* See sign for JELLY.

jeans *pl. n.* See sign for PANTS.

jelly *n.* Same sign used for: **jam.**

[Initialized sign miming spreading jelly on bread] Strike the extended little finger of the right *J hand* on the upturned left *open hand* as it moves upward in an arc with a double movement.

jest *v.* See sign for TEASE.

jet *n.* See sign for AIRPLANE.

job *n.* See sign for WORK.

join[1] *v.* Same sign used for: **participate.**

[Represents a person's legs entering a place where there are other people with whom one can have social exchanges] Beginning with the right *H hand* in front of the chest, palm facing left and fingers pointing forward,

and the left *C hand* in front of the lower left side of the chest, palm facing right, bring the right hand down in an arc into the palm side of the left hand while closing the left fingers around the fingers of the right *H hand.*

join[2] *v.* See sign for BELONG.

joint *n.* See sign for BELONG.

jolly *adj.* See sign for HAPPY.

journal *n.* See sign for MAGAZINE.

journey *n.* See sign for TRIP.

joy *n.* See sign for HAPPY.

judge *v.* Same sign used for: **court, justice, trial.**

[The hands move up and down indicating weighing a decision] Move both *F hands,* palms facing each other, up and down in front of each side of the chest with a repeated alternating movement.

juice *n.*

[**drink**[1] + initialized sign] Beginning with the thumb of the right *C hand* near the chin, palm facing left, tip the hand up toward the face. Then form a *J* near the right side of the face with the right hand.

jump *v., n.*

[Demonstrates the action of jumping] Beginning with the extended fingers of the right *V hand,* palm facing in, pointing down and touching the open left palm, move the right hand up and down in front of the chest with a double movement.

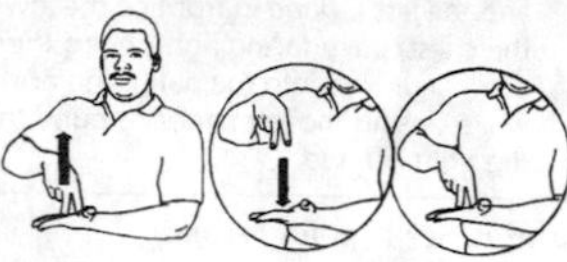

jury *n.*
[Represents people in a jury box] Beginning with the little-finger sides of both *bent 4 hands,* palms in, together in front of the chest, move the hands apart to each side.

just *adv.* Same sign used for: **recently, while ago, a.**
[Indicates something in the recent past] Wiggle the index finger of the right *X hand,* palm facing back, up and down with a repeated movement on the lower right cheek.

justice *n.* See sign for JUDGE.

justify *v.* See sign for CHANGE[1].

keen *adj.* See sign for SHARP.

keep *v.* Same sign used for: **maintain.**

[Eyes looking in different directions] Tap the little-finger side of the right *K hand* across the index-finger side of the left *K hand* palms facing in opposite directions.

keep quiet *v. phrase.* See sign for SHUT UP (*informal*).

ketchup or **catsup** *n.*

[Initialized sign] Shake the right *K hand,* palm facing left, up and down with a short repeated movement in front of the right side of the body.

key[1] *n.*

[Mime turning a key in a lock] Twist the knuckle of the right *X hand,* palm facing down, in the palm of the left *open hand,* palm facing right and fingers pointing forward, with a repeated movement.

key[2] *n.* Same sign used for: **keystroke.**

[Action of pressing on a key] Push the extended thumb of the right *10 hand* downward a short distance in front of the right side of the body.

keystroke *n.* See sign for KEY[2].

kick *v.* Same sign used for: **kick off.**

[Demonstrates the action of kicking something] Bring the right *B hand* from in front of the right side of the body, palm facing left and fingers angled down, upward to strike the index-finger side of the right hand against the little-finger side of the left *B hand* held in front of the body, palm facing in and fingers pointing right.

kick off *n.* See sign for KICK.

kid[1] *n.*

[Suggests a child's runny nose] With the right index finger and little finger extended, palm facing down, put the extended index finger under the nose, and twist the hand up and down with a small repeated movement.

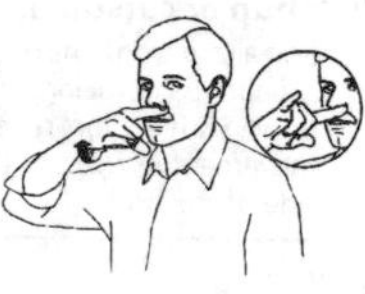

kid[2] *v.* See sign for TEASE. Related form: **kidding** *n.*

kill *v.* Same sign used for: **murder, slaughter.**

[Represents a knife being inserted] Push the side of the extended right index finger, palm facing down, across the palm of the left *open hand,* palm facing right, with a deliberate movement.

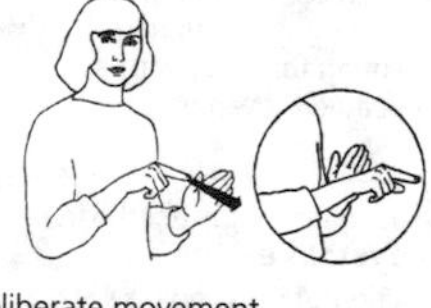

kind[1] *adj.* Same sign used for: **generous, gentle, gracious.**

[A comforting movement] Bring the right *open hand,* palm facing in near the middle of the chest, in a forward circle around the back of the left *open hand,* palm facing in, as it moves in a circle around the right hand.

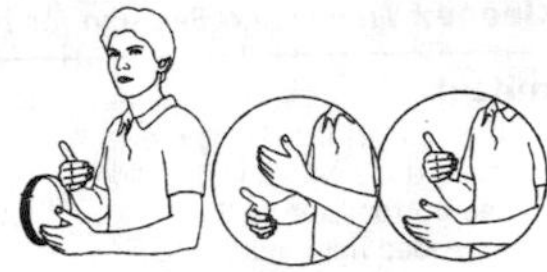

kind[2] *n.* Same sign used for: **sort, type.**

[Initialized sign similar to sign for **world**] Move the right *K hand,* palm facing left, in a forward circle around the left *K hand,* palm facing right, as it moves in a circle around the right hand, ending with the little-finger side of the right hand landing on the index-finger side of the left hand.

kiss *v., n.*

[The hand takes a kiss from the mouth and puts it on the cheek] Touch the fingertips of the right *flattened O hand,* palm facing in, to the right side of the mouth, and then open the right hand and lay the palm of the right *open hand* against the right side of the face.

kitchen *n.*

[Initialized sign similar to sign for **cook**] Beginning with the palm side of the right *K hand* on the upturned left *open hand,* flip the right hand over, ending with the back of the right hand in the left palm.

Kleenex *Trademark.* See sign for TISSUE.

knife *n.*

[Represents the slicing movement done with a knife] Slide the bottom side of the extended right index finger, palm facing in, with a double movement at an angle down the length of the extended left index finger, palm facing right, turning the right palm down each time as it moves off the end of the left index finger.

know *v.*

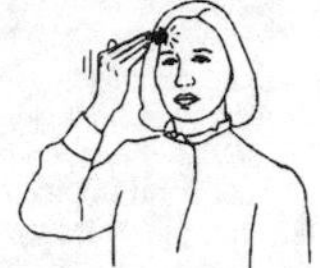

[Location of knowledge in the brain] Tap the fingertips of the right *bent hand,* palm facing down, on the right side of the forehead.

knowledge *n.* See sign for AWARE[1].

label *n., v.* Same sign used for: **apply, brand, decal, tag.**

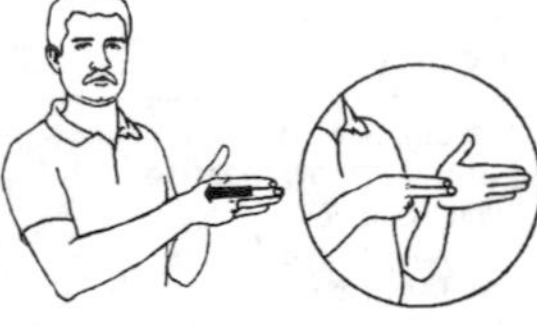

[Demonstrates applying a label] Wipe the extended fingers of the right *H hand,* palm facing left, from the fingers to the heel of the left *open hand,* palm facing right and fingers pointing forward.

---

labor *v.* See sign for WORK.

---

lack *n.* See sign for SKIP[1].

---

ladder *n.* See sign for CLIMB.

---

lady *n.* Same sign used for: **female.**

[**girl** + **polite**] Bring the thumb of the right *A hand,* palm facing left, downward from the right side of the chin while opening, ending by tapping side of the thumb of the right *open hand* in the center of the chest.

---

land *n.* See sign for DIRT.

---

language *n.*

[Initialized sign] Beginning with the thumbs of both *L hands* near each other in front of the chest, palms angled down, bring the hands outward with a wavy movement to in front of each side of the chest.

lapse *n.* See sign for BETWEEN.

large *adj.* See also sign for BIG. Same sign used for: **grand, great, massive.**

[Initialized sign showing a large size] Move both *L hands* from in front of each side of the chest, palms facing each other, in large arcs beyond each side of the body.

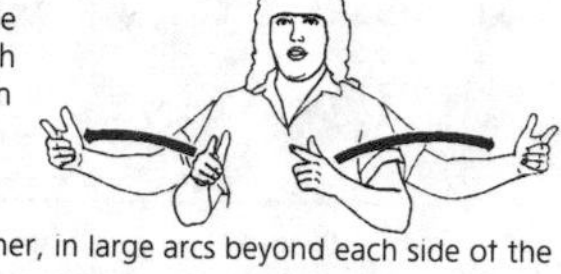

last[1] *adj., adv., n.* Same sign used for: **end, final, finally.**

[Indicates the last thing] Move the extended little finger of the right *I hand,* palm facing left, downward in front of the chest, striking the extended little finger of the left *I hand,* palm facing in, as it passes.

last[2] *adj., adv.* See signs for AGO, BEFORE, CONTINUE[1].

late *adj., adv.* Same sign used for: **delay, tardy.**

[Hand moves into the past] Bend the wrist of the right *open hand,* palm facing back and fingers pointing down, back near the right side of the waist with a double movement.

lately *adv.* See sign for SINCE[1].

later or **later on** *adv.* Same sign used for: **after a while, afterward.**

[Initialized sign representing the minute hand on a clock moving to indicate the passing of time] With the thumb of the right *L hand,* palm facing forward, on the palm of the left *open hand,* palm facing right and fingers pointing forward, twist the right hand forward, keeping the thumb in place and ending with the right palm facing down.

laugh *v.*

[Initialized sign showing the shape of the mouth when one laughs] Beginning with the extended index fingers of both *L hands* at each corner of the mouth, palms facing back, pull the hands outward to each side of the head with a double movement while closing the hands into *10 hands* each time.

lavatory *n.* See sign for TOILET.

law *n.* Same sign used for: **legal.**

[Initialized sign representing recording laws on the books] Place the palm side of the right *L hand,* palm facing left, first on the fingers and then the heel of the left *open hand,* palm facing right and fingers pointing up.

lay off *v. phrase. Informal.* See sign for DISMISS.

layer *n.* Same sign used for: **plush.**

[Shows the shape of a layer on top of something] Slide the thumb of the right *modified C hand,* palm facing left, from the heel to off the fingers of the upturned palm of the left *open hand* held in front of the chest.

lazy *adj.* Same sign used for: **slothful.**

[Initialized sign] Tap the palm side of the right *L hand* against the left side of the chest with a double movement.

lead *v.* Same sign used for: **conduct, guide, head, host, steer.**

[One hand leads the other by pulling it] With the fingers of the left *open hand,* palm facing right, being held by the fingers and thumb of the right hand, palm facing in, pull the left hand forward a short distance.

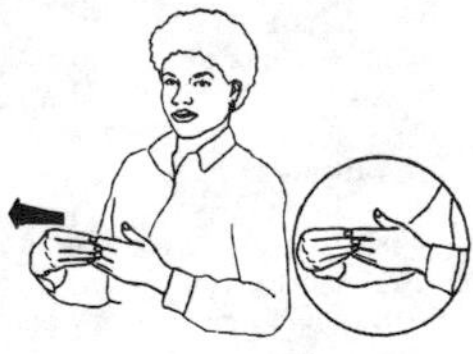

leak[1] *v., n.* Same sign used for: **drain, run.**

[Represents the flow of a leaking liquid] Beginning with the index-finger side of the right *4 hand,* palm facing in and fingers pointing left, touching the palm of the left *open hand,* palm facing down and fingers pointing right, move the right hand down with a double movement.

leak[2] *n.,v.* See sign for DRIP.

lean *adj.* See signs for DIET, THIN[2].

learn *v.* Same sign used for: **educate, education.**

[Represents taking information from paper and putting it in one's head] Beginning with the fingertips of the right *curved 5 hand,* palm facing down, on the palm of the upturned left *open hand,* bring the right hand up while closing the fingers and thumb into a *flattened O hand* near the forehead.

leave[1] *v.* Same sign used for: **depart, desert, withdraw.**

[The hands move from one location to another] Beginning with both *curved 5 hands* in front of each side of the chest, palms facing down, pull the hands back toward the right shoulder while closing the fingers and thumbs into *flattened O hands.*

leave[2] *v.* Same sign used for: **leftover, rest.**

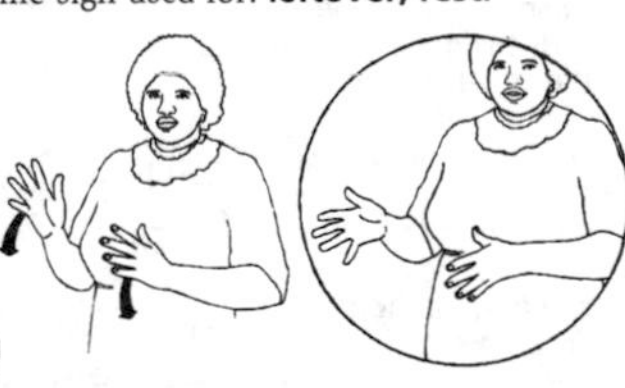

[The hands seem to leave something by thrusting it down] Beginning with both *5 hands* in front of each side of the body, palms facing each other and fingers angled up, thrust the fingers downward with a deliberate movement.

leave[3] *v.* See sign for GO.

lecture *v., n.* See sign for SPEAK[2].

left *adj., adv., n.*

[Initialized sign indicating a direction to the left] Beginning with the right *L hand* in front of the right side of the chest, palm facing forward and index finger pointing up, move the hand deliberately to the left.

leftover *n., adj.* See sign for LEAVE[2].

legal *adj.* See sign for LAW.

leisure *n.* See sign for ENJOY.

lemon *n.*

[Initialized sign pointing to puckered lips from eating a sour lemon] Tap the thumb of the right *L hand,* palm facing left, against the chin with a double movement.

lend *v.* Same sign used for: **loan.**

[Directional sign toward the person to whom something is lent] With the little-finger side of the right *V hand* across the index-finger side of the left *V hand,* move the hands from near the chest forward and down a short distance.

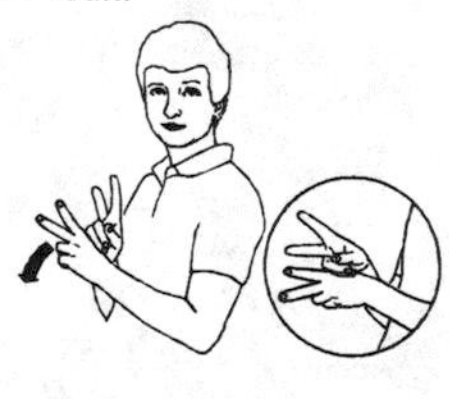

lend me *v. phrase.* See sign for BORROW.

length *n.* See sign for LONG.

lessen *v.* See signs for DECREASE.

lesson *n.* See sign for COURSE.

let *v.* Same sign used for: **allow, grant, permit.**

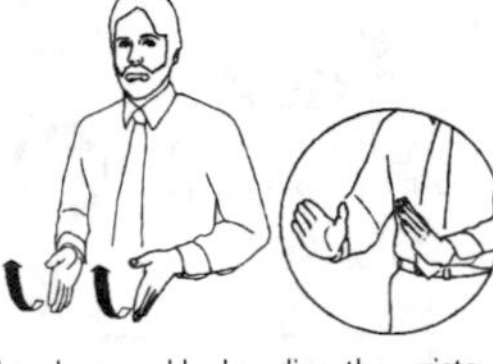

[The hands outline a path for a person to pass] Beginning with both *open hands* in front of the waist, palms facing each other and fingers pointing down, bring the fingers forward and upward by bending the wrists.

let know *v. phrase.* See sign for INFORM.

letter *n.* Same sign used for: **mail.**

[Shows licking a stamp and placing it on an envelope] Touch the extended thumb of the right *10 hand* to the lips, palm facing in, and then move the thumb downward to touch the fingertips of the left *open hand* held in front of the body, palm facing up.

lettuce *n.*

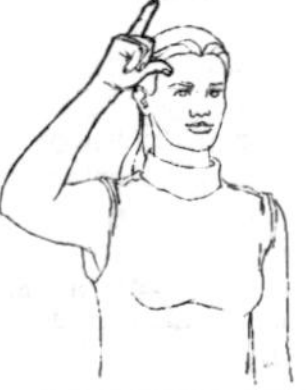

[Initialized sign formed on the head, representing a head of lettuce] Touch the thumb of the right *L hand,* palm facing forward and index finger pointing up, to the right side of the forehead.

level *adj.* See sign for EVEN[1].

lever *n.* See sign for PIPE[1].

liability *n.* See sign for BURDEN.

liberate *v.* See sign for SAVE[1].

liberty *n.* See sign for SAVE[1].

library *n.*

[Initialized sign] Move the right *L hand,* palm facing forward, in a circle in front of the right shoulder.

license *n.*

[Initialized sign similar to sign for **certificate**] Tap the thumbs of both *L hands* with a double movement in front of the chest, palms facing forward.

lie *v., n.* Same sign used for: **fib.**

[The hand movement indicates that a person is speaking out of the side of the mouth when telling a lie] Slide the index-finger side of the right *bent hand,* palm facing down, with a double movement across the chin from right to left.

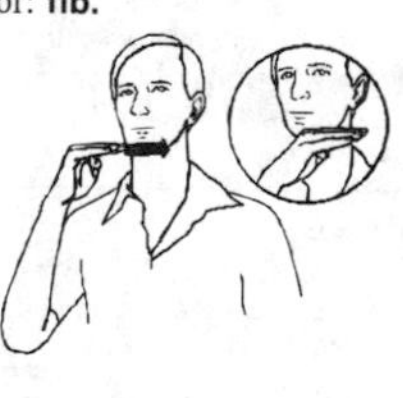

lift *v.* See sign for RAISE[1].

light[1] *adj., n.*

[The snap of a light being turned on] Beginning with the fingertips of the right *8 hand* near the chin, palm facing in, flick the middle finger upward and forward with a double movement while opening into a *5 hand* each time.

light[2] *adj.*

[The gesture represents something light floating upward] Beginning with both *5 hands* with bent middle fingers in front of the waist, palms facing down, twist the wrists to raise the hands quickly toward each other and upward, ending with the hands in front of each side of the chest, bent middle fingers pointing in.

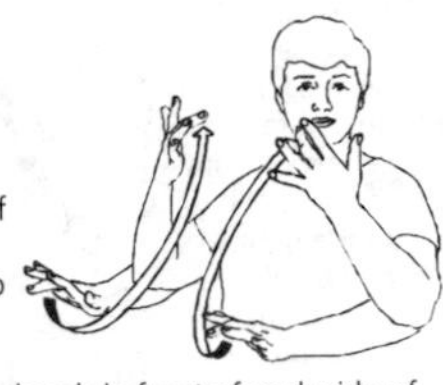

light[3] *adj.* See sign for BRIGHT.

like[1] *v.*

[Pulling out feelings] Beginning with the bent thumb and middle finger of the right *5 hand* touching the chest, palm facing in, bring the hand forward while closing the fingers to form an *8 hand.*

like[2] *v.* See sign for ENJOY.

like[3] *prep.* See sign for SAME.

line *n.* Same sign used for: **string, thread.**

[Shows shape of a line] Beginning with the extended little fingers of both *I hands* touching in front of the chest, palms facing in, move both hands outward.

line up *v. phrase.* Same sign used for: **align, queue, row.**

[Represents people lined up in a row] Beginning with the little finger of the right *4 hand,* palm facing left, touching the index finger of the right *4 hand,* palm facing right, move the right hand back toward the chest and the left hand forward.

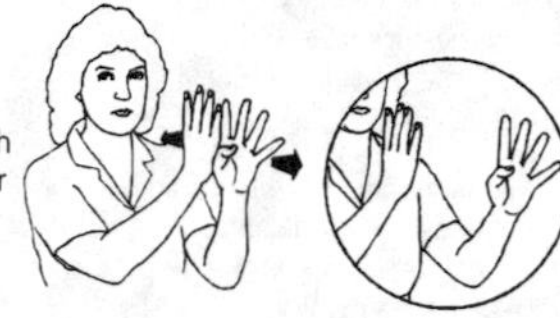

link *v.* See signs for BELONG, RELATIONSHIP.

list *n., v.* Same sign used for: **record, score.**

[The finger points out items on a list] Touch the bent middle finger of the right *5 hand,* palm facing left, several times on the palm of the left *open hand,* palm facing right and fingers pointing up, as it moves from the fingers downward to the heel.

listen *v.* Same sign used for: **eavesdrop.**

[The fingers bring sound to the ear] With the thumb of the right *curved 3 hand,* palm facing left, touching the right ear, bend the extended index and middle fingers down with a short double movement.

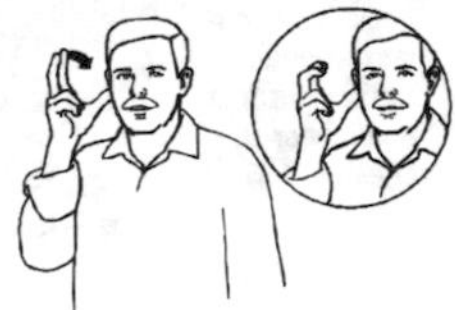

little *adj.* See also sign for SMALL[1]. Same sign used for: **short.**

[Shows someone or something short in size] Move the right *bent hand,* palm facing down, with a short double movement in front of the right side of the body.

little bit *n.* See sign for TINY.

live *v.* Same sign used for: **alive, dwell, survival, survive.**

[Outlines life within one's body] Move both *A hands,* palms facing in, upward on each side of the chest.

load *n.* See sign for PILE.

loan *v.* See sign for LEND.

local *adj.* See sign for LOCATION.

location *n.* Same sign used for: **local.**

[Initialized sign similar to sign for **area**] Beginning with the thumbs of both *L hands* touching in front of the body, palms facing down, move the hands apart and back in a circular movement until they touch again near the chest.

lock *n., v.*

[Represents the wrists locked together] Beginning with both *S hands* in front of the body, right hand above left and both palms facing down, turn the right hand over by twisting the wrist, ending with the back of the right *S hand,* palm facing up, on the back of the left *S hand,* palm facing down.

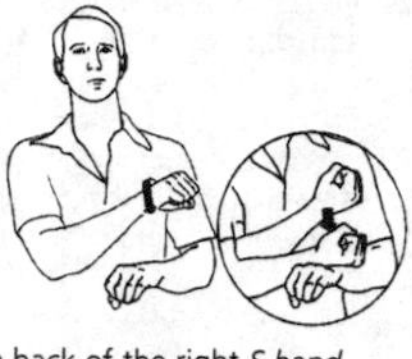

lone *adj.* See sign for ALONE. Related form: **lonely** *adj.*

lonely or **lonesome** *adj.*

[Suggests that someone living alone is silent] Bring the side of the extended right index finger, palm facing left, from near the nose slowly downward in front of the mouth.

long *adj.* Same sign used for: **length.**

[The finger measures out a long length] Move the extended right index finger from the wrist up the length of the extended left arm to near the shoulder.

long ago *n., adj.* Same sign used for: **ancient.**

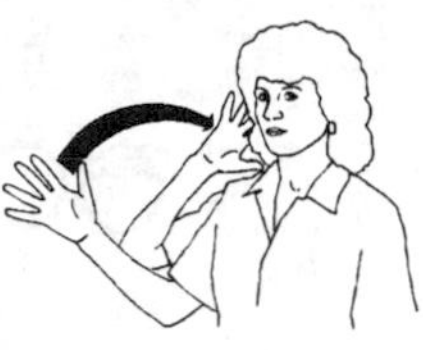

[The hand indicates a time far in the past] Beginning with the right *5 hand* in front of the right shoulder, palm facing left, bring the hand back to behind the right shoulder.

look alike *v. phrase* See sign for ALIKE.

look at *v. phrase.*

[Represents the eyes directed toward something] Move the right *V hand,* palm facing down and extended fingers pointing forward, forward a short distance in the direction of the referent.

look for *v. phrase.* Same sign used for: **check for, examine, hunt for, search for.**

[Shows repeated searching for something] Move the right *C hand,* palm facing left, with a double movement in a circle in front of the face.

look like *v. phrase.* See sign for SEEM.

look over *v. phrase.* Same sign used for: **browse, observe, view.**

[Represents the eyes surveying something] Beginning with both *V hands* in front of each side of the chest, right hand higher than the left hand, both palms facing down, and fingers pointing forward, move the hands in double alternating circles.

looks *n.*

Same sign used for: **good-looking, handsome.**

[The location of a person's face] Move the right extended index finger in a circle in front of the face, palm facing in.

loose *adj.* See sign for DISCONNECT.

lose[1] *v.*

[The hands seem to drop something as if to lose it] Beginning with the fingertips of both *flattened O hands* touching in front of the body, palms facing up, drop the fingers quickly downward and away from each other while opening into *5 hands,* ending with both palms and fingers angled downward.

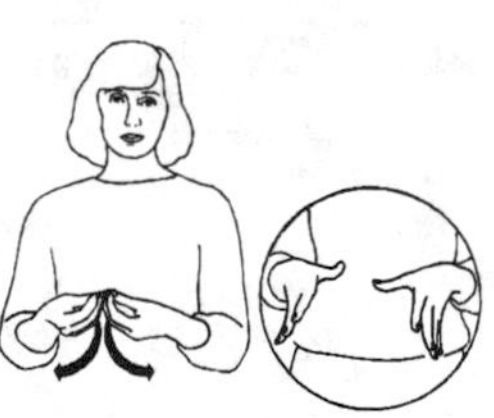

lose[2] *v.* See sign for DECREASE.

lots *n.* See sign for MUCH.

loud *adj.* See sign for NOISE.

lousy *adj. Slang.* Related form: **louse** *n.*

[Suggests that someone with a runny nose feels lousy] Beginning with the thumb of the right *3 hand* touching the nose, palm facing left, bring the hand downward in front of the chest.

love *v., n.*

[The hands bring something that is loved close to oneself] With the wrists of both *S hands* crossed in front of the chest, palms facing in, bring the arms back against the chest.

lovely *adj.* See signs for BEAUTIFUL, PRETTY.

lover *n.* See sign for SWEETHEART.

low *adj.* Related form: **lower** *adj.* Same sign used for: **demote.**

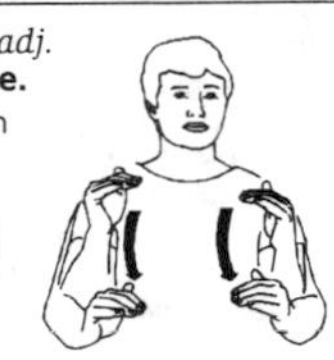

[Indicates a location lower than another location] Beginning with both *bent hands* in front of each shoulder, palms facing each other, move them downward in front of each side of the chest.

luck *n.* Related form: **lucky** *adj.* Same sign used for: **fortunate.**

[Similar to sign for **favorite**[1] but directed toward another] Beginning with the bent middle finger of the right *5 hand,* palm facing in, touching the chin, twist the wrist to swing the hand forward with a quick movement, ending with the palm angled forward.

luggage *n.* See sign for BAGGAGE.

lump[1] *n.* Same sign used for: **bump.**

[Shows the size of a small amount or swelling] Beginning with the side of the extended right index finger, palm facing left and finger pointing forward, on the back of the left *open hand,* palm facing down and fingers pointing right, bring the right finger upward in a small arc, ending farther back on the back of the left hand.

lump[2] *n.* See sign for AMOUNT.

lunch *n.*

[**eat** + **noon**] Bring the fingers of the right *flattened O hand* to the lips, palm facing in. Then place the elbow of the bent right arm, arm extended up and open right palm facing forward, on the back of the left *open hand* held in front of the body, palm facing down.

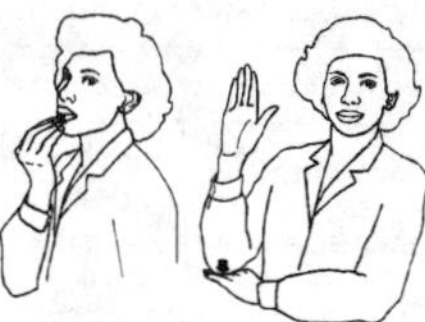

luxury *adj.* See sign for FANCY.

machine *n.* Same sign used for: **factory, industry, manufacture, mechanism, motor, run.**

[Represents movement of gears meshing together] With the fingers of both *curved 5 hands* loosely meshed together, palms facing in, move the hands up and down in front of the chest with a repeated movement.

mad *adj.* See signs for ANGER, CROSS[1].

magazine *n.* Same sign used for: **brochure, journal, pamphlet.**

[Shows the spine of a magazine] Grasp the little-finger side of the left *open hand,* palm angled up, with the index finger and thumb of the right *A hand,* and slide the right hand from heel to fingertips of the left hand with a double movement.

mail[1] *n., v.* Alternate form: **mail out.** Same sign used for: **send, send out.**

[Shows sending something forward] Flick the fingertips of the right *bent hand* forward across the back of the left *open hand,* both palms facing down, with a quick movement, straightening the right fingers as the right hand moves forward.

mail[2] *n.* See signs for EMAIL[1,2], LETTER.

main *adj.* See sign for IMPORTANT.

maintain *v.* See signs for FIX, KEEP.

major *v.* See sign for SPECIALIZE.

make *v.* Same sign used for: **create, manufacture, produce.**

[The hands seem to be molding something] Beginning with the little-finger side of the right *S hand* on the index-finger side of the left *S hand,* twist the wrists in opposite directions with a small, quick, grinding movement.

make believe *v. phrase.* See sign for IMAGINE.

make-up or **makeup** *n.* Same sign used for: **cosmetics.**

[Mime dabbing make-up on one's face] Move the fingertips of both *flattened O hands,* palms facing each other, in double alternating circles near each cheek.

make up *v. phrase.* See sign for INVENT.

make up your mind *v. phrase.* See sign for DECIDE.

malady *n.* See sign for SICK.

male *n.* See signs for BOY, MAN.

mama *n.* See sign for MOTHER.

man *n.* Same sign used for: **male.**

[A combination of **boy** and a gesture indicating the height of a man] Beginning with the thumb side of the right *flattened C hand* in front of the right side of the forehead, palm facing left, bring the hand straight forward while closing the fingers to the thumb.

manage *v.* Same sign used for: **administer, control, direct, govern, handle, in charge of, operate, preside over, reign, rule.**

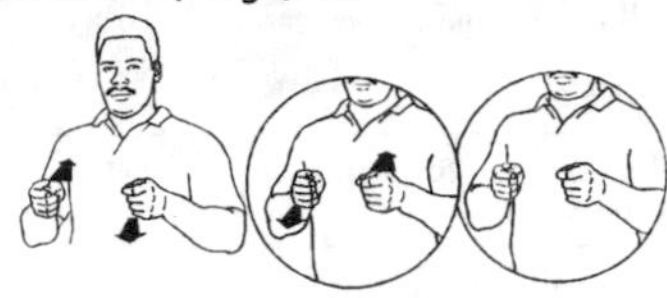

[Mime holding a horse's reigns indicating being in a position of management] Beginning with both *modified X hands* in front of each side of the body, right hand forward of the left hand and palms facing each other, move the hands forward and back with a repeated alternating movement.

manners *n.* See sign for POLITE.

mantel *n.* See sign for SHELF.

manufacture *v.* See signs for MACHINE, MAKE.

many *adj., pron.* Same sign used for: **a lot, numerous.**

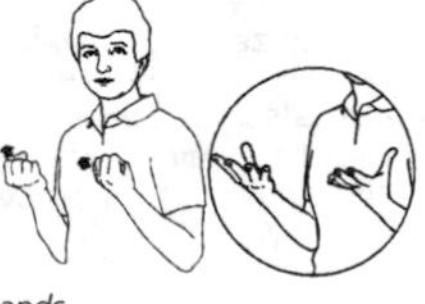

[Natural gesture for indicating many things] Beginning with both *S hands* in front of each side of the chest, palms facing up, flick the fingers open quickly with a double movement into *5 hands.*

margarine *n.* See sign for BUTTER.

market *n.* See sign for STORE[1].

marry *v.*
[Symbolizes joining hands in marriage] Bring the right *curved hand,* palm facing down, downward in front of the chest to clasp the left *curved hand,* palm facing up.

marshall *n.* See sign for POLICE.

mart *n.* See sign for STORE[1].

marvel *n.* See sign for WONDERFUL. Related form: **marvelous** *adj.*

mass *n.* See sign for CLASS.

massive *adj.* See signs for EXCESS, LARGE.

match *v., n.* Same sign used for: **combine, fit, merge, suit.**
[The fingers move together to match with each other] Beginning with both *5 hands* in front of each side of the chest, palms facing in, bring the hands together, ending with the bent fingers of both hands meshed together in front of the chest.

materialize *v.* See sign for SHOW UP.

materials *pl. n.* Same sign used for: **media.**
[Initialized sign similar to sign for **thing**] Beginning with the right *M hand* in front of the body, palm facing up,

move the hand in a double arc to the right.

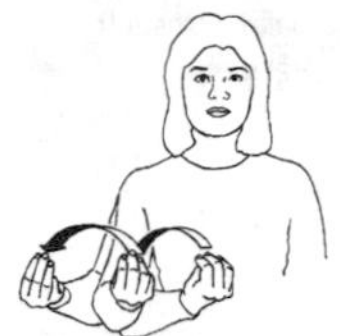

matinee *n.* See sign for AFTERNOON.

maximum *n., adj.* Same sign used for: **up to.**

[Shows reaching the top] Beginning with the right *B hand,* palm facing down and fingers pointing left, a few inches under the left *open hand,* palm facing down and fingers pointing right, bring the back of the right hand up against the left palm.

may *v.* See signs for CAN[1], MAYBE.

maybe *adv.* Same sign used for: **may, might, perhaps, probability, probable, probably.**

[Indicates weighing possibilities] Beginning with both *open hands* in front of each side of the chest,

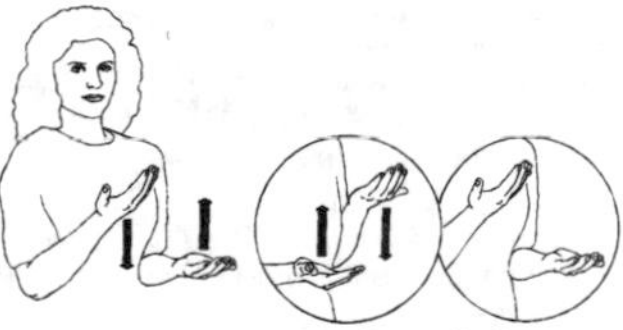

palms facing up and fingers pointing forward, alternately move the hands up and down with a double movement.

mayonnaise *n.*

[Initialized sign miming spreading mayonnaise on bread] Move the fingers of the right *M hand,* palm facing down, in a double circular movement on the palm of the left *open hand,* palm facing up.

me *pron.* Same sign used for: **I.**
[Directional sign toward self] Point the extended right index finger to the center of the chest.

meager *adj.* See sign for SMALL[1].

mean[1] *adj.* Related form: **meanness** *n.* Same sign used for: **bust, cruel, rude.**
[Shows a rough movement against another] Beginning with both *5 hands* in front of the body, palms facing in opposite directions and the right hand above the left hand, close the hands into *A hands* while quickly moving the right hand down brushing the knuckles against the left knuckles as it passes.

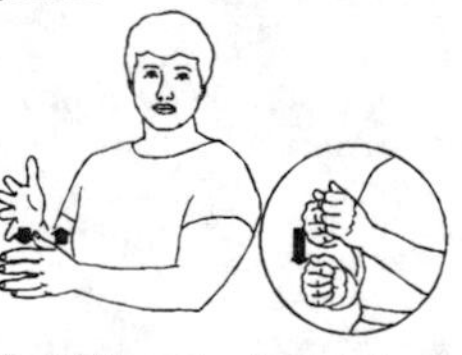

mean[2] *v.* Related form: **meaning** *n.* Same sign used for: **intend, purpose, stand for.**
[Exchanging things to look at their relative standing] Touch the fingertips of the right *V hand,* palm facing down, in the palm of the left *open hand,* palm facing up

and fingers pointing forward, and then twist the right wrist and touch the fingertips down again.

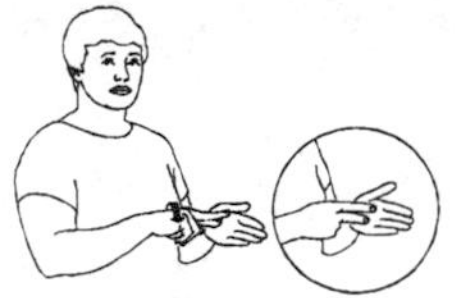

meanwhile *n.* See sign for DURING.

measure *v.* Related form: **measurement** *n.* Same sign used for: **size.**

[The fingers seem to measure something] Tap the thumbs of both *Y hands,* palms facing down, together in front of the chest with a double movement.

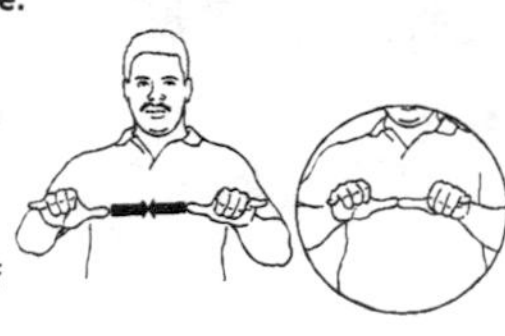

measure up *v. phrase.* See sign for MEET.

meat *n.*

[Indicates the meaty part of the hand] With the bent index finger and thumb of the right *5 hand,* palm facing down, grasp the fleshy part of left *open hand* near the thumb, palm facing right and fingers pointing forward, and shake the hands forward and back with a double movement.

mechanism *n.* See sign for MACHINE.

meddle *v.* See sign for NOSY.

media *pl. n.* See sign for MATERIALS.

medical *adj.* See sign for DOCTOR.

medicine *n.* Related forms: **medical** *adj.*, **medication** *n.*

[Represents mixing a prescription with a mortar and pestle] With the bent middle finger of the right *5 hand,* palm facing down, in the palm of the left *open hand,* rock the right hand from side to side with a double movement while keeping the middle finger in place.

meditate *v.* See sign for WONDER. Related form: **meditation**.

meet *v.* Same sign used for: **greet, measure up.**

[Represents two people approaching each other when meeting] Beginning with the extended index fingers of both hands pointing up in front of each shoulder, palms facing each other, bring the hands together in front of the chest.

meeting *n.* Related form: **meet** *v.* Same sign used for: **assembly, conference, convention, convocation, council.**

[Represents many people coming together for a meeting] Beginning with both open hands in front of the chest, palms facing each other and fingers pointing up, close the fingers with a double movement into *flattened O hands* while moving the hands together.

mellow *adj.* See sign for SOFT.

melody *n.* See sign for MUSIC.

melt *v.* See sign for DISSOLVE.

memorize *v.* Related form: **memory** *n.*
[The hand seems to take information from the brain and then hold on to it tightly, as if to keep it in the memory] Beginning with the fingertips of the right *curved hand* touching the right side of the forehead, palm facing in, bring the hand forward and down while closing the fingers into an *S hand,* palm facing in.

mend *v.* See sign for FIX.

merchandise *n.* See sign for SELL.

mercy *n.* Related form: **merciful** *adj.* Same sign used for: **poor thing**.
[The finger used to show feeling is directed toward another] Beginning with the bent middle finger of the right *5 hand* pointing forward in front of the right shoulder, move the hand forward in a repeated circular movement.

merge *v.* See signs for CIRCULATE, MATCH, MESH.

merry *adj.* See sign for HAPPY.

mesh *v.* Same sign used for: **blend, combine, infuse, integrate, merge.**
[Shows the fingers coming together to merge] Beginning with both *curved 5 hands* in front of each side of the chest, palms facing in, drop the hands down while meshing the fingers together, and then drop them apart in front of each side of the body.

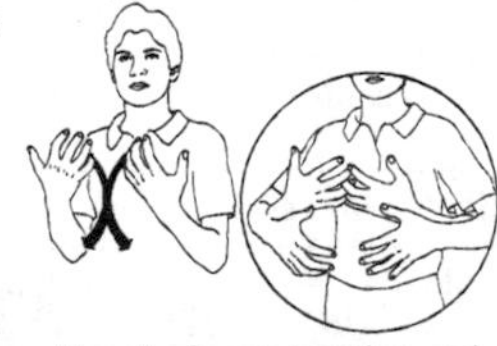

messy *adj.* Same sign used for: **chaos, disorder, garbled, riot, stir, storm.**

[Represents something turned upside down, causing a mess] Beginning with both *curved 5 hands* in front of the body, right hand over the left hand, twist the hands with a deliberate movement, reversing the positions.

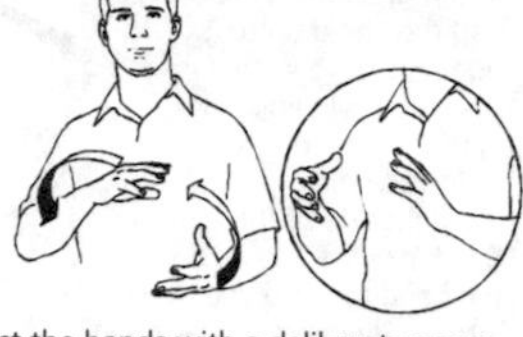

metal *n., adj.* Same sign used for: **rock, steel.**

[Striking the chin which represents a hard substance] Bring the top of the bent index finger of the right *X hand,* palm facing left, forward from under the chin with a double movement.

microwave *n.* Alternate form: **microwave oven.**, *v.*

[Abbreviation **m-w**] Beginning with both *M hands* in front of each side of the chest, palms facing in, move the hands toward each other while extending the fingers toward each other with a double movement, changing into *W hands* each time.

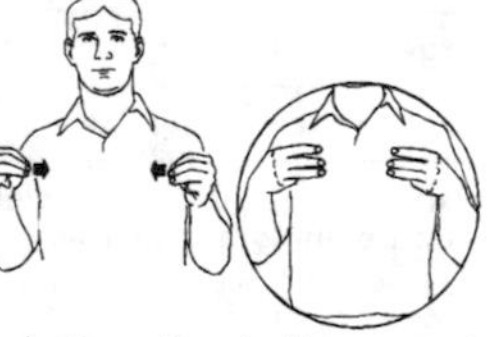

midday *n.* See sign for NOON.

middle *adj., n.* Same sign used for: **center.**

[Indicates the middle of something] Move the bent middle finger of the right *5 hand,* palm facing down, in a circular movement and then down into the palm of the left *open hand* held in front of the chest, palm facing up.

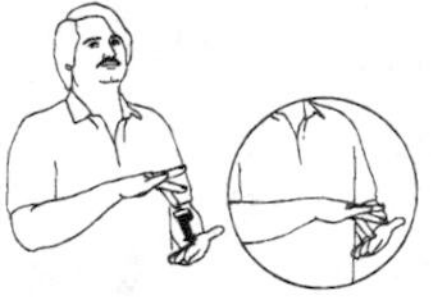

midst *prep.* See sign for AMONG.

might *v.* See sign for MAYBE.

mighty *adj.* See sign for POWER[1].

migraine *n.* See sign for HEADACHE.

milk *n.*

[Mime squeezing a cow's udder to get milk] Beginning with the right *C hand,* palm facing left, in front of the right side of the body, squeeze the fingers together with a double movement, forming an *S hand* each time.

million *adj.*

[Initialized sign similar to sign for **thousand** except repeated] Touch the fingertips of the right *M hand,* palm facing down, first on the heel, then in the middle, and then on the fingers of the upturned left *open hand.*

mind *n.* Same sign used for: **brain, sense.**

[Location of the mind] Tap the bent extended right index finger, palm facing in, against the right side of the forehead with a double movement.

mine *pron.* See sign for MY.

mingle *v.* See sign for ASSOCIATE.

mini *adj.* See sign for SMALL[1].

minor *adj.*

[Shows something taking a lesser position under another] Slide the index-finger side of the right *B hand*, palm facing left and fingers pointing forward, forward under the little-finger side of the left *B hand*, palm facing right and fingers pointing forward.

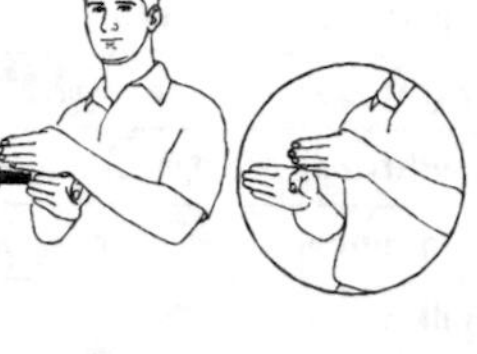

minus *prep.*

[Shape of a minus sign] Touch the thumb side of the extended right index finger, palm facing down and finger pointing forward, against the palm of the left open hand, palm facing right.

minute *n.* Same sign used for: **moment, momentarily, one minute.**

[The finger represents the movement of the minute hand on a clock] Move the extended right index finger, palm facing left, forward a short distance, pivoting the closed fingers of the right hand on the palm of the left *open hand,* palm facing right and fingers pointing up.

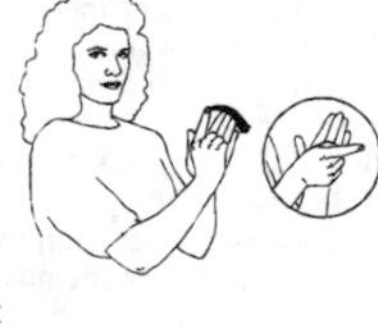

mirror *n.*

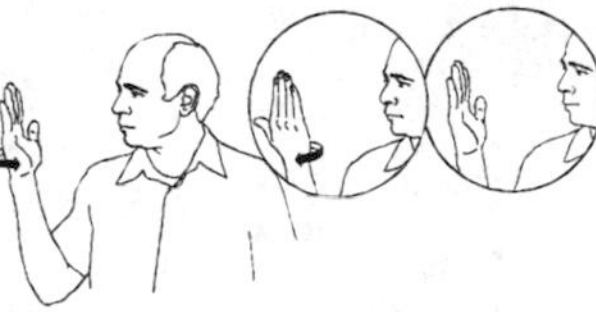

[The hand represents a mirror] Beginning with the right *open hand* held up near the right shoulder, palm facing left, twist the wrist to turn the palm in and back with a double movement.

misconception *n.* See sign for MISUNDERSTAND.

miss[1] *v.*

[The hand seems to snatch at something as it passes] Move the right *C hand,* palm facing left, from near the right side of the forehead in a quick downward arc in front of the face while closing into an *S hand,* ending with the palm facing down in front of the left shoulder.

miss[2] *Slang.* Same sign used for: **You're too late.**

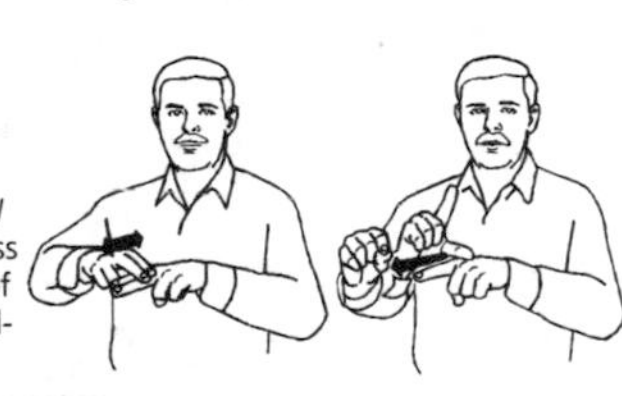

[**train** + **zoom**[1]] Rub the extended fingers of the right *H hand* across the back of the extended fingers of the left *H hand,* both palms facing down. Then beginning with the thumb of the right *L hand,* palm facing forward, on the base of the extended left index finger, palm facing down, move the right hand quickly to the right while closing the index finger to the thumb.

miss[3] *v.* See signs for ABSENT, DISAPPOINTED, SKIP[1]. Related form: **missing** *adj.*

mistake *n.* Related form: **mistaken** *adj.*
[Similar to sign for **wrong** but made with a double movement] Tap the middle fingers of the right *Y hand,* palm facing in, against the chin with a double movement.

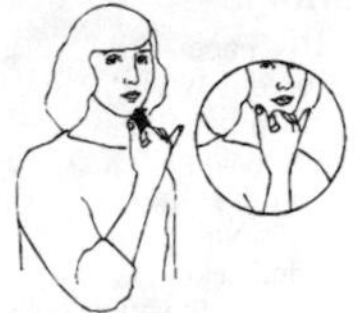

misty *adj.* See sign for WET.

misunderstand *v.* Related form: **misunderstanding** *n.* Same sign used for: **misconception.**
[The fingers indicate something turned around in the mind] Touch the index finger of the right *V hand* to the right side of the forehead, palm facing forward, and then twist the wrist and touch the middle finger to the forehead, ending with the palm facing back.

mix[1] *v.* Same sign used for: **blend, complex, confuse, disorder, scramble, stir.**
[Mime mixing things up] Beginning with the right *curved 5 hand* over the left *curved 5 hand,* palms facing each other, move the hands in repeated circles in opposite directions in front of the chest.

mix[2] *v.* See signs for BEAT[1], CIRCULATE.

mixed up *v. phrase.* See sign for CONFUSE[1].

mobilize *v.* See sign for TRIP.

modify *v.* See sign for CHANGE[1].

moist *adj.* See sign for WET. Related forms: **moisten** *v.*, **moisture** *n.*

mom *n.* See sign for mother. Alternate form: **mommy** *n.*

moment *n.* See sign for MINUTE. Related form: **momentarily** *adv.*

Monday *n.*
[Initialized sign] Move the right *M hand,* palm facing in, in a double circle in front of the right shoulder.

money *n.* Same sign used for: **fund.**
[Represents putting money in one's hand] Tap the back of the right *flattened O hand,* palm facing up, with a double movement against the palm of the left *open hand,* palm facing up.

monitor *v.* See sign for CARE[1].

month *n.* Same sign used for: **one month.**
[The finger moves down the weeks on a calendar] Move the extended right index finger, palm facing in and finger pointing left, from the tip to the base of the extended left index finger, palm facing right and finger pointing up in front of the chest.

moon *n.*

[The shape of the crescent moon] Tap the thumb of the right *modified C hand,* palm facing left, against the right side of the forehead with a double movement.

more *adj., adv.*

[The hands seem to add more and more things together] Tap the fingertips of both *flattened O hands,* palms facing each other, together in front of the chest with a double movement.

more than *adj.* See sign for EXCESS.

morning *n.*

[Represents the sun coming up over the horizon] With the left *open hand* in the crook of the bent right arm, bring the right *open hand* upward, palm facing in.

most *adj., adv., n.*

[The hand rises to a higher level] Beginning with the palm sides of both *10 hands* together in front of the chest, bring the right hand upward, ending with the right hand in front of the right shoulder, palm facing left.

mother *n.* Same sign used for: **mama, mom, mommy.**

[Formed in the female area of the head] Tap the thumb of the right *5 hand,* palm facing left, against the chin with a double movement.

motion *v.* See sign for SUGGEST.

motive *n.* See signs for FEEL, ZEAL. Related form: **motivation.**

motor *n.* See sign for MACHINE.

mount *v.* See sign for PUT.

mountain *n.*

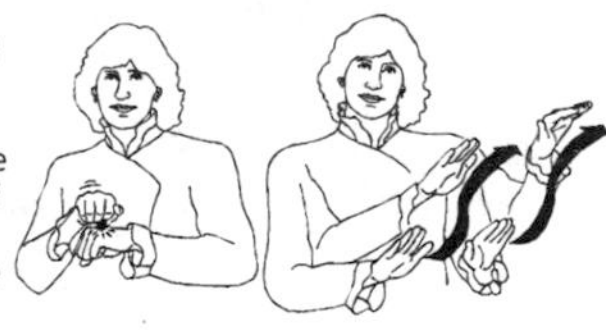

[**rock**[1] + the shape of a mountainside] Tap the palm side of the right *S hand* on the back of the left *S hand,* both palms facing down in front of the body. Then, beginning with both *open hands* in front of each side of the waist, palms facing down and fingers angled up, move the hands upward and forward at an angle with a large wavy movement.

mouse[1] *n.*

[Represents the twitching of a mouse's nose] Flick the extended right index finger, palm facing left, across the tip of the nose with a double movement.

mouse[2] *n.*
[Action of moving a computer mouse] Move the right *modified C hand*, palm forward, around in front of the right side of the body.

mouth *n.*
[Location of the mouth] Draw a circle around the mouth with the extended right index finger, palm facing in.

move *v.* Related form: **movement** *n.* Same sign used for: **relocate.**
[The hands seem to move something from one place to another] Beginning with both *flattened O hands* in front of the body, palms facing down, move the hands in large arcs to the right.

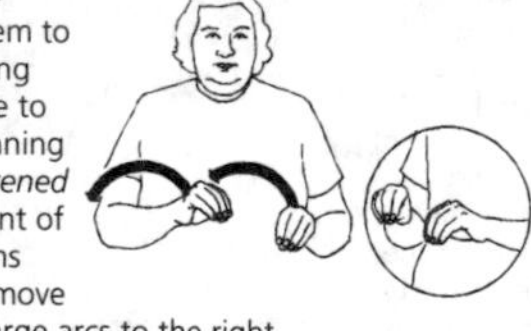

movie *n.* See sign for FILM.

much *n., adj., adv.* Same sign used for: **a lot, lots.**
[The hands expand to encompass something large] Beginning with the fingertips of both *curved 5 hands* touching each other in front of the body, palms facing each other, bring the hands outward to in front of each side of the chest.

mule *n.* See sign for DONKEY.

mull or **mull over** *v.* Same sign used for: **cogitate, deliberate, ponder.**

[Represents the brain as it cogitates] Wiggle the fingers of the right *4 hand* in a small repeated circle near the forehead, palm facing in.

multiplication *n.* See sign for ARITHMETIC.

multiply *v.* Same sign used for: **estimate, figure, figure out.**

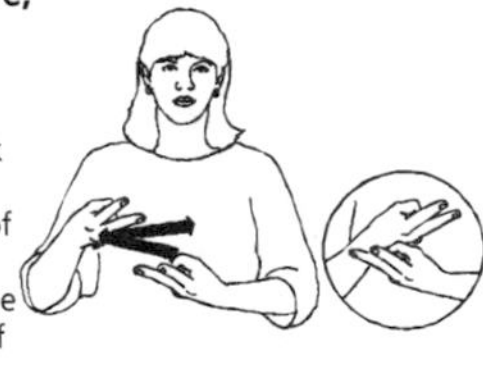

[The movement suggests combining things] Brush the back of the right *V hand* across the palm side of the left *V hand,* both palms facing up, as the hands cross in front of the chest.

murder *v.* See sign for KILL.

music *n.* Same sign used for: **chant, melody, sing, song.**

[Demonstrates the rhythm of music] Swing the little-finger side of the right *open hand,* palm facing left, back and forth with a double movement across the length of the bent left forearm held in front of the chest.

must *auxiliary v.* Same sign used for: **have to, necessary, ought to.**

[Suggests standing firm on a position] Move the bent index finger of the right *X hand,* palm facing forward, downward with a deliberate movement in front of the right side of the body by bending the wrist down.

mute *adj.* See sign for SILENT.

my *pron.* Same sign used for: **mine, own.**

[Pulling something to oneself] Place the palm of the right *open hand* on the chest, fingers pointing left.

myself *pron.*

[Sign moves toward oneself] Tap the thumb side of the right *A hand,* palm facing left, against the chest with a double movement.

mystery *n.* See sign for HIDE.

nab *v.* See signs for CAPTURE, CATCH[1].

nag *v.* See sign for PREACH.

naked *n.* See sign for NUDE.

name[1] *n., v.*

[The hands form an "X," which is used by illiterate people to sign their names] Tap the middle-finger side of the right *H hand* across the index-finger side of the left *H hand*.

name[2] *v.* See sign for CALL[2].

napkin *n.*

[Mime wiping one's mouth with a napkin] Wipe fingertips of the right *open hand* from side to side over the lips with a double movement, palm facing in.

narrow *adj.*

[The hands demonstrate something getting narrower] Bring both *open hands* from in front of each side of the body, palms facing each other, toward each other in front of the waist.

narrow down *v. phrase.* Same sign used for: **convey, focus on.**

[The hands move downward from wider to narrower] Beginning with both *open hands* in front of each shoulder, palms facing each other and fingers pointing forward, bring the hands downward toward each other in front of the body.

nasty *adj.* See signs for BAD, DIRTY.

nation *n.* Same sign used for: **native, natural, nature, normal, of course.** Related form: **national** *adj.*

[Initialized sign] Beginning with the right *N hand,* palm facing down, over the left *open hand,* palm facing down, move the right hand in a small circle and then straight down to land on the back of the left *open hand.*

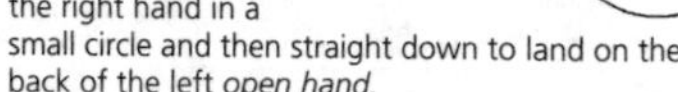

native *n.* See sign for NATION.

natural *n.* See sign for NATION.

nature *n.* See sign for NATION.

naughty *adj.* See sign for BAD.

nay *archaic.* See sign for NEVER MIND.

near *adv.* See sign for CLOSE.

near future, in the See sign for SOON[1].

nearly *adv.* See sign for ALMOST.

neat *adj.*

[Initialized sign similar to sign for **clean**] Slide the extended fingers of the right *N hand,* palm facing down, from the heel to the fingers of the upturned left *open hand,* fingers pointing forward.

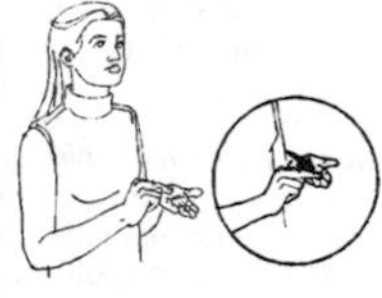

necessary *adj.* See sign for MUST, NEED.

neck *n.*

[Location of the neck] Tap the fingertips of the right *bent hand,* palm facing down, against the neck with a double movement.

necklace[1] *n.*

[Location of a necklace] Beginning with both extended index fingers touching near each side of the neck, bring the hands downward to touch near the middle of the chest.

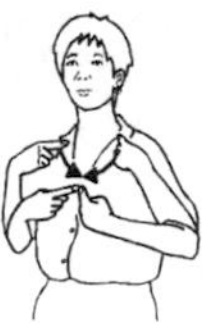

necklace[2] *n.* See sign for BEADS.

necktie *n.* Same sign used for: **tie.**

[Initialized sign showing the location of a necktie] Touch the fingertips of the right *N hand* first to near the neck and then to the lower chest, palm facing in.

need *v., n.* Same signs used for: **necessary, supposed to.**

[A forceful movement to emphasize need] Tap the bent index finger of the right *X hand,* palm facing down, with a short, repeated downward movement in front of the right side of the body, by bending the wrist down.

negative *adj.*
[Shape of a minus sign] Tap the thumb side of the extended right index finger, palm facing down and finger pointing forward, against the palm of the left *open hand,* palm facing right and fingers pointing up, with a double movement.

neglect *v.* See sign for IGNORE. Related forms: **negligence** *n.*, **negligent** *adj.*

neighbor *n.*
[**next door** + **person marker**] Beginning with the palm of the right *bent hand,* palm facing in and fingers pointing left, touching the back of the left *bent hand,* palm facing in and fingers pointing right, move the right hand forward in a small arc. Then move both *open hands,* palms facing each other, downward along each side of the body.

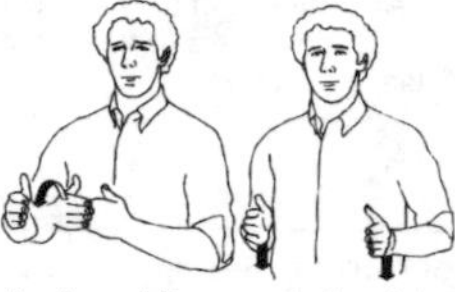

nephew *n.*
[Initialized sign formed near the male area of the head] Beginning with the extended fingers of the right *N hand* pointing toward the right side of the forehead, palm facing left, twist the wrist to point the fingers forward with a double movement.

nervous *adj.* Related form: **nervously** *adv.* Same sign used for: **anxiety, anxious.**

[Natural gesture of shaking when nervous] Shake both *5 hands* with a loose, repeated movement in front of each side of the body, palms facing each other and fingers pointing forward.

never *adv.*

[Natural gesture used to wave an unwanted thing away] Move the right *open hand* from near the right side of the face, palm facing left, downward with a large wavy movement to in front of the right side of the body, ending with the palm facing down.

never mind *slang.* Same sign used for: **blah** *(slang),* **nay** *(archaic).*

[Natural gesture] Beginning with the right *open hand* in front of the right shoulder, palm facing forward and fingers pointing up, bend the wrist to bring the hand downward to the right side of the body, ending with the fingers pointing down and the palm facing back.

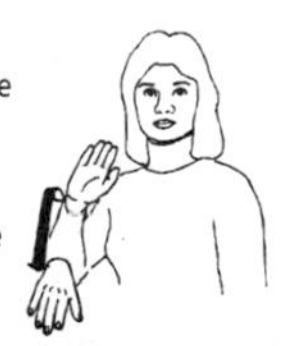

nevertheless *adv.* See sign for ANYWAY.

new *adj.*

[One hand presents the other hand with something new] Slide the back of the right *curved hand,* palm facing up, from the fingertips to the heel of the upturned left *open hand.*

newspaper *n.* Same sign used for: **issue, press, print, publication.**

[Represents putting movable type into place to set up a newspaper] Beginning with the right *G hand,* palm facing forward, above the left *open hand,* palm facing up, pull the right hand down toward the heel of the left hand with a double movement, closing the right thumb and index finger together each time.

next[1] *adj., adv., prep.* Same sign used for: **next to.**

[Demonstrates one hand overcoming an obstacle to move on to the next thing] Beginning with the right *bent hand,* palm facing in and fingers pointing left, closer to the chest than the left *open hand,* palm facing in and fingers pointing right, move the right hand up and over the left hand, ending with the right palm on the back of the left hand.

next[2] *adj.* See sign for TURN.

next door or **next-door** *adv.*

[Shows a location next to another thing] Beginning with the palm of the right *bent hand,* palm facing in and fingers pointing left, touching the back of the left *curved hand,* palm facing in and fingers pointing right, move the right hand forward in a small arc.

next to *prep.* See signs for BESIDE, NEXT[1].

nickel *n.* Same sign used for: **five cents.**

[The sign **cent** is formed with a *5 hand*] Beginning with the bent index finger of the right *5 hand,* palm facing left, touching the right side of the forehead, bring the hand forward with a double movement.

niece *n.*

[Initialized sign formed near the female area of the head] Beginning with the extended fingers of the right *N hand* pointing toward the right cheek, palm facing left, twist the wrist to point the fingers forward with a double movement.

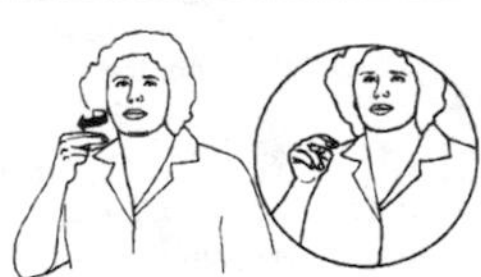

niggardly *adj.* See sign for GREEDY.

night *n.* Same sign used for: **tonight.**

[Represents the sun going down over the horizon] Tap the heel of the right *bent hand,* palm facing down, with a double movement on the back of the left *open hand* held across the chest, palm facing down.

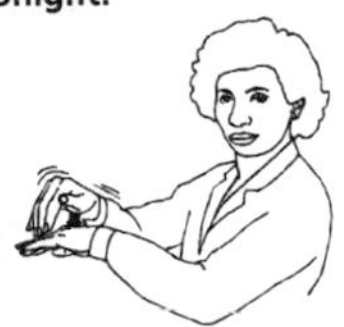

no[1] *adv.*

[Fingerspell **n-o** quickly] Snap the extended right index and middle fingers closed to the extended right thumb, palm facing down, while moving the hand down slightly.

no[2] *adv.* See sign for NONE.

nod *v.* See sign for BOW[1].

noise *n.* Same sign used for: **aloud, loud, sound.**
[Indicates the vibration of a loud sound coming from the ears] Beginning with the bent index fingers of both *5 hands* touching each ear, palms facing in, move the hands forward with a deliberate movement while shaking the hands.

nominate *v.* See signs for APPLY[2], SUGGEST.

nonchalant *adj.* See sign for DON'T CARE.

none[1] *pron.* Same sign used for: **no.**
[Indicates zero amount of something in the hand] Move both *flattened O hands,* palms facing forward, from side to side with a repeated movement in front of each side of the chest.

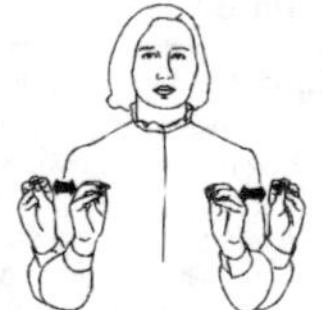

noon *n.* Alternate form: **noontime.** Same sign used for: **midday.**
[Represents the sun straight overhead at noon] Place the right elbow, arm extended up and right *open hand* facing forward, on the back of the left *open hand* held across the body, palm facing down.

normal *n., adj.* See sign for NATION.

north *n., adj., adv.*

[Initialized sign moving in the direction of north on a map] Move the right *N hand,* palm facing forward, upward in front of the right shoulder.

nose *n.*

[Location of the nose] Touch the extended right index finger to the right side of the nose, palm facing down.

nosy *adj. Informal.* Same sign used for: **butt in, meddle, peek, pry, snoop.**

[Represents one's nose extending to insert it into another's business] Beginning with the bent index finger of the right *X hand* beside the nose, palm facing left, bring the right hand downward and insert the bent index finger in the thumb-side opening of the left *O hand,* palm facing right.

not *adv.* Same sign used for: **don't.**

[Flicking away something distasteful] Bring the extended thumb of the right *10 hand* from under the chin, palm facing left, forward with a deliberate movement.

nothing *n.*

[The hand opens to reveal nothing in it] Beginning with the index-finger side of the right *O hand* under the chin, palm facing forward, bring the hand downward and forward while opening into a *5 hand,* palm facing down.

notice[1] *v.* Same sign used for: **aware, recognize.**

[Brings the eye down to look at something in the hand] Bring the extended curved right index finger from touching the cheek near the right eye, palm facing left, downward to touch the palm of the left *open hand,* palm facing right in front of the chest.

notice[2] *v.* See sign for INFORM.

notify *v.* See sign for INFORM.

not my fault *adj.* See sign for NOT RESPONSIBLE.

notorious *adj.* See sign for FAMOUS.

not responsible *adj.* Same sign for: **hands off, not my fault.**

[Natural gesture for flicking away responsibility] Beginning with the fingertips of both *8 hands* touching each shoulder, palms facing each other, flick the hands quickly forward while opening into *5 hands.*

now *adv.* Same sign used for: **current, present, prevailing, urgent.**

[Indicates a presence right before you] Bring both *bent hands,* palms facing up, downward in front of each side of the body.

nude *adj.* Same sign used for: **bare, naked.**

[The sign **empty** formed downward on the hand representing a person's body] Move the bent middle finger of the right *5 hand,* palm facing in, downward on the back of the left *open hand,* palm facing in and fingers pointing down, from the wrist to off the fingertips.

number *n.* Alternate form: **numeral.** Related form: **numeric** *adj.*

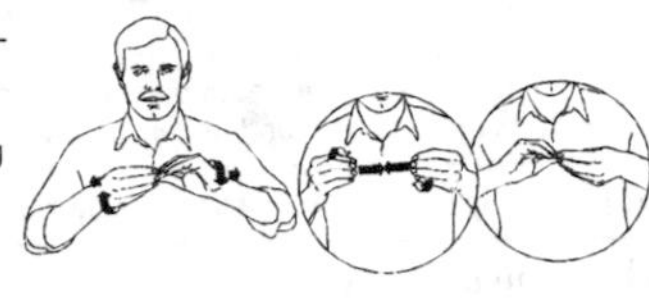

[Adding two quantities together] Beginning with the fingertips of both *flattened O hands* touching, left palm angled forward and right palm facing in, bring the hands apart while twisting the wrists in opposite directions and touch the fingertips again, ending with the left palm facing in and the right palm angled forward.

numerous *adj.* See sign for MANY.

nurse *n.*

[Initialized sign similar to sign for **doctor**] Tap the extended fingers of the right *N hand,* palm facing down, with a double movement on the wrist of the left *open hand* held in front of the body, palm facing up.

nut *n.* See sign for PEANUT.

obey *v.* Related forms: **obedience, obedient.**
[Represents placing one's own ideas in a position subservient to another's] Beginning with the right *O hand* in front of the forehead and the left *O hand* in front of the left shoulder, both palms facing in, bring the hands downward simultaneously while opening the fingers, ending with both *open hands* in front of the body, palms facing up and fingers pointing forward.

---

object *v.* See signs for COMPLAIN, DISAGREE.

---

objection *n.* See sign for PROTEST[1].

---

objective *n.* See sign for GOAL.

---

obligation *n.* See sign for BURDEN.

---

observe *v.* See sign for LOOK OVER.

---

obsession *n.* Related forms: **obsess** *v.*, **obsessive** *n, adj.* Same sign for: **persevere, persistent.**
[The finger used for feeling remains on the other hand during a movement that signifies duration] With the bent middle finger of the right *5 hand* on the back of the left *open hand,* both palms facing down, move the hands forward in a repeated circular movement in front of the body.

---

obstruct *v.* See sign for PREVENT.

---

obtain *v.* See sign for GET.

occasional[1] *adj.* Related form: **occasionally** *adv.* Same sign used for: **once in a while, periodically.**

[**next-next-next**] Beginning with the right *bent hand* in front of the right side of the chest, palm facing left and fingers pointing left, move the hand forward in a deliberate double arc.

occasional[2] *adj.* See sign for SOMETIMES.

occupation *n.* See sign for WORK.

occupy *v.* See sign for CAPTURE.

occur *v.* See signs for HAPPEN, SHOW UP. Related form: **occurrence** *n.*

odd *adj.* See sign for STRANGE.

odor *n.* See sign for SMELL.

of course See sign for NATION.

off *prep., adv.*

[Shows moving one hand off the other hand] Beginning with the palm of the right *open hand* across the back of the left *open hand* at an angle, both palms facing down in front of the body, raise the right hand upward in front of the chest.

offer *v.* See sign for SUGGEST.

office *n.*
[Initialized sign similar to sign for **box**] Beginning with both *O hands* in front of each side of the body, palms facing each other, move the hands deliberately in opposite directions, ending with the left hand near the chest and the right hand several inches forward of the left hand, both palms facing in.

officer *n.* See signs for CAPTAIN, CHIEF.

officially *adv.* See sign for DECIDE.

often *adv.* Same sign used for: **frequently.**
[The sign **again** formed with a repeated movement to indicate frequency of occurrence] Touch the fingertips of the right *bent hand,* palm facing left, first on the heel and then on the fingers of the left *open hand,* palm angled up.

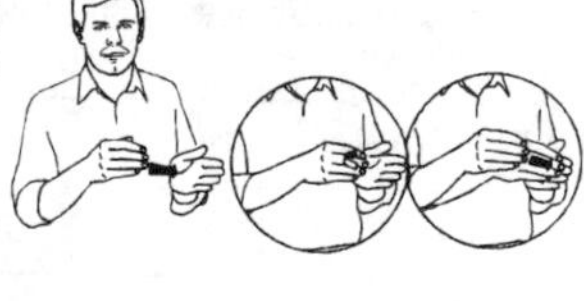

Oh or **Oh, I see** *interj.*
Move the right *Y hand* downward, palm angled down, with a small double movement in front of the right side of the body.

okay *adj.* See sign for SUPERB.

old *adj.*

[Shows the shape of a beard on an old man] Move the right *C hand* from near the chin, palm facing left, downward a short distance while closing into an *S hand.*

omit *v.* See sign for ELIMINATE[1].

on *prep.*

[Shows moving one hand on the other] Bring the palm of the right *open hand* downward on the back of the left *open hand* held in front of the body, both palms facing down.

once *adv.*

Beginning with the extended right index finger touching the left *open hand* held in front of the body, palm facing right and fingers pointing forward, bring the right finger upward with a quick movement while twisting the right wrist in, ending with the palm facing in and finger pointing up in front of the right side of the chest.

once in a while *adv.* See sign for OCCASIONAL[1].

one another *pron.* See sign for ASSOCIATE.

one dollar *n. phrase.* See sign for FIRST.

one fourth *n.* Related form: **one-fourth** *adj.* Same sign used for: **quarter.**

[**one** + **four** formed over each other as in a fraction] Beginning with the extended right index finger pointing up in front of the right side of the chest, palm facing in, drop the hand while opening into a *4 hand.*

one half *n.* Related form: **one-half** *adj.* Same sign used for: **half**.

[**one** + **two** formed over each other as in a fraction] Beginning with the extended right index finger pointing up in front of the right side of the chest, palm facing in, drop the hand while opening into a *2 hand.*

one minute *n.* See sign for MINUTE.

one month *n.* See sign for MONTH.

one third *n.* Related form: **one-third** *adj.* Same sign used for: **third.**

[**one** + **three** formed over each other as in a fraction] Beginning with the extended right index finger pointing up in front of the right side of the chest, palm facing in, drop the hand while opening into a *3 hand.*

one week *n.* See sign for WEEK.

onion *n.*

[As if wiping a tear away from onion fumes] Twist the knuckle of the bent index finger of the right *X hand,* palm facing forward, with a double movement near the outside corner of the right eye.

only[1] *adj., adv.*

[Emphasizes one alone] Beginning with the extended right index finger pointing up in front of the right shoulder, palm facing forward, twist the wrist in, ending with the palm facing in near the right side of the chest.

only[2] *adj., adv.* See sign for ALONE.

onward *adv.* See sign for GO ON.

open *adj., v.*

[Represents doors opening] Beginning with the index-finger sides of both *B hands* touching in front of the chest, palms facing forward, twist both wrists while bringing the hands apart to in front of each side of the chest, ending with the palms facing each other and the fingers pointing forward.

operate[1] *v.* Related form: **operation** *n.* Same sign used for: **surgery.**

[Represents the action of cutting during surgery] Move the thumb of the right *A hand,* palm facing down, from the fingers to the heel of the left *open hand,* palm facing right and fingers pointing forward.

operate[2] *v.* See signs for MANAGE, RUN[2].

opinion *n.*

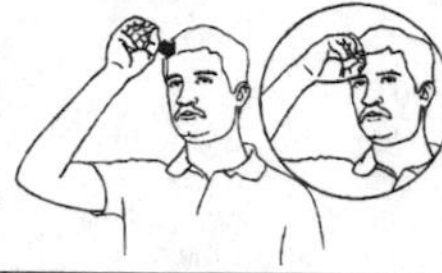

[Initialized sign] Move the right *O hand,* palm facing left in front of the forehead, toward the head with a double movement.

opponent *n.* See sign for ENEMY.

opportunity *n.*

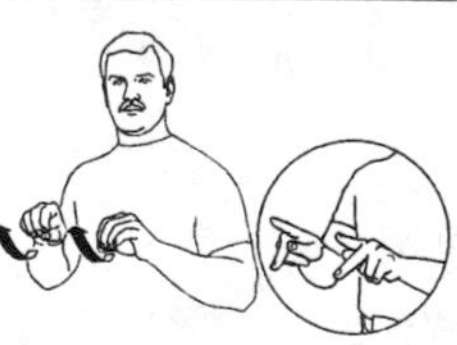

[Abbreviation **o-p** formed in a way that is similar to the sign for **let**] Beginning with both *O hands* in front of the chest, palms facing down, move the hands forward and upward in an arc while changing into *P hands.*

opposed to *v. phrase.* See sign for AGAINST.

opposite *adj.* Related form: **oppose** *v.* Same sign used for: **contrary, contrast, counter.**

[Shows two things repelled by each other] Beginning with the fingertips of both extended index fingers touching in front of the chest, palms facing in, bring the hands straight apart to in front of each side of the chest.

opposition *n.* See sign for STRUGGLE.

or[1] *conj.* Same sign used for: **then.**

[Touches two choices] Tap the extended right index finger, palm facing in, first to the thumb tip and then to the end of the index finger of the left *L hand,* palm facing right and index finger pointing forward.

or[2] *conj.* Same sign used for: EITHER.

orange *n., adj.*

[The hand seems to squeeze an orange] Beginning with the right *C hand* in front of the mouth, palm facing left, squeeze the fingers open and closed with a repeated movement, forming an *S hand* each time.

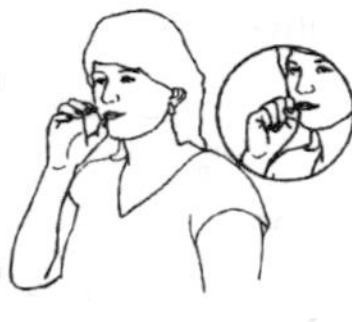

ordeal *n.* See sign for EXPERIENCE.

order *n., v.* Same sign used for: **command, direct.**

[Represents taking words from the mouth and directing them at another] Move the extended right index finger, palm facing left and finger pointing up, from in front of the mouth straight forward while turning the palm down, ending with the finger pointing forward.

ordinary *adj.* See sign for DAILY.

organize *v.* See sign for PREPARE.

origin *n.* See sign for START. Related form: **origination** *n.*

originate *v.* See sign for INVENT.

other[1] *adj., n.* Same sign used for: **else.**

[The thumb points over to another person, object, etc.] Beginning with the right *10 hand* in front of the chest, palm facing down, twist the hand upward to the right, ending with the palm facing up and the extended thumb pointing right.

other[2] *adj.* See sign for ANOTHER.

ought to *v. phrase.* See sign for MUST.

our *adj.* Related form: **ours** *pron.*

[The hand seems to draw a possession to oneself] Beginning with the thumb side of the right *C hand* on the right side of the chest, palm facing left, bring the hand forward in an arc across the chest, ending with the little-finger side of the left hand on the left side of the chest, palm facing right.

ourselves *pl. pron.*

[Uses the handshape used for reflexive pronouns] Beginning with the thumb of the right *A hand* touching the right side of the chest, palm facing left, bring the hand in an arc across the chest and touch again on the left side of the chest.

out *adv.* Same sign used for: **go out.**

[Demonstrates a movement out of something] Beginning with the right *5 hand,* palm facing down, inserted in the thumb side opening of the left *C hand,* palm facing right, bring the right hand upward, closing the fingers and thumb together into a *flattened O hand.*

outdoors *adv.* See sign for OUTSIDE.

outrage *n.* See sign for ANGER.

outside *n., adj., adv., prep.* Same sign used for: **external, outdoors.**

[An exaggerated form of the sign for **out**] Beginning with the right *5 hand,* palm facing down, inserted in the thumb side opening of the left *C hand,* palm facing right, bring the right hand upward and forward in an arc while closing the fingers and thumb together into a *flattened O hand* in front of the chest, fingers pointing in.

over[1] *prep.* Same sign used for: **exceed, too much.**

[Shows a location higher than another] Beginning with the fingertips of the right *bent hand* on the fingertips of the left *bent hand,* palms facing each other and fingers pointing in opposite directions, bring the right hand upward a short distance in a small arc.

over[2] *prep., adv.* See signs for ABOVE, ACROSS, END[1], FINISH[1].

overcome *v.* See sign for DEFEAT.

overflow *v.* Same sign used for: **plenty, run over.**

[Demonstrates a substance flowing over the sides of a container] Slide the fingers of the right *open hand,* palm facing forward, over the index-finger side of the left *open hand,* palm facing in, while opening into a *5 hand* as it goes over to the back of the left hand.

overlook *v.* Same sign used for: **oversight.**

[Represents something passing in front of the eyes without notice] Beginning with the right *open hand* near the right side of the head, palm facing left and fingers pointing up, move the hand in an arc in front of the face to the left while turning the fingers down, ending with the fingers pointing left and the palm facing in, in front of the left side of the chest.

owe *v.* See sign for AFFORD.

own[1] *adj., pron.* Same sign used for: **self.**

[The hand moves back toward oneself] Bring the knuckles of the right *10 hand,* palm facing right, back against the center of the chest.

own[2] *adj., pron.* See sign for MY.

pace *n.* See sign for PROCEDURE. Shared idea of taking orderly steps.

pack *v.*
[Mime putting things into a suitcase] Beginning with both *flattened O hands* in front of each side of the chest, palms facing down, move the hands downward with an alternating double movement.

package *n.* See signs for BOX, ROOM.

page *n.* Same sign used for: **dictionary.**
[The thumb seems to flip through the pages of a book] Strike the extended thumb of the right *A hand*, palm facing down, against the left open palm with a double circular upward movement.

pain *n.* See also sign for HURT. Same sign used for: **ache, injury.**
[Similar to sign for **hurt** except with a twisting movement] Beginning with both extended index fingers pointing toward each other in front of the chest, right palm facing down and left palm facing up, twist the wrist in opposite directions, ending with right palm facing up and the left palm facing down.

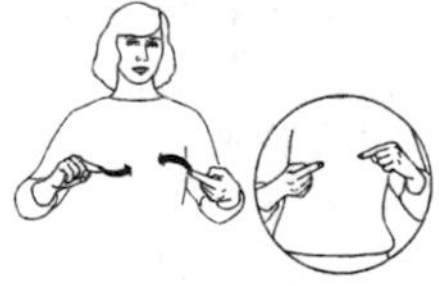

paint *n.*, *v.* Same sign used for: **brush.**

[Mime the action of a paintbrush's bristles moving when painting] Bring the fingertips of the right *open hand* down the length of the left palm from the fingertips to the base with a double movement, pulling the back of the right fingers up the left palm to the fingertips each time.

pair *n.* See signs for BOTH, COUPLE.

pal *n.* See sign for FRIEND.

pamphlet *n.* See sign for MAGAZINE.

panic *n.*,*v.* See sign for AFRAID.

panties *n.*

[Mime pulling up panties] Beginning with the fingertips of both *F hands,* palms facing in, touching each hip, move the hands up to touch the fingertips again at the waist.

pants *n.* Same sign used for: **jeans, slacks, trousers.**

[Shows location of pants on both legs] Beginning with the fingertips of both *open hands* touching each hip, palms facing in, move the hands upward toward the waist with a double movement.

papa *n.* See sign for FATHER.

paper *n., adj.*
[The pressing of pulp to make paper] Brush the heel of the right *open hand,* palm facing down, on the heel of the left *open hand,* palm facing up, in front of the body with a double movement.

paper clip *n.*
[Demonstrates clipping a paper clip on the edge of paper] Beginning with the extended thumb of the right *U hand* against the palm side of the left *B hand,* palm facing down, close the extended right middle and index fingers down against the back of the left hand.

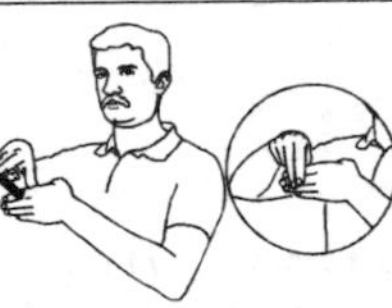

parable *n.* See sign for STORY.

paradox *n.* See sign for PUZZLED.

parched *adj.* See sign for THIRSTY.

pardon *v.* See signs for DISMISS, FORGIVE.

parents *pl. n.*
[**mother** + **father**] Touch the thumb of the right *5 hand,* palm facing left, first to the chin, then to the forehead.

park *v.*
[The handshape represents a vehicle that is set on the other hand as if to park] Tap the little-finger side of the right *3 hand,* palm facing left and fingers pointing forward, on the palm of the left *open hand,* palm facing up, with a repeated movement.

parole *n.,v.* See sign for DISMISS.

part[1] *n.* Related form: **partial** *adj.* Same sign used for: **piece, section, segment.**

[The hand seems to divide what is in the other hand into parts] Slide the little-finger side of the right *open hand,* palm facing left, across the palm of left *open hand,* palm facing up, with a curved movement.

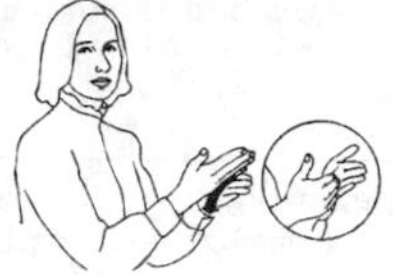

part[2] *n., adj.* See sign for SOME.

part from *v. phrase.* See sign for DISCONNECT.

partial to *adj.* Same sign used for: **favorite.**

[Pointing out a favorite] Tap the fingertips of the right *B hand,* palm facing left, with a double movement against the index finger of the left *B hand* held up in front of the chest, palm facing right.

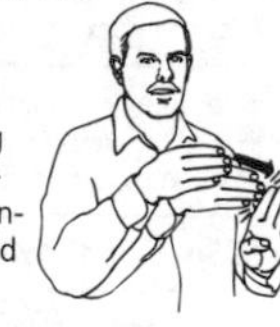

participate *v.* See sign for JOIN[1].

particular *adj.* See sign for POINT[2].

party *n.*

[Initialized sign] Beginning with both *P hands* in front of the right side of the body, palms facing down, swing the hands from side to side in front of the body with a large double arc.

pass *v.* Same sign used for: **by, past.**

[One hand moves past the other hand] Beginning with both *A hands* in front of the body, palms facing in opposite directions and left hand somewhat forward of the right hand, move the right hand forward, striking the knuckles of the left hand as it passes.

pass around *v. phrase.* Same sign used for: **deal, pass out.**

[Mime passing something around] Beginning with the fingers of both *flattened O hands* together in front of the body, palms facing up, move the right hand forward and then twist it around to the right, ending with the palm facing left.

passion *n.* See sign for WANT.

passive *adj.* See sign for QUIET.

pass out *v. phrase* See sign for PASS AROUND.

password *n.* Same sign used for: **access code.**

[**secret + word**] Tap the thumb side of the right *A hand*, palm left, against the mouth with a repeated movement. Then touch the extended fingers of the right *G hand,* palm left, against the extended left index finger pointing up in front of the chest, palm right.

past *adv.* See signs for AGO, BEFORE, PASS.

path *n.* See sign for ROAD. Related form: **pathway** *n.*

patient[1] *adj.* Related form: **patience** *n.* Same sign used for: **bear, tolerant, tolerate.**

[The thumb seems to seal the lips as a person tolerates something] Move the right *A hand,* palm facing left, downward in front of the chin.

patient[2] *n.*

[Initialized sign similar to sign for **hospital**] Move the extended middle finger of the right *P hand,* palm facing in, first down and then forward on the left upper arm.

patrol *v.* See sign for CARE[1].

pauper *n.* See sign for POOR.

pause *v.* See sign for HOLD[2].

pay *v.*

[Represents directing money from the hand to pay another person] Beginning with the extended right index finger touching the palm of the left *open hand,* palms facing each other, move the right finger forward and off the left fingertips.

pay attention *v. phrase.* See sign for ATTENTION.

peace *n.* Related form: **peaceful** *adj.*

[The hands seem to calm down what is before them] Beginning with the palms of both *open hands* together in front of the chest, right palm facing forward and left palm facing in, twist the wrist to reverse positions.

Then move the hands downward, ending with both *open hands* in front of each side of the waist, palms facing down and fingers pointing forward.

peach *n.*
[The fingers seem to feel peach fuzz] Beginning with the fingertips of the right *curved 5 hand* on the right cheek, palm facing left, bring the fingers down with a double movement, forming a *flattened O hand* near the right side of the chin.

peanut *n.* Same sign used for: **nut.**
[Represents peanut butter sticking to the back of one's teeth] Flick the extended right thumb, palm facing left, forward off the edge of the top front teeth with an upward double movement.

peculiar *adj.* See sign for STRANGE.

peddle *v.* See sign for SELL.

peek *v.* See sign for NOSY.

penalty *n.* See sign for PUNISH. Related form: **penalize** *v.*

pencil *n.*
[Indicates wetting the tip of a pencil and then writing with it] Touch the fingertips of the right *modified X hand,* palm facing in, near the mouth. Then move the right hand smoothly down and across the upturned left *open hand* from the heel to off the fingertips.

penitent *adj.* See sign for SORRY. Related form: **penitence** *n.*

penniless *adj.* Same sign used for: **broke** (*informal*).
[Gesture indicates a broken neck to signify being broke] Bring the little-finger side of the right *bent hand,* palm facing down and fingers pointing back, against the right side of the neck with a deliberate movement while bending the head down to the left.

penny *n.* See sign for CENT.

pension *n.* Same sign used for: **allowance, royalty, subscribe, welfare.**
[Collecting money out of nowhere] With right *curved hand* in front of the right shoulder, palm facing back, bring the hand downward and inward toward the right side of the chest with a double movement, closing the fingers to form an *A hand* each time.

people *n.* Same sign used for: **folk, public.**
[Initialized sign] Move both *P hands,* palms facing down, in alternating forward circles in front of each side of the body.

pepper *n.*

[The hand seems to drop pepper on food] Shake the right *F hand,* palm facing down, up and down in front of the right side of the body with a repeated movement.

per *prep.* See sign for EACH.

perceive *v.* See signs for PREDICT, UNDERSTAND. Related form: **perception** *n.*

percent *n.* Related form: **percentage** *n.*

[Draw the shape of a percent sign in the air] Move the right *O hand* from near the right side of the face, palm facing forward, a short distance to the right, then down at an angle to in front of the right side of the chest.

perfect *adj.* Related form: **perfection** *n.* Same sign used for: **accurate, ideal.**

[Initialized sign showing things matching perfectly] Move the right *P hand,* palm facing left, in a small circle above the left *P hand,* palm facing up. Then move the right hand downward to touch both middle fingers together in front of the chest.

perform *n.* See sign for ACT[2]. Related form: **performance** *n.*

perhaps *adv.* See sign for MAYBE.

period *n.* Same sign used for: **decimal, dot.**

[Draw a period in the air] With the right index finger and thumb pinched together, palm facing forward in front of the right side of the chest, push the right hand forward a short distance.

periodically *adv.* See sign for OCCASIONAL[1].

perish *v.* See signs for DIE, DISSOLVE.

permit[1] *v.* Related form: **permission** *n.* Same sign used for: **privilege.**

[Initialized sign similar to sign for **try**] Beginning with both *P hands* in front of the body, palms facing down, swing the wrists to move both hands forward and upward in small arcs.

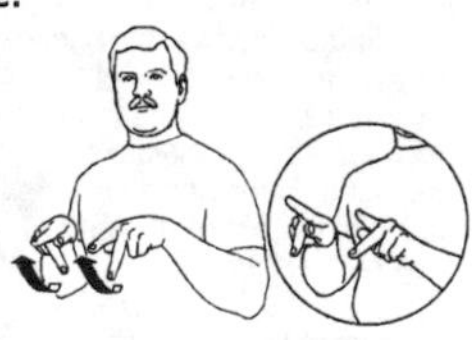

permit[2] *v.* See sign for LET.

perplexed *adj.* See sign for PUZZLED.

persevere *v.* See sign for OBSESSION.

persistent *adj.* See signs for CONSTANT, OBSESSION. Related form: **persistence** *n.*

person *n.*

[Initialized sign following the shape of a person] Bring both *P hands,* palms facing each other, downward along the sides of the body with a parallel movement.

personal *adj.* Same sign used for: **personnel.**
[Initialized sign] Move the right *P hand,* palm facing down, in a small double circle on the left side of the chest with a double movement.

personality *n.*
[Initialized sign similar to sign for **character**[1]] Move the right *P hand,* palm facing down, in a small circle in front of the left side of the chest. Then bring the thumb side of the right *P hand* back against the left side of the chest.

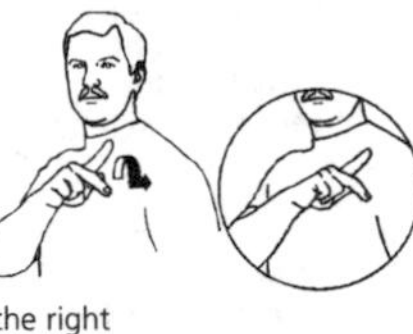

person marker *n.*
[The hands follow the shape of a person] Move both *open hands,* palms facing each other, downward along each side of the body.

personnel *n.* See sign for PERSONAL.

perspire *v.* See sign for SWEAT. Related form: **perspiration** *n.*

petition *n.* See sign for SUGGEST.

philander *v.* See sign for FLIRT.

phone *n., v.* See sign for TELEPHONE.

photo *n.* See sign for PICTURE. Alternate form: **photograph.**

photograph *v.* See sign for TAKE PICTURES.

phrase *n.* See sign for STORY.

physician *n.* See sign for DOCTOR.

pick *v.* See sign for CHOOSE.

picnic *n.*

[Represents eating a sandwich at a picnic] With the left *bent hand* over the back of the right *bent hand,* both palms facing down and fingers pointing toward the mouth, move the hands toward the mouth with a repeated movement.

picture *n.* Same sign used for: **photo, photograph.**

[The hand seems to focus the eyes on an image and then record it on paper] Move the right *C hand,* palm facing forward, from near the right side of the face downward, ending with the index-finger side of the right *C hand* against the palm of the left *open hand,* palm facing right.

pie *n.*

[Demonstrates cutting a pie into slices] Slide the fingertips of the right *open hand,* palm facing left, from the fingers to the heel of the upturned left hand, fingers pointing forward, and then perpendicularly across the left palm.

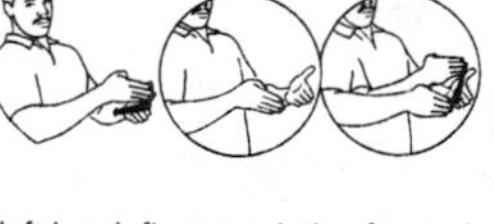

piece *n.* See sign for PART[1].

pig *n.*

[Similar to sign for **dirty**] With the back of the right *open hand* under the chin, palm facing down, bend the right fingers down and up again with a double movement.

pile[1] *n.* Same sign used for: **batch, bulk, load.**

[The shape and size of a pile] Move the right *5 hand* from in front of the left side of the chest, palm facing right and fingers pointing forward, upward in an arc in front of the right shoulder, ending near the right side of the body, palm facing left.

pile[2] *n.* See sign for AMOUNT.

pill *n.*

[Represents flicking a pill into the mouth] Beginning with the index finger of the right *A hand* tucked under the thumb, palm facing in, flick the right index finger open toward the mouth with a double movement.

pillage *v.* See sign for STEAL.

pillow *n.*

[The hands seem to squeeze a soft pillow] With the fingers of both *flattened C hands* pointing toward each other near the right ear, palms facing each other, close the fingers to the thumbs of each hand with a repeated movement.

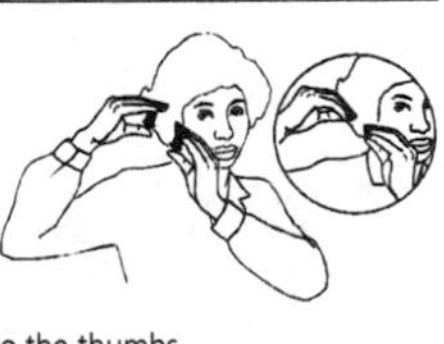

pin *n.*

[Represents clipping on a pin] Beginning with the thumb of the right *modified C hand* against the left side of the chest, palm facing left, pinch the right index finger to the thumb.

pink *adj.*

[Initialized sign similar to **red**] Brush the middle finger of the right *P hand*, palm facing in, downward across the lips with a short repeated movement.

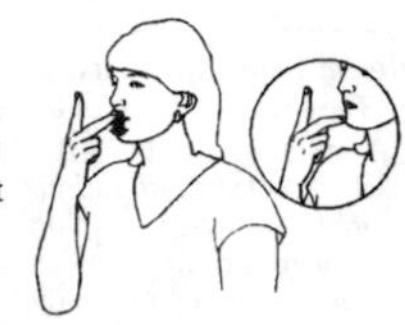

pinpoint *n.* See sign for POINT[1].

pipe[1] *n.* Same sign used for: **handle, lever, pole, rod.**

[The shape of a pipe] Beginning with the index-finger sides of both *O hands* touching in front of the chest, palms facing forward, move the hands apart to in front of each side of the chest.

pipe[2] *n.* See sign for STICK[2].

pistol *n.* See sign for GUN.

pitch *v.* See sign for THROW.

pizza *n.*

[**z** formed with *P hand*] Form a *Z* with the right *P hand*, palm facing left, in front of the right side of the chest.

place[1] *n.* Same sign used for: **position.**

[Initialized sign outlining an area] Beginning with the middle fingers of both *P hands* touching in front of the body, palms facing each other, move the hands apart in a circular movement back until they touch again near the chest.

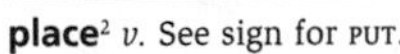

place[2] *v.* See sign for PUT.

place[3] *n.* See sign for AREA.

plan *n., v.* Same sign used for: **arrange, prepare, schedule.**

[The hands show a smooth and orderly flow of events] Move both *open hands* from in front of the left side of the body, palms facing each other and fingers pointing forward, in a long smooth movement to in front of the right side of the body.

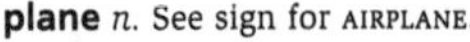

plane *n.* See sign for AIRPLANE.

plant *n.*

[Represents a seed sprouting and growing as it emerges from the ground] Bring the right *flattened O hand,* palm facing in, with a repeated movement upward through the left *C hand,* palm facing in and fingers pointing right, while spreading the right fingers into a *5 hand* each time.

plate *n.* Same sign used for: **saucer.**

[The shape of a plate] Move both *modified C hands* downward with a short repeated movement in front of each side of the body, palms facing each other.

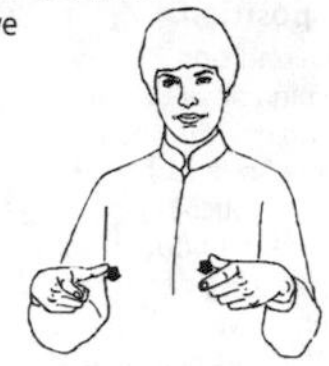

play[1] *v., n.* Same sign used for: **romp.**

[The movement is loose and playful] Swing both *Y hands* up and down by twisting the wrists in front of each side of the body with a repeated movement.

play[2] *n.* See sign for ACT[2].

play cards *v. phrase.* See sign for CARDS.

plead *v.* See sign for BEG.

pleasant *adj.* See signs for COOL, FRIENDLY.

please[1] *adv.*

[Rubbing the heart, indicating a feeling of well-being] Rub the palm of the right *open hand* in a large circle on the chest.

please[2] *v.* See sign for ENJOY. Related form: **pleasure** *n.*

plenty *n.* See signs for ENOUGH, OVERFLOW.

plush *adj.* See sign for LAYER.

pocketbook *n.* See sign for PURSE.

point[1] *n.* Same sign used for: **particular, pinpoint, specific, target.**

[Demonstrates pointing at a specific thing] Bring the right extended index finger from in front of the right shoulder, palm facing left and finger pointing up, downward to touch the left extended index finger held in front of the left side of the chest, palm facing right and finger pointing up.

point[2] *v.* See sign for THERE.

pole *n.* See signs for PIPE[1], STICK[2].

police *n.* Same sign used for: **badge, cop, marshall, security, sheriff.**

[Shows the location of a police badge] Tap the thumb side of the right *modified C hand,* palm facing left, against the left side of the chest with a double movement.

polite *adj.* Same sign used for: **courteous, courtesy, gentle, manners, prim.**

[The ruffles on an old-fashioned shirt worn in polite society] Tap the thumb of the right *5 hand,* palm facing left, with a double movement against the center of the chest.

politics *n.* Related form: **political** *adj.*

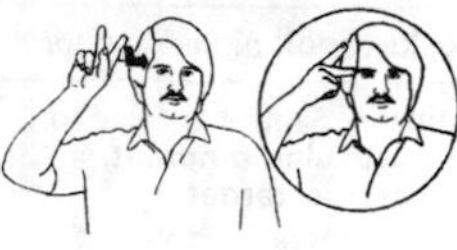

[Initialized sign similar to sign for **government**] Beginning with the right *P hand* near the right side of the head, palm facing forward, twist the wrist to turn the palm back and touch the middle finger of the right *P hand* against the right side of the forehead.

pollution *n.* See sign for DIRTY.

ponder *v.* See signs for MULL, WONDER.

poor *adj.* Same sign used for: **pauper, poverty.**

[Represents the tattered sleeves on the elbows of poor people] Beginning with the fingertips of the right *curved 5 hand,* palm facing up, touching the elbow of the bent left arm, pull the right hand downward while closing the fingers to the thumb with a double movement, forming a *flattened O hand* each time.

poor thing *n. phrase.* See sign for MERCY.

pop *v.* See sign for SODA POP.

popcorn *n.*

[Shows action of popcorn popping] Beginning with both *S hands* in front of each side of the body, palms facing up, alternately move each hand upward while flicking out each index finger with a repeated movement.

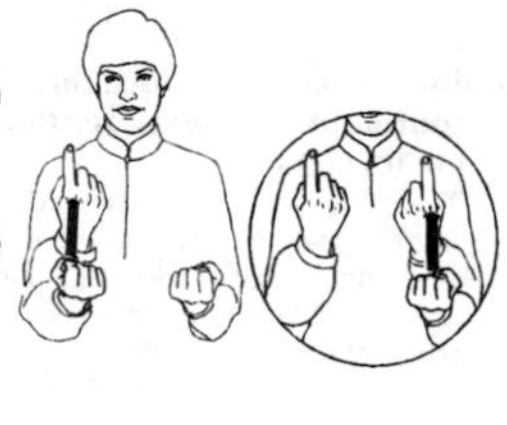

popular *adj.*

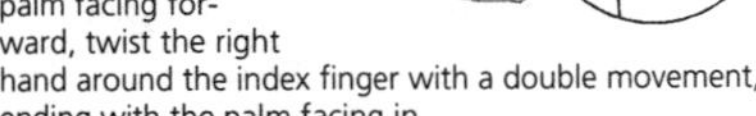

[Represents many people surrounding a popular person] With the extended left index finger against the palm of the right *5 hand,* palm facing forward, twist the right hand around the index finger with a double movement, ending with the palm facing in.

pop up *v. phrase.* See sign for SHOW UP.

portray *v.* See sign for SHOW[1].

position *n.* See sign for PLACE.

possess *v.* See signs for CAPTURE, GREEDY.

post *v.* See sign for APPLY[1].

postage *n.* See sign for STAMP[1].

postage stamp *n.* See sign for STAMP[1].

postpone *v.* Same sign used for: **defer, delay, put off.**

[Represents taking something and putting it off until the future] Beginning with both *F hands* in front of the body, palms facing each other and the left hand nearer to the body than the right hand, move both hands forward in small arcs.

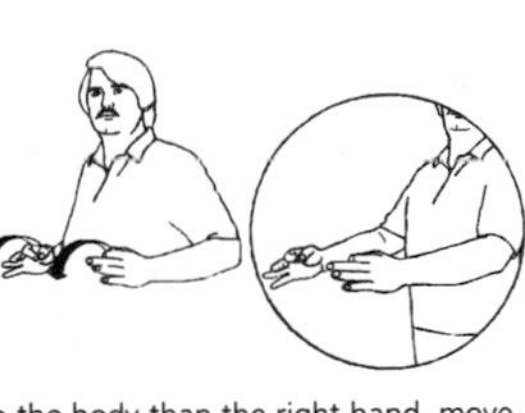

pot *n.* See sign for BOWL.

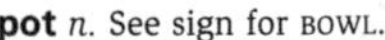

potato *n.*

[Represents putting fork tines into a baked potato to see if it is done] Tap the fingertips of the right *bent V hand,* palm facing down, with a double movement on the back of the left *open hand,* palm facing down.

potent *adj.* See sign for POWER[1].

pound *n.* See sign for WEIGH.

pour *v.*

[Mime holding a large container and pouring from it] Beginning with both *C hands* in front of the body, palms facing each other, tip the hands so that the right hand is above the left hand, palm facing down, and the left hand is in front of the body, palm facing up.

poverty *n.* See sign for POOR.

power[1] *n.* Related form: **powerful** *adj.* Same sign used for: **mighty, potent, strength, sturdy.**

[Demonstrate power in one's arms] Move both S hands, palms facing in, forward with a short deliberate movement from in front of each shoulder.

power[2] *n.* See sign for STRONG[1].

practice *n.*, *v.* Same sign used for: **exercise, rehearse, training.**

[The repetitive action symbolizes doing something again and again] Rub the knuckles of the right *A hand,* palm facing down, back and forth on the extended left index finger held in front of the chest, palm facing down and finger pointing right, with a repeated movement.

pray[1] *v.* Related form: **prayer** *n.*

[Natural gesture for praying] With the palms of both *open hands* together in front of the chest, fingers angled upward, move the hands forward with a double circular movement.

pray[2] *v.* See signs for AMEN, ASK, WORSHIP. Related form: **prayer** *n.*

preach *v.* Same sign used for: **nag.**

[Information is directed emphatically toward another] Move the right *F hand,* palm facing forward, with a short double movement forward in front of the right shoulder.

precise *adj.* Same sign used for: **concise, exact.**

[Demonstrates something coming together precisely] Beginning with the right *modified X hand* near the left *modified X hand,* move the right hand in a small circle and then forward to touch the hands together in front of the chest.

predict *v.* Same sign used for: **forecast, foresee, perception, prophecy.**

[Represents the eyes looking forward into the future] Beginning with the fingers of the right *V hand* pointing to each eye, move the right hand forward under the palm of the left *open hand.*

prefer[1] *v.* Same sign used for: **rather.**

[**favorite**[1] + **better**] Beginning with the bent middle finger of the right *5 hand* touching the chin, palm facing in, bring the hand forward to the right while closing into a *10 hand.*

prefer[2] *v.* See sign for FAVORITE[1]. Related form: **preference** *n.*

pregnant[1] *adj.* Same sign used for: **breed, conceive.**

[The shape of a pregnant woman's stomach] Bring both *5 hands* from in front of each side of the body, palms facing in, toward each other, entwining the fingers in front of the stomach.

pregnant[2] *adj.* See sign for STUCK. This sign is used only when referring to an unwanted pregnancy.

prejudice *n.* See sign for AGAINST.

prepare[1] *v.* Same sign used for: **arrange, organize, put in order, sequence, sort.**

Beginning with both *open hands* in front of the left side of the body, palms facing each other and fingers pointing forward, move the hands in double downward arcs to in front of the right side of the body.

prepare[2] *v.* See sign for PLAN.

present[1] *n.* See signs for BOX, GIFT, ROOM.

present[2] *adv.* See signs for HERE, NOW.

present[3] *v.* See sign for GIVE.

presentation *n.* See sign for SPEAK[2].

preserve *v.* See sign for SAVE[2]. Related form: **preservation** *n.*

preside over *v. phrase.* See sign for MANAGE.

president *n.* Same sign used for: **horns, superintendent.**

[The horns of authority, as on a stag] Beginning with the index-finger sides of both *C hands* near each side of the forehead, palms facing forward, move the hands outward to above each shoulder while closing into *S hands.*

press *n.* See sign for NEWSPAPER.

pretty *adj.* See also sign for BEAUTIFUL. Same sign used for: **lovely.**

[The hand encircles the beauty of the face] Beginning with the right *5 hand* in front of the face, palm facing in, move it in a circular movement, closing the fingers to the thumb in front of the chin, forming a *flattened O hand.*

prevailing *adj.* See sign for NOW.

prevent *v.* Same sign used for: **ban, barrier, block, blockage, hinder, impair, obstruct.**

[The hands seem to shield the body with a barrier] With the little-finger side of the right *B hand,* palm facing down, against the index-finger side of the left *B hand,* palm facing right, move the hands forward a short distance.

previous[1] *adj.*

[The hand indicates a time in the past] Tap the fingertips of the right *bent hand* on the right shoulder with a double movement.

previous[2] *adj.* See sign for BEFORE.

price *n.* See sign for COST.

prim *adj.* See sign for POLITE.

print *v., n.* See sign for NEWSPAPER.

prior *adj.* See sign for BEFORE.

private *adj.* See sign for SECRET. Related form: **privacy** *n.*

privilege *v.* See signs for PERMIT, RIGHT[2].

probably *adv.* See sign for MAYBE. Related forms: **probability** *n.*, **probable** *adj.*

problem[1] *n.*
[The knuckles rub together with friction] Beginning with the knuckles of both *bent V hands* touching in front of the chest, twist the hands in opposite directions with a deliberate movement, rubbing the knuckles against each other.

problem[2] *n.* See sign for DIFFICULT.

procedure *n.* Related form: **procedural** *adj.* Same sign used for: **pace, process, progress, take steps.**

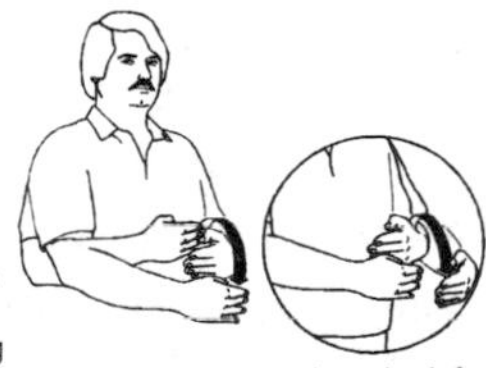

[Represents the progression of activities in a procedure] Beginning with both *open hands* in front of the body, palms facing in, left fingers pointing right and right fingers pointing left, and the right hand closer to the chest than the left hand, move the right hand over the left hand and then the left hand over the right hand in an alternating movement.

proceed *v.* See sign for GO ON.

process *n.* See sign for PROCEDURE.

proclaim *v.* See sign for ANNOUNCE. Related form: **proclamation** *n.*

produce *v.* See sign for MAKE.

proficient *adj.* See signs for GOOD AT, SKILL.

profit *n.* Same sign used for: **gross.**

[The hand seems to put a profit into one's pocket] Move the right *F hand,* palm facing down, downward with a double movement near the right side of the chest.

program *n.*

[Initialized sign] Move the middle finger of the right *P hand,* palm facing left, from the fingertips to the base of the left *open hand,* palm facing right and fingers pointing up. Repeat the movement on the back side of the left hand.

progress *n.* See sign for PROCEDURE.

prohibit *v.* See sign for FORBID.

prolong *v.* See sign for EXAGGERATE.

prominent *adj.* See signs for ADVANCED, CHIEF[1].

promise *n., v.* Same sign used for: **commit.**

[**true** + a gesture seeming to seal a promise in the hand] Bring the extended right index finger, palm facing left and finger pointing up, from in front of the lips downward, changing into an *open hand* and placing the palm of the right hand on the index-finger side of the left *S hand* held in front of the body, palm facing right.

promote[1] *v.* Related form: **promotion** *n.* Same sign used for: **rank.**

[**advanced** formed with a repeated movement to indicate levels of promotion] Move both *bent hands,* palms facing each other, from near each side of the head upward in a series of deliberate arcs.

promote[2] *v.* See sign for ADVANCED. Related form: **promotion** *n.*

promptly *adv.* See sign for REGULAR. Related form: **prompt** *adj.*

prone *v.* See sign for CATCH[2].

proof *n.* Related form: **prove** *v.* Same sign used for: **evidence.**

[The hand seems to bring something forward to present to another as proof] Move the fingertips of the right *open hand,* palm facing in, from in front of the mouth downward, ending with the back of the right hand on the palm of the left *open hand,* both palms facing up in front of the chest.

propaganda *n.* See sign for ADVERTISE.

prophecy *n.* See sign for PREDICT.

proposal *n.* See sign for SUGGEST. Related form: **propose** *v.*

prose *n.* See sign for STORY.

prosper *v.* See sign for SUCCESSFUL.

protect *v.* See sign for DEFEND.

protest[1] *n.* Same sign used for: **complaint, grievance, objection.**

[Similar to sign for **complain** but formed with a single movement] Strike the fingertips of the right *curved 5 hand* against the center of the chest with a double movement.

protest[2] *v., n.* Same sign used for: **rebel, rebellion, revolt, revolution, strike.**

[Natural gesture indicating that a person is on strike] Beginning with the right *S hand* in front of the right shoulder, palm facing back, twist the hand sharply forward.

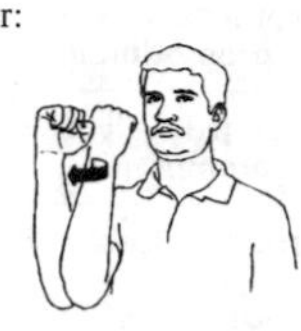

protest[3] *v.* See sign for COMPLAIN.

proud *adj.* Related form: **pride** *n.* Same sign used for: **arrogant.**

[Feelings of self-worth welling up in the body] Move the thumb of the right *10 hand,* palm facing down, from the center of the lower chest upward with a smooth movement.

provide *v.* See signs for GIVE, SUGGEST.

pry *v.* See sign for NOSY.

pseudo *adj.* See sign for FAKE.

public *n.* See sign for PEOPLE.

publication *v.* See sign for NEWSPAPER.

publicize *v.* See sign for ADVERTISE. Related form: **publicity** *n.*

pull *v.* See sign for DRAG.

punish *v.* Same sign used for: **penalize, penalty.**

[The arm is struck] Strike the extended right index finger, palm facing left, downward across the elbow of the left bent arm.

puny *adj.* See sign for TINY[1].

pupil[1] *n.* Same sign used for: **student.**

[**learn** + **person marker**] Beginning with the fingertips of the right *flattened C hand,* palm facing down, on the upturned palm of the left open hand, bring the right hand up while closing the fingers and thumb into a *flattened O hand* near the forehead. Then move both open hands, palms facing each other, downward along each side of the body.

pupil[2] *n.*

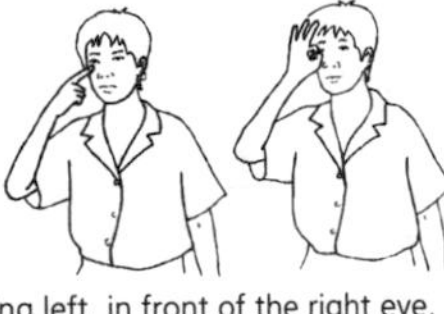

[**eye**[1] + the shape of one's pupil in the eye] Point the extended right index finger to the right eye, palm facing in. Then place the thumb side of the right *F hand,* palm facing left, in front of the right eye.

purchase *v.* See sign for BUY.

purple *n., adj.*

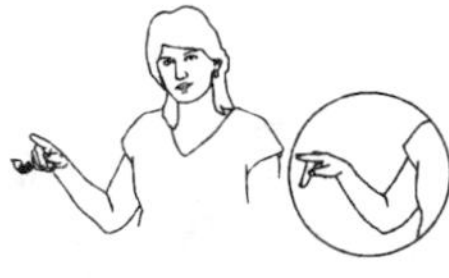

[Initialized sign] Shake the right *P hand,* palm facing down, back and forth in front of the right side of the body with a double movement.

purpose *n.* See sign for MEAN[2].

purse *n.* Same sign used for: **pocketbook, suitcase.**

[Mime holding a purse] Shake the right *S hand,* palm facing left, up and down near the right side of the waist with the elbow bent.

pursue *v.* See sign for CHASE.

push *v.*

[Mime pushing something] Move the palms of both *open hands,* palms facing forward, with a deliberate movement forward in front of the chest.

put *v.* Same sign used for: **install, mount, place, set.**

[The hands seem to take an object and put it in another location] Beginning with both *flattened O hands* in front of the body, palms facing down, move the hands upward and forward in a small arc.

put down *v. phrase.* Same sign used for: **document, record.**

[The hand seems to put something on a list] Touch the fingertips of the right *flattened O hand,* palm facing down, to the palm of the left *open hand,* palm facing up. Then slap the palm of the right *open hand* against the left palm.

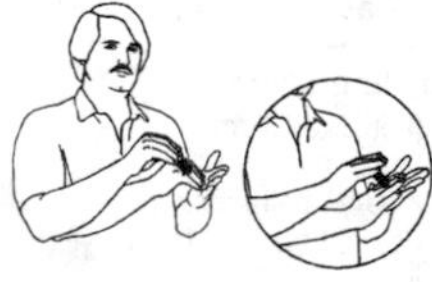

put in order *v. phrase.* See sign for PREPARE.

put off *v. phrase.* See sign for POSTPONE.

puzzled *adj.* Same sign used for: **bewildered, paradox, perplexed.**

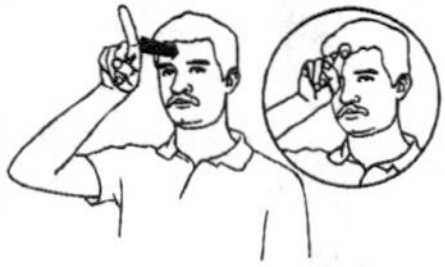

[Indicates a question in the mind] Beginning with the extended right index finger in front of the forehead, palm facing forward and finger angled up, bring the back of the right hand against the forehead while bending the finger into an *X hand.*

qualification *n.* Related form: **qualify.**

[Initialized sign similar to sign for **character**] Move the right *Q hand* in a small circle and then back against the right side of the chest, palm facing down.

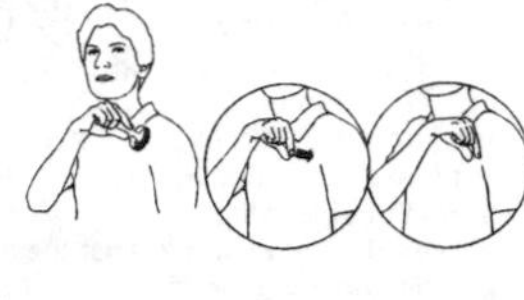

quarrel *v.* See sign for ARGUE.

quarter[1] *n.* Same sign used for: **twenty-five cents.**

[**cent** + **twenty-five**] Beginning with the extended right index finger touching the right side of the forehead, palm facing left and finger pointing up, twist the hand forward while changing into a *5 hand* with a wiggling bent middle finger, palm facing forward.

quarter[2] *n.* See sign for ONE FOURTH.

queer[1] *adj.* See sign for STRANGE.

queer[2] *n.* See sign for GAY[1]. (Slang, disparaging and offensive).

question *n., v.* See also sign for QUERY.

[Draw a question mark in the air] Move the extended right index finger from pointing forward in front of the right shoulder, palm facing down, downward with a curving movement while retracting the index finger and then pointing it straight forward again at the bottom of the curve.

queue *v.* See sign for LINE UP.

quick *adj., adv.* See sign for FAST. Related form: **quickly** *adv.*

quick-witted *adj.* See sign for SMART.

quiet *adj.* Same sign used for: **calm, calm down, passive, silence, silent, still, tranquil.**

[Natural gesture requesting others to be quiet] Beginning with both *B hands* crossed in front of the upper chest, palms angled outward in either direction, bring the hands downward and outward, ending with both *B hands* in front of each side of the waist, palms facing down.

quiet down *v. phrase.* See sign for SETTLE.

quit[1] *v.*

[Formed with the opposite movement as **join**[1] and indicates withdrawing involvement with others] Beginning with the extended fingers of the right *H hand* inside the opening of the left *O hand* held in front of the body, palm facing right, bring the right hand upward, ending in front of the right shoulder, palm facing left and fingers pointing up.

quit[2] *v.* See signs for RESIGN, STOP[1].

quiz *n., v.* See sign for TEST.

quotation *n.* Related form: **quote** *n., v.* Same sign used for: **theme.**

[Natural gesture forming quotation marks in the air] Beginning with both *V hands* held near each side of the head, palms angled forward and fingers pointing up, bend the fingers downward with a double movement.

quotes *pl. n.* See sign for TITLE.

race *v.*

[The hands move back and forth as if in contention with each other in a race] With an alternating movement, move both *A hands* forward and back past each other quickly, palms facing each other in front of the body.

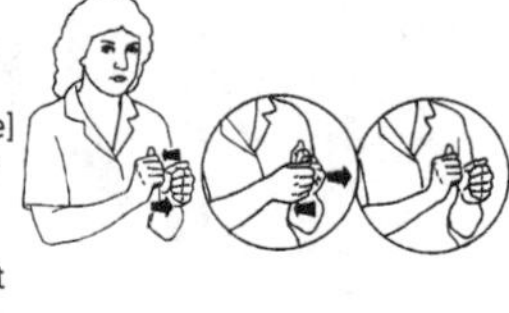

radiant *adj.* See sign for BRIGHT.

radio *n.*

[Represents radio headphones on the ears] With the fingers of the right *curved 5 hand* near the right ear, twist the hand forward with a double movement.

rage *n.* See sign for ANGER.

raid *v.* See sign for ROB.

railroad *n.* See sign for TRAIN.

rain *n., v.*

[Represents raindrops falling] Bring both *curved 5 hands,* palms facing down, from near each side of the head downward to in front of each shoulder with a double movement.

rainbow *n.*
[The shape of a rainbow] Beginning with the right *4 hand* in front of the left shoulder, palm facing in and fingers pointing left, bring the hand upward in front of the face, ending in front of the right shoulder, palm facing in and fingers pointing up.

raise[1] *v.* Same sign used for: **get up, lift, rise.**
[Natural gesture of raising something] Beginning with both *open hands* in front of each side of the body, palms facing up, lift the hands upward to in front of each shoulder.

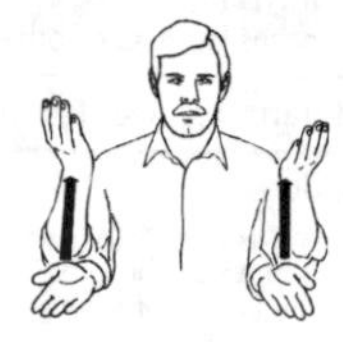

raise[2] *v.* See sign for GROW UP.

raise[3] *n.* See sign for INCREASE.

random *adj.* See signs for CIRCULATE, VARIETY.

range *n.* See sign for VARIETY.

rank *n.* See sign for PROMOTE.

rape *v.* See sign for STUCK.

rather *adv.* See signs for FAVORITE, PREFER[1].

rational *adj.* See sign for REASON.

rationale *n.* See sign for REASON.

razor *n.* See sign for SHAVE.

reach[1] *v.*

[Demonstrates reaching for something] Move the right *curved 5 hand*, palm facing down, from in front of the right side of the body forward while changing into an *S hand*.

reach[2] *v.* See sign for ARRIVE.

react *v.* See signs for ANSWER, REPORT. Related form: **reaction** *n.*

read *v.*

[Represents the movement of the eyes down a page to read it] Move the fingertips of the right *V hand*, palm facing down, from the fingertips to the heel of the left *open hand*, palm facing right.

ready *adj.* Related form: **readiness.**

[Initialized sign] Move both *R hands* from in front of the left side of the body, palms facing each other and fingers pointing forward, in a smooth movement to in front of the right side of the body.

real *adj.* Same sign used for: **actual, genuine.**

[Movement emphasizes validity of one's statement] Move the side of the extended right index finger from in front of the mouth, palm facing left and finger pointing up, upward and forward in an arc.

realize *v.* See sign for REASON. Related form: **realization** *n.*

really *adj.* See sign for TRUTH.

rear[1] *v.* See sign for GROW UP.

rear[2] *n.* See sign for BACK.

reason *n.* Related form: **reasonable** *adj.* Same sign used for: **rational, rationale, realization, realize.**

[Initialized sign similar to sign for **think**[1]] Move the fingertips of the right *R hand,* palm facing in, in a double circular movement in front of the right side of the forehead.

rebel *v.* See sign for PROTEST. Related form: **rebellion** *n.*

rebuke *v.* See sign for WARN.

receive *v.* See sign for GET.

recently[1] *adv.* Related form: **recent** *adj.* Same sign used for: **a while ago.**

[Represents the minute hand on a clock moving a short distance into the past] With the little-finger side of the right *1 hand,* palm facing in and finger pointing up, against the palm of the left *open hand,* palm facing right and fingers pointing up, bend the extended right index finger back toward the chest with a double movement.

recently[2] *adv.* See sign for JUST.

recess *n.* See sign for REST[1].

reckless *adj.* See sign for CARELESS.

recognize *v.* See sign for NOTICE.

record[1] *n.*, *v.* See sign for LIST.

record[2] *v.* See sign for PUT DOWN.

recover[1] *v.*

[**again** + **well**[1]] Beginning with the bent right hand beside the left *curved hand,* both palms facing up, bring the right hand up while turning it over, ending with the fingertips of the right hand touching the palm of the left hand. Then, beginning with the fingertips of both *curved 5 hands* touching each shoulder, palms facing in, bring the hands forward with a deliberate movement while closing into *S hands.*

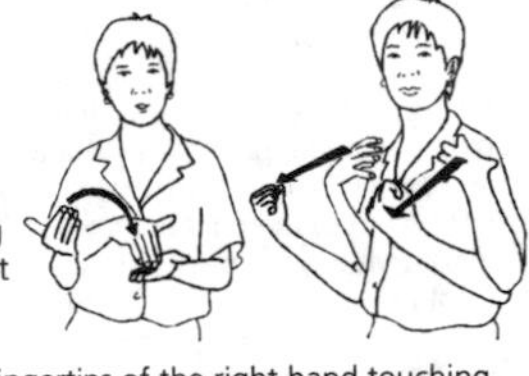

recover[2] *v.* See sign for SET UP.

red *adj.*

[Shows the redness of the lips] Bring the extended right index finger, palm facing in, from the lips downward with a short double movement.

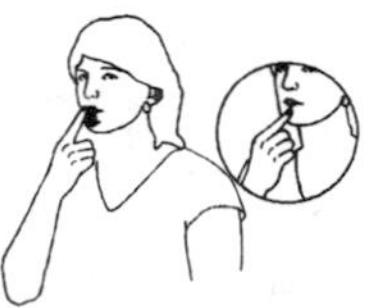

reduce *v.* See signs for BRIEF, DECREASE. Related form: **reduction** *n.*

refer *v.*

[Initialized sign] Beginning with the fingers of the right *R hand,* palm facing in, on the back of the left *open hand,* palm facing in, twist the right hand forward, ending with the right palm facing down.

reflect *v.* See sign for WONDER.

refresh *v.* See sign for COOL.

refrigerator *n.*

[Initialized sign similar to sign for **door**] Beginning with the thumb side of the right *R hand*, palm facing forward and fingers pointing up, against the palm side of the left *open hand*, palm facing right and fingers pointing up, move the right hand to the right in an arc while twisting the palm back in front of the right side of the chest.

refund *v., n.* Same sign used for: **come back, return.**

[Shows the direction that something takes in coming back to oneself] Beginning with both extended index fingers pointing up in front of the chest, palms facing in, bring the fingers back to point at each side of the chest, palms facing down.

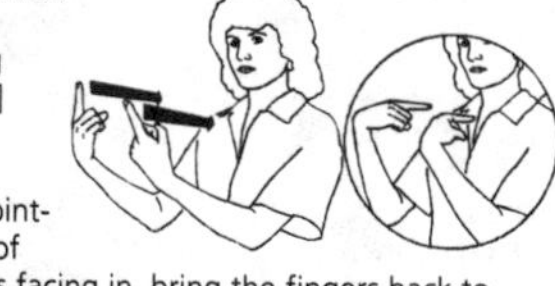

refuse *v.* See sign for WON'T.

register[1] *v.* Related form: **registration** *n.*

[Initialized sign similar to sign for **sign**[2]] Touch the fingertips of the right *R hand*, palm facing down, first to the heel and then to the fingertips of the palm of the left *open hand*.

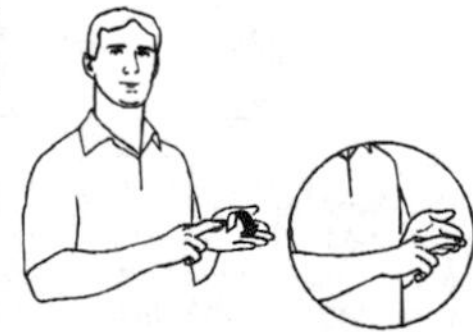

register[2] *v.* See sign for SIGN[2].

regret *n.* See sign for SORRY.

regular *adj.* Related form: **regularly** *adv.* Same sign used for: **prompt, promptly.**

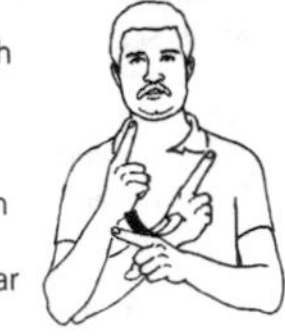

[The fingers hit with regularity] With the right index finger extended, brush the little-finger side of the right hand, palm facing in, across the extended left index finger, palm facing in, as the right hand moves toward the chest in a double circular movement.

rehearse *v.* See sign for PRACTICE.

reign *v.* See sign for MANAGE.

reindeer *n.* See sign for DEER.

reiterate *v.* See sign for AGAIN.

reject *v.* Same sign used for: **turn down, veto.**

[Natural gesture indicating turning down something] Beginning with the right *10 hand* in front of the right shoulder, elbow extended and palm facing down, twist the wrist downward, ending with the thumb pointing down and the palm facing right.

rejoice *v.* See sign for CELEBRATE.

relate *v.* See sign for COORDINATE.

relationship *n.* Related form: **relate** *v.* Same sign used for: **ally, connection, link, tie.**

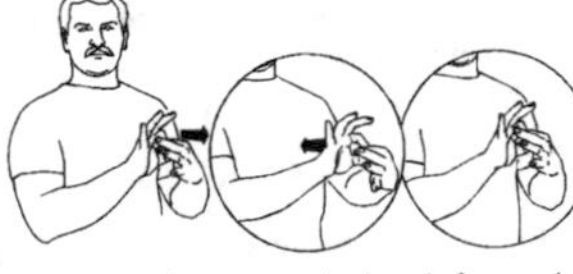

[Represents a link between two persons or things] With the thumbs and index fingers of both *F hands* intersecting, move the hands forward and back toward the chest with a double movement.

relax *v.* See signs for REST[1], SETTLE.

relief *n.* Related form: **relieved** *v.*

[Shows feeling being calmed in the body] With the index-finger sides of both *B hands* against the chest, left hand above the right hand, move the hands downward simultaneously.

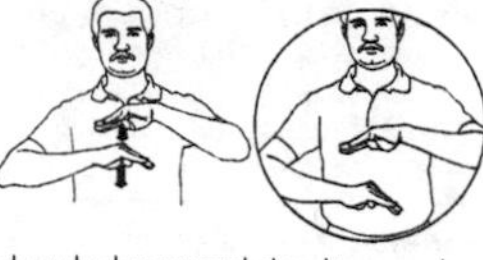

relocate *v.* See sign for MOVE.

rely *v.* See sign for DEPEND.

remain *v.* See signs for CONTINUE[1], STAY.

remark *v.* See sign for SAY.

remarkable *adj.* See sign for WONDERFUL.

remarks *pl. n.* See sign for STORY.

remember *v.*

[Bringing a thought from the mind forward to examine it] Move the thumb of the right *10 hand* from the right side of the forehead, palm facing left, smoothly down to touch the thumb of the left *10 hand* held in front of the body, palm facing down.

remind *v.*

[Natural gesture to tap someone to remind them of something] Tap the fingertips of the right *bent hand* with a double movement on the right shoulder, palm facing down.

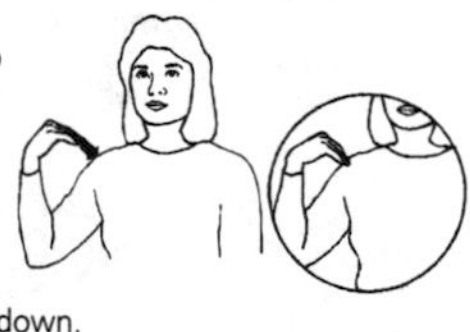

remodel *v.* See sign for IMPROVE[2].

remote *adj.* See sign for FAR.

remote control *n.*
[Mime operating a remote control with one's thumb] Bend the extended thumb of the right *10 hand,* palm facing in, up and down with a repeated movement in front of the right shoulder.

remove[1] *v.* Related form: **removal** *n.* Same sign used for: **abolish, abort, abortion.**
[Demonstrates picking something up and tossing it away to remove it] Bring the fingertips of the right *curved hand* against the palm of the left *open hand* while changing into an *A hand,* palms facing each other. Then move the right hand downward off the left fingertips while opening into a *curved 5 hand* in front of the right side of the body.

remove[2] *v.* See signs for ELIMINATE[1], TAKE OFF.

rent *v., n.*
[Initialized sign similar to sign for **month**] Move the middle finger side of the right *R hand,* palm facing down and fingers pointing left, downward with a double movement from the tip to the base of the extended left index finger, palm facing right and finger pointing up in front of the chest.

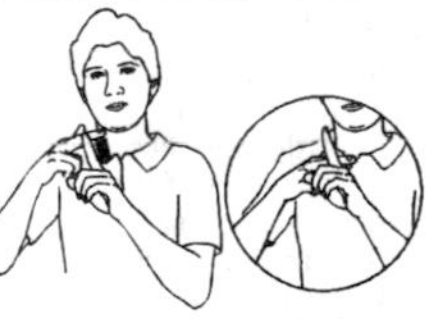

repair *v.* See sign for FIX.

repeat *v.* See sign for AGAIN.

repel *v.* See sign for ELIMINATE[1].

repent *v.* See sign for SORRY.

replace *v.* See sign for TRADE.

reply *n., v.* See signs for ANSWER, REPORT.

report *n., v.* Same sign used for: **react, reaction, reply, respond, response.**

[Initialized sign similar to sign for **answer**] Beginning with fingers of both *R hands* pointing up, right hand closer to the mouth than the left hand and the palms facing in opposite directions, move the hands forward and downward with a deliberate movement, ending with the palms facing down and fingers pointing forward.

repossess *v.* See sign for CAPTURE.

reptile *n.* See sign for SNAKE.

request *v.* See sign for ASK.

require *v.* See sign for DEMAND.

research *v., n.*

[Initialized sign similar to sign for **investigate**] Move the fingertips of the right *R hand*, palm facing down, across the open left palm from the heel to the fingertips with a double movement.

reservation *n.* See sign for APPOINTMENT.

resign *v.* Same sign used for: **back out, draw back, drop out, quit.**

[Represents pulling one's legs out of a situation] Beginning with the fingers of the right *bent U hand,* palm facing down, in the opening of the left *O hand,* palm facing right, pull the right fingers out to the right.

resist *v.* Same sign used for: **anti-, defensive, immune, uncertain.**

[Natural gesture for resisting something] Move the right *S hand,* palm facing down, from in front of the right side of the body outward to the right with a deliberate movement.

respiration *n.* See sign for BREATH.

respond *v.* See sign for REPORT. Related form: **response** *n.*

response *n.* See sign for ANSWER.

responsibility *n.* See sign for BURDEN. Related form: **responsible** *adj.*

rest[1] *v., n.* Same sign used for: **recess, relax.**

[Shows laying one's hands on one's chest as if in repose] With the arms crossed at the wrists, lay the palm of each *open hand* on the chest near the opposite shoulder.

rest[2] *v.* See sign for LEAVE[2].

restaurant *n.*
[Initialized sign similar to sign for **cafeteria**] Touch the fingers of the right *R hand,* palm facing in, first to the right and then to the left side of the chin.

restless *adj.*
[Represents one's legs turning over restlessly during a sleepless night] With the back of the right *bent V hand* laying across the open left palm, both palms facing up, turn the right hand over and back with a double movement.

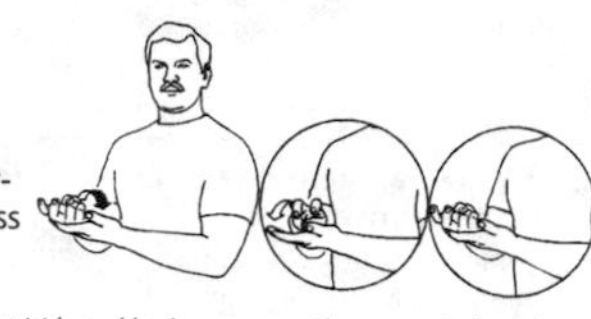

rest of See sign for AFTER[1].

restore *v.* See sign for SAVE[2].

restrain *v.* See sign for CONTROL[1]. Related form: **restraint** *n.*

rest room[1] *n.*
[Abbreviation **r-r**] Tap the right *R hand,* palm facing down and the fingers pointing forward, downward first in front of the right side of body and then again slightly to the right.

rest room[2] *n.* See sign for TOILET.

result *n.*
[Initialized sign similar to sign for **end**[1]] Move the fingertips of the right *R hand,* palm facing down, along the length of the index finger of the left *B hand,* palm facing in, and then down off the fingertips.

retail *v.* See sign for SELL.

retain *v.* See sign for SAVE[2].

retaliate *v.* See sign for REVENGE.

retire *v.*

[Initialized sign similar to sign for **holiday**] Touch the extended thumbs of both *R hands,* palms facing each other, against each side of the chest.

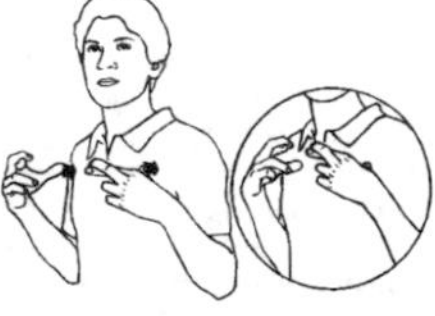

retirement *n.* Similar to sign for RETIRE but made with a double movement.

return *v.* See sign for BRING, REFUND.

reveal *v.* See signs for ANNOUNCE, TELL[1].

revenge *n.* Same sign used for: **avenge, get even, retaliate, vengeance.**

[Suggests two people striking each other] Beginning with both *modified X hands* in front of the chest, left hand above the right hand and palms facing each other, bring the right hand upward until the knuckles of both the hands touch.

revenue *n.* See sign for INCOME[1].

reverberate *v.* See sign for BELL. Related form: **reverberation** *n.*

reverse *n., adj., v.* Same sign used for: **revert, swap, switch.**

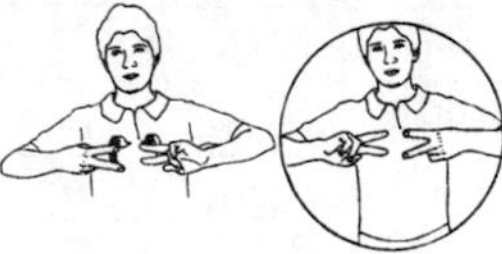

[The fingers seem to reverse positions] Beginning with both *V hands* in front of the chest, right palm facing in and fingers pointing left, and left palm facing out and fingers pointing right, twist the hands in opposite directions to turn the palms the opposite direction.

revert *v.* See sign for REVERSE.

revoke *v.* See sign for TEAR.

revolt *v.* See sign for PROTEST. Related form: **revolution.** *n.*

reward *n.,v.* See sign for GIFT.

ribbon *n.* See sign for BOW[2].

rich *adj.* Same sign used for: **wealth.**

[Represents a pile of money in one's hand] Beginning with the little-finger side of the right *S hand,* palm facing left, in the open left palm held in front of the body, raise the right hand a short distance while opening into a *curved 5 hand,* palm facing down.

rid *v.* See sign for ELIMINATE[1].

ride in a car, truck, etc. *v. phrase.*

[Represents a person sitting in a vehicle] With the fingers of the right *bent U hand,* palm facing down, hooked over the thumb of the left *C hand,* palm facing right, move the hands forward from in front of the body.

ridiculous *adj.* See sign for SILLY.

right[1] *n., adj., adv.*

[Initialized sign showing a right direction] Move the right *R hand,* palm facing forward, from in front of the right side of the body to the right a short distance.

right[2] *n.* Same sign used for: **all right, privilege.**

[Shows the approved path] Slide the little-finger side of the right *open hand,* palm facing left, in an upward arc across the upturned left palm held in front of the body.

right[3] *adj.* Same sign used for: **accurate, correct.**

With the index fingers of both hands extended forward at right angles, palms angled in and right hand above left, bring the little-finger side of the right hand sharply down across the thumb side of the left hand.

rigid *adj.* See sign for FREEZE.

ring[1] *n.*

[The location of a ring on the ring finger] Move the bent thumb and index finger of the right *5 hand,* palm facing down, back and forth the length of the ring finger of the left *5 hand,* palm facing down, with a repeated movement.

ring[2] *v., n.* See sign for BELL.

riot *v., n.* See signs for COMPLAIN, MESSY.

rip *v.* See sign for TEAR.

rise *v., n.* See sign for RAISE.

risk *n.* See sign for DANGER.

rival *n.* See sign for ENEMY.

river *n.*

[**water** + a gesture showing the movement of waves] Tap the index-finger side of the right *W hand,* palm facing left, against the chin with a double movement. Then move both *5 hands,* palms facing down, forward from in front of the chest with an up-and-down wavy movement.

road *n.* Same sign used for: **path, route, street, way.**

[Indicates the shape of a road] Move both *open hands* from in front of each side of the body, palms facing each other, forward with a parallel movement.

roam *v.* Same sign used for: **adrift, wander.**

[Represents the aimless movement of a roaming person] Beginning with the extended right index finger pointing up in front of the right shoulder, palm facing forward, move the hand to in front of the chest and then outward again in a large arc.

roar *v.*, *n.* See sign for SCREAM.

rob *v.* Related form: **robbery.** Same sign used for: **burglary, hold up, raid.**

[Represents pulling out one's guns for a robbery] Beginning with both *H hands* in front of each side of the waist, palms facing each other and fingers pointing down, twist the wrists upward, bringing the hands up in front of each side of the body, palms facing each other and fingers pointing forward.

rock[1] *n.* Same sign used for: **stone.**

[Indicates the hardness of a rock] Tap the back of the right *S hand,* palm facing up, on the back of the left *S hand* held in front of the chest, palm facing down, with a repeated movement.

rock[2] *n.* See sign for METAL.

rod *n.* See signs for PIPE[1], STICK[2].

romp *v.*, *n.* See sign for PLAY[1].

room *n.* See sign for BOX. Same sign used for: **package, present.**

[Shows the four walls of a room] Beginning with both *open hands* in front of each side of the chest, palms facing each other and fingers pointing forward, move the hands in opposite directions by bending the wrists, ending with the left hand near the chest and the right hand several inches forward of the left hand, both palms facing in.

rot *v., n.* See sign for WEAR OUT. Related form: **rotten** *adj.*

rough *adj.* Same sign used for: **approximate, coarse, draft, estimate.**

[Indicates a rough, scratchy surface] Move the fingertips of the right *curved 5 hand,* palm facing down, from the heel to the fingertips of the upturned left *open hand* held in front of the body.

round[1] *n.*

[Initialized sign similar to sign for **circle**[1]] Move the extended fingers of the right *R hand* from pointing down in front of the body in a large flat circle in front of the body.

round[2] *adj.* See sign for CIRCLE[1].

route *n.* See sign for ROAD.

routine *n.* See sign for DAILY.

row[1] *n.*

[Represents legs sitting in a row] Beginning with the index–finger sides of both *bent V hands* touching in front of the body, palms facing down, move the hands apart to in front of each side of the body.

row[2] *n.* See sign for LINE UP.

royalty *n.* See sign for PENSION.

rub *v.* See signs for WASH, WIPE.

rude *adj.* See sign for MEAN[1].

ruin[1] *v.* Same sign used for: **spoil.**

[A ripping movement] Slide the little-finger side of the right *X hand,* palm facing left, across the index–finger side of the left *X hand,* palm facing right.

ruin[2] *v.* See sign for DAMAGE.

rule *v.* See sign for MANAGE.

rumor *n.* See sign for GOSSIP[1].

run[1] *v.* Related form: **running** *v.*

[Represents one's legs moving when running] With the index finger of the right *L hand,* palm facing left and index finger pointing forward, hooked on the thumb of the left *L hand,* palm facing right and index finger pointing forward, move both hands forward.

run[2] *v.* See sign for LEAK[1].

run[3] *v.* Same sign used for: **operate.**

[Represents the smooth operation of an assembly line] Brush the palm of the right *open hand* upward with a double movement across the left *open hand,* palms facing each other and fingers pointing forward.

run[4] *v.* See sign for MACHINE.

run around *v. phrase.* Same sign used for: **fool around, tour, travel.**

[Shows movement in different directions] With the left extended index finger pointing up in front of the body and the right extended index finger pointing down above it, both palms facing in, move both hands in alternate circles in front of the body.

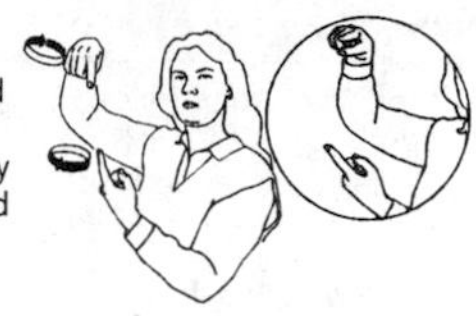

run away *v. phrase.* Same sign used for: **escape, get away, split** (*slang*).

[Represents one moving away quickly] Move the extended right index finger, palm facing left and finger pointing up, from between the index and middle fingers of the left *5 hand,* palm facing down in front of the chest, forward with a deliberate movement.

run out of *v. phrase.* Same sign used for: **all gone, deplete, used up.**

[Indicates grabbing everything so that nothing is left] Beginning with the little-finger side of the right *5 hand,* palm facing in, on the heel of the left *open hand,* palm facing up, bring the right hand forward to the left fingertips while changing into an *S hand.*

run over *v. phrase.* See sign for OVERFLOW.

rush *v., n.* See sign for HURRY.

sad *adj.* Same sign used for: **grave.**

[The hands seem to pull the face down to a sad expression] Move both *5 hands* from in front of each side of the face, palms facing in and fingers pointing up, downward a short distance.

safe *adj.* See sign for SAVE[1].

sail *n.* See sign for BOAT. Related form: **sailing** *n.*

salad *n.*

[Mime tossing a salad] Move both *curved hands,* palms facing up and fingers pointing toward each other, from in front of each side of the body toward each other with a double movement.

salary *n.* See signs for EARN, INCOME[1].

sale *n.* See sign for SELL.

salt *n.*

[Represents tapping out salt from a shaker on one's food] Alternately tap the fingers of the right *V hand* across the back of the fingers of the left *V hand,* both palms facing down.

salvation *n.* See sign for SAVE[1].

same[1] *adj.* or **the same** *adv.* Same sign used for: **like, such as.**

[The fingers come together to show that they are the same] Beginning with both extended index fingers pointing forward in front of each side of the body, palms facing down, bring the hands together, ending with the index fingers together in front of the body.

same[2] *adj.* See sign for ALIKE.

sandwich *n.*

[Represents a sandwich being eaten] With the palms of both *open hands* together, right hand above left, bring the fingers back toward the mouth with a short double movement.

satisfy *v.* Related form: **satisfaction** *n.* Same sign used for: **appease, content, contentment.**

[A settling down of feelings] Beginning with both *B hands* in front of the chest, right hand above the left hand and both palms facing down, bring the index-finger sides of both hands against the chest.

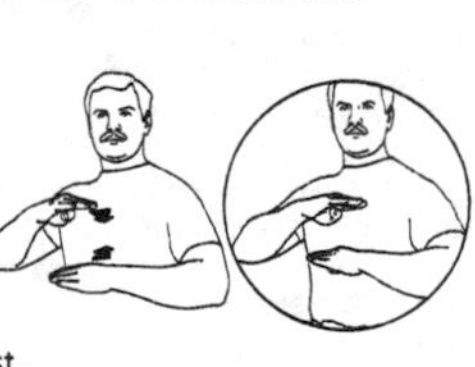

Saturday *n.*

[Initialized sign] Move the right *S hand,* palm facing back, in a small circle in front of the right shoulder.

saucer *n.* See sign for PLATE.

save[1] *v.* Same sign used for: **free, freedom, liberate, liberty, safe, salvation, secure, security.**

[Initialized sign representing breaking the chains of captivity] Beginning with both *S hands* crossed at the wrists in front of the chest, palms facing in opposite directions, twist the wrists and move the hands apart, ending with the hands in front of each shoulder, palms facing forward.

save[2] *v.* Related form: **savings** *pl. n.* Same sign used for: **preservation, preserve, restore, retain, storage, store, stuff.**

[The *S hand* holds one's savings behind the bars of a bank cage] Tap the fingers of the right *V hand* with a double movement on the back of the fingers of the left *V hand,* both palms facing in.

saw *n.* See sign for WOOD.

say *v.* Same sign used for: **comment, remark, remarks, state.**

[Points to where words are said] Tap the extended right index finger, palm facing in, on the chin with a double movement.

scalp *n.* See sign for BALD.

scant *adj.* See sign for TINY.

scared *adj.* See signs for AFRAID, FEAR.

scent *n., v.* See sign for SMELL.

schedule[1] *n.* Same sign used for: **chart, graph.**

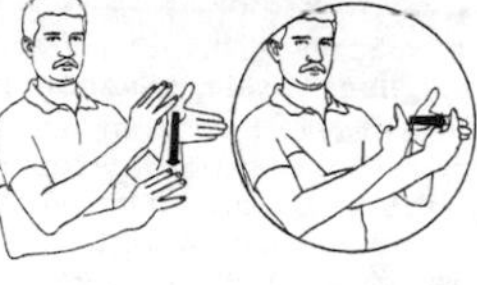

[Shows the rows and columns on a schedule] Beginning with the left *open hand* held in front of the left shoulder, palm facing right and fingers pointing forward, bring the fingers of the right *4 hand,* palm facing left, down the heel of the left hand, and then drag the back of the right fingers across the length of the left palm from the heel to the fingertips.

schedule[2] *n.* See signs for PLAN.

school *n.*

[A teacher claps for attention] Tap the fingers of right *open hand,* palm facing down, with a double movement on the upturned palm of left *open hand.*

scissors *n.*

[Mime cutting with scissors] Open and close the index and middle fingers of the right *V hand,* palm facing in and fingers pointing left, with a repeated movement.

scold *v.* Same sign used for: **admonish.**

[Natural gesture for scolding someone] Move the extended right index finger from in front of the right shoulder, palm facing left and finger pointing up, forward with a double movement.

score *n.*, *v.* See sign for LIST.

scramble *v.* See sign for MIX[1].

scream *v.*, *n.* Same sign used for: **cry, roar, shout, yell.**

[The hand seems to take a loud sound from the mouth and direct it outward] Beginning with the fingers of the right *C hand* close to the mouth, palm facing in, bring the hand forward and upward in an arc.

scribble *v.* See sign for WRITE.

seal *n.*, *v.* See sign for STAMP[2].

seal one's lips *v. phrase.* See sign for SHUT UP.

search for *v. phrase.* See sign for LOOK FOR.

seasoning *n.*

[Mime shaking seasoning on food] Shake the right *curved hand,* palm facing forward and fingers pointing left, downward in front of the chest with a double movement.

seat *n.* See sign for CHAIR.

second-hand *adj.* Same sign used for: **used.**

[Two fingers turned over, indicating a second use] Beginning with the right *L hand* in front of the right side of the chest, palm facing down and index finger pointing forward, twist the wrist up and down with a double movement.

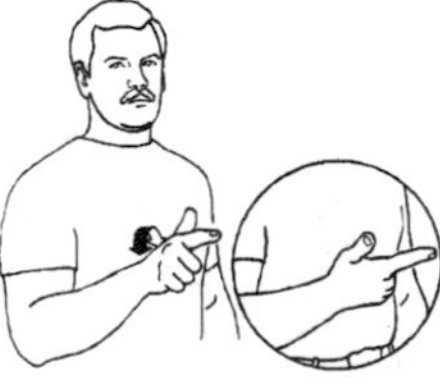

second the motion *v. phrase.* [Two fingers waving for attention during a parliamentary procedure] Beginning with the right *L hand* in front of the right side of the head, palm facing left and index finger pointing up, move the hand deliberately forward while tipping the hand downward, ending with the index finger pointing forward.

secret *adj., n.* Same sign used for: **classified, confidential, privacy, private.**

[The movement seems to silence the lips to keep a secret] Tap the thumb side of the right *A hand,* palm facing left, against the mouth with a repeated movement.

secretary *n.* [The hand seems to take words from the mouth and write them on paper] Bring the right *modified X hand* from near the right side of the chin downward across the palm of the left *open hand* from the heel to off the fingertips.

section *n.* See signs for CLASS, PART[1].

secure *v.* See sign for SAVE[1]. Related form: **security** *n.*

security *n.* See signs for DEFEND, POLICE, SAVE[1].

see *v.* Same sign used for: **sight, visualize.**

[The fingers follow the direction of vision from the eyes] Bring the fingers of the right *V hand* from pointing at the eyes, palm facing in, forward a short distance.

seem *v.* Same sign used for: **apparently, appear, look like.**

[Looking in a mirror] Beginning with the right *open hand* near the right shoulder, palm facing forward and fingers pointing up, turn the hand so the palm faces back.

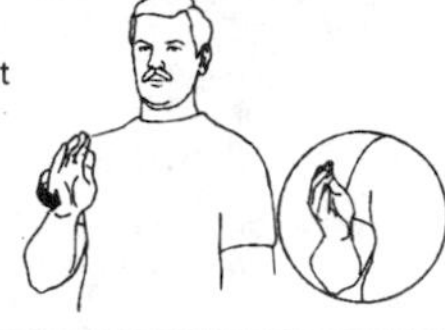

segment *n.* See sign for PART[1].

seize *v.* See sign for CAPTURE.

seldom *adv.*

[**once** formed with a rhythmic repeated movement] Bring the extended right index finger, palm facing in, downward against the upturned palm of the left *open hand* and then swing it upward in a slow upward arc with a double movement.

select *v.* See signs for APPOINT, CHOOSE.

self *n.* See sign for OWN.

selfish *n.* See sign for GREEDY.

sell *v.* Same sign used for: **distribute, merchandise, peddle, retail, sale.**

[The hands seem to hold something out for inspection in order to sell it] Beginning with both *flattened O hands* held in front of each side of the chest, palms facing down and fingers pointing down, swing the fingertips forward and back by twisting the wrists upward with a double movement.

send *v.* See sign for MAIL[1].

send out *v. phrase.* See sign for MAIL[1].

senior *n., adj.*

[Shows top year in school] Place the palm of the right *5 hand,* palm facing down and fingers pointing left, on the thumb of the left *5 hand,* palm facing in and fingers pointing right.

sensation *n.* See sign for FEEL.

sense *v., n.* See signs for FEEL, MIND.

sensitive *adj.*

[Formed with the finger used for feeling] Beginning with the bent middle finger of the right *5 hand* touching the right side of the chest, flick the wrist forward, ending with the palm facing down.

sentence *n.* Same sign used for: **statement.**

[Represents stretching out words into a sentence] Beginning with the thumbs and index fingers of both *F hands* touching in front of the chest, palms facing each other, pull the hands apart with a wiggly movement, ending in front of each side of the chest.

separate *v., adj.* Related form: **separation** *n.*

[Things pulled apart] Beginning with the knuckles of both *A hands* touching in front of the chest, palms facing in, bring the hands apart.

sequence *v.* See sign for PREPARE.

series *n.* See sign for CLASS.

serious *adj.* Same sign used for: **severe.**

[Drilling a serious point in] With the extended right index finger touching the chin, palm facing left, twist the right hand, ending with the palm facing back.

serpent *n.* See sign for SNAKE.

serve *v.* Related form: **service** *n.* Same sign used for: **host.**

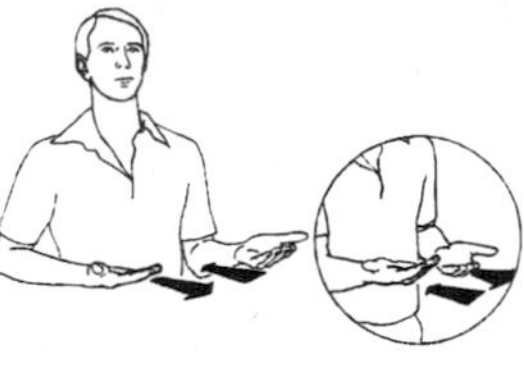

[The hands seem to carry something to serve it] Beginning with both *open hands* in front of each side of the body, palms facing up and right hand closer to the body than the left, move the hands forward and back with an alternating movement.

set *v.* See sign for PUT.

set off *v. phrase.* See sign for ZOOM.

settle or **settle down** *v.* Same sign used for: **calm, calm down, quiet down, relax.**

[Natural gesture for calming someone down] Beginning with both *5 hands* in front of each side of the chest, palms facing down, move the hands slowly down to in front of each side of the waist.

set up *v. phrase.* Same sign used for: **erect, founded, recover.**

[The movement represents setting up something] Beginning with the fingertips of both *curved hands* touching in front of the chest, palms facing down, bend the fingers upward, ending with the fingers angled upward and touching each other.

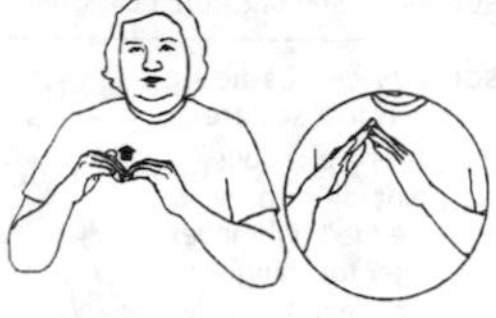

several *adj.* See sign for FEW.

severe *adj.* See sign for SERIOUS.

sex *n.* Related form: **sexual** *adj.*

[Denotes the male and female areas of the head] Touch the index-finger side of the right *X hand,* first to near the right eye and then to the lower chin, palm facing forward.

sham *n.* See sign for FAKE.

shame *n.* See sign for ASHAMED. Related form: **shameful** *adj.*

shampoo *n., v.* Same sign used for: **wash one's hair.**

[Mime shampooing one's hair] Move both *curved 5 hands,* palms facing each other, in and out near each side of the head with a repeated movement.

shape *n.* Same sign used for: **form, image.**

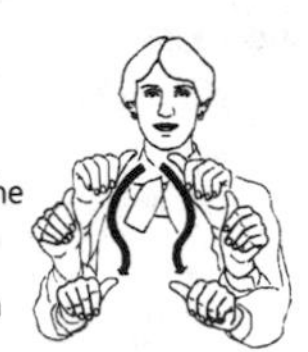

[The hands outline the image of a shape] Beginning with both *10 hands* in front of each side of the chest, palms facing forward, bring the hands downward with a wavy movement, ending in front of each side of the waist.

share *v.* Same sign used for: **change.**

[The hand moves back and forth as if to share a portion of something] Move the little-finger side of the right *open hand,* palm facing in, back and forth with a double movement at the base of the index finger of the left *open hand,* palm facing in.

sharp *adj.* Same sign used for: **keen.**

[Feeling something sharp] Flick the bent middle finger of the right *5 hand,* palm facing down, forward off the back of the left *open hand* held in front of the body.

shave *v.* Same sign used for: **razor.**

[Represents holding a hand razor to shave] Move the knuckles of the right *Y hand,* palm facing left, downward on the right cheek with a repeated movement.

she *pron.* See sign for HE.

shed *v.* See sign for BLOOD.

shelf *n.* Same sign used for: **mantel.**

[The shape of a shelf] Beginning with the index-finger sides of both *B hands* touching in front of the chest, palms facing down and fingers pointing forward, bring the hands apart to in front of each side of the chest.

sheriff *n.* See sign for POLICE.

shield *v.* See sign for DEFEND.

shift *v.* See sign for CHANGE[1].

shiny *adj.* Related form: **shine** *n., v.* Same sign used for: **glitter, glossy, glow, sparkle.**

[Indicates the glare reflecting off something shiny] Beginning with the bent middle finger of the right *5 hand,* palm facing down, touching the back of the left *open hand,* palm facing down, bring the right hand upward in front of the chest with a wiggly movement.

ship *n.* See sign for BOAT.

shirk *v.* See sign for AVOID.

shirt *n.*

[Indicates the location of a shirt] Pull a small portion of clothing from the upper right chest forward with the fingers of the right *F hand,* palm facing in, with a double movement.

shiver *v.*, *n.* See sign for COLD[2].

shoe *n.*

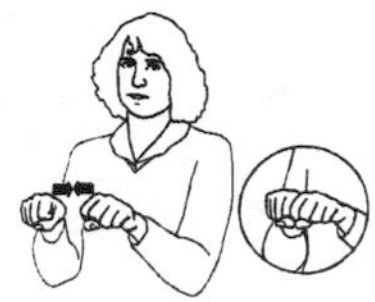

[Represents clicking the heels of shoes together] Tap the index-finger sides of both *S hands* together in front of the chest with a double movement, palms facing down.

shoot *v.* See sign for TAKE PICTURES.

shop[1] *v.* Related form: **shopping** *n.*

[The hand takes money and gives it in payment] Beginning with the back of the right *flattened O hand,* palm facing up, across the palm of the left *open hand,* palm facing up, move the right hand forward and slightly upward with a double movement.

shop[2] *n.* See sign for STORE.

shoplift *v.* See sign for STEAL.

short[1] *adj.* Related form: **shortage** *n.* See also sign for BRIEF[1]. Same sign used for: **soon, temporary.**

[The fingers measure off a short distance] Rub the middle-finger side of the right *H hand,* palm angled left, back and forth with a repeated movement on the index-finger side of the left *H hand,* palm angled right.

short[2] *adj.* See signs for LITTLE[1], THIN[1].

shortly *adv.* See sign for SOON[1].

shout *v.* See sign for SCREAM.

show[1] *v.* Same sign used for: **demonstrate, example, expose, indicate, indication, portray.**

[The finger points to something in the hand and moves it to show it to someone else] With the extended right index finger, palm facing in, touching the open left palm, move both hands forward a short distance.

show[2] *v.* (*alternate sign, used when something is shown to many people*) Same sign used for: **exhibit.**

[Represents showing something around to many people] With the extended right index finger, palm facing in, touching the open left palm, move both hands in a flat circle in front of the body.

show[3] *n.* See sign for ACT[2], FILM.

shower *n., v.*

[Represents water coming down from a shower head] Beginning with the right *O hand* above the right side of the head, palm facing down, open the fingers into a *5 hand* with a double movement.

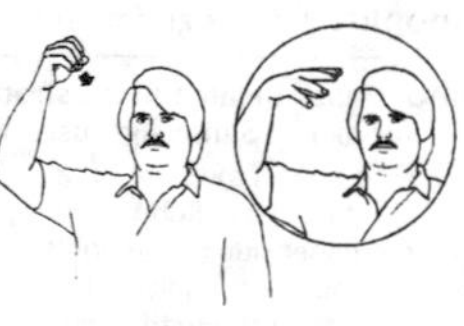

show off *v. phrase.* See sign for BRAG.

show up *v. phrase.* Same sign used for: **appear, come up, incident, materialize, occur, pop up, surface, turn up.**

[Represents something popping up into sight] Push the extended right index finger, palm angled left, upward between the index finger and middle finger of the left *open hand,* palm facing down.

shrink *v.* See sign for DIET.

shut up *v. phrase.* Same sign used for: **keep quiet, seal one's lips.**

[Represents closing one's mouth to shut it up] Beginning with the thumb of the *flattened C hand* touching the chin, palm facing in, close the fingers to the thumb, forming a *flattened O hand.*

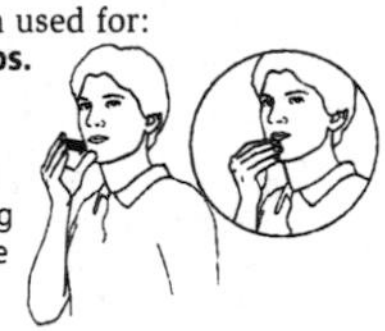

shy[1] *adj.*

Beginning with the palm side of the right *A hand* against the lower right cheek, twist the hand forward, ending with the palm facing back.

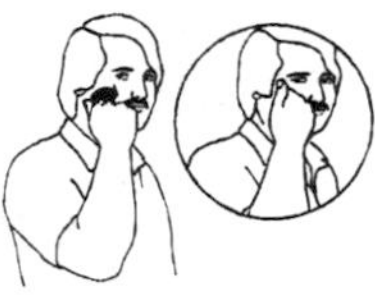

shy[2] *adj.* See sign for ASHAMED.

sick *adj.* Related form: **sickness** *n.* Same sign used for: **ill, illness, malady.**

[The finger used to indicate feeling touches the forehead to show that a person doesn't feel well] Touch the bent middle finger of the right *5 hand,* palm facing in, to the forehead.

side *n.*

[Shows the shape of the side of a wall] Bring the right *open hand,* palm facing left and fingers pointing forward, downward in front of the right side of the body.

sight *n.* See sign for SEE.

sign[1] *v., n.*

[Represents one's hands moving when using sign language] Beginning with both extended index fingers pointing up in front of each side of the chest, palms facing forward and the left hand higher than the right hand, move the hands in large alternating circles toward the chest.

sign[2] *v.* Same sign used for: **register.**

[Represents placing one's name on a piece of paper] Place the extended fingers of the right *H hand,* palm facing down, firmly down on the upturned palm of the left *open hand* held in front of the chest.

sign[3] *n.* See sign for SQUARE.

signature *n.* Same sign as for SIGN[2] but made with a double movement.

significant *adj., n.* See sign for IMPORTANT. Related form: **significance** *n.*

silence *n.* See sign for QUIET.

silent *adj.* Same sign used for: **calm, calm down, mute, quiet, still.**

[The fingers seem to silence the mouth, and the hands move down as if to show quiet] Beginning with both extended index fingers pointing up in front of the mouth, right hand closer to the face than the left hand and palms facing in opposite directions, bring the hands downward and outward, ending with both *open hands* in front of each side of the chest, palms angled down.

silky *adj.* See sign for SMOOTH.

silly *adj.* Same sign used for: **ridiculous.**

[Looking past something worthless] Beginning with the right *Y hand* in front of the face, palm facing in, twist the wrist outward with a double movement, brushing the right thumb across the nose with each movement.

similar *adj.* See signs for ALIKE.

simple[1] *adj.*

[A simple movement] Beginning with both *F hands* in front of the body, right hand higher than the left hand and palms facing in opposite directions, bring the right hand down, striking the fingertips of the left hand as it passes.

simple[2] *adj.* See sign for EASY.

sin *n., v.* Same sign used for: **trespass.**

[The fingers move in opposition to each other as do good and evil] Beginning with both extended index fingers angled upward in front of each side of the chest, palms facing in, move the hands toward each other in double circular movement.

since[1] *prep.* Same sign used for: **been, ever since, lately.**

[Shows passage of time from the past to the present] Move the extended index fingers of both hands from touching the upper right chest, palms facing in, forward in an arc, ending with the index fingers angled forward and the palms angled up.

since[2] *conj.* See sign for BECAUSE.

sing *v.* See sign for MUSIC.

sister *n.*

[The female area of the head plus a sign similar to **same** indicating a girl in the same family] Beginning with the thumb of the right *L hand* touching the right side of the chin, palm facing left, move the right hand downward, ending with the little-finger side of the right *L hand* across the thumb side of the left *L hand* held in front of the chest, palms facing right.

sit *v.*

[The bent fingers represent one's legs dangling from the edge of a seat] Hook the fingers of the right *curved U hand,* palm facing down, perpendicular to the fingers of the left *U hand* held in

front of the chest, palm facing down and fingers pointing right.

size[1] *n.* [The hands seem to measure out a size] Beginning with the thumbs of both *Y hands* touching in front of the chest, palms facing down, bring the hands apart to in front of each side of the chest.

size[2] *n.* See sign for MEASURE.

sketch *n.* See sign for ART.

skill *n.* Related form: **skilled** *adj.* Same sign used for: **ability, able, agile, capable, efficient, enable, expert, handy, proficient, talent.**

[The edge of the hand is honed as are skills] Grasp the little-finger side of the left *open hand* with the curved right fingers. Then pull the right hand forward while closing the fingers into the palm.

skin *n.* Same sign used for: **flesh.**

[The location of skin on one's hand] Pinch and shake the loose skin on the back of the left *open hand*, palm facing down, with the bent thumb and index finger of the right *5 hand*.

skinny *adj.* See sign for THIN[2].

skip *v.* Same sign used for: **lack, miss.**

[Points out the hiding finger] Beginning with the left *5 hand* held across the chest, middle finger bent downward, move the extended right index finger, palm facing left and finger pointing forward, from right to left in front of the chest, hitting the bent left middle finger as it passes.

skirt *n.*

[The location of a skirt] Brush the thumbs of both *5 hands,* palms facing in and fingers pointing down, from the waist downward and outward with a repeated movement.

slacks *pl. n.* See sign for PANTS.

slaughter *v.* See sign for KILL.

sleep *v., n.* Same sign used for: **doze, slumber.**

[The hand brings the eyes and face down into a sleeping position] Bring the right *open hand,* palm facing left and fingers point up, in against the right cheek.

slice *v., n.*

[Demonstrates the action of slicing off the end of something] Bring the palm side of the right *open hand,* palm facing left and fingers pointing forward, from in front of the chest straight down near the thumb side of the left *S hand* held in front of the body, palm facing down.

slide *v.* See sign for SLIP.

slim *adj.* See signs for DIET, THIN[2].

slip *v.* Same sign used for: **slide.**

[Represents a person's legs slipping] Beginning with the fingertips of the right *V hand* touching the upturned palm of the left *open hand,* push the right fingers forward, ending with the right palm on the left palm.

slipper *n.*

[Represents sliding one's foot into a slipper] Slide the right *open hand,* palm facing down, forward across the palm of the left *curved hand,* palm facing up, while closing the left fingers around the right fingers.

slothful *adj.* See sign for LAZY.

slow *adj.* Related form: **slowly** *adj.*

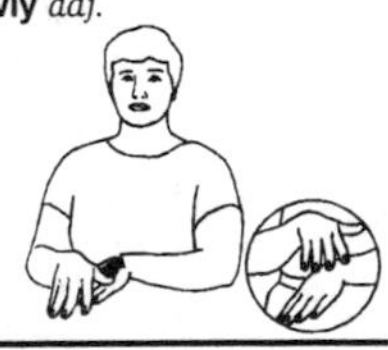

[Demonstrates a slow movement] Pull the fingertips of the right *5 hand,* palm facing down, from the fingers toward the wrist of the back of the left *open hand,* palm facing down.

slumber *n.* See sign for SLEEP.

small *adj.* See also signs for LITTLE[1], TINY. Same sign used for: **meage mini.**

[Shows a small size] Beginning with both *open hands* in front of each side of the chest, palms facing each other and fingers pointing forward, bring the palms close to each other in front of the chest.

smart *adj.* See also sign for SCHOLARLY. Same sign used for: **brilliant. clever, intelligence, intelligent, quick-witted.**

[Indicates brightness coming from the brain] Bring the bent middle finger of the right *5 hand* from touching the forehead, palm facing in, forward with a wavy movement.

smell *v., n.* Same sign used for: **fragrance, fume, odor, scent.**

[Represents bringing something from in front of the nose to smell it] Brush the fingers of the right *open hand,* palm facing in, upward in front of the nose with a double movement.

smile *v., n.* Same sign used for: **grin.**

[The shape of the mouth when smiling] Beginning with both *flattened C hands* near each side of the mouth, palms facing each other, pull the fingers back and upward past each cheek in the shape of a smile while pinching the fingers together, forming *flattened O hands* near each side of the head, palms facing down.

smoke[1] *v.* Related form: **smoking** *n.*

[Mime smoking a cigarette] Beginning with the fingers of the right *V hand* touching the right side of the mouth, palm facing in and fingers pointing up, bring the hand forward with a double movement.

---

smoke[2] *n.*

[Shows the movement of smoke upward from a fire] Beginning with the right *curved 5 hand* above the left *curved 5 hand,* palms facing each other in front of the chest, move the hands in repeated flat circles in opposite directions.

---

smooth[1] *adj.*

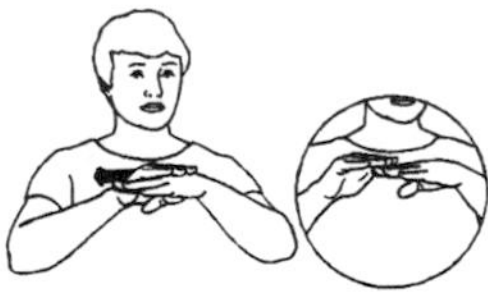

[Demonstrates a smooth flat surface] Move the fingers of the right *open hand,* palm facing down, from the wrist to the fingertips across the top of the left *open hand* held in front of the body, palm facing down.

---

smooth[2] *adj.* Related form: **smoothly** *adv.* Same sign used for: **fluent, fluently, go smoothly, silky.**

[The fingertips seem to feel something smooth] Beginning with both *flattened O hands* in front of each side of the chest, palms facing up, slide the thumb of each hand across the fingertips from the little fingers to the index fingers with a smooth movement, ending with *A hands.*

snack *v., n.*

[Demonstrates picking up a snack to eat it] Move the fingertips of the right *F hand* from touching the open left palm held in front of the chest, palms facing each other, upward to the mouth with a double movement.

snake *n.* Same sign used for: **reptile, serpent.**

[Represents a snake striking with its fangs] Beginning with the back of the right *bent V hand* in front of the mouth, palm facing forward, move the hand forward in a double spiral movement.

snoop *v.* See sign for NOSY.

snow *n.,v.*

[Represents snow on one's shoulder + the movement of snow falling] Beginning with the fingers of both *5 hands* touching each shoulder, palms facing down, turn the hands forward and bring the hands slowly down to in front of each side of the body while wiggling the fingers as the hands move.

soap *n.*

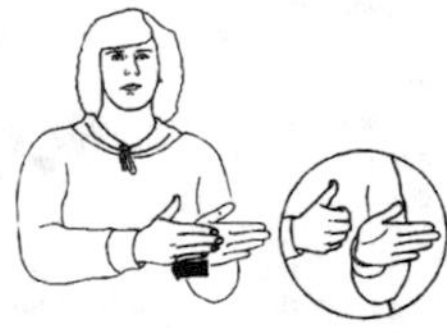

[Represents rubbing soap on one's hands] Wipe the fingers of the right *bent hand* on the palm of the left *open hand* from the fingers to the heel with a double movement, bending the right fingers back into the palm each time.

so-called *adj.* See sign for TITLE.

soccer *n.*

[Formed similar to **kick** but with a double movement] Move the right *B hand* upward in front of the body to hit the index-finger side of the right hand against the little-finger side of the left *B hand* with a double movement, both palms angled in.

socialize *v.* See sign for ASSOCIATE.

sock *n.* or **socks** *pl. n.*

[Suggests needles used for knitting socks] Rub the sides of both extended index fingers back and forth with an alternating movement, palms facing down and fingers pointing forward in front of the body.

soda pop *n.* Alternate forms: **soda, pop.** Same sign used for: **soft drink.**

[Represents recapping a soda pop bottle] Insert the bent middle finger of the right *5 hand,* palm facing down, into the hole formed by the left *O hand,* palm facing right. Then slap the right *open hand,* palm facing down, sharply on the thumb side of the left *O hand.*

soft *adj.* Same sign used for: **gentle, mellow, tender.**

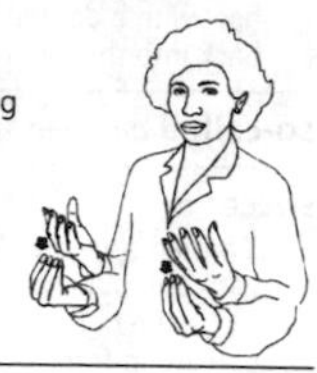

[The hands seem to feel something soft] Beginning with both *curved 5 hands* in front of each side of the chest, palms facing up, bring the hands down with a double movement while closing the fingers to the thumbs each time.

softball *n.* See sign for BASEBALL.

soft drink *n.* See sign for SODA POP.

soil *n.* See sign for DIRT.

soiled *adj.* See sign for DIRTY.

solely *adv.* See sign for ALONE.

solid *adj.* See signs for HARD[1], STRONG[1], STURDY[1].

solidify *v.* See sign for FREEZE.

some *adj.* Same sign used for: **part.**

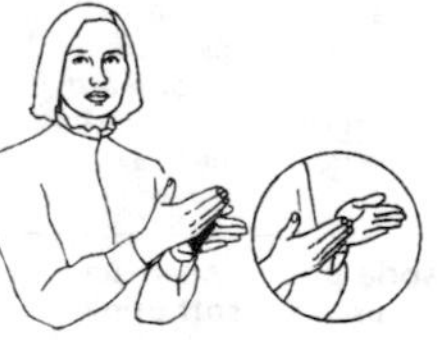

[The hand seems to divide an object] Pull the little-finger side of the right *bent hand,* palm facing left, across the palm of the left *open hand,* palm facing up and fingers pointing forward.

sometimes *adv.* Same sign used for: **occasional.**

[Similar to sign for **once** except repeated to indicate reoccurrence] Bring the extended right index finger, palm facing in, downward against the upturned palm of the left *open hand* and up again in a rhythmic repeated circular movement.

son *n.*

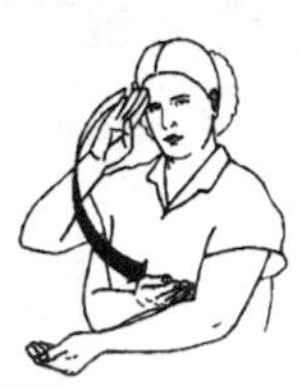

[A shortened form of the combination of the signs for **boy** and **baby**] Beginning with the fingertips of the right *B hand* against the forehead, palm facing left, bring the right hand downward, ending with the bent right arm cradled in the bent left arm held across the body, both palms facing up.

song *n.* See sign for MUSIC.

soon[1] *adv.* Same sign used for: **near future, in the; shortly.**

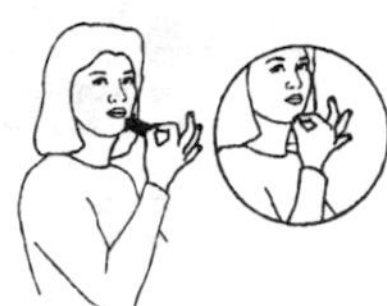

[The movement is close, indicating immediacy] Touch the fingertips of the right *F hand,* palm facing in, to the middle of the chin.

soon[2] *adv.* See sign for SHORT[1].

sordid *adj.* See sign for AWFUL.

sorry *adj.* Related form: **sorrow** *n.* Same sign used for: **apologize, apology, penitence, penitent, regret, repent.**

[Indicates rubbing the chest in sorrow] Rub the palm side of the right *A hand* in a large circle on the chest with a repeated movement.

sort[1] *n.* See sign for KIND[2].

sort[2] *v.* See signs for FILE[1], PREPARE.

sort of See sign for FAIR[1].

so-so *adj.* See sign for FAIR[1].

sound *n.* See signs for HEAR, NOISE.

soup *n.*
[Mime eating soup with a spoon] With the thumb extended, move the fingers of the right *U hand* from touching the palm of the left *open hand* upward to the mouth, both palms facing up.

sour *adj.* Same sign used for: **bitter.**
[Points to puckered lips from eating something sour] With the tip of the extended right index finger on the chin near the mouth, palm facing left, twist the hand, ending with the palm facing back.

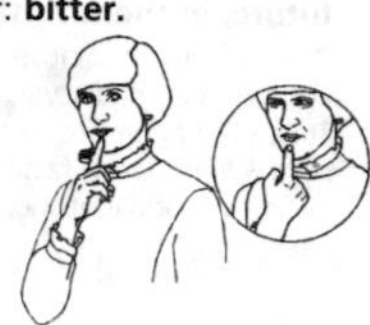

source *n.* See sign for START.

south *n., adj.* Related form: **southern** *adj.*
[Initialized sign indicating a southern direction on a map] Move the right *S hand*, palm facing in, downward in front of the right side of the chest.

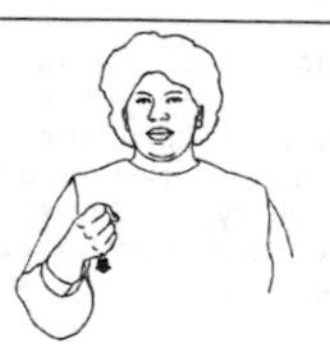

space *n.* See sign for AREA.

spaghetti *n.*
[The shape of spaghetti] Beginning with both extended little fingers touching in front of the chest, palms facing in, bring the hands apart in small arcs, ending in front of each shoulder.

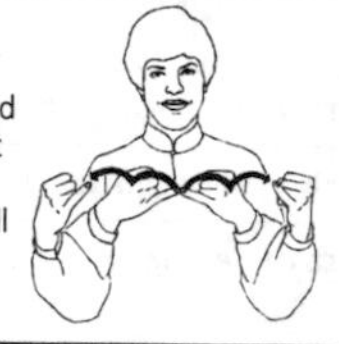

sparkle *v.* See sign for SHINY.

speak[1] *v.* Same sign used for: **talk.**

[Represents words coming from the mouth] Beginning with the index-finger side of the right *4 hand* touching the chin, palm facing left, move the hand forward with a repeated movement.

speak[2] *v.* Same sign used for: **address, lecture, presentation, speech.**

[Waving the hand when making a point] Beginning with the right *open hand* near the right side of the head, palm facing left and fingers pointing up, twist the wrist to move the fingers forward and back with a short repeated movement.

special *adj.* Same sign used for: **especially, unique.**

[Demonstrates pulling one thing out that is special] Grasp the left extended index finger, palm facing in and finger pointing up, with the fingers of the right *G hand* and pull upward in front of the chest.

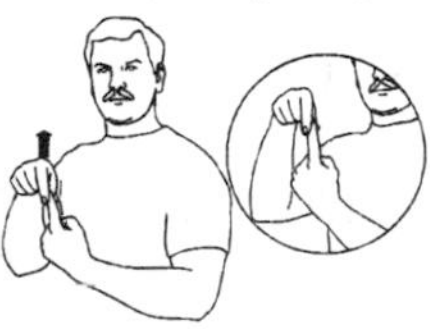

specialize *v.* Related form: **specialty** *n.* Same sign used for: **field, major, straight.**

[Suggests going in a specific direction] Slide the little-finger side of the right *B hand,* palm facing left and fingers pointing forward, along the index-finger side of the left

B hand held in front of the chest, palm facing right and fingers pointing forward.

specific *adj.* See sign for POINT[1].

speech *n.* See sign for SPEAK[2].

spend *v.*

[Represents money slipping through one's hands] Beginning with both *curved hands* in front of each side of the chest, right hand nearer the chest than the left hand and both palms facing up, move the hands forward while moving the thumbs across the fingers, ending with *10 hands.*

split[1] *n., v.* See sign for DIVIDE.

split[2] *Slang.* See sign for RUN AWAY.

split up *v. phrase.* See sign for DIVIDE.

spoil *v.* See sign for RUIN[1].

sponsor *v.* See sign for SUPPORT.

spoon *n.*

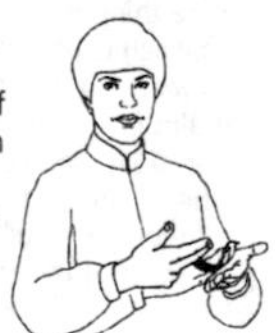

[The fingers represent a spoon scooping up food] Wipe the backs of the fingers of the right *U hand,* palm facing up and thumb extended, across the upturned palm of the left *open hand* from the fingers to the heel with a double movement.

spot *n.* Same sign used for: **stain.**

[Shape and location of a spot] Touch the thumb side of the right *F hand* to the left side of the chest, palm facing left.

spread *v.* Same sign used for: **disseminate, distribute.**

[Demonstrates something spreading outward] Beginning with the fingertips of both *flattened O hands* touching in front of the chest, palms facing down, move the hands forward and away from each other while opening into *5 hands* in front of each side of the body, palms facing down.

spring *n.*

[Similar to sign for **grow** except with a double movement] Beginning with the right *flattened O hand,* palm facing up, being held by the left *C hand,* palm facing in, move the right hand upward with a double movement, opening into a *5 hand* each time.

sprout *v.* See sign for GROW.

squabble *v.* See sign for ARGUE.

square *n., adj.* Same sign used for: **sign.**

[Draw a square in the air] Beginning with both extended index fingers touching in front of the upper chest, palms angled forward and fingers pointing upward, bring the hands straight out to in front of each shoulder then straight down, and finally back together in front of the waist.

squeeze *n.* See sign for BRIEF.

stain *n.* See sign for SPOT .

staircase *n.* See sign for STAIRS.

stairs *n.* Same signs used for: **staircase, stairway.**

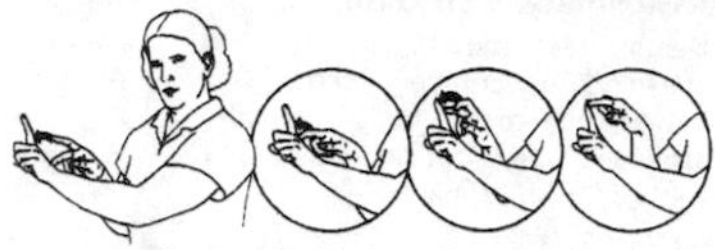

[Demonstrates the action of walking up stairs] Move the fingertips of the right *bent V hand,* palm facing forward, in an alternating crawling movement up the extended left index finger, palm facing forward.

---

stairway *n.* See sign for STAIRS.

---

stall *v.* See sign for HOLD[2].

---

stamp[1] *n., v.* Same sign used for: **postage, postage stamp.**

[The fingers seem to lick a stamp and place it on an envelope] Move the fingers of the right *H hand* from the mouth, palm facing in, down to land on the fingers of the left *open hand,* palm facing up, in front of the body.

---

stamp[2] *n., v.* Same sign used for: **brand, guarantee, seal.**

[Mime stamping something with a rubber stamp] Move the right *S hand,* palm facing left, from in front of the chest downward, ending with the little-finger side of the right *S hand* on the upturned palm of the left *open hand.*

---

stand *v.*

[The fingers represent erect legs] Place the fingertips of the right *V hand,* palm facing in and fingers pointing down, on the up-turned palm of the left *open hand* held in front of the body.

standard *n., adj.* Related form: **standardized** *adj.* Same sign used for: **common.**

[**same**[1] formed with a large circular movement to indicate everything is the same] Beginning with both *Y hands* in front of the body, palms facing down, move the hands in a large flat circle.

stand for *v. phrase.* See sign for MEAN[2].

staple *v.* Same sign as for STAPLER but formed with a single movement.

stapler *n.*

[Mime pushing down on a stapler] Press the heel of the right *curved 5 hand,* palm facing down, on the heel of the left *open hand,* palm facing up, with a double movement.

star *n.*

[Striking flints to create sparks that look like stars] Brush the sides of both extended index fingers against each other, palms facing forward, with an alternating movement as the hands move upward in front of the face.

start *n.* Same sign used for: **beginning, origin, origination, source.**

[Represents turning a key to start ignition] Beginning with the extended right index finger, palm facing in, inserted between the index and middle fingers of the left *open hand,* palm facing right and fingers pointing forward, twist the right hand back, ending with the palm angled forward.

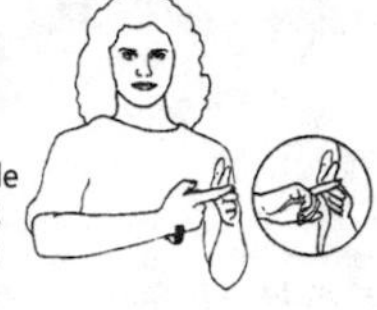

startle *v.* See sign for SURPRISE.

starved *adj.* See sign for HUNGRY.

state[1] *n.*

[Initialized sign similar to sign for **law**] Move the index-finger side of the right *S hand,* palm facing forward, down from the fingers to the heel of the left *open hand,* palm facing right and fingers pointing up.

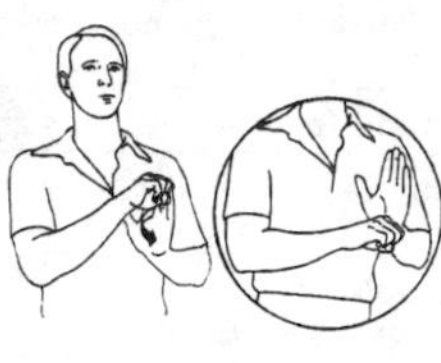

state[2] *v.* See sign for SAY.

statement *n.* See sign for SENTENCE.

stay *v.* Same sign used for: **remain.**

[Continuity of movement] With the thumb of the right *10 hand* on the thumb-nail of the left *10 hand,* both palms facing down in front of the chest, move the hands forward and down a short distance.

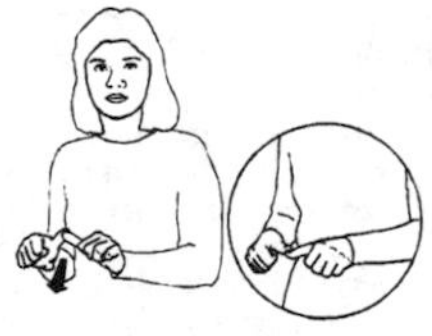

steadfast *adj.* See sign for CONSTANT.

steady *adj.* See sign for CONSTANT.

steal *v.* Same sign used for: **burglary, pillage, shoplift, theft.**

[The fingers seem to snatch something] Beginning with the index-finger side of the right *V hand,* palm facing down, on the elbow of the bent left arm, held at an upward angle across the chest, pull the right hand upward toward the left wrist while bending the fingers in tightly.

steel *n.* See sign for METAL.

steer *v.* See sign for LEAD.

stern *adj.* See sign for STRICT.

stick[1] *v.* Related form: **sticky** *adj.* Same sign used for: **adhere, adhesive, expose, fasten.**

[Demonstrates something sticky causing the finger and thumb to stick together] With the thumb of the right *5 hand,* palm facing down, touching the palm of the left *open hand,* palm facing up, close the right middle finger down to the thumb.

stick[2] *n.* Same sign used for: **pipe, pole, rod.**

[Shape of a stick] Beginning with the thumb sides of both *F hands* touching in front of the chest, palms facing forward, move the hands apart.

sticky *adj.* Same sign as for STICK[1] but formed with a double movement.

still[1] *adv.* See also sign for YET.
[Formed with a continuing movement to show passage of time] Move the right *Y hand,* palm facing down, from in front of the right side of the body forward and upward in an arc.

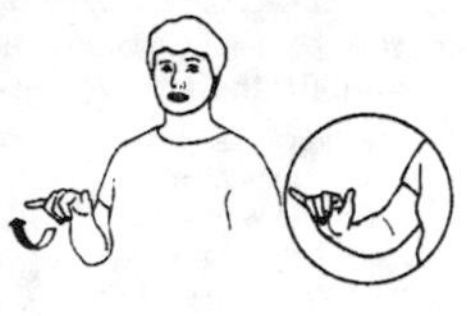

still[2] *adj.* See signs for QUIET, SILENT.

sting *v., n.*
[Represents the stinger of an insect penetrating to wound] Beginning with the right *X hand* held in front of the right side of the chest, palm facing left, bring the bent index finger down deliberately against the back of the left *S hand,* palm facing down, and then back upward quickly.

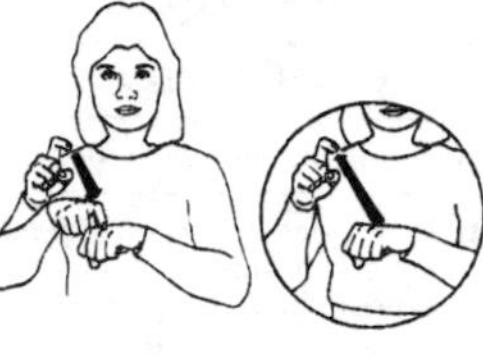

stingy *adj.* (alternate sign)
Same sign used for: **tightwad** (*informal*).
[Clutching a prized item] Beginning with the fingers of the right *curved 5 hand* in front of the chin, palm facing in, bring the hand downward while closing into an *S hand.*

stir *v.* See signs for BEAT[1], MESSY, MIX[1].

stocks *pl. n.* See sign for INVEST.

stomachache *n.*
[**hurt** formed near the stomach] Beginning with both extended index fingers pointing toward each other in front of the body, palms facing up, jab the fingers toward each other with a short double movement.

stone *n.* See sign for ROCK[1].

stop[1] *v.* Same sign used for: **cease, halt, quit.**
[Demonstrates an abrupt stopping movement] Bring the little-finger side of the right *open hand,* palm facing left and fingers pointing up, sharply down on the upturned palm of the left *open hand* held in front of the body.

stop[2] *v.* See sign for DESIST.

storage *n.* See sign for SAVE[2].

store[1] *n.* Same sign used for: **market, mart, shop.**
[The hands seem to hold merchandise out for inspection and sale] Beginning with both *flattened O hands* in front of each side of the body, palms facing down and fingers pointing down, swing the fingers forward and back from the wrists with a repeated movement.

store[2] *v.* See sign for SAVE[2].

storm *n.* See signs for MESSY, WIND.

story *n.* Same sign used for: **parable, phrase, prose, remarks, tale.**

[The hands seem to pull out sentences to form a story] Beginning with both *flattened C hands* in front of the chest, palms facing each other and the right hand slightly over the left hand, close the fingertips to the thumbs of each hand and then pull the hands straight apart in front of each shoulder with a double movement.

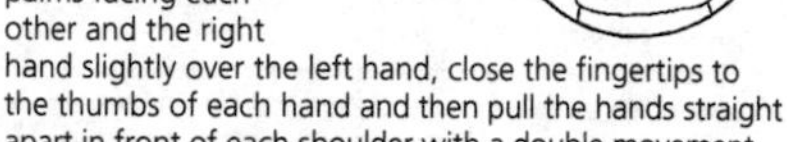

straight[1] *adj., adv.* Same sign used for: **direct.**

[Indicates a straight direction] Beginning with the index-finger side of the right *B hand* against the right shoulder, palm facing left and fingers pointing up, move the hand straight forward by bending the wrist down.

straight[2] *adj., adv.* See sign for SPECIALIZE.

stranded *adj.* See sign for STUCK.

strange *adj.* Same sign used for: **bizarre, freak, odd, peculiar, queer, unusual.**

[Something distorting one's vision] Move the right *C hand* from near the right side of the face, palm facing left, downward in an arc in front of the face, ending near the left side of the chin, palm facing down.

street *n.* See sign for ROAD.

strength *n.* See signs for POWER[1], STRONG[1], WELL[1].

stress *n.* See sign for IMPRESSION.

stretch[1] *v.* Same sign used for: **elastic.**

[Mime stretching out some elastic] Beginning with the knuckles of both *S hands* touching in front of the chest, palms facing in, bring the hands apart to in front of each side of the chest with a double movement.

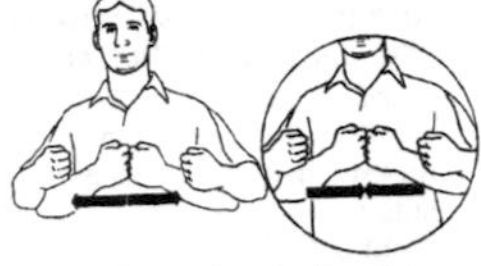

stretch[2] *v.* See sign for EXAGGERATE.

strict *adj.* Same sign used for: **bold, firm, stern.**

Strike the index-finger side of the right *bent V hand* against the nose with a deliberate movement, palm facing left.

strike *v.* See signs for COMPLAIN, HIT, PROTEST.

string *n.* See sign for LINE.

strip *v.* See sign for TEAR.

strive *v.* See sign for TRY.

stroll *v.* See sign for WALK.

strong[1] *adj.* Same sign used for: **power, solid, strength.**

[Initialized sign formed similar to **power**[1]] Beginning with the index-finger side of the right *S hand* near the left shoulder, palm facing left, move the right hand down in an arc, ending with the little-finger side of the right *S hand* touching near the crook of the left arm, palm facing up.

strong[2] *adj.* See sign for POWERFUL, WELL[1].

struggle *v., n.* Same sign used for: **antagonism, at odds, banter, conflict, controversy, opposition.**

[Represents opposing forces struggling] Beginning with both extended index fingers pointing toward each other in front of the chest, palms facing in and right hand closer to the body than the left hand, move the hands back and forth simultaneously with a double movement.

stubborn *adj.* See sign for DONKEY.

stuck *adj.* Same sign used for: **confined, pregnant, rape, stranded, trapped.**

[Indicates where food gets stuck in the throat] Move the fingertips of the right *V hand,* palm facing down, against the throat with a deliberate movement.

student *n.* See sign for PUPIL[1].

study *v., n.*

[Eyes scanning information held in the hand in order to learn it] While wiggling the fingers, move the right *5 hand,* palm facing down, with a double movement toward the left *open hand* held in front of the chest, palm facing up.

stuff *n.* See sign for SAVE[2].

stuffed *adj.* See sign for FULL[1].

stupid *adj.* See sign for DUMB.

sturdy[1] *adj.* Same sign used for: **solid, tough.**

[Striking something that is sturdy] Move the right *S hand* from in front of the right side of the chest, palm facing in, in a downward arc across the back of the left *S hand* held in front of the chest, palm facing down, and back again.

sturdy[2] *adj.* See sign for POWER[1].

subdue *v.* See sign for DEFEAT.

subject *n.* See sign for TITLE.

submit *v.* See signs for ADMIT, SUGGEST. Related form: **submission** *n.*

subscribe *v.* See sign for PENSION.

substitute *v.* See sign for TRADE. Related form: **substitution** *n.*

subtract *v.* Same sign used for: **deduct, discount, eliminate, exempt.**

[Demonstrates removing something] Beginning with the fingertips of the right *curved 5 hand* touching the palm of the left *open hand* held in front of the left side of the chest, palm facing right and fingers pointing up, bring the right hand down off the base of the left hand while changing into an *S hand.*

subway *n.*

[Initialized sign formed under the left hand representing moving under street level] Move the right *S hand,* palm facing left, forward and back under the palm of the left *open hand* held across the chest, palm facing down and fingers pointing right.

succeed *v.* See sign for FINALLY.

success *n.* See sign for ACHIEVE.

successful *adj.* Related forms: **succeed** *v.*, **success** *n.* See also sign for ACHIEVE. Same sign used for: **accomplish, accomplishment, achievement, prosper, triumph.**

[Moving to higher stages] Beginning with both extended index fingers pointing up in front of each shoulder, palms facing back, move the hands in double arcs upward and back, ending near each side of the head.

such as See sign for SAME.

sudden *adj., adv.* See sign for FAST.

suffer *v.*

[Similar to **patient**[1] except formed with a double movement] Beginning with the thumb of the right *A hand* touching the chin, palm facing left, twist the hand to the left with a double movement.

sufficient *adj.* See sign for ENOUGH.

sugar *n.* See sign for CANDY.

suggest *v.* Related form: **suggestion** *n.* Same sign used for: **appeal, bid, motion, offer, nominate, petition, proposal, propose, provide, submit, submission.**

[The hands seem to put forward a suggestion] Beginning with both *open hands* in front of each side of the chest, palms facing up and fingers pointing forward, move the hands simultaneously upward in an arc.

suit[1] *n.* See signs for FIT[1], MATCH.

suit[2] *n.* See sign for CLOTHES.

suitcase *n.* See sign for PURSE.

summarize *v.* See sign for BRIEF.

summer *n.*

[Represents wiping sweat from the brow] Bring the thumb side of the extended right index finger, palm facing down and finger pointing left, across the forehead while bending the index finger into an *X hand.*

summon *v.* See sign for CALL[1].

sun *n.*

[Represents shielding one's eyes from the sun] Tap the thumb and index finger of the right *C hand,* palm facing forward, against the right side of the head with a double movement.

Sunday *n.*

[The movement of the hands shows reverence and awe] Beginning with both *open hands* in front of each shoulder, palms facing forward and fingers pointing up, move the hands forward and back with a small double movement.

sundown *n.* See sign for SUNSET.

sunrise *n.* Same sign used for **dawn**.

[Represents the sun coming up over the horizon] Bring the index-finger side of the right *F hand,* palm facing left, upward past the little-finger side of the left *open hand,* palm facing down and fingers pointing right, held across the chest, ending with the right *F hand* in front of the face.

sunset *n.* Same sign used for: **sundown.**

[Represents the sun going down below the horizon] Move the thumb side of the right *F hand*, palm facing left, downward past the little-finger side of the left *open hand* held across the chest, palm facing down and fingers pointing right.

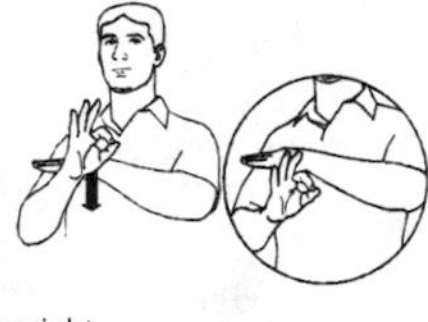

superb *adj.* Same sign used for: **excellent, fantastic, okay.**

[Natural gesture to indicate something is superb] Move the right *F hand,* palm facing left, forward with a short double movement in front of the right shoulder.

superintendent *n.* See sign for PRESIDENT.

superior *n.* See sign for CHIEF[1].

supervise *v.* See sign for CARE[1].

supplement *v.* See sign for ADD.

supply *v.* See sign for FEED.

support *v., n.* Same sign used for: **advocate, allegiance, backup, boost, fund, in behalf of, in favor of, sponsor.**

[Initialized sign similar to sign for **help**] Push the knuckles of the right *S hand,* palm facing left, upward under the little-finger side of the left *S hand,* palm facing in, pushing the left hand upward a short distance in front of the chest.

suppose *v.* Same sign used for: **if, in case of.**

[Indicates a thought coming from the mind] Move the extended little finger of the right *I hand,* palm facing in, forward from the right side of the forehead with a short double movement.

supposed to *v.phrase.* See sign for NEED.

suppress *v.* See sign for CONTROL[1]. Related form: **suppression** *n.*

supreme *adj.* See sign for ADVANCED.

sure[1] *adj.* Same sign used for: **cer**

[Indicates that facts are coming straight from the mouth] Move the extended right index finger from in front of the mouth, palm facing left and finger pointing up, forward with a deliberate movement.

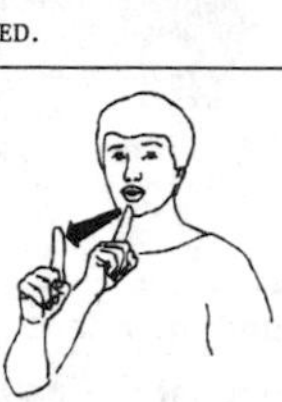

sure[2] *adj.* See sign for HONEST.

surface *v.* See sign for SHOW UP.

surgery *n.* See sign for OPERATE[1].

surprise *n., v.* Same sign used for: **amaze, amazement, astound, bewilder, startle.**

[Represents the eyes widening in surprise] Beginning with the index fingers and thumbs of both hands pinched together near the outside of each eye, palms facing each other, flick the fingers apart, forming *L hands* near each side of the head.

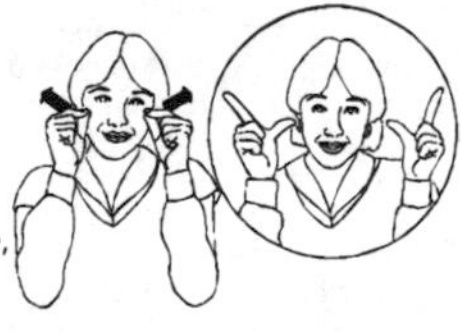

survive *v.* See sign for LIVE. Related form: **survival** *n.*

suspect *v.* Related forms: **suspicion** *n.*, **suspicious** *adj.*

Beginning with the extended right index finger touching the right side of the forehead, palm facing down, bring the hand forward a short distance with a double

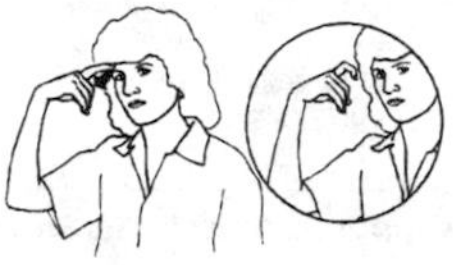

movement, bending the index finger into an *X hand* each time.

suspend v. See sign for HOLD[2].

swap *v.* See signs for REVERSE, TRADE.

swear *v.* See sign for CURSE.

sweat *v., n.* Same sign used for: **perspire, perspiration, toil.**

[Represents sweat coming from one's brow] Beginning with both *S hands* in front of each side of the forehead, move the hands forward while opening into *curved hands,* palms facing down and fingers pointing toward each other.

sweep *v.* See sign for BROOM.

sweet *adj.* Same sign used for: **gentle.**

[Licking something sweet from the fingers] Wipe the fingertips of the right *open hand,* palm facing in and fingers pointing up, downward off the chin while bending the fingers.

sweetheart *n.* Same sign used for: **beau, lover.**

[Two people nodding toward each other] With the knuckles of both *10 hands* together in front of the chest, palms facing in and thumbs pointing up, bend the thumbs downward toward each other with a double movement.

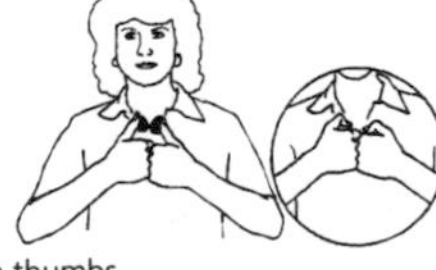

swim *v.* Related form: **swimming** *n.*

[Demonstrates the movement of the hands when swimming] Beginning with the fingers of both *open hands* crossed in front of the chest, palms facing down, move the hands apart to each side with a double movement.

switch *v.* See signs for CHANGE[1], REVERSE, TRADE.

syrup *n.* See sign for GRAVY.

table[1] *n.*
[Represents the flat surface of a table top] Beginning with the bent arms of both *open hands* across the chest, right arm above the left arm, move the right arm down with a short double movement.

table[2] *n.* See sign for DESK.

tag *n.* See sign for LABEL.

take *v.* Same sign used for: **acquire, adopt, assume, assumption, takeover, take up.**
[The hands seem to take up something] Beginning with both *curved 5 hands* in front of each side of the body, palms facing down, move the hands upward toward the body while changing into *S hands.*

take advantage of *v. phrase.* See signs for ADVANTAGE[1].

take care of *v. phrase.* See sign for CARE[1].

take off *v. phrase.* Same sign for: **remove, undress.**
[Mime taking off one's clothes] Beginning with the fingers of both *curved hands* on each side of the chest, palms facing in, bring the hands outward to in front of each shoulder while closing into *S hands,* palms facing each other.

takeover *n.* See signs for CAPTURE, TAKE.

take pictures *v. phrase.* Same sign used for: **photograph, shoot.**

[Represents the shutter on a camera opening and closing] Beginning with both *modified C hands* near the outside of each eye, palms facing each other, bend the right index finger downward.

take up *v. phrase.* See sign for TAKE.

tale *n.* See sign for STORY.

talent *n.* See sign for SKILL.

talk[1] *v.*

[Shows words coming from the mouth] Beginning with the index-finger side of the right *4 hand* in front of the mouth, palm facing left and fingers pointing up, move the hand forward with a double movement.

talk[2] *v.* See signs for BLAB, CHAT[1], SPEAK[1]. Related form: **talkative** *adj.*

tall[1] *adj.* (Used to describe things)

[Indicates the height of a tall thing] Move the extended right index finger, palm facing forward and finger pointing up, from the heel upward to off the fingertips of the left *open hand,* palm facing right and fingers pointing up, ending with the right hand in front of the head.

tall[2] *adj.* (Use to describe people) Same sign used for: **height.**

[Shows height of a tall person] Raise the right *open hand*, palm facing down, upward from in front of the right shoulder.

tardy *adj.* See sign for LATE.

target *n.* See signs for GOAL, POINT.

task *n.* See sign for WORK.

taste *n., v.*

[The finger used for feeling points toward the sense of taste] Touch the bent middle finger of the right *5 hand,* palm facing in, to the lips.

tasty *adj.* See sign for DELICIOUS.

tax *adj.* See sign for COST.

taxi *n.* See sign for CAB.

tea *n.*

[Mime dipping a tea bag in hot water] With the fingertips of the right *F hand,* palm facing down, inserted in the hole formed by the left *O hand* held in front of the chest, palm facing in, move the right hand in a small circle.

teach *v.* Same sign used for: **educate, education, indoctrinate, indoctrination, instruct, instruction.**

[The hands seem to take information from the head and direct it toward another person] Move both *flattened O hands,* palms facing each other, forward with a small double movement in front of each side of the head.

team *n.*

[Initialized sign similar to sign for **class**] Beginning with the index-finger sides of both *T hands* touching in front of the chest, palms angled forward, bring the hands away from each other in outward arcs while turning the palms in, ending with the little fingers touching.

tear *v.* Same sign used for: **revoke, rip, strip, torn.**

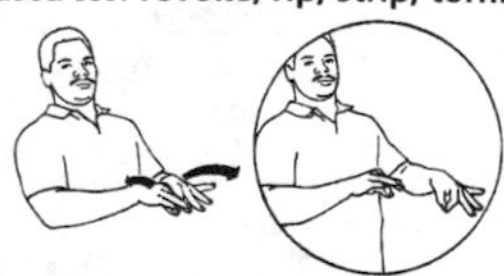

[Mime ripping a piece of paper] Beginning with the index-finger sides of both *F hands* touching in front of the chest, palms facing down, move the right hand back toward the body with a deliberate movement while moving the left hand forward.

tear apart *v. phrase.* See sign for BREAK.

tear down *v. phrase.* See sign for BREAK DOWN.

tease *v.* Related form: **teasing** *n.* Same sign used for: **jest, kid, kidding.**

[The hand seems to direct jabbing remarks at someone] Push the little-finger side of the right *X hand,* palm facing left, forward with a repeated movement across the index-finger side of the left *X hand,* palm facing right.

technical *adj.* Related forms: **technology** *n.*, **technique** *n.*

Tap the bent middle finger of the right *5 hand*, palm facing up, upward on the little-finger side of the left *open hand*, palm facing right and fingers pointing forward, with a double movement.

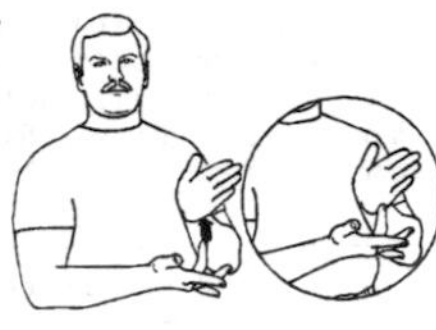

teeny *adj.* See sign for TINY.

teeth *n.*

[Location of the teeth] Move the curved index finger of the right *X hand* from right to left across the top front teeth, palm facing in.

telephone *n.*, *v.* Same sign used for: **call, phone.**

[Represents holding a telephone receiver to the ear] Tap the knuckles of the right *Y hand,* palm facing in, with a double movement on the lower right cheek, holding the right thumb near the right ear and the little finger in front of the mouth. The same sign is used for the verb, as in *to telephone my sister*, but the sign is made with a single movement.

television or **TV** *n.*
[Abbreviation T-V] Form a *T* and then a *V* in front of the right shoulder with the right hand, palm facing forward.

tell[1] *v.* Same sign used for: **reveal.**
[Represents words coming from the mouth toward another person] Beginning with the extended right index finger near the chin, palm facing in and finger pointing up, move the finger forward in an arc by bending the wrist, ending with the finger angled forward.

tell[2] *v.* See sign for ANNOUNCE.

temporary *adj.* See sign for SHORT[1].

ten cents *pl. n.* See sign for DIME.

tender *adj.* See sign for SOFT.

terminate *v.* See signs for ELIMINATE[1], FIRE[2].

terrible *adj.* See sign for AWFUL.

test *n., v.* Same sign used for: **examine, examination, inquire, quiz.**
[Draw a question mark in the air + a gesture representing distributing the test to a group] Beginning with both extended index fingers pointing up in front of the head, palms facing forward, bring the hands in arcs to the side and then downward while bending the index fingers into *X hands* and continuing down while throwing the

fingers open into *5 hands* in front of the body, palms facing down and fingers pointing forward.

text *n.* See sign for WORD.

text message *n.* Related form: **text** *v.*

[Mime action of thumbs when text messaging]. With the knuckles of both *curved 5 hands* together in front of the body, bend the extended thumbs with a random up and down movement.

thank or **thanks** *v.* Same sign used for: **thank you.**

[The hand takes gratitude from the mouth and presents it to another] Move the fingertips of the right *open hand,* palm facing in and fingers pointing up, from the mouth forward and down, ending with the palm angled up in front of the chest.

thank you See sign for THANK.

Thanksgiving *n.*

[Represents the shape of a turkey's wattle] Beginning with the right *G hand* in front of the nose, palm facing left, bring the hand downward in an arc with a double movement, bringing the hand forward in front of the chest each time.

that *pron., adj.*

[Points out something in the hand] Bring the palm side of the right *Y hand* with a deliberate movement down to land on the palm of the left *open hand* held in front of the chest, palm facing up.

theater *n.* See sign for ACT[2].

theft *n.* See sign for STEAL.

their *pron.* Related form: **theirs** *pron.*

[Points toward the referents being discussed] Move the right *open hand,* palm facing forward and fingers pointing up, from in front of the right side of the body outward to the right.

them *pron.* Same sign used for: **these, they.**

[Points toward the referents being discussed] Move the extended right index finger, palm facing down and finger pointing forward, from in front of the right side of the body outward to the right.

theme *n.* See signs for QUOTATION, TITLE.

themselves *pl. pron.*

[This hand shape is used for reflexive pronouns and is directed toward the referents being discussed] Move the right *10 hand* from in front of the right side of the body, palm facing left, outward to the right.

then *adv.* See signs for FINISH[1], OR.

there *adv.* Same sign used for: **point.**

[Points to a specific place away from the body] Push the extended right index finger from in front of the right shoulder forward a short distance, palm facing forward and finger pointing forward.

these *pron.* See sign for THEM.

they *pron.* See sign for THEM.

thick *adj.*

[Shows the thickness of a thick layer] Slide the thumb side of the right *modified C hand,* palm facing forward, from the wrist across the back of the left *open hand* held in front of the chest, palm facing down.

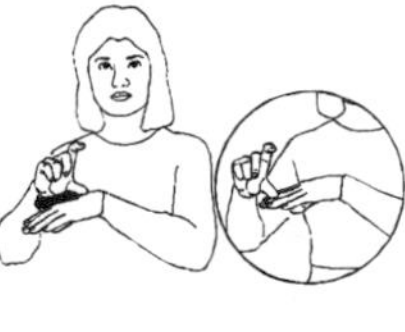

thin[1] *adj.* Same sign used for: **short.**

[Shows the thickness of a thin layer] Slide the thumb side of the right *G hand,* palm facing forward, from the wrist to the fingers of the left *open hand* held in front of the chest, palm facing down.

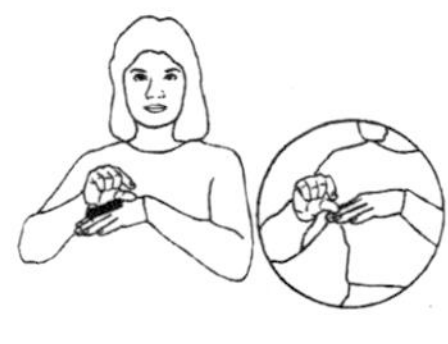

thin[2] *adj.* Same sign used for: **lean, skinny, slim.**

[Indicates something or someone that is very thin] Beginning with the extended little fingers of both *I hands* touching in front of the chest, right hand above the left hand and palms facing in, bring the right hand upward and the left hand downward.

thin[3] *adj.* See sign for DIET.

thing *n.*

[Something in the hand] Bring the right *open hand,* palm facing up and fingers pointing forward, from in front of the body in a large arc to the right.

think[1] *v.* Alternate form: **thought** *v., n.*

[Indicates the location of the mind] Tap the extended right index finger, palm facing in, to the right side of the forehead with a short double movement.

think[2] *v.* See signs for CONCERN[1], WONDER.

think about *v. phrase.* See sign for WONDER.

thinking *n.* See sign for WONDER.

third *adj.* See sign for ONE THIRD.

thirsty *adj.* Related form: **thirst** *n.* Same sign used for: **parched.**

[Indicates a dry throat] Move the extended right index finger, palm facing in and finger pointing up, downward on the length of the neck, bending the finger down as it moves.

this *pron., adj.*

[Points to a specific thing held in the hand] Move the extended right index finger, palm facing down and finger pointing down, from in front of the chest in a circular movement and then down to touch the left *open hand* held in front of the body, palm facing up.

thousand *n., adj.*

[An *M hand* representing *mille*, the Latin word for thousand] Bring the fingertips of the right *bent hand*, palm facing left, against the palm of the left *open hand* held in front of the body, palm facing right and fingers pointing forward.

thread *n.* See signs for CORD, LINE.

threat *n.* See sign for DANGER.

thrifty *adj.* See sign for GREEDY.

through *prep.* Same sign used for: **via.**

[Demonstrates movement through something] Slide the little-finger side of the right *open hand*, palm facing in and fingers angled to the left, between the middle finger and ring finger of the left *open hand* held in front of the chest, palm facing right and fingers pointing up.

throw *v.* Same sign used for: **cast, dump, pitch, throw away, toss.**

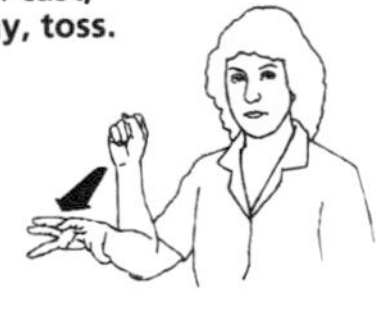

[Mime throwing something] Beginning with the right *S hand* in front of the right shoulder, palm facing forward, move the hand forward and downward while opening into a *5 hand*, palm facing down.

throw away *v. phrase.* See sign for THROW.

throw out *v. phrase.* See sign for ABANDON.

Thursday *n.*

[Abbreviation **t-h**] Beginning with the right *T hand* in front of the right shoulder, palm facing left, flick the index and middle fingers forward, forming an *H hand.*

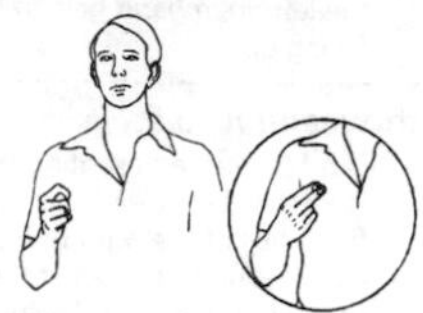

tie *v.* See sign for NECKTIE.

tight *adj.* See sign for GREEDY.

tightwad *n. Informal.* See sign for STINGY.

time *n.*

[Indicates the location of a person's watch] Tap the bent index finger of the right *X hand,* palm facing down, with a double movement on the wrist of the left wrist held in front of the chest, palm facing down.

timepiece *n.* See sign for WATCH.

timid *adj.* See sign for AFRAID.

tiny *adj.* See also sign for SMALL[1]. Same sign used for: **little bit, puny, scant, teeny.**

[Shows a tiny movement] Beginning with the right *6 hand* in front of the right side of the chest, palm facing up, flick the thumb off the little finger with a quick movement.

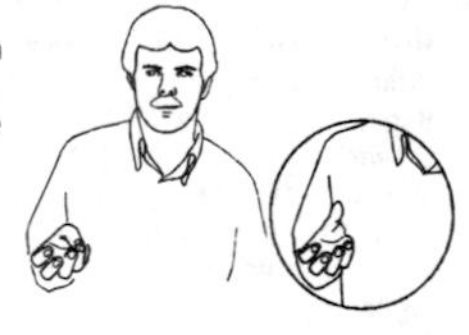

tired *adj.* Same sign used for: **exhausted, fatigue, weary.**

[The hands show that energy has dropped in the body] Beginning with the fingertips of both *bent hands* on each side of the chest, palms facing in, roll the hands downward on the fingertips, ending with the little-finger sides of both hands touching the chest, palms facing outward.

tissue *n.* Same sign used for: **Kleenex** (*trademark*).

[**cold**[1] + **paper**] Bring the index finger and thumb of the right *G hand,* palm facing in, downward on each side of the nose with a double movement, pinching the fingers together each time. Then brush the heel of the right *open hand,* palm facing down and fingers pointing left, with a double movement on the heel of the left *open hand* held in front of the body, palm facing up and fingers pointing right.

title *n.* Same sign used for: **entitle, quotes, so-called, subject, theme, topic.**

[Represents quotation marks around a title] Beginning with both *bent V hands* near each side of the head, palms facing forward, twist the hands while bending the fingers down, ending with the palms facing back.

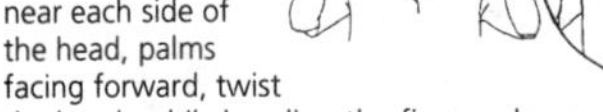

today *n., adv.*

[Sign similar to **now**] Bring both *Y hands,* palms facing up, with a short double movement downward in front of each side of the body.

together *adv.*
[Sign similar to **with** except with a circular movement indicating duration] With the palm sides of both *A hands* together in front of the body, move the hands in a flat circle.

toil *n.* See sign for SWEAT.

toilet *n.* Same sign used for: **bathroom, lavatory, rest room, washroom.**
[Initialized sign] Move the right *T hand,* palm facing forward, from side to side in front of the right shoulder with a repeated shaking movement.

tolerant *adj.* See sign for PATIENT[1].

tolerate *v.* See sign for CONTROL[1]. Related form: **tolerant** *adj.*

tomorrow *n., adv.*
[The sign moves forward into the future] Move the palm side of the right *10 hand,* palm facing left, from the right side of the chin forward while twisting the wrist.

tonight *n.* See sign for NIGHT.

too much *adj.* See signs for EXCESS, OVER[1].

top *n., adj.*

[The location on the top of something] Bring the palm of the right *open hand,* palm facing down and fingers pointing left, downward on the fingertips of the left *open hand* held in front of the chest, palm facing right and fingers pointing up.

---

topic *n.* See sign for TITLE.

---

torn *adj.* See sign for TEAR.

---

toss *v.* See sign for THROW.

---

touch *v., n.*

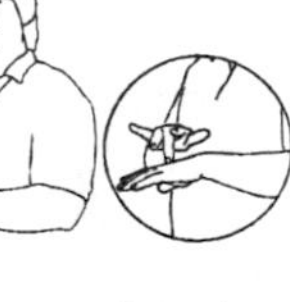

[Demonstrates touching something, with the middle finger used frequently to indicate feelings] Bring the bent middle finger of the right hand, palm facing down, downward to touch the back of the left *open hand* held in front of the body, palm facing down.

---

tough *adj.* See sign for STURDY[1].

---

tour *n.* See signs for RUN AROUND, TRIP.

---

tow *v.* See sign for DRAG.

---

toward *prep.*

[Demonstrates a movement toward something] Beginning with the extended right index finger in front of the right shoulder, palm facing left, move the hand in an arc to the left, ending with the right extended index finger touching the left extended index finger pointing up in front of the left side of the body, palm facing right.

towel *n.*

[Mime drying one's back with a towel] Beginning with the right *S hand* above the right shoulder, palm facing forward, and the left *S hand* near the left hip, palm facing back, move the hands simultaneously upward and downward at an angle with a repeated movement.

town *n.* Same sign used for: **community, village.**

[Represents the rooftops in a town] Tap the fingertips of both *open hands* together in front of the chest with a double movement, palms facing each other at an angle.

trade *v.* Same sign used for: **budget, exchange, replace, substitute, substitution, swap, switch.**

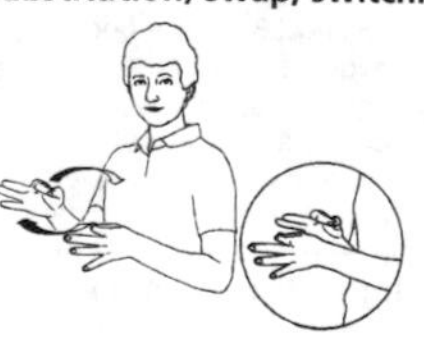

[Demonstrates moving something into another thing's place] Beginning with both *F hands* in front of the body, palms facing each other and right hand somewhat forward of the left hand, move the right hand back toward the body in an upward arc while moving the left hand forward in a downward arc.

traffic *n.*

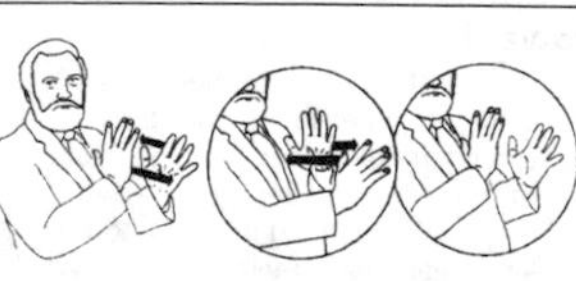

[Represents many vehicles moving quickly past each other in both directions] With both *5 hands* in front of the chest, palms facing each other and fingers pointing up, move the right hand forward and the left hand back with a repeated alternating movement, brushing palms as they pass each time.

trail *v.* See sign for FOLLOW.

trailer *n.* See sign for TRUCK.

train *n.* Same sign used for: **go by train, railroad, travel by train.**

[Represents the crossties on a railroad track] Rub the fingers of the right *H hand* back and forth with a repeated movement on the fingers of the left *H hand* held in front of the body, both palms facing down.

training *n.* See sign for PRACTICE.

tranquil *adj.* See sign for QUIET.

transport *v.* See sign for BRING.

trapped *adj.* See sign for STUCK.

travel *v.* See signs for RUN AROUND, TRIP.

travel by train *v. phrase.* See sign for TRAIN.

tree *n.*

[Represents a tree trunk and branches at the top] Beginning with the elbow of the bent right arm resting on the back of the left *open hand* held across the body, twist the right *5 hand* forward and back with a small repeated movement.

trespass *n.* See sign for SIN.

trial *n.* See sign for JUDGE.

tribute *n.* See sign for GIFT.

trip *n.* Same sign used for: **journey, mobilize, tour, travel.**

[Represents legs moving as if on a trip] Move the right *bent V hand,* palm facing down, from in front of the right side of the body upward and forward in an arc, ending with the palm facing forward.

triumph *n.* See sign for SUCCESSFUL.

trouble[1] *n.* Same sign used for: **anxious, care, concern, worry.**

[Represents problems coming from all directions] Beginning with both *B hands* near each side of the head, palms facing each other, bring the hands toward each other with a repeated alternating movement, crossing the hands in front of the face each time.

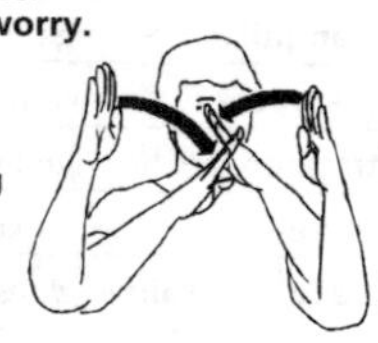

trouble[2] *n.* See sign for DIFFICULT.

trousers *n.* See sign for PANTS.

truck *n.* Same sign used for: **trailer.**

[Initialized sign similar to sign for **bus**] Beginning with the little-finger side of the right *T hand,* palm facing left, touching the index-finger side of the left *T hand,* palm facing right, move the right hand back toward the chest while the left hand moves forward.

true *adj.* Same sign used for: **actual, actually, certain, certainly, truly.**

[Represents words coming from the mouth] Move the side of the extended right index finger from in front of the mouth, palm facing left and finger pointing up, forward in an arc.

truly *v.* See sign for TRUE.

trust *n.* See sign for CONFIDENT.

truth *n.* Same sign used for: **fact, really.**

[Represents the truth coming straight from the mouth] Move the extended right index finger from pointing up in front of the mouth, palm facing left, forward with a deliberate movement.

try *v.* Same sign used for: **attempt, strive.**

[The hands push forward indicating effort] Move both *S hands* from in front of each side of the body, palms facing each other, downward and forward in simultaneous arcs.

Tuesday *n.*

[Initialized sign] Move the right *T hand,* palm facing in, in a circle in front of the right shoulder.

turn *n.* See also sign for CHANGE[1].
Same sign used for:
alternate, next.

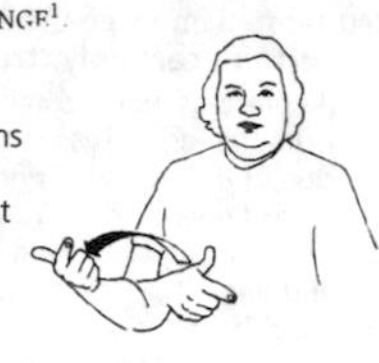

[Indicates alternating positions in order to take turns] Move the right *L hand* from in front of the body, palm angled left, to the right by flipping the hand over, ending with the palm facing up.

turn down *v. phrase.* See sign for REJECT.

turn into *v. phrase.* See sign for BECOME.

turn over *v. phrase.* See sign for COOK.

turn up *v. phrase.* See sign for SHOW UP.

twenty-five cents *pl. n.* See sign for QUARTER[1].

twin *n.*

[Initialized sign] Touch the index-finger side of the right *T hand,* palm facing left, first to the right side of the chin and then to the left side of the chin.

type[1] *v.* Related form: **typing** *v.*

[Mime typing] Beginning with both *curved 5 hands* in front of the body, palms facing down, wiggle the fingers with a repeated movement.

type[2] *n.* See sign for FAVORITE[1]. Related form: **typical** *adj.*

type[3] *n.* See sign for KIND[2].

ugly *adj.*
Beginning with the extended right index finger in front of the left side of the face, palm facing left and finger pointing left, move the hand to the right side of the face while bending the index finger to form an *X hand.*

unaware *adj.* See sign for DON'T KNOW.

uncertain *adj.* See sign for RESIST.

uncle *n.*
[Initialized sign formed near the male area of the head] Shake the right *U hand,* palm facing forward and fingers pointing up, near the right side of the forehead.

unconscious *adj.* See sign for DON'T KNOW.

under *prep.*
[Shows a location under something else] Move the right *10 hand,* palm facing left, from in front of the chest downward and forward under the left *open hand* held in front of the chest, palm facing down and fingers pointing right.

understand *v.* Same sign used for: **apprehend, comprehend, perceive.**

[Comprehension seems to pop into one's head] Beginning with the right *S hand* near the right side of the forehead, palm facing left, flick the right index finger upward with a sudden movement.

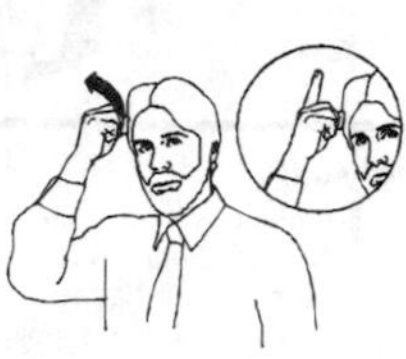

undress *v.* See sign for TAKE OFF.

union *n.* See sign for COOPERATION.

unique *adj.* See sign for SPECIAL.

unite *v.* See sign for BELONG.

unity *n.* See sign for COOPERATION.

universal *adj.* See sign for COOPERATION.

university *n.*

[Initialized sign similar to sign for **college**] Beginning with the palm side of the right *U hand* on the left *open hand* in front of the chest, palm facing up, move the right hand in a circular movement upward and forward.

unknown *adj.* See sign DON'T KNOW.

unusual *adj.* See sign for STRANGE.

up *adv., prep.*
[Points up] With the right extended index finger pointing up in front of the right shoulder, palm facing forward, move the right hand upward a short distance.

upstairs *adv.* Same sign as for UP but made with a double movement. Same sign used for: **upward.**

up to *prep.* See sign for MAXIMUM.

urgent *adj.* See signs for HURRY, NOW.

us *pron.*
[Initialized sign similar to sign for **we**] Touch the index-finger side of the right *U hand,* palm facing left and fingers pointing up, to the right side of the chest. Then twist the wrist and move the hand around to touch the little-finger side of the right *U hand* to the left side of the chest, palm facing right.

use *v.*
[Initialized sign] Move the right *U hand,* palm facing forward and fingers pointing up, in a repeated circle over the back of the left *S hand* held in front of the chest, palm facing down, hitting the heel of the right hand on the left hand each time as it passes.

used *adj.* See sign for SECOND-HAND.

used to *adj. phrase.* Same sign used for: **usual, usually.**

[Initialized sign similar to sign for **habit**] With the heel of the right *U hand,* palm facing forward and fingers pointing up, on the back of the left *S hand* held in front of the chest, palm facing down, move both hands downward.

used up *v. phrase.* See sign for RUN OUT OF.

usual *adv.* See signs for DAILY, USED TO. Related form: **usually** *adv.*

vacant *adj.* See sign for EMPTY. Related form: **vacancy** *n.*

vacation *n.*

[Thumbs in the straps of one's overalls as a symbol of leisure] With the thumbs of both *5 hands* near each armpit, palms facing in and fingers pointing toward each other, wiggle the fingers with a repeated movement.

vacuum *v.*

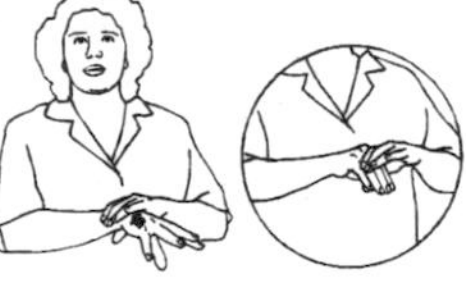

[Demonstrates the action of a vacuum drawing in dirt] With the fingertips of the right *flattened C hand* on the fingers of the left *open hand* held in front of the chest, palm facing up and fingers pointing forward, close the right fingers with a double movement while sliding across the left palm, forming a *flattened O hand* each time.

vague *adj.* Same sign used for: **ambiguous, blurry, fade, hazy, illegible.**

[Represents a blurring of the facts] With the palms of both *5 hands* together at angles in front of the chest, move both hands in circular movements going in opposite directions rubbing the palms against each other.

value *adj.* See sign for IMPORTANT.

vanilla *n., adj.*
[Initialized sign] Shake the right *V hand,* palm facing forward and fingers pointing up, from side to side with a small double movement in front of the right shoulder.

vanish *v.* See sign for DISAPPEAR[1].

vanquish *v.* See sign for DEFEAT.

variety *n.* Same sign used for: **and so-forth, random, range.**
[Pointing out many things] Beginning with the extended index fingers of both hands touching in front of the chest, palms facing down, move the hands apart while bending the index fingers downward, forming *X hands* with a repeated movement, ending with the hands in front of each side of the chest.

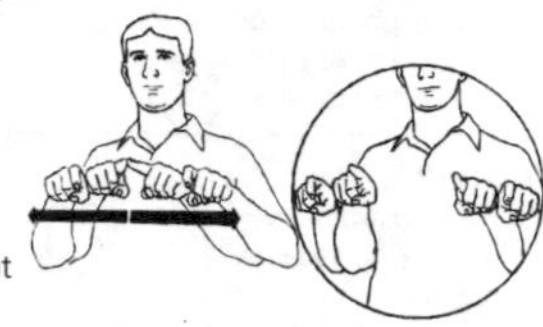

vegetable *n.*
[Initialized sign] Beginning with the index finger of the right *V hand,* palm facing forward, touching the right side of the chin, twist the wrist to turn the palm back and touch the middle finger to the right side of the chin, ending with the palm facing back.

vengeance *n.* See sign for REVENGE.

versus *prep.* See sign for CHALLENGE.

very *adv.*

[Initialized sign similar to sign for **much**] Beginning with the fingertips of both *V hands* touching in front of the chest, palms facing each other, bring the hands apart to in front of each shoulder.

veto *v.* See sign for REJECT.

via *prep.* See sign for THROUGH.

view *v.* See sign for LOOK OVER.

village *n.* See sign for TOWN.

visit *v.*, *n.*

[Initialized sign] Beginning with both *V hands* in front of each side of the chest, palms facing in and fingers pointing up, move the hands in alternating repeated movements.

visualize *adj.* See sign for SEE.

voice *n.* Related forms: **vocal, vocalize.**

[Initialized sign showing the location of one's voice] Move the fingertips of the right *V hand,* palm facing down, upward on the throat with a double movement.

void *adj.* See sign for EMPTY.

volunteer *v.* See sign for APPLY[2].

wacky *Slang. adj.* See sign for CRAZY.

wager *n.* See sign for BET.

wages *pl. n.* See signs for EARN, INCOME[1].

wait *v., n.*

[Seems to be twiddling the finger while waiting impatiently] Beginning with both *curved 5 hands* in front of the body, palms facing up, wiggle the fingers with a repeated motion.

waive *v.* See sign for DISMISS.

wake up *v. phrase.* See sign for AWAKE.

walk *v.* Same sign used for: **stroll, wander.**

[Represents a person's legs moving when walking] Beginning with both *open hands* in front of each side of the body, left palm facing in and fingers pointing down and right palm facing down and fingers pointing forward, move the fingers of both hands up and down with an alternating movement by bending the wrists.

wander *v.* See signs for ROAM, WALK.

want *v.* Same sign used for: **desire, passion.**

[Represents bringing a wanted thing toward oneself] Beginning with both *5 hands* in front of the body, palms facing up and fingers pointing forward, bring the hands back toward the chest while constricting the fingers toward the palms.

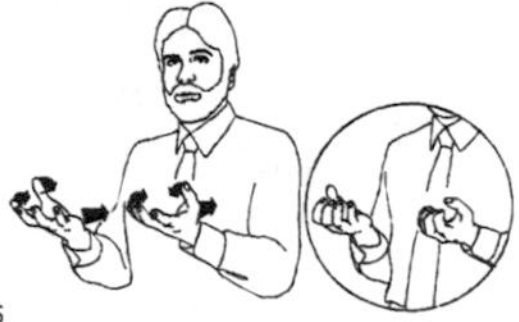

war *n.* See sign for BATTLE.

warm *adj.* Related form: **warmth** *n.*

[Using one's breath to warm the hand] Beginning with the fingers of the right *E hand* near the mouth, palm facing in, move the hand forward in a small arc while opening the fingers into a *C hand.*

warn *v.* Related form: **warning** *n.* Same sign used for: **caution, rebuke.**

[Indicates tapping someone on the hand as a warning] Tap the palm of the right *open hand* with a double movement on the back of the left *open hand* held in front of the chest, both palms facing down.

was *v.* See sign for AGO.

wash *v.* Same sign used for: **rub.**

[Demonstrates the action of rubbing something to wash it] Rub the palm side of the right *A hand* with a repeated movement across the palm side of the left *A hand,* palms facing each other.

wash one's hair *v. phrase.* See sign for SHAMPOO.

washroom *n.* See sign for TOILET.

watch[1] *v.*

[Represents the eyes looking at something] Beginning with the right *V hand* in front of the right side of the face, palm facing down and fingers pointing forward, move the hand forward.

watch[2] *n.* Same sign used for: **timepiece, wristwatch.**

[The shape of a watch's face] Place the palm side of the right *F hand* on the back of the left wrist.

watch[3] *v.* See sign for ATTENTION.

water *n.*

[Initialized sign] Tap the index-finger side of the right *W hand,* palm facing left, against the chin with a double movement.

way *n.* See sign for ROAD.

we *pron.*

[Points to self and encompasses others in near area] Touch the extended right index finger, palm facing down, first to the right side of the chest and then to the left side of the chest.

weak *adj.* Related form: **weakness** *n.* Same sign used for: **fatigue, feeble.**

[The fingers collapse as if weak] Beginning with the fingertips of the right *5 hand,* palm facing in, touching the palm of the left *open hand* held in front of the chest, move the right hand downward with a double movement, bending the fingers each time.

wealth *n.* See sign for RICH.

wear out *v. phrase.* Same sign used for: **decay, rot, rotten.**

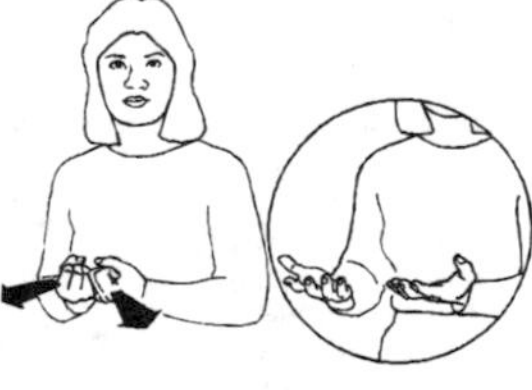

[Shows something coming apart] Beginning with both *S hands* together in front of the chest, palms facing up, move the hands forward with a sudden movement while opening into *5 hands,* palms facing up.

weary *adj.* See sign for TIRED.

weather *n.*

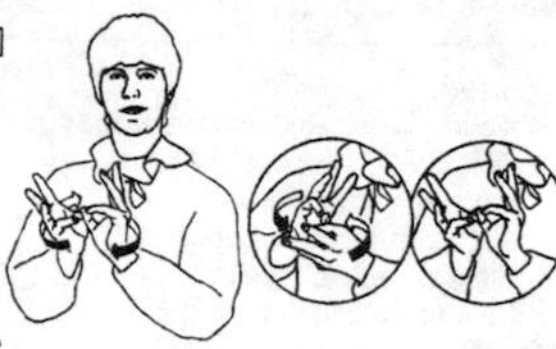

[Initialized sign] With the fingertips of both *6 hands* together in front of the chest, palms facing each other, twist the hands in opposite directions with a double movement.

wedding *n.* Related form: **wed** *v.*

[Represents bringing the bride's and groom's hands together during a wedding] Beginning with both *open hands* hanging down in front of each side of the chest, palms facing in and fingers pointing down, bring the fingers upward toward each other, meeting in front of the chest.

Wednesday *n.*

[Initialized sign] Move the right *W hand,* palm facing in and fingers pointing up, in a circle in front of the right shoulder.

week *n.* Same sign used for: **one week.**

[The finger moves along the days of one week on an imaginary calendar] Slide the palm side of the right *1 hand* from the heel to the fingers of the left *open hand* held in front of the chest, palm facing in.

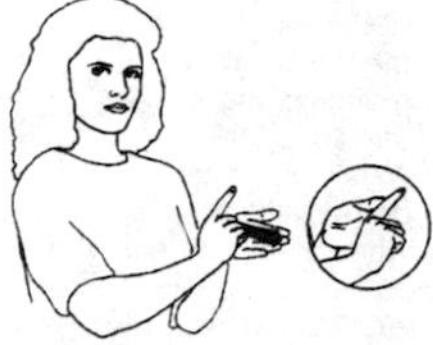

weekend *n.*
[**week** + **end**[1]] Slide the palm side of the right *1 hand* from the heel to the fingertips of the left *open hand* held in front of the chest, palm facing in. Then move the palm side of the right *open hand* downward along the fingertips of the left *open hand* held in front of the chest, palm facing right.

weep *v.* See sign for CRY[1].

weigh *v.* Related form: **weight** *n.* Same sign used for: **pound.**
[The fingers seem to balance something as if on a scale] With the middle-finger side of the right *H hand* across the index-finger side of the left *H hand,* palms angled toward each other, tip the right hand up and down with a repeated movement.

welcome *v., n., adj., interj.* See sign for INVITE.

welfare *n.* See sign for PENSION.

well[1] *adj., adv.* Same sign used for: **bold, cure, heal, healthy, strength, strong.**
[The hands seem to pull health from the body] Beginning with the fingertips of both *5 hands* on each side of the chest, palms facing in and fingers pointing up, bring the hands forward with a deliberate movement while closing into *S hands.*

well[2] *adj.* See sign for GOOD.

were *v.* See sign for AGO.

west *n., adj.* Related form: **western** *adj.*

[Initialized sign indicating a western direction on a map] Move the right *W hand*, palm facing forward, to the left in front of the right side of the chest.

wet *adj.* Same sign used for: **damp, dew, humid, misty, moist, moisten, moisture.**

[The hands seem to feel something wet] Beginning with the right *5 hand* near the right side of the chin, palm facing left, and the left *5 hand* in front of the left side of the chest, palm facing up, bring the hands downward while closing the fingers to the thumbs.

what *pron.*

[The fingers on the left hand are choices pointed out by the right hand] Bring the extended right index finger, palm facing left, downward across the left *open hand* held in front of the chest, palm facing up.

whatever *pron.* See sign for ANYWAY.

when *adv.*
[A continuous movement showing duration of time] Beginning with the extended right index finger in front of the chest, palm facing down and finger pointing forward, and the left extended index finger in front of the lower chest, palm facing in and finger pointing right, move the right index finger in a circular movement down to land on the left index finger.

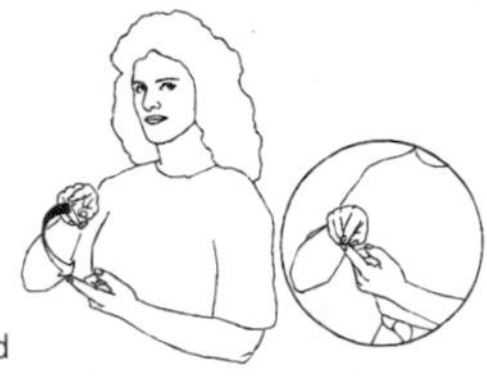

where *adv.*
[Indicates one direction and then another] Move the extended right index finger, palm facing forward and finger pointing up, with a short double movement from side to side in front of the right shoulder.

whether *pron.* See sign for WHICH.

which *pron., adj.* Same sign used for: **either, whether.**

[The movement indicates indecision] Beginning with both *10 hands* in front of each side of the chest, palms facing each other and right hand higher than the left hand, move the hands up and down with an alternating movement.

while *conj.* See sign for DURING.

while ago, a *adv.* See sign for JUST.

white *adj.*

[The downy breast of a swan] Beginning with the fingertips of the right *5 hand* on the chest, palm facing in, pull the hand forward while closing the fingers into a *flattened O hand.*

who *pron.* Same sign used for: **whom.**

[Outlines the verbal formation of the word **who**] With the thumb of the *modified C hand* touching the chin, palm facing left, bend the index finger up and down with a double movement.

whole *adj., n.* See sign for ALL.

whom *pron.* See sign for WHO.

why *adv.*

[Taking information and presenting it for examination] Beginning with the fingertips of the right *bent hand* touching the right side of the forehead, palm facing down, move the hand forward with a deliberate movement while changing into a *Y hand.*

wicked *adj.* See sign for BAD.

wide *adj.* Related form: **width** *n.* Same sign used for: **broad, general.**

[Indicates a wide space] Beginning with both *open hands* in front of each side of the body, palms facing each other and fingers pointing forward, move the hands away from each other outward to the sides of the body.

wife *n.*

[The hand moves from near the female area of the head + **marry**] Move the right *curved hand* from near the right side of the chin, palm facing forward, downward to clasp the left *curved hand* held in front of the body.

will *v.*

[The hand moves into the future] Move the right *open hand,* palm facing left and fingers pointing up, from the right side of the chin forward while turning the fingers forward.

willing *adj.* See sign for ADMIT.

will not See sign for WON'T.

win *v., n.*

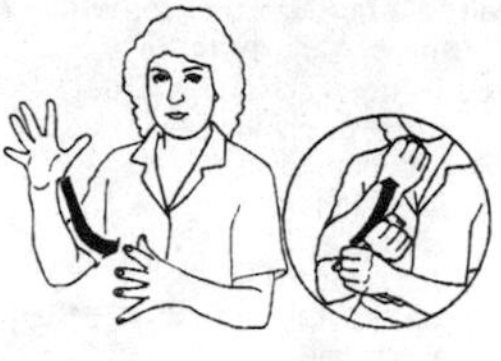

[Grabbing the golden ring on a carousel] Beginning with the right *5 hand* in front of the right shoulder, palm facing forward and fingers pointing up, and the left *5 hand* in front of the body, palm facing right and fingers pointing forward, sweep the right hand downward in an arc across the index-finger side of the left hand while changing both hands into *S hands* and bringing the right hand upward in front of the chest.

wind *n.* Alternative form: **windy** *adj.* Same sign used for: **storm.**

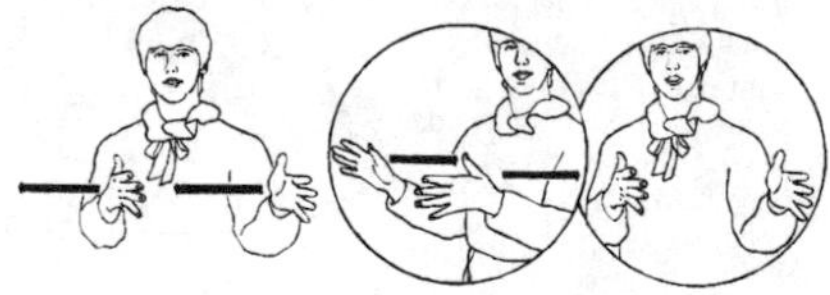

[Represents the action of wind blowing] Beginning with both *5 hands* in front of the left side of the body, palms facing each other and fingers pointing forward, move the hands back and forth in front of the chest with a repeated movement.

wind up *v. phrase.* See sign for END[1].

window *n.*

[Represents closing a window] Bring the little-finger side of the right *open hand* down sharply with a double movement on the index-finger side of the left *open hand,* both palms facing in and fingers pointing in opposite directions.

wine *n.*
[Initialized sign] Move the right *W hand,* palm facing left, in a small circle near the right side of the chin.

wings *pl. n.*, See sign for FLY.

winter[1] *n.*
[Initialized sign similar to sign for **cold**[2]] Beginning with both *W hands* in front of the body, palms facing each other, move the hands toward each other with a shaking repeated movement.

winter[2] *n.* See sign for COLD[2].

wipe *v.* Same sign used for: **rub**.
[Demonstrates the action of wiping something] Wipe the palm side of the right *A hand* with a repeated movement back and forth on the left *open hand* held in front of the body, palm facing up.

wire[1] *n.* Same sign used for: **cable.**
[Shape of a wire] Beginning with both extended little fingers pointing toward each other in front of the chest, palms facing in, move the hands apart from each other.

wire[2] *n.* See sign for CORD.

wireless *adj.*
[**none**[2] + **wire**[1]] Beginning with both *flattened O hands,* palms facing forward, in front of the chest, move the hands apart to each side. Then beginning with both extended little fingers pointing toward each other in front of the chest, palms facing in, move the hands apart from each other.

wise *adj.* Related form: **wisdom** *n.*
[Shows the depth of wisdom in the brain] Move the right *X hand,* palm facing left, up and down with a double movement in front of the right side of the forehead.

wish *v., n.* Same sign used for: **desire.**
[The fingers outline the path of craving for something] Move the fingers of the right *C hand,* palm facing in, downward on the chest a short distance.

with *prep.*
[Indicates two things coming together so they are with one another] Beginning with both *A hands* in front of the chest, palms facing each other, bring the hands together.

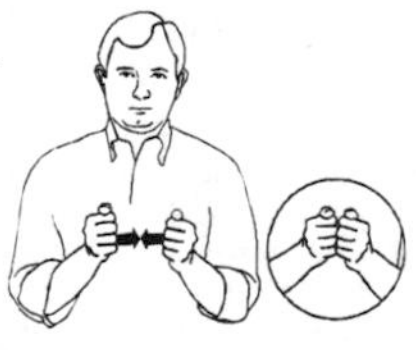

withdraw *v.* See signs for DISCONNECT, LEAVE[1].

within *prep.* See sign for INCLUDE.

woman *n.*

[A gesture beginning near the female area of the head + **polite**] Beginning with the extended thumb of the right *open hand* touching the right side of the chin, palm facing left, bring the hand downward to touch the thumb again in the center of the chest.

wonder *v.* Same sign used for: **consider, contemplate, meditate, ponder, reflect, think, think about, thinking.**

[Represents thoughts going around in one's head] Move the extended right index finger, palm facing in, in a small circle near the right side of the forehead with a repeated movement.

wonderful *adj.* Same sign used for: **amaze, excellent, fantastic, great, incredible, marvel, marvelous, remarkable.**

[A gesture of awe and wonder] Move both *5 hands,* palms facing forward and fingers pointing up, from in front of each side of the head forward with a short double movement.

won't *contraction.* Same sign used for: **refuse, will not.**

[Natural gesture for refusing to do something] Beginning with the right *10 hand* in front of the right shoulder, palm facing left, move the hand deliberately back toward the shoulder while twisting the wrist up.

wood *n.* Related form: **wooden** *adj.* Same sign used for: **saw.**

[Shows action of sawing wood] Slide the little-finger side of the right *open hand,* palm facing left and fingers pointing forward, forward and back with a double movement on the index finger side of the left *open hand* held in front of the chest, palm facing in and fingers pointing right.

word *n.* Same sign used for: **text.**

[Measures the size of a word] Tap the extended fingers of the right *G hand,* palm facing left, with a double movement against the extended left index finger pointing up in front of the left side of the chest, palm facing right.

work *n., v.* Same sign used for: **active, employment, job, labor, occupation, task.**

[Demonstrates repetitive action] Tap the heel of the right *S hand,* palm facing forward, with a double movement on the back of the left *S hand* held in front of the body, palm facing down.

work out *v. phrase.* See sign for EXERCISE[1].

world *n.*

[Initialized sign indicating the movement of the earth around the sun] Beginning with both *W hands* in front of the body, palms facing each other, move the right hand upward and forward in

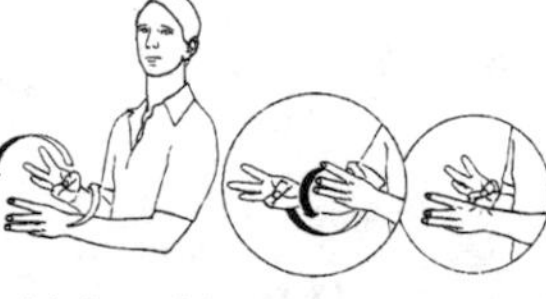

an arc as the left hand moves back and upward around the right hand, exchanging positions.

worry *v.* See sign for TROUBLE[1].

worship *n., v.* Same sign used for: **adore, beg, pray.**

[Similar to sign for **amen** except formed with a double movement] With the right fingers cupped over the left *A hand,* bring the hands downward and in toward the chest with a double movement.

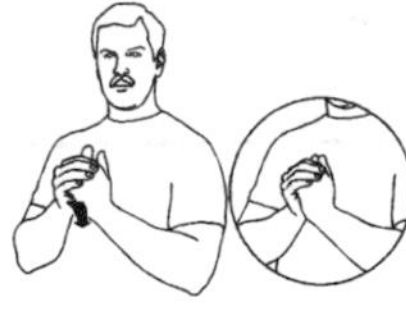

worth *n., prep.* See sign for IMPORTANT.

wound *v., n.* See sign for HURT.

wow *interj.*

[Natural gesture] Swing the right *5 hand*, palm facing in, limply up and down in front of the right side of the body.

wristwatch *n.* See sign for WATCH.

write *v.* Related form: **written** *adj.* Same sign used for: **edit, scribble.**

[Mime writing on paper] Bring the fingers of the right *modified X hand*, palm facing left, with a wiggly movement from the heel to the fingers of the left *open hand* held in front of the body, palm facing up.

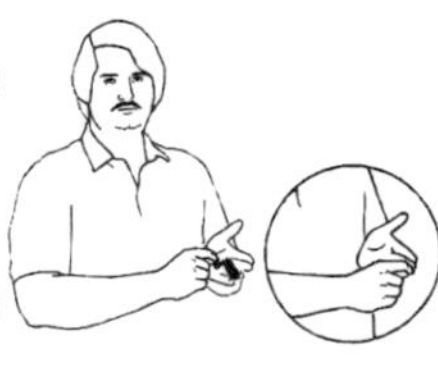

wrong *adj.* Same sign used for: **incorrect.**

[Similar to sign for **mistake** but with a single movement] Place the middle fingers of the right *Y hand,* palm facing in, against the chin with a deliberate movement.

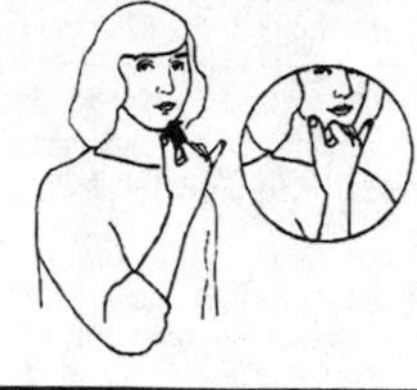

xylophone *n.*

[Mime playing a xylophone] Beginning with the palms of both *modified X hands* facing each other in front of each side of the body, move the hands up and down with an alternating movement.

yeah *adv. Informal.* See sign for YES.

year *n.*

[Represents the movement of the earth around the sun] Beginning with the right *S hand,* palm facing left, over the left *S hand,* palm facing right, move the right hand forward in a complete circle around the left hand while the left hand moves in a smaller circle around the right hand, ending with the little-finger side of the right hand on the thumb side of the left hand.

yearn *v.* See sign for HUNGRY.

yell *v.* See sign for SCREAM.

yellow *adj.*

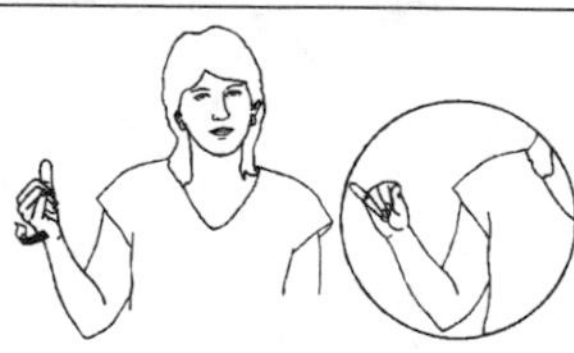

[Initialized sign] Move the right *Y hand,* palm facing left, with a twisting double movement.

yes *adv.* Same sign used for: **yeah** (*informal*).

[Represents a person's head nodding in approval] Move the right *S hand,* palm facing forward, up and down in front of the right shoulder by bending the wrist with a repeated movement.

yesterday *n., adv.*

[Initialized sign moving back into the past] Move the thumb of the right *Y hand,* palm facing forward, from the right side of the chin up to the right cheek.

yet *adv.* See also sign for STILL[1].

[The hand gestures back into the past] Bend the wrist of the right *open hand,* palm facing back and fingers pointing down, back with a double movement near the right side of the waist.

you *pron.*

[Point toward the referent] Point the extended right index finger, palm facing down, toward the person being talked to.

young *adj.* Same sign used for: **youth.**

[Represents bringing up youthful feelings in the body] Beginning with the fingers of both *bent hands* on each side of the chest, palms facing in, brush the fingers upward with a double movement.

your *pron.* Related form:
yours *pron.*
[The hand moves toward the referent] Push the palm of the right *open hand,* palm facing forward and fingers pointing up, toward the person being talked to.

you're too late. *v. phrase.* See sign for MISS[2].

yourself *pron.*
[This hand shape is used for reflexive pronouns and moves toward the referent] Push the extended thumb of the right *10 hand,* palm facing left, forward with a double movement toward the person being talked to.

youth *n.* See sign for YOUNG.

zeal *n.* Same sign used for: **aspiration, aspire, eager, enthusiastic, motivation, motive.**

[Rubbing the hands together in eagerness] Rub the palms of both *open hands,* palms facing each other, back and forth against each other with a double alternating movement.

zip *v.* Same sign as for **zipper** but formed with a single movement.

zipper *n.*

[Mime pulling a zipper up and down] With the right *modified X hand,* palm facing down, move the right hand up and down with a double movement in front of the chest.

zoom *v.* Same sign used for: **set off.**

[Represents something getting smaller as it goes off into the distance] Beginning with the thumb of the right *G hand,* palm facing forward, at the base of the extended left index finger held in front of the chest, palm facing down and finger pointing right, move the right thumb across the length of the left index finger, closing the right index finger and thumb together as the hand moves to the right.